BATMAN TALES
ONCE UPON A CRIME

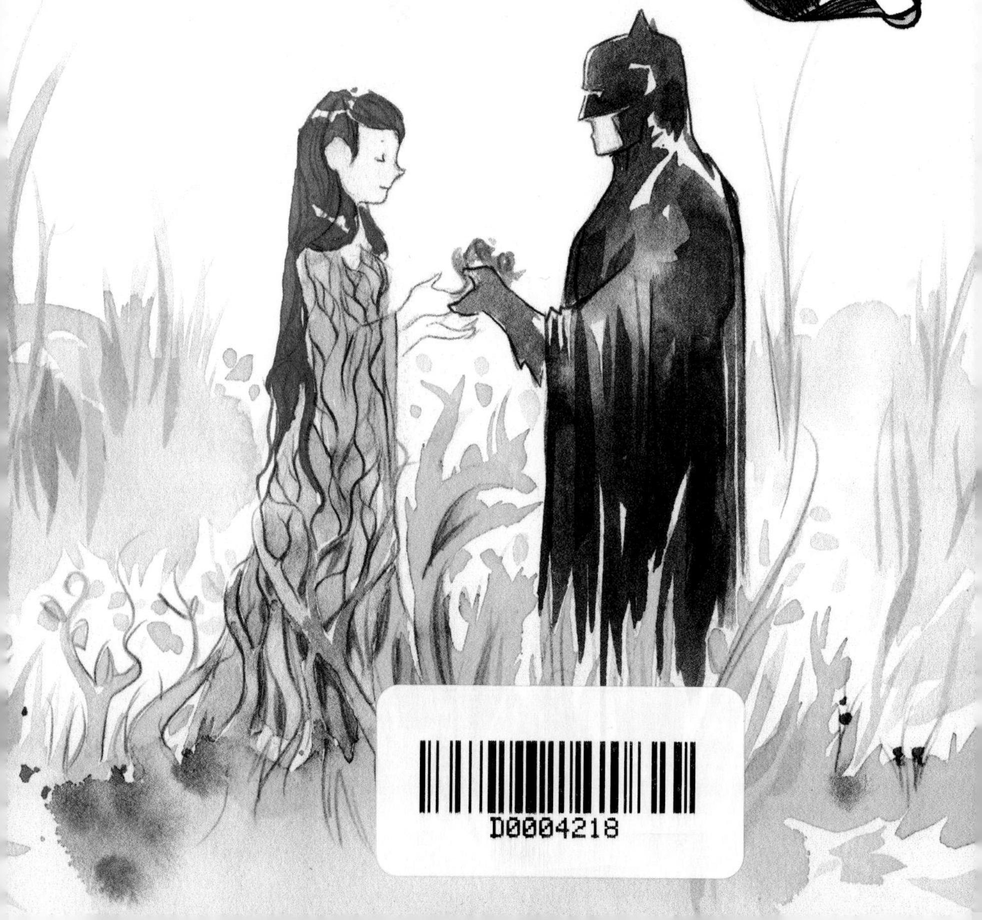

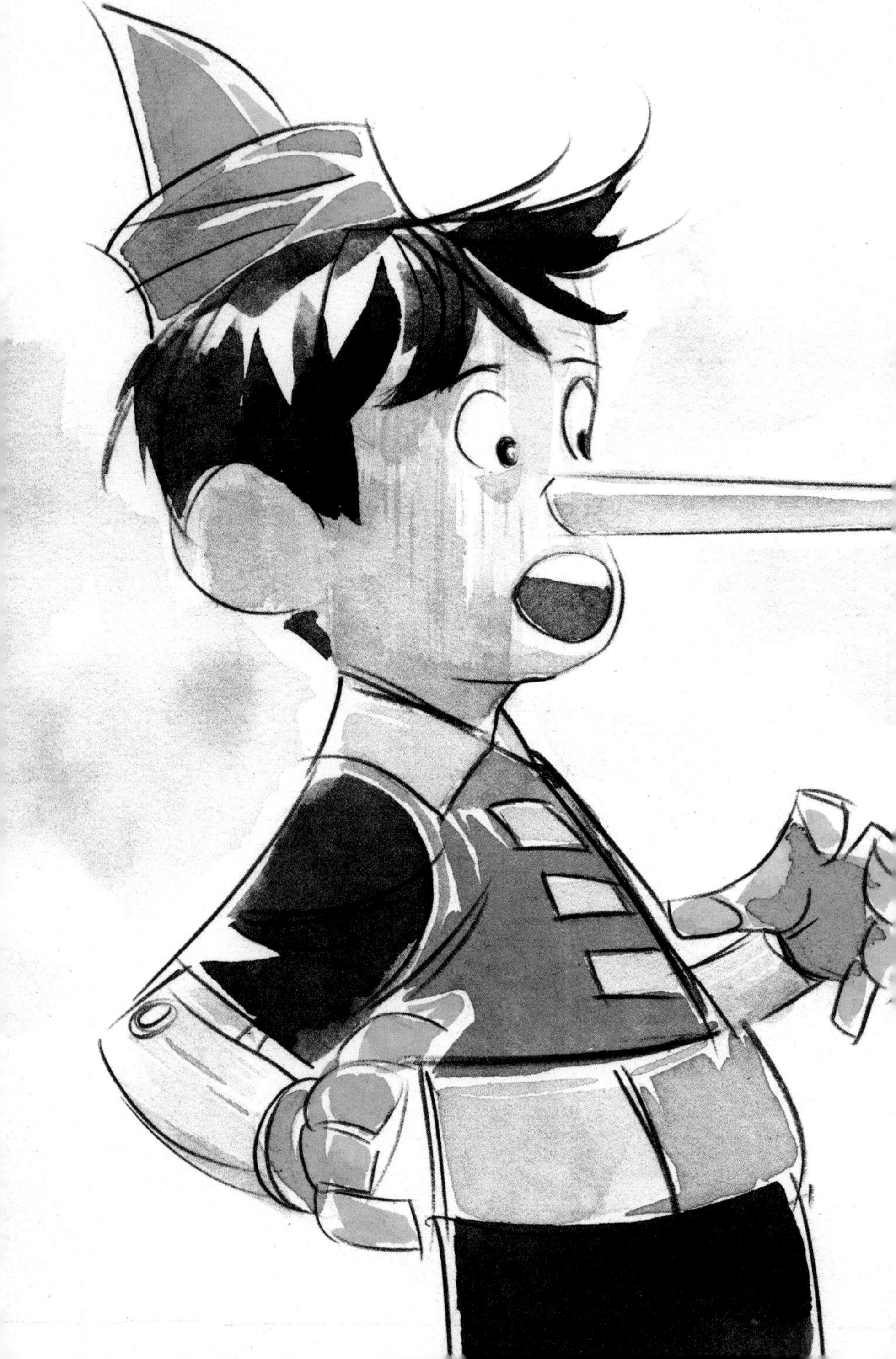

BATMAN TALES:
ONCE UPON A CRIME

Written by
DEREK FRIDOLFS

Painted by
DUSTIN NGUYEN

Lettered by
STEVE WANDS

Batman created by Bob Kane with Bill Finger

KRISTY QUINN Editor
STEVE COOK Design Director - Books
LORI JACKSON & GABE MALDONADO Publication Design

BOB HARRAS Senior VP - Editor-in-Chief, DC Comics
MICHELE R. WELLS VP & Executive Editor, Young Reader

DAN DiDIO Publisher
JIM LEE Publisher & Chief Creative Officer
BOBBIE CHASE VP - New Publishing Initiatives & Talent Development
DON FALLETTI VP - Manufacturing Operations & Workflow Management
LAWRENCE GANEM VP - Talent Services
ALISON GILL Senior VP - Manufacturing & Operations
HANK KANALZ Senior VP - Publishing Strategy & Support Services
DAN MIRON VP - Publishing Operations
NICK J. NAPOLITANO VP - Manufacturing Administration & Design
NANCY SPEARS VP - Sales

Batman Tales: Once Upon a Crime

Published by DC Comics. Copyright © 2020 DC Comics. All
Rights Reserved. All characters, their distinctive likenesses,
and related elements featured in this publication are trade-
marks of DC Comics. The stories, characters, and incidents
featured in this publication are entirely fictional. DC Comics
does not read or accept unsolicited submissions of ideas,
stories, or artwork.

DC - a WarnerMedia Company.

DC Comics, 2900 West Alameda Ave., Burbank, CA 91505
Printed by LSC Communications, Crawfordsville, IN, USA
12/27/2019
First Printing
ISBN: 978-1-4012-8340-7

Library of Congress Cataloging-in-Publication Data

Names: Fridolfs, Derek, writer. | Nguyen, Dustin, illustrator. | Wands,
    Steve, letterer.
Title: Batman tales : once upon a crime / written by Derek Fridolfs ;
    painted by Dustin Nguyen ; lettered by Steve Wands.
Description: Burbank, CA : DC Comics, [2020] | Audience: Ages 8-12 |
    Audience: Grades 4-6 | Summary: Collection of short stories with a
    classic fairy-tale twist set in Batman's Gotham City.
Identifiers: LCCN 2019040280 (print) | LCCN 2019040281 (ebook) | ISBN
    9781401283407 (paperback)
Subjects: LCSH: Graphic novels. | CYAC: Graphic novels. | Fairy tales. |
    Superheroes--Fiction.
Classification: LCC PZ7.7.F784 Bat 2020 (print) | LCC PZ7.7.F784 (ebook)
    | DDC 741.5/973--dc23
LC record available at https://lccn.loc.gov/2019040280
LC ebook record available at https://lccn.loc.gov/2019040281

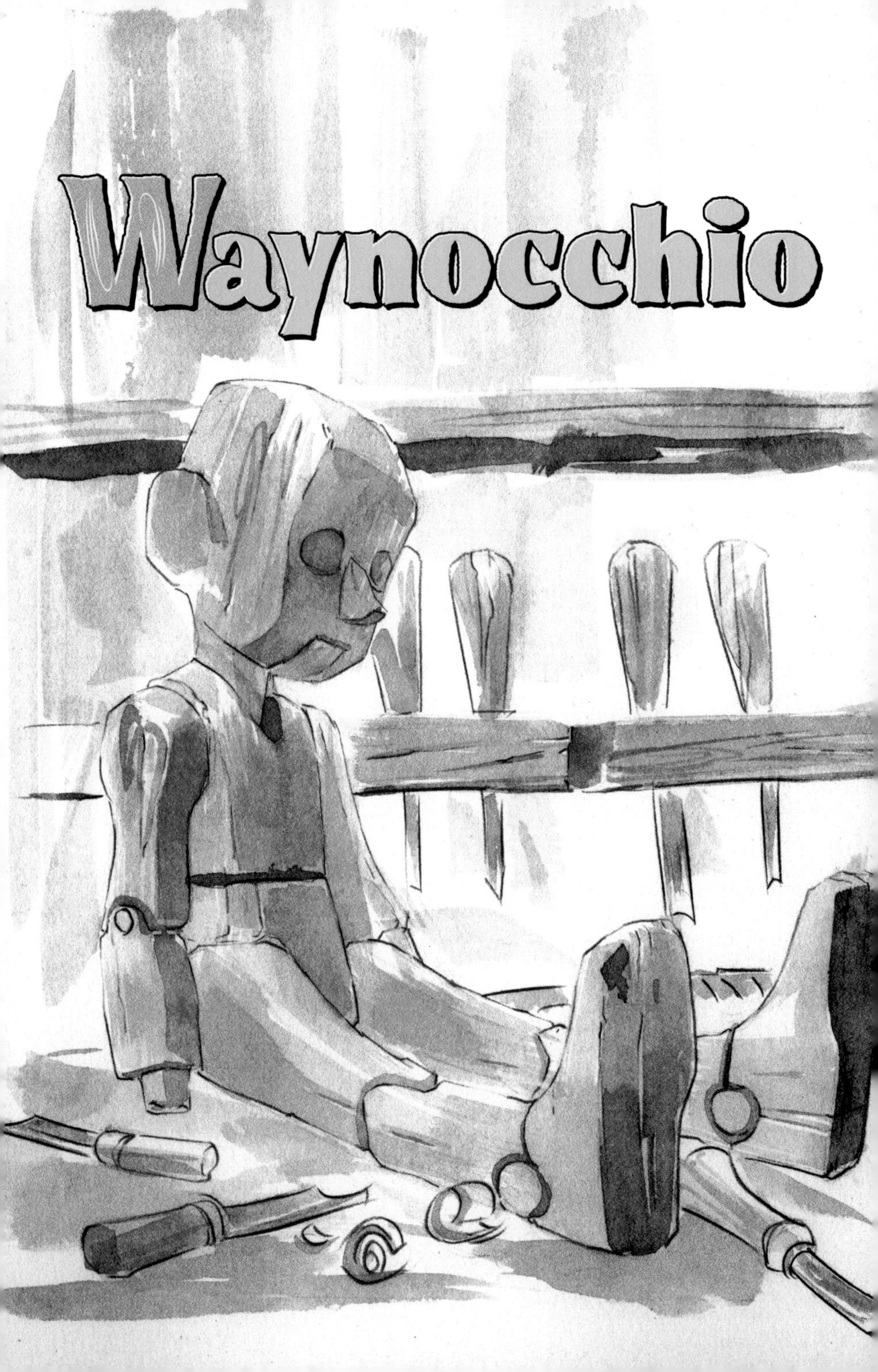
Waynocchio

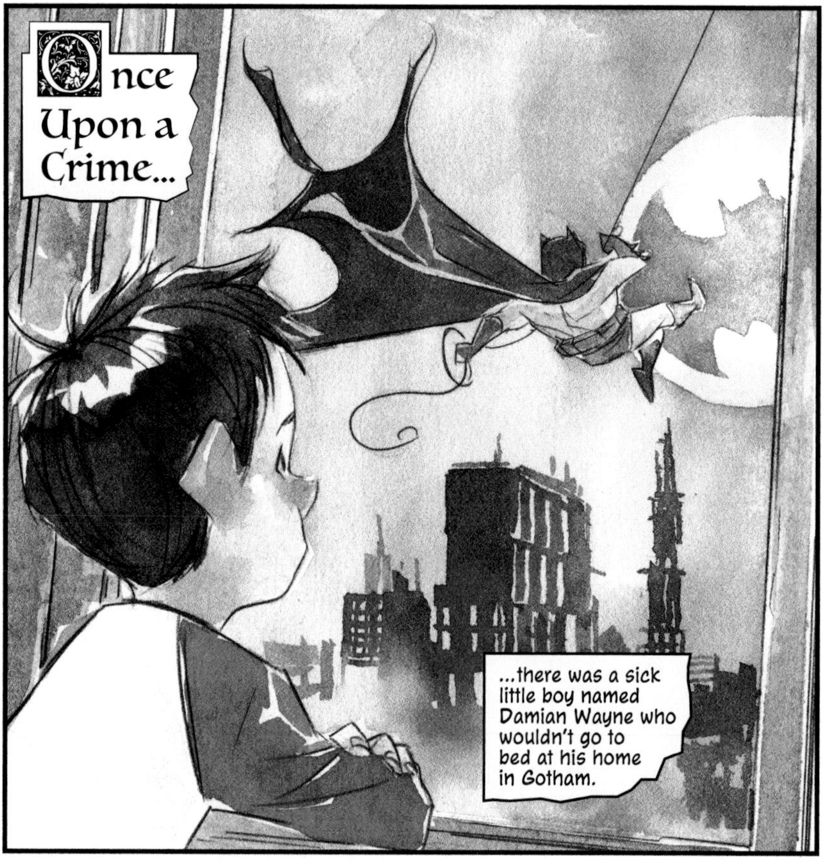
Once Upon a Crime...
...there was a sick little boy named Damian Wayne who wouldn't go to bed at his home in Gotham.

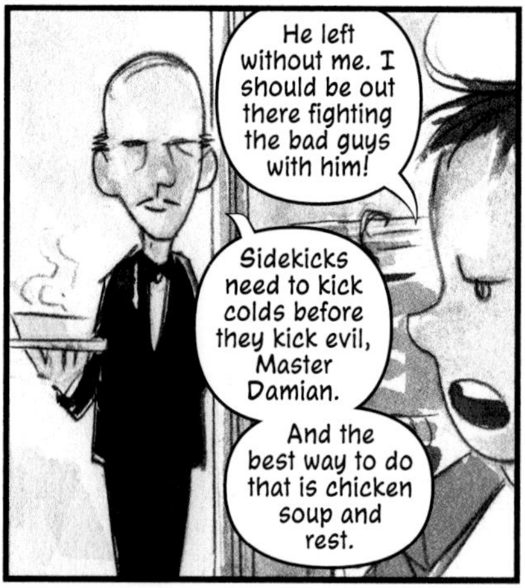
He left without me. I should be out there fighting the bad guys with him!
Sidekicks need to kick colds before they kick evil, Master Damian.
And the best way to do that is chicken soup and rest.

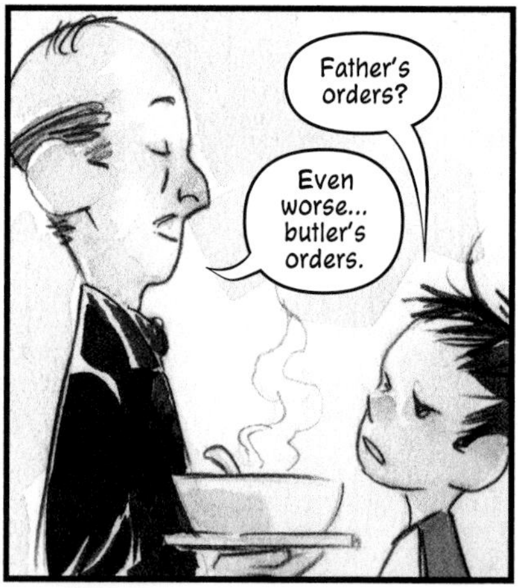
Father's orders?
Even worse... butler's orders.

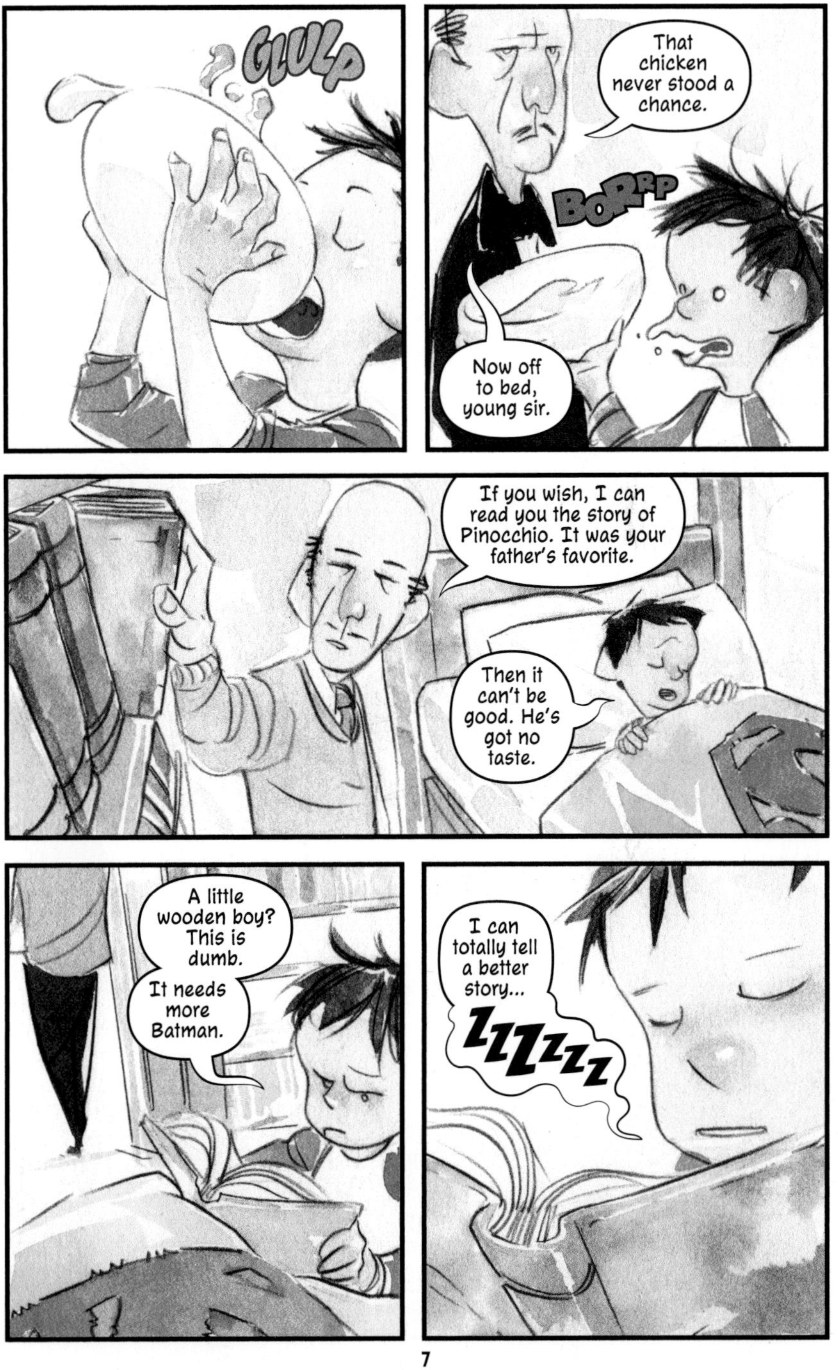
GLULP
That chicken never stood a chance.
BORRP
Now off to bed, young sir.
If you wish, I can read you the story of Pinocchio. It was your father's favorite.
Then it can't be good. He's got no taste.
A little wooden boy? This is dumb.
It needs more Batman.
I can totally tell a better story...
ZZZZZZ

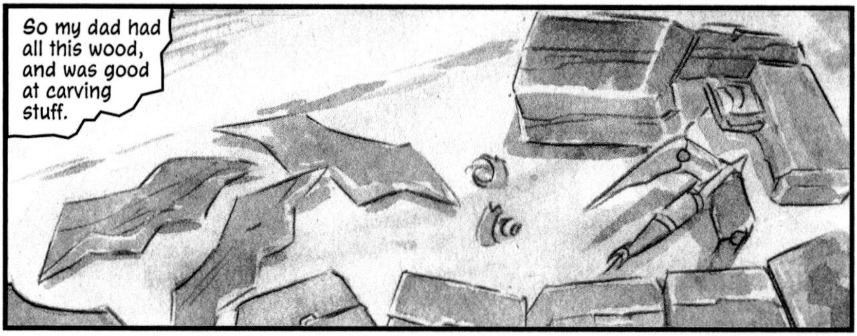
So my dad had all this wood, and was good at carving stuff.

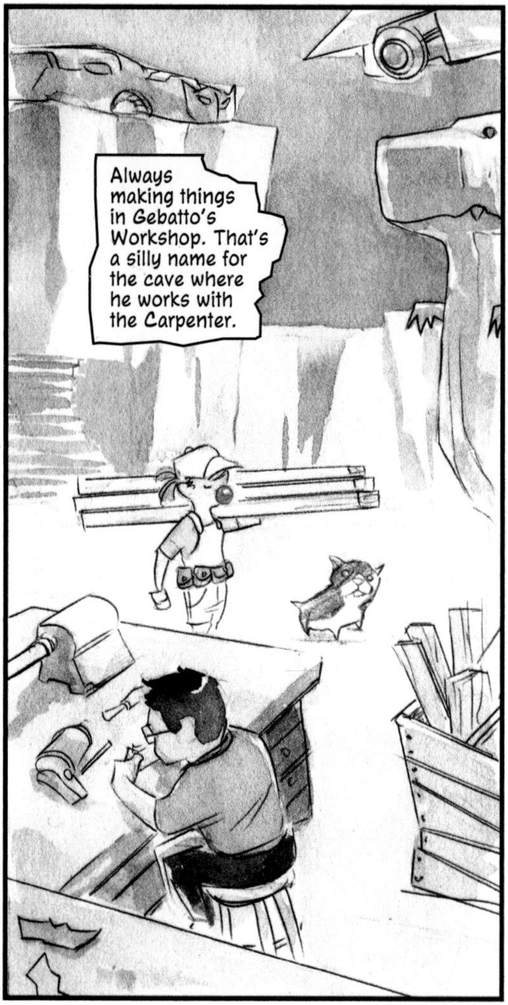
Always making things in Gebatto's Workshop. That's a silly name for the cave where he works with the Carpenter.

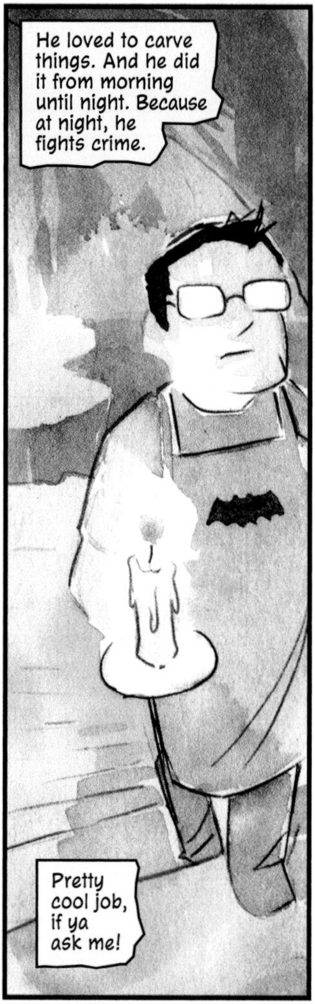
He loved to carve things. And he did it from morning until night. Because at night, he fights crime.
Pretty cool job, if ya ask me!

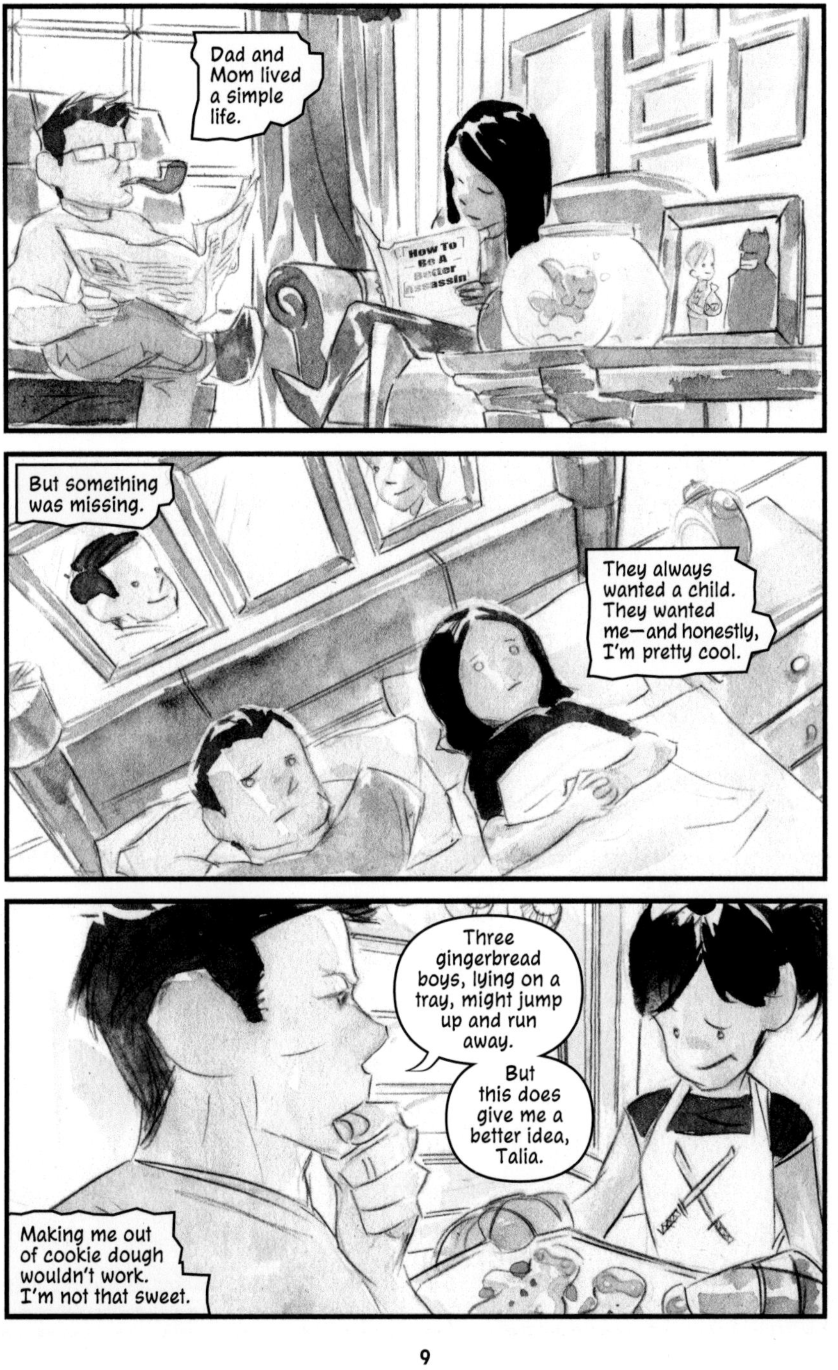
Dad and Mom lived a simple life.
How To Be A Better Assassin
But something was missing.
They always wanted a child. They wanted me—and honestly, I'm pretty cool.
Three gingerbread boys, lying on a tray, might jump up and run away.
But this does give me a better idea, Talia.
Making me out of cookie dough wouldn't work. I'm not that sweet.

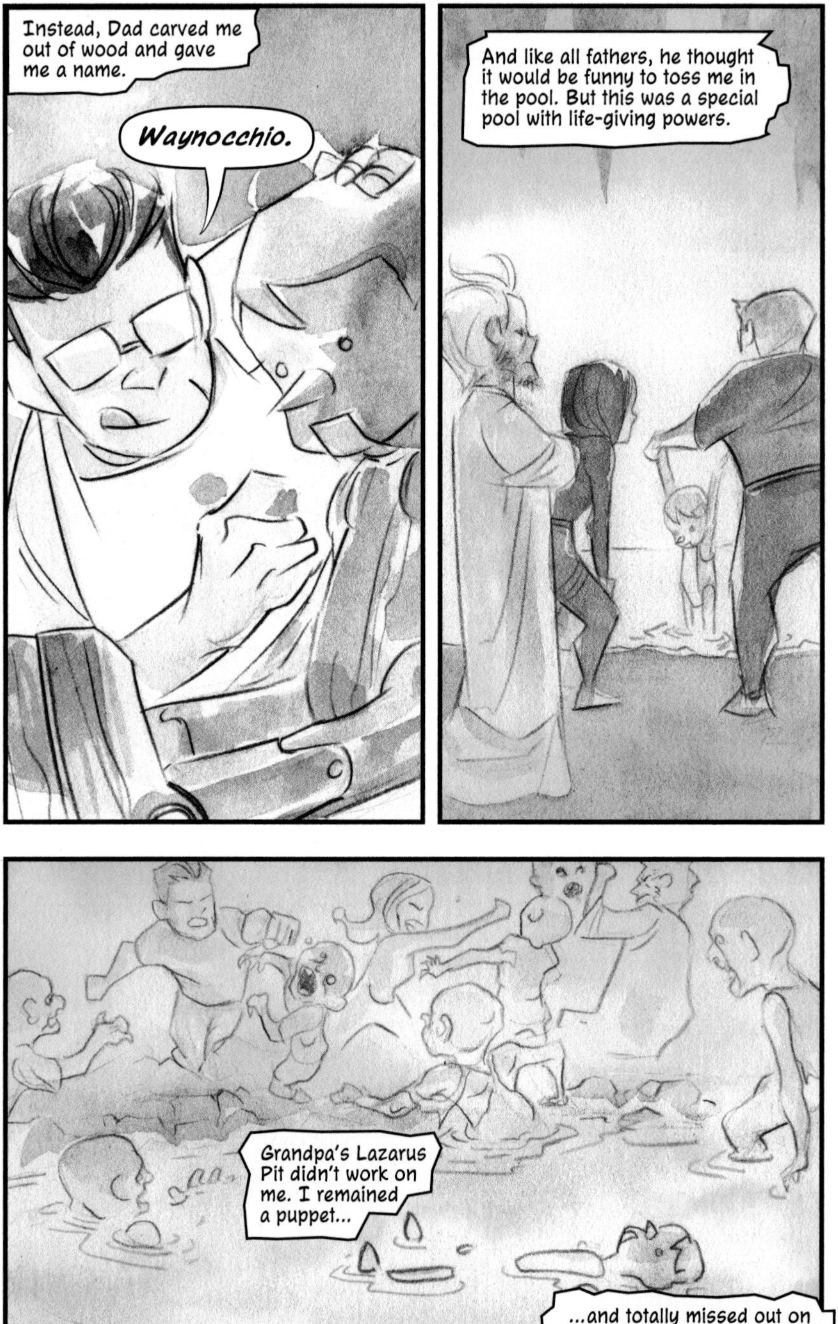
Instead, Dad carved me out of wood and gave me a name.
Waynocchio.
And like all fathers, he thought it would be funny to toss me in the pool. But this was a special pool with life-giving powers.
Grandpa's Lazarus Pit didn't work on me. I remained a puppet...
...and totally missed out on some zombie-fighting action!

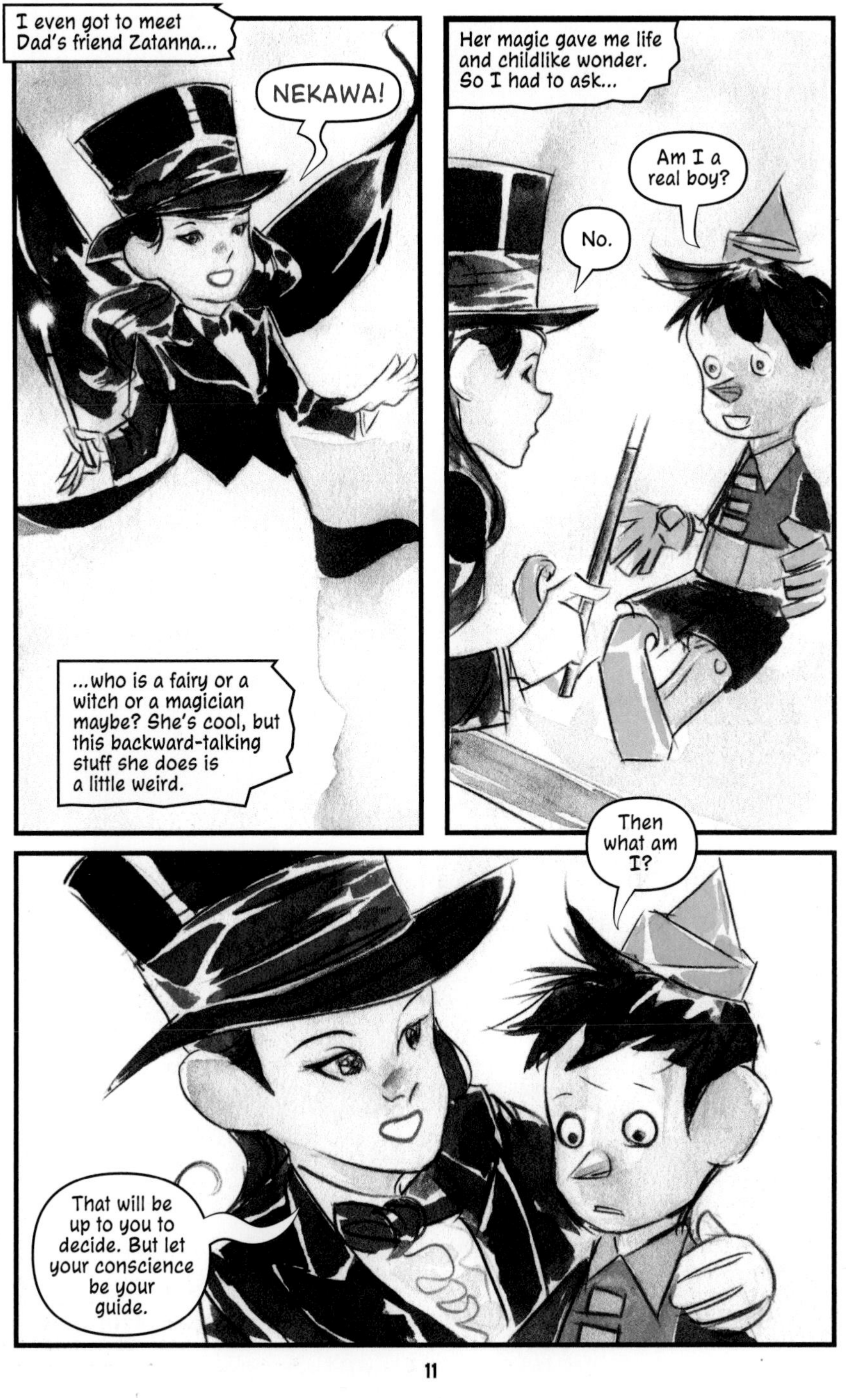

I even got to meet Dad's friend Zatanna...
NEKAWA!
...who is a fairy or a witch or a magician maybe? She's cool, but this backward-talking stuff she does is a little weird.
Her magic gave me life and childlike wonder. So I had to ask...
Am I a real boy?
No.
Then what am I?
That will be up to you to decide. But let your conscience be your guide.

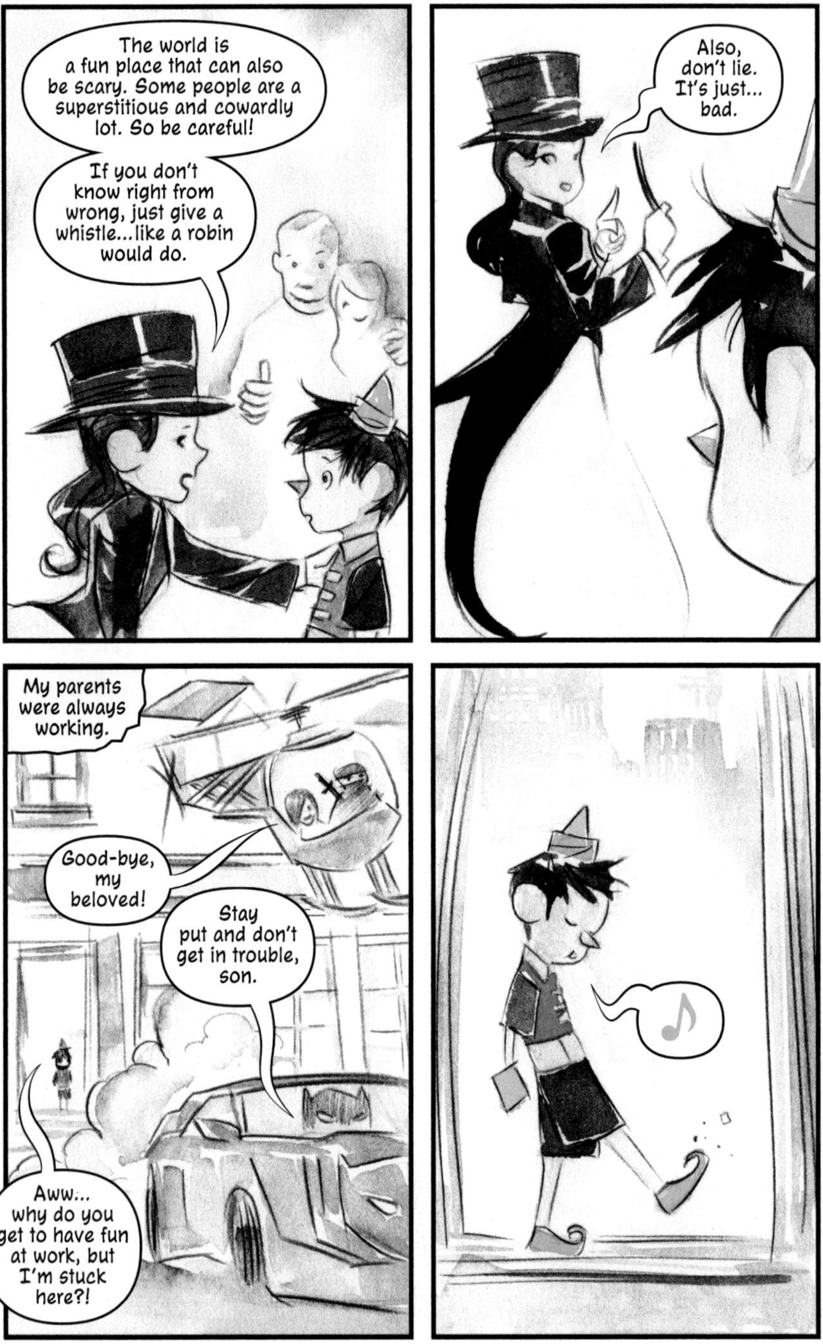
The world is a fun place that can also be scary. Some people are a superstitious and cowardly lot. So be careful!
If you don't know right from wrong, just give a whistle...like a robin would do.
Also, don't lie. It's just... bad.
My parents were always working.
Good-bye, my beloved!
Stay put and don't get in trouble, son.
Aww... why do you get to have fun at work, but I'm stuck here?!
♪

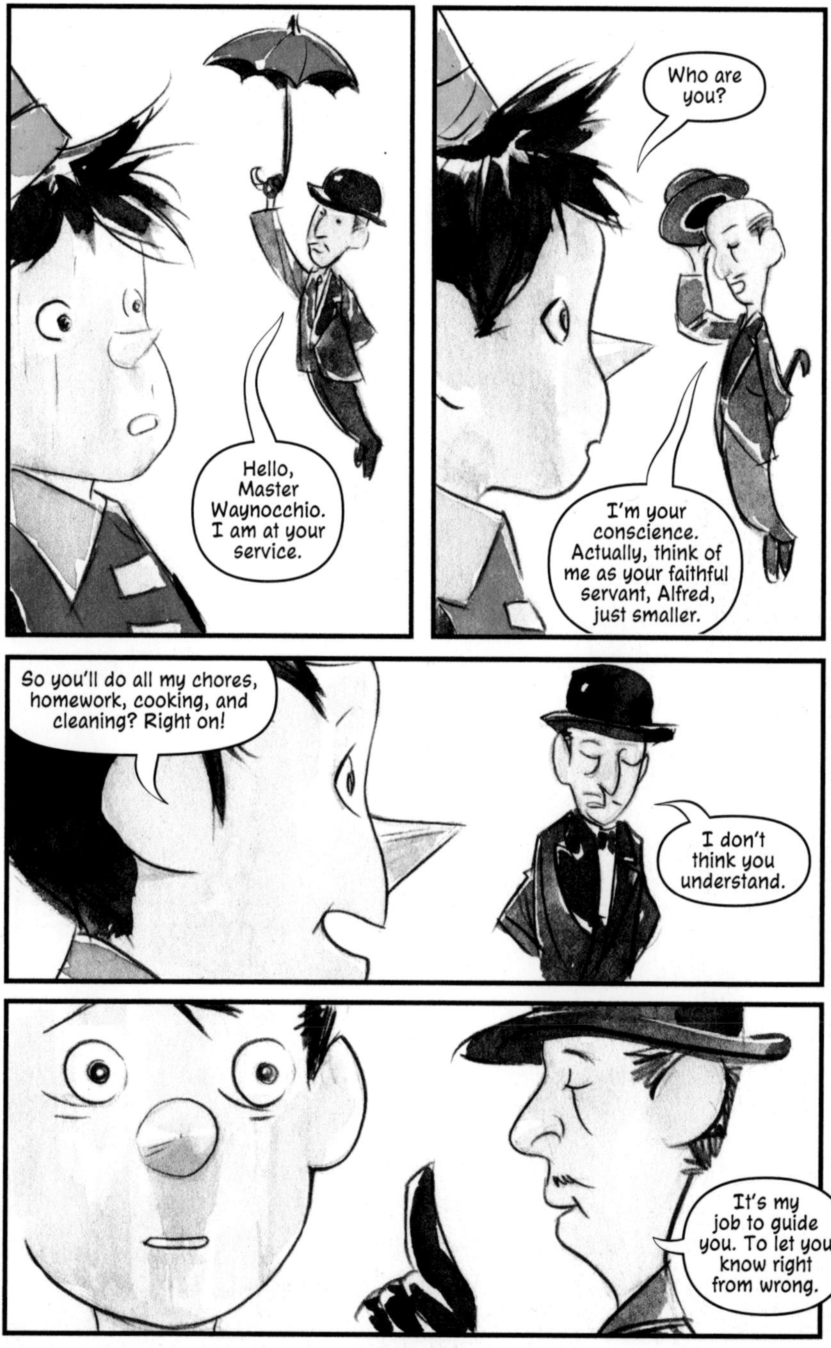
Hello, Master Waynocchio. I am at your service.
Who are you?
I'm your conscience. Actually, think of me as your faithful servant, Alfred, just smaller.
So you'll do all my chores, homework, cooking, and cleaning? Right on!
I don't think you understand.
It's my job to guide you. To let you know right from wrong.

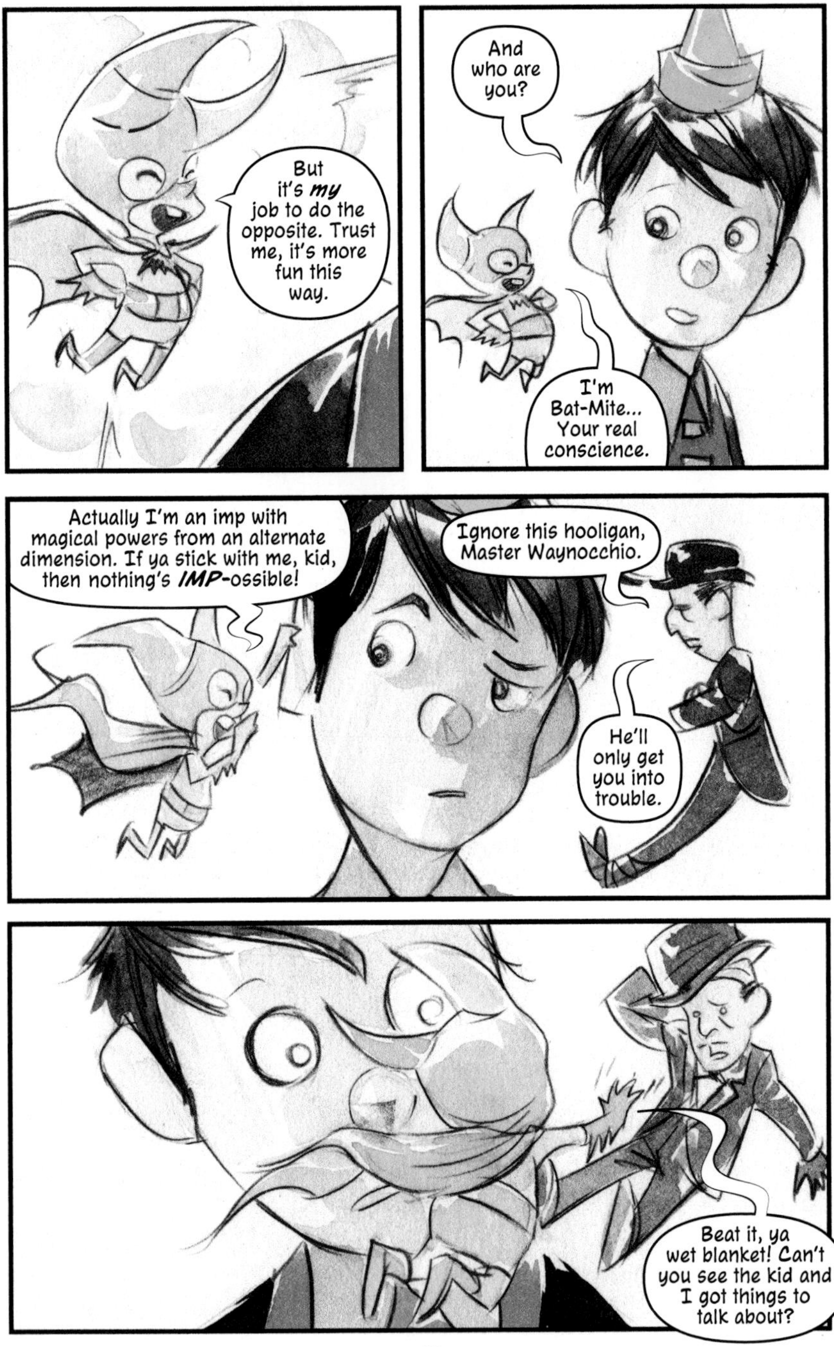
But it's *my* job to do the opposite. Trust me, it's more fun this way.
And who are you?
I'm Bat-Mite... Your real conscience.
Actually I'm an imp with magical powers from an alternate dimension. If ya stick with me, kid, then nothing's *IMP*-ossible!
Ignore this hooligan, Master Waynocchio.
He'll only get you into trouble.
Beat it, ya wet blanket! Can't you see the kid and I got things to talk about?

Soooo, kid...what is it you want?

To be a real boy.

No wait! A real **BOY Wonder!** And to fight alongside my dad.

WHAT?!

Why do you want to settle for second place sidekick, when you can be *numero uno**?

Trust me... be Batman. Always be Batman!

And I know a thing or two about how you can do that. Because I'm his biggest fan.

I don't know. I think I can handle this by myself.

Besides... when you're as perfect as I am, you don't need anyone's help.

*Number one.

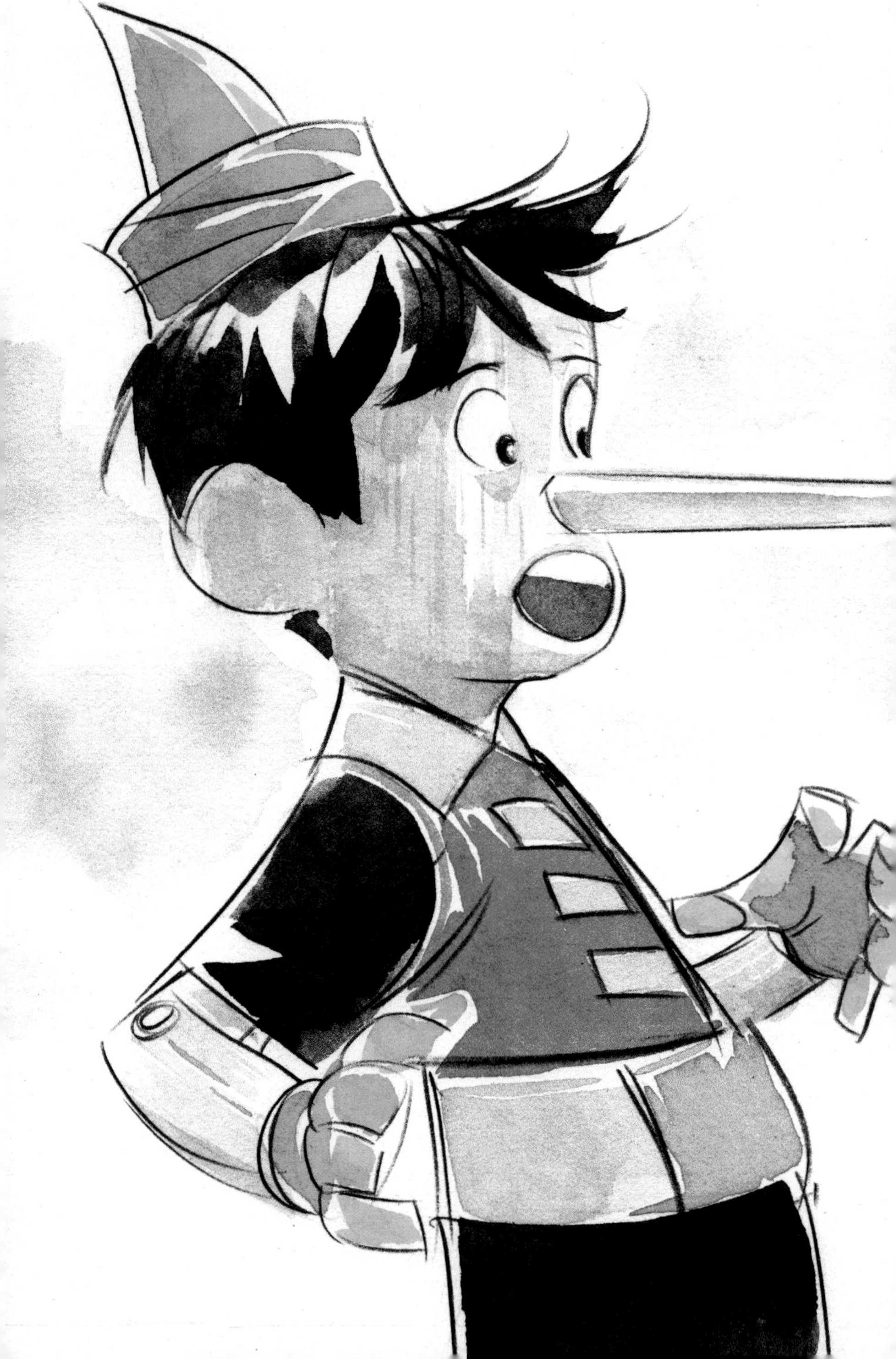

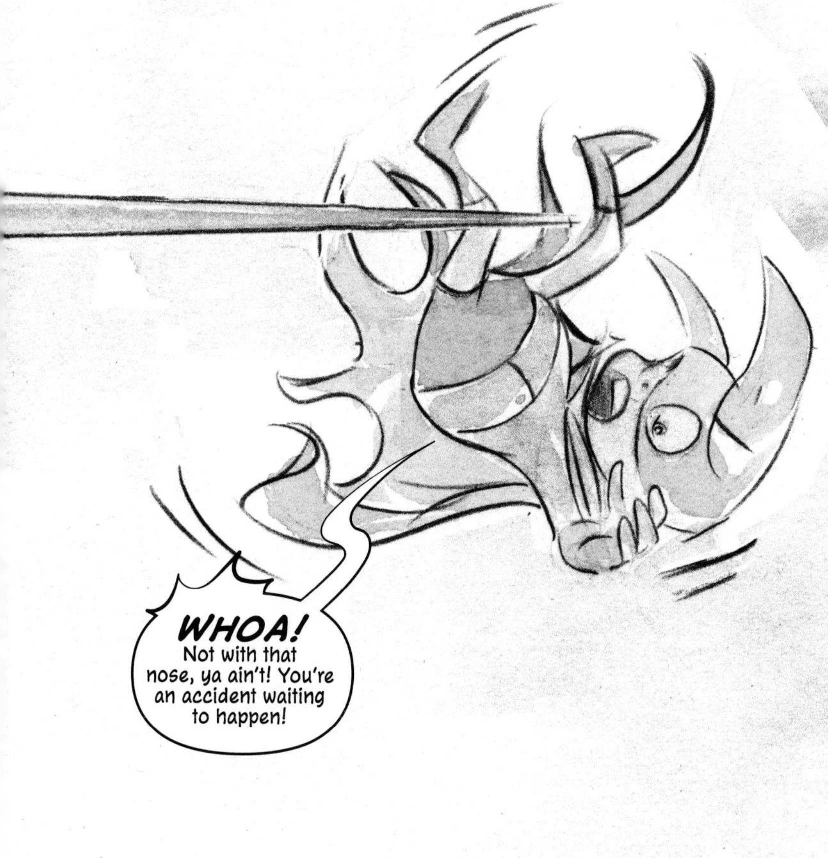
WHOA!
Not with that nose, ya ain't! You're an accident waiting to happen!

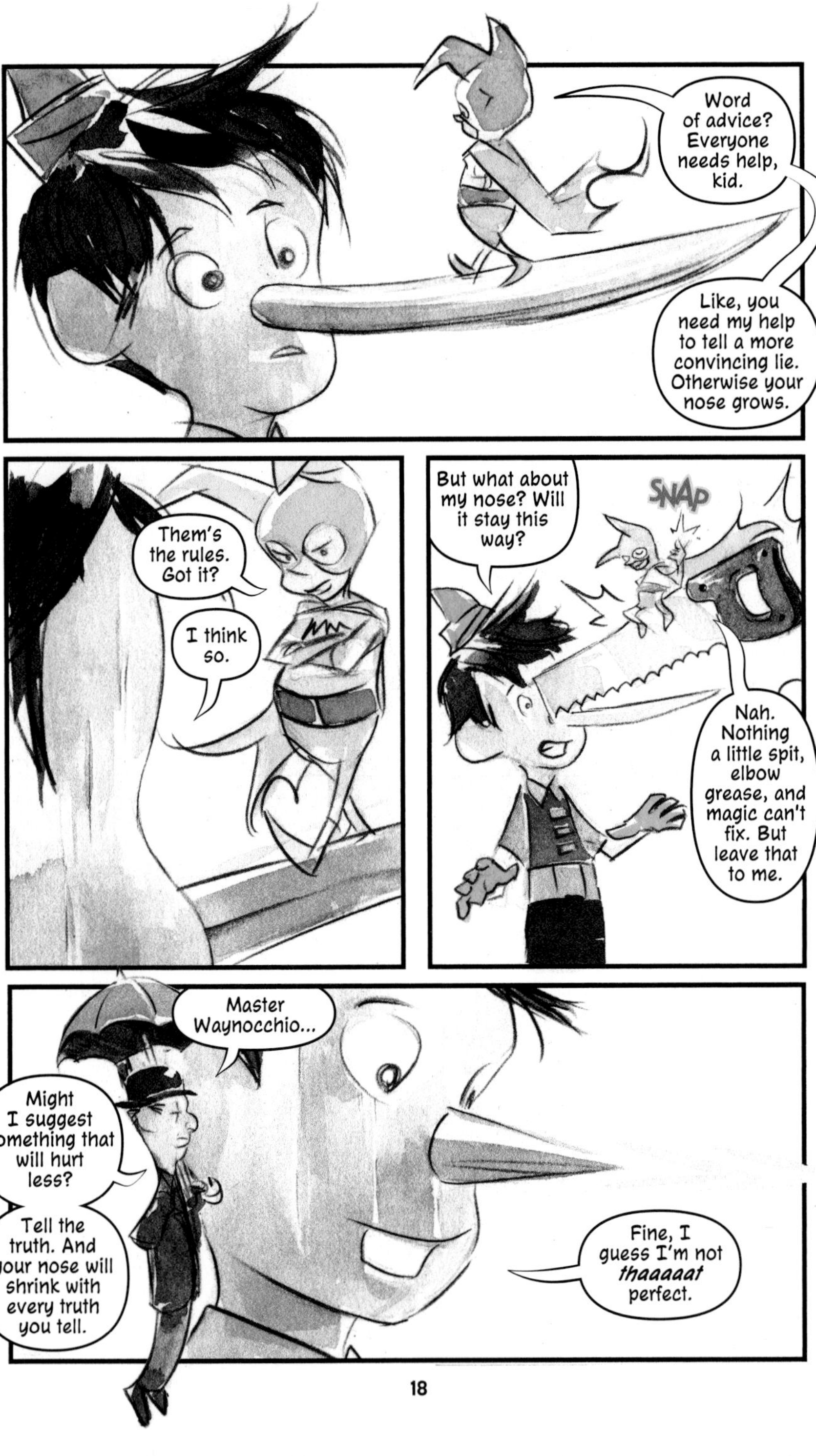
Word of advice? Everyone needs help, kid.
Like, you need my help to tell a more convincing lie. Otherwise your nose grows.
Them's the rules. Got it?
I think so.
But what about my nose? Will it stay this way?
SNAP
Nah. Nothing a little spit, elbow grease, and magic can't fix. But leave that to me.
Master Waynocchio...
Might I suggest something that will hurt less?
Tell the truth. And your nose will shrink with every truth you tell.
Fine, I guess I'm not *thaaaaat* perfect.

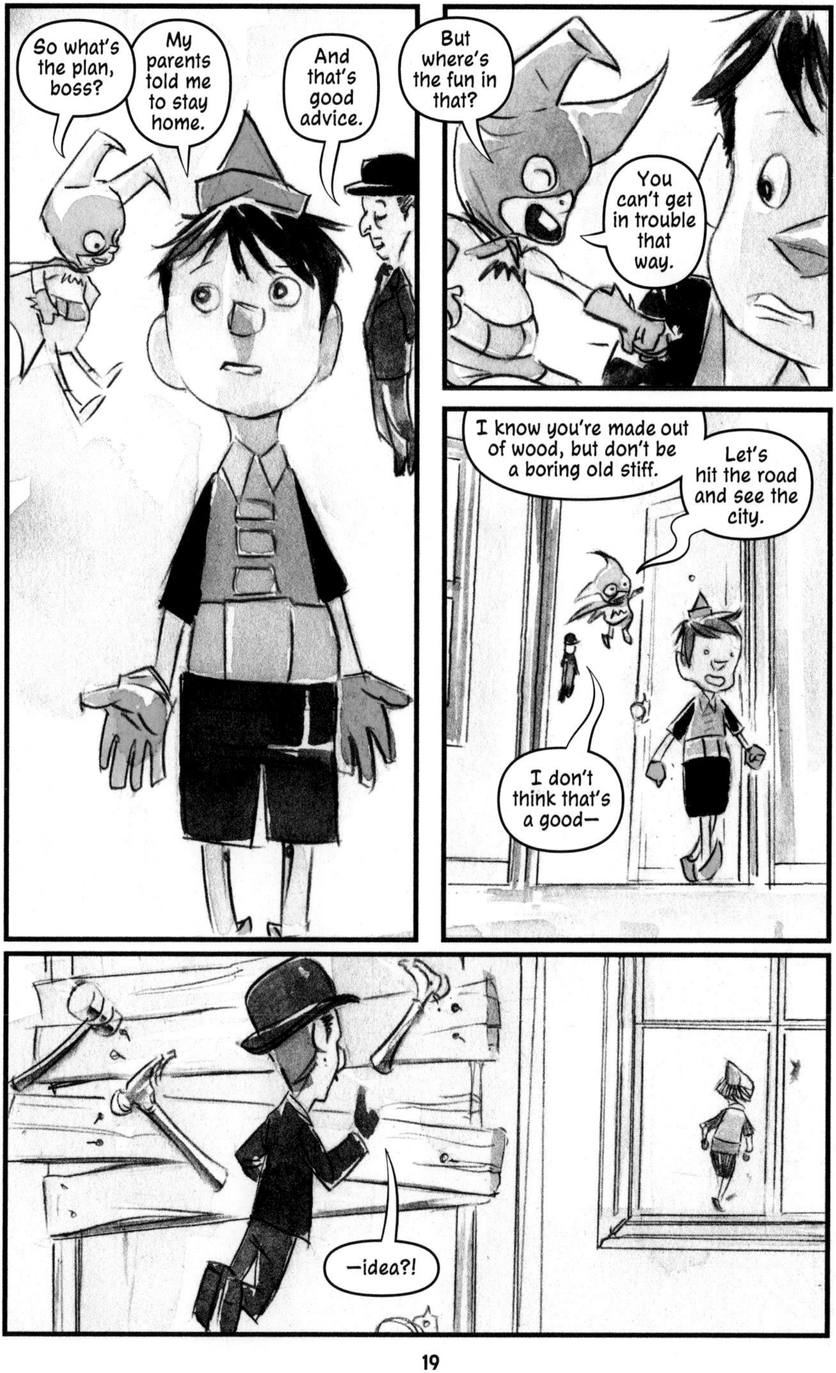

So what's the plan, boss?
My parents told me to stay home.
And that's good advice.
But where's the fun in that?
You can't get in trouble that way.
I know you're made out of wood, but don't be a boring old stiff.
Let's hit the road and see the city.
I don't think that's a good—
—idea?!

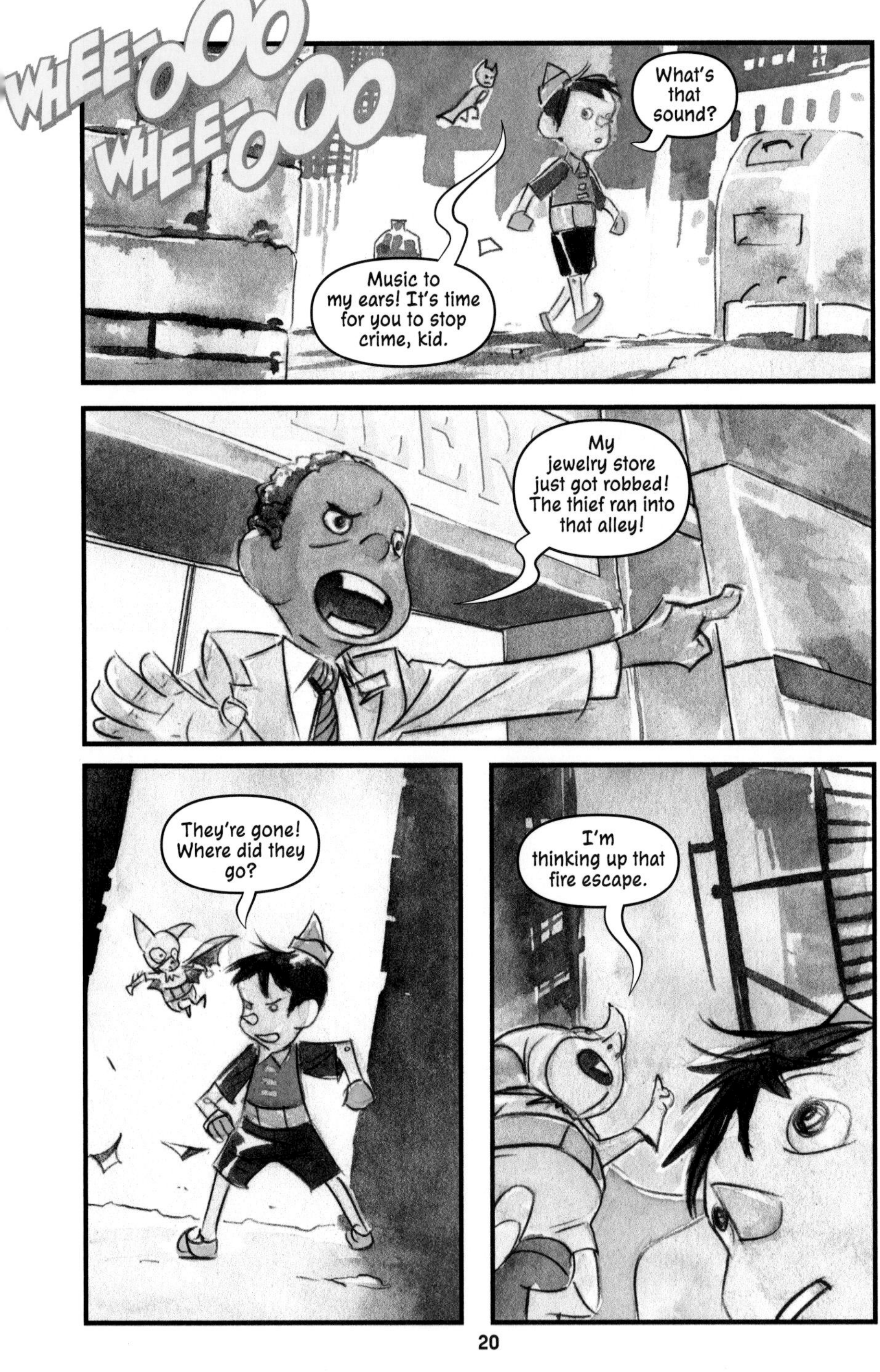
WHEE-OOO
WHEE-OOO
What's that sound?
Music to my ears! It's time for you to stop crime, kid.
My jewelry store just got robbed! The thief ran into that alley!
They're gone! Where did they go?
I'm thinking up that fire escape.

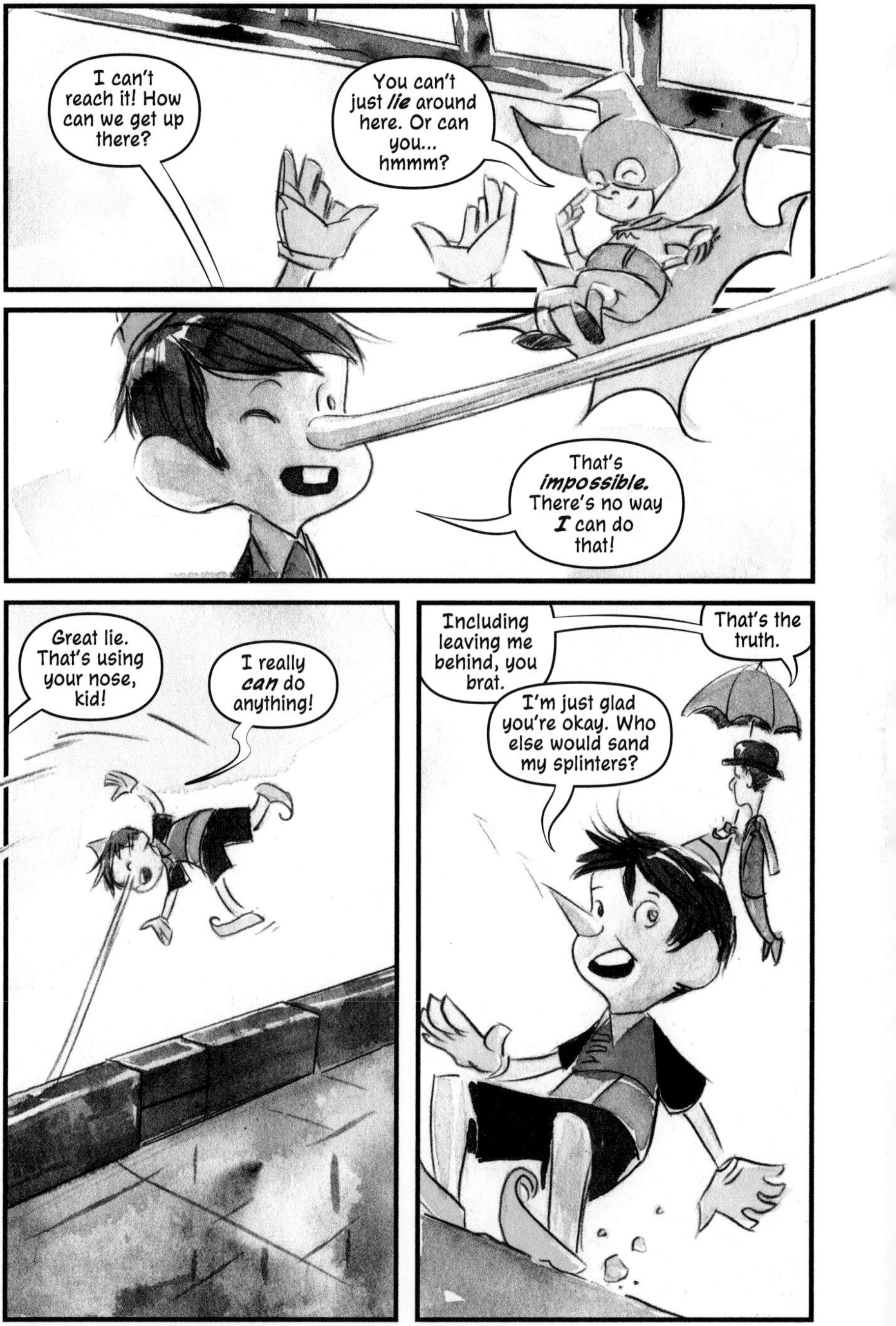
I can't reach it! How can we get up there?
You can't just *lie* around here. Or can you... hmmm?
That's *impossible.* There's no way *I* can do that!
Great lie. That's using your nose, kid!
I really *can* do anything!
Including leaving me behind, you brat.
That's the truth.
I'm just glad you're okay. Who else would sand my splinters?

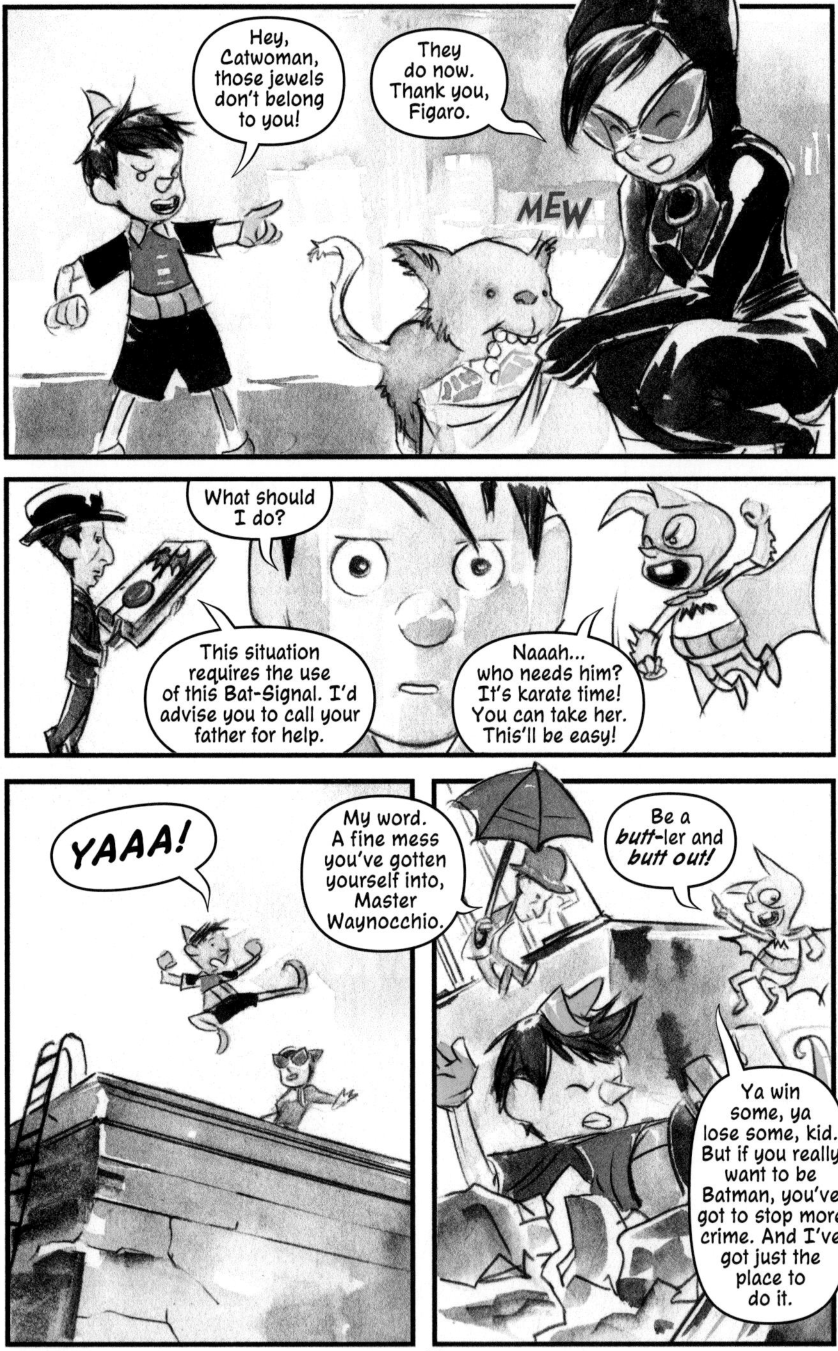
Hey, Catwoman, those jewels don't belong to you!
They do now. Thank you, Figaro.
MEW
What should I do?
This situation requires the use of this Bat-Signal. I'd advise you to call your father for help.
Naaah... who needs him? It's karate time! You can take her. This'll be easy!
YAAA!
My word. A fine mess you've gotten yourself into, Master Waynocchio.
Be a *butt*-ler and *butt out!*
Ya win some, ya lose some, kid. But if you really want to be Batman, you've got to stop more crime. And I've got just the place to do it.

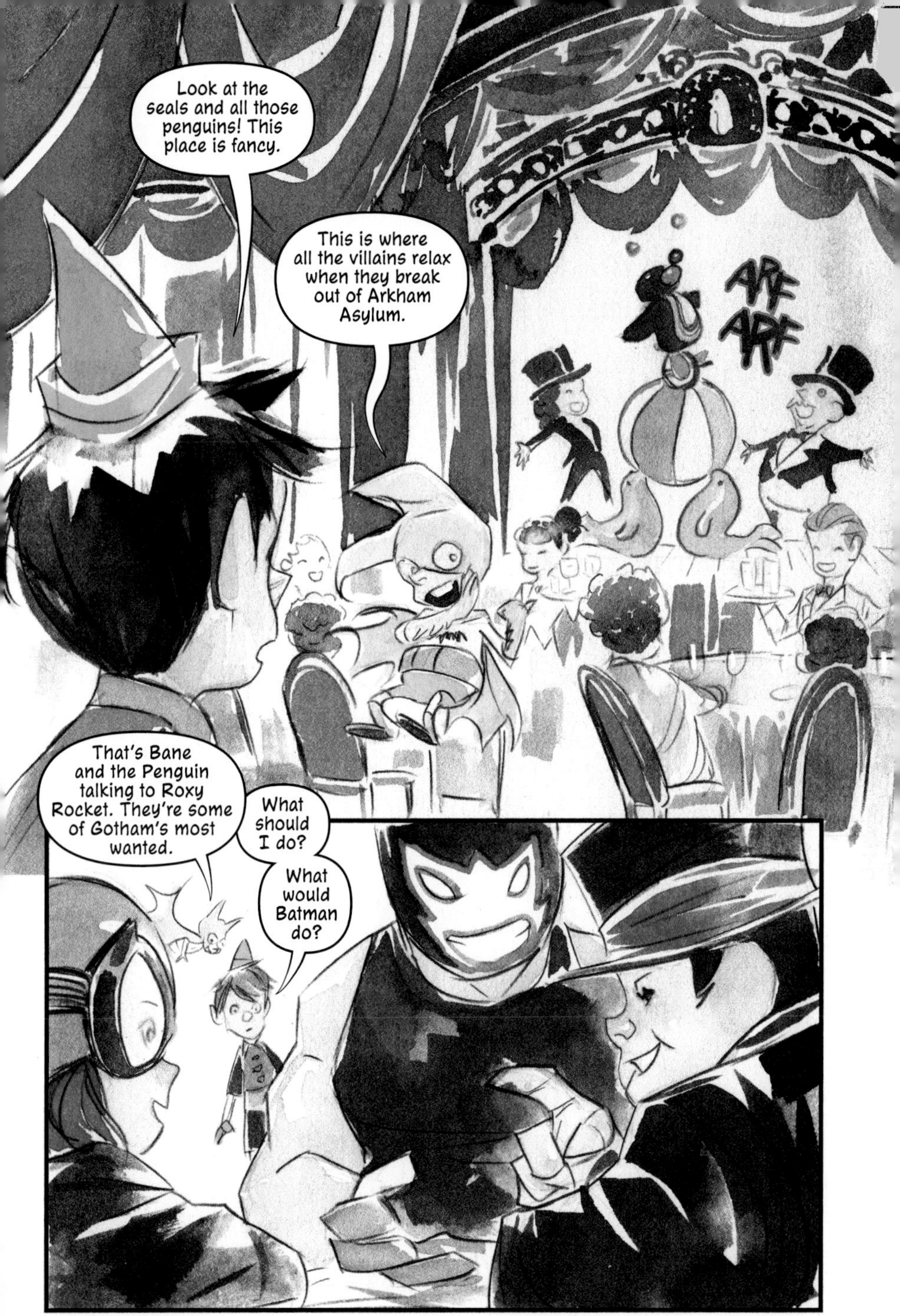
Look at the seals and all those penguins! This place is fancy.
This is where all the villains relax when they break out of Arkham Asylum.
ARF ARF
That's Bane and the Penguin talking to Roxy Rocket. They're some of Gotham's most wanted.
What should I do?
What would Batman do?

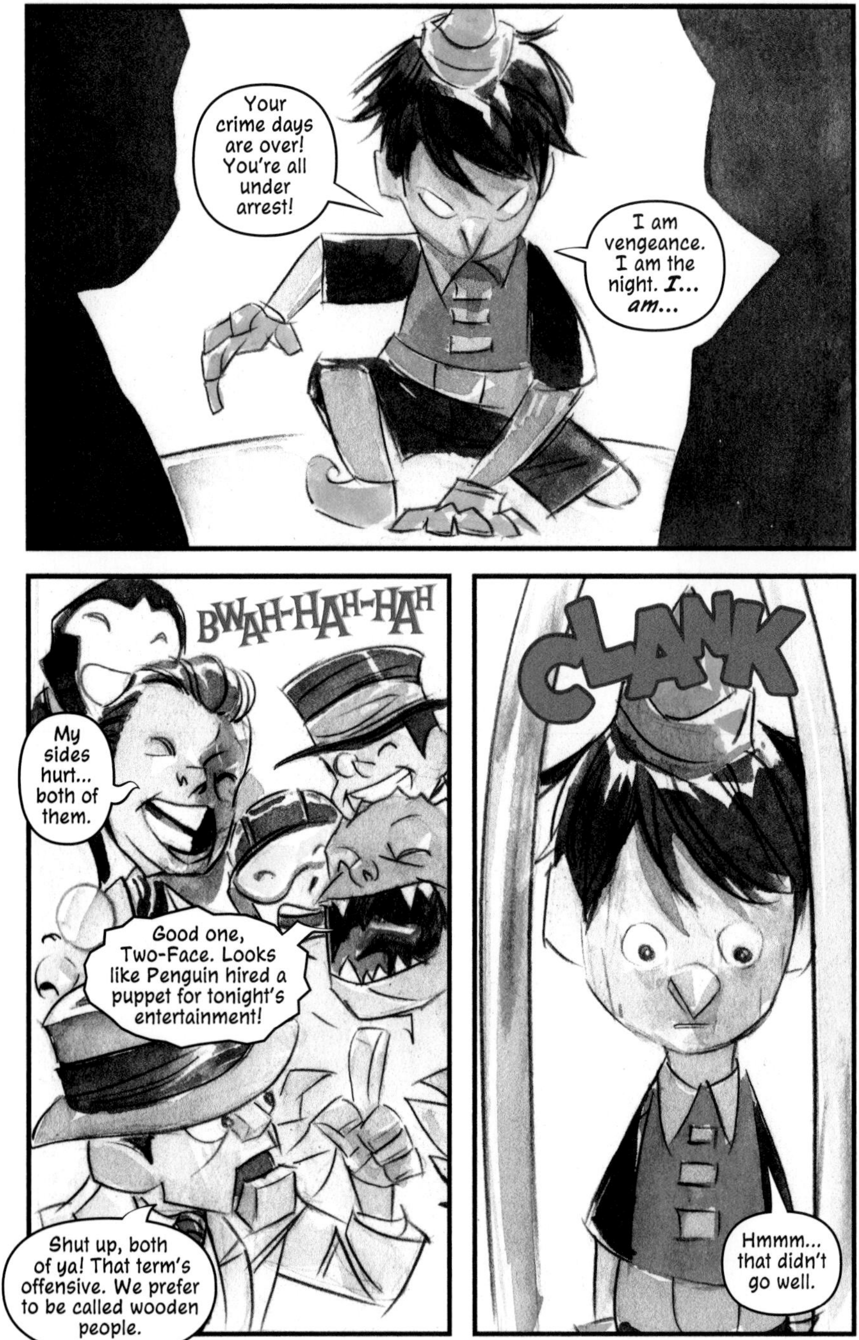
Your crime days are over! You're all under arrest!
I am vengeance. I am the night. ***I... am...***
BWAH-HAH-HAH
My sides hurt... both of them.
Good one, Two-Face. Looks like Penguin hired a puppet for tonight's entertainment!
Shut up, both of ya! That term's offensive. We prefer to be called wooden people.
CLANK
Hmmm... that didn't go well.

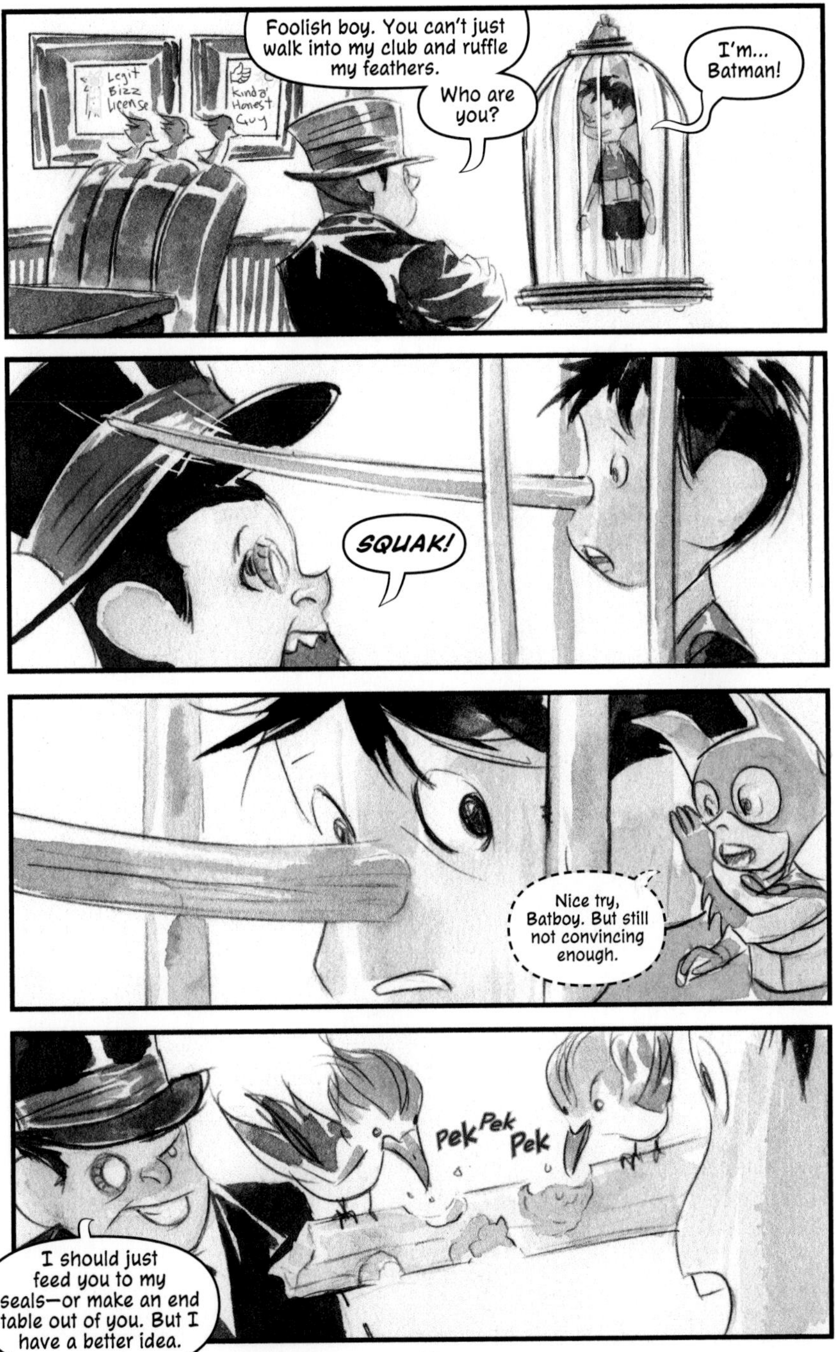
Legit Bizz License
Kinda' Honest Guy
Foolish boy. You can't just walk into my club and ruffle my feathers.
Who are you?
I'm... Batman!
SQUAK!
Nice try, Batboy. But still not convincing enough.
Pek Pek Pek
I should just feed you to my seals—or make an end table out of you. But I have a better idea.

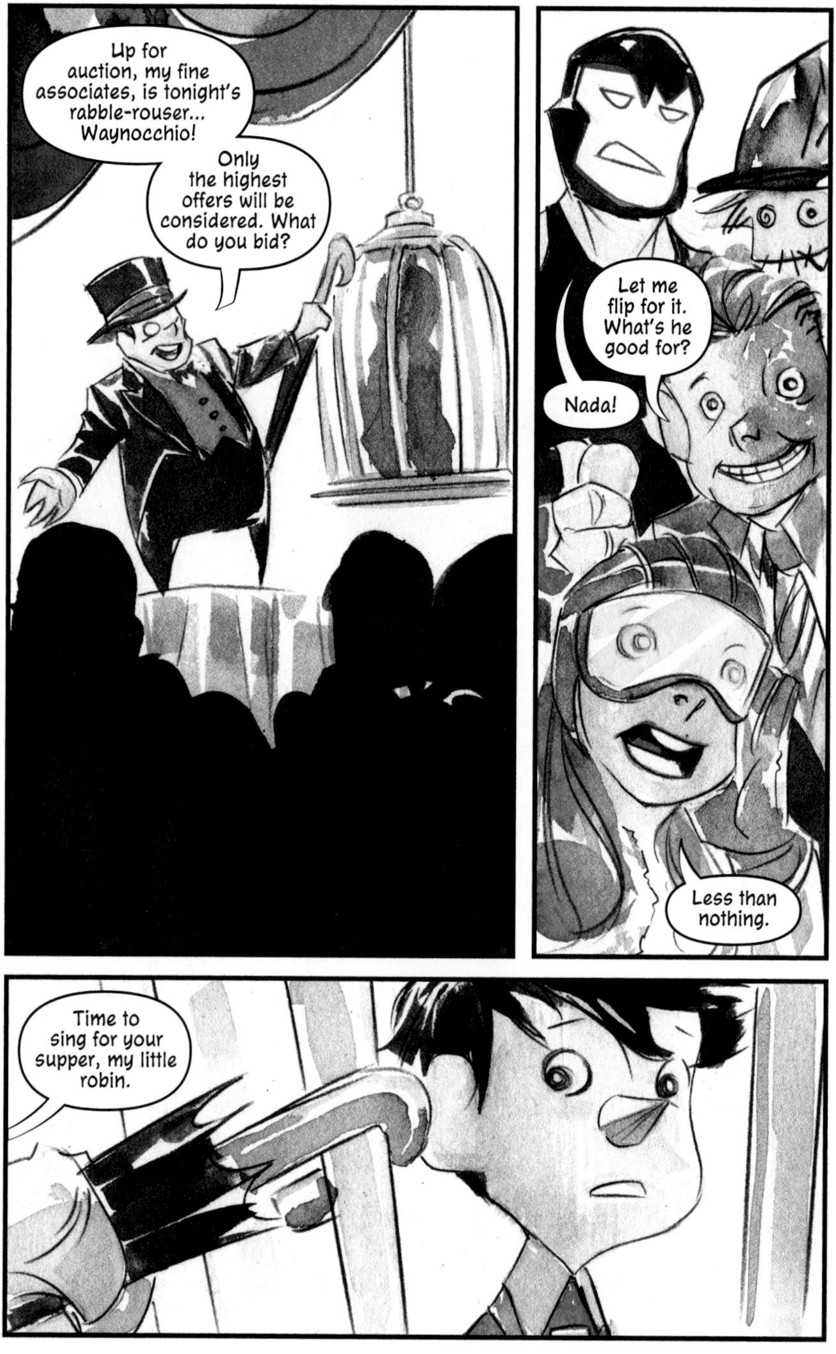
Up for auction, my fine associates, is tonight's rabble-rouser... Waynocchio!
Only the highest offers will be considered. What do you bid?
Let me flip for it. What's he good for?
Nada!
Less than nothing.
Time to sing for your supper, my little robin.

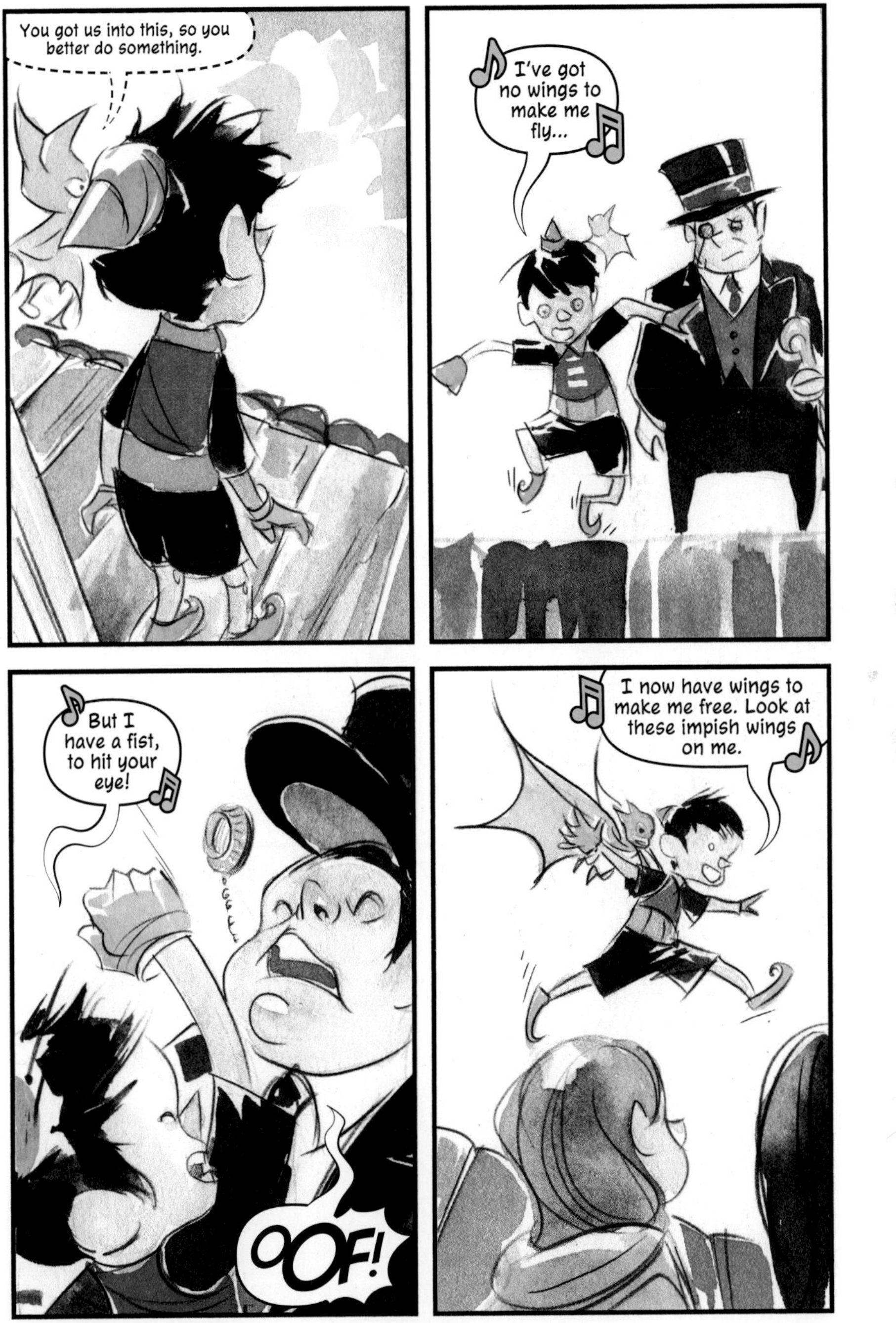
You got us into this, so you better do something.
I've got no wings to make me fly...
But I have a fist, to hit your eye!
OOF!
I now have wings to make me free. Look at these impish wings on me.

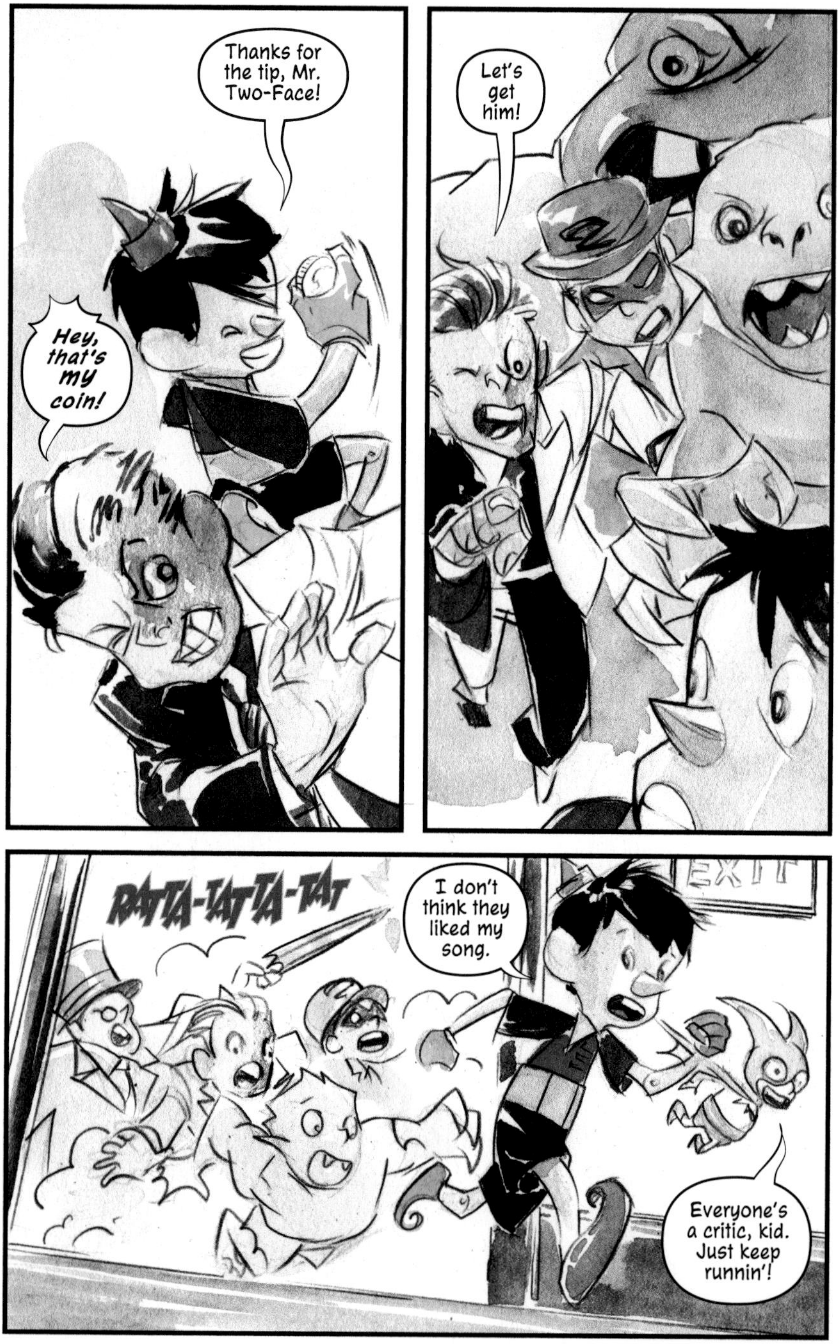
Thanks for the tip, Mr. Two-Face!
Hey, that's my coin!
Let's get him!
RATTA-TAT-TA-TAT
I don't think they liked my song.
EXIT
Everyone's a critic, kid. Just keep runnin'!

Waynocchio! Waynocchio!

I can't find him anywhere.

Did you try using your Son Dial?

It's on, but he's not responding.

Then we should go out and find him. Together.

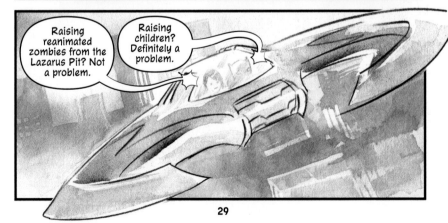

Raising reanimated zombies from the Lazarus Pit? Not a problem.

Raising children? Definitely a problem.

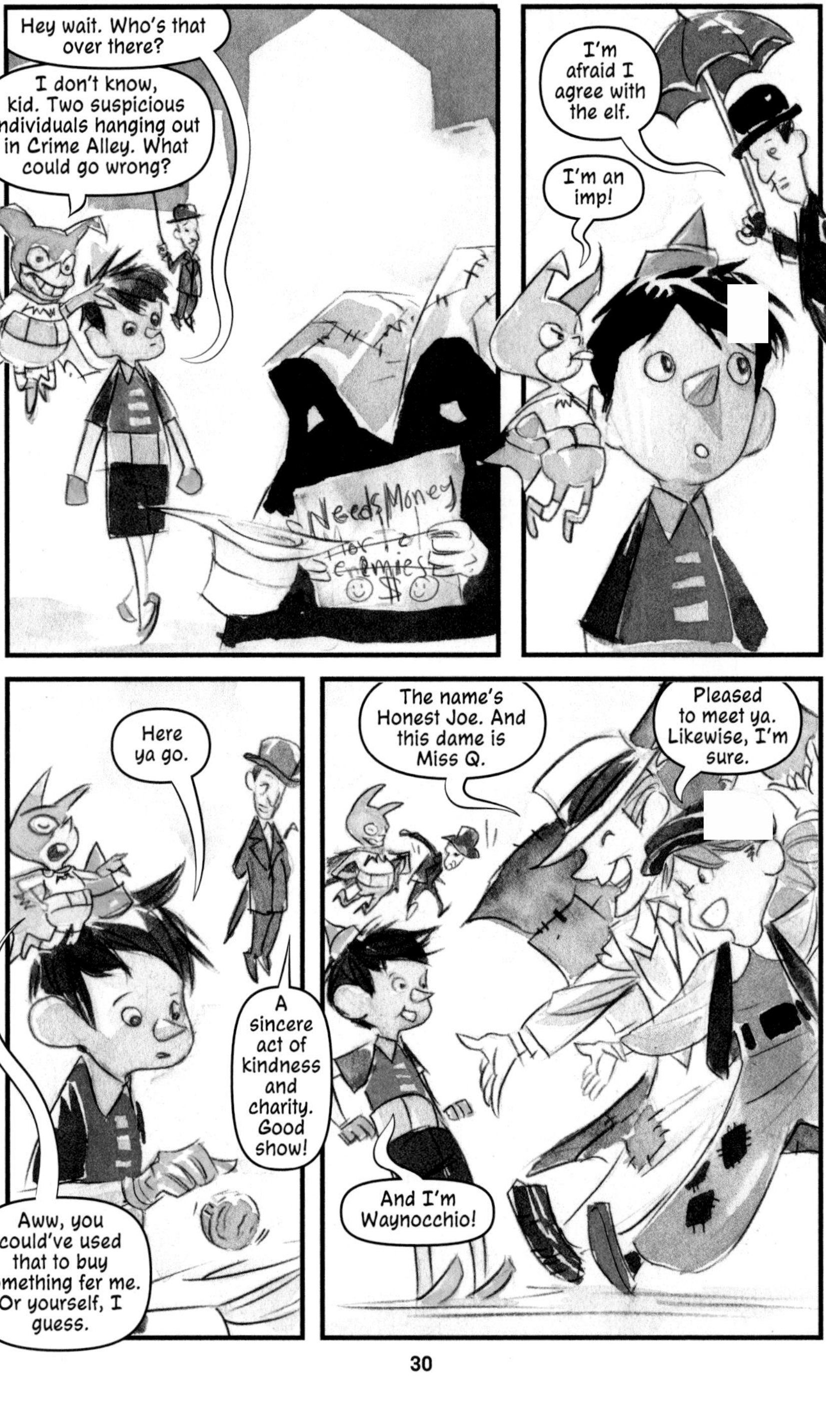
Hey wait. Who's that over there?
I don't know, kid. Two suspicious individuals hanging out in Crime Alley. What could go wrong?
Needs Money
I'm afraid I agree with the elf.
I'm an imp!
Here ya go.
A sincere act of kindness and charity. Good show!
Aww, you could've used that to buy something fer me. Or yourself, I guess.
The name's Honest Joe. And this dame is Miss Q.
Pleased to meet ya. Likewise, I'm sure.
And I'm Waynocchio!

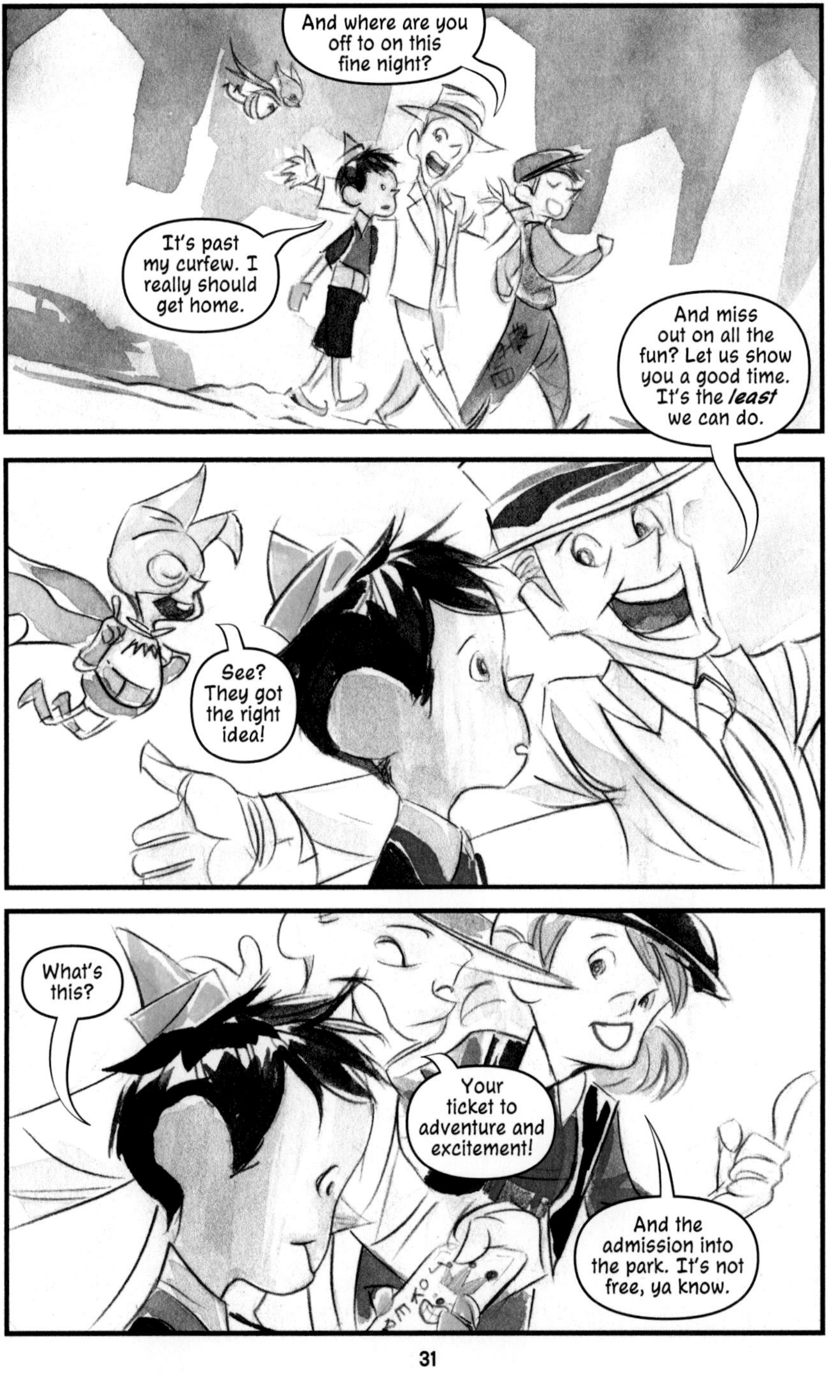

And where are you off to on this fine night?
It's past my curfew. I really should get home.
And miss out on all the fun? Let us show you a good time. It's the *least* we can do.
See? They got the right idea!
What's this?
Your ticket to adventure and excitement!
And the admission into the park. It's not free, ya know.

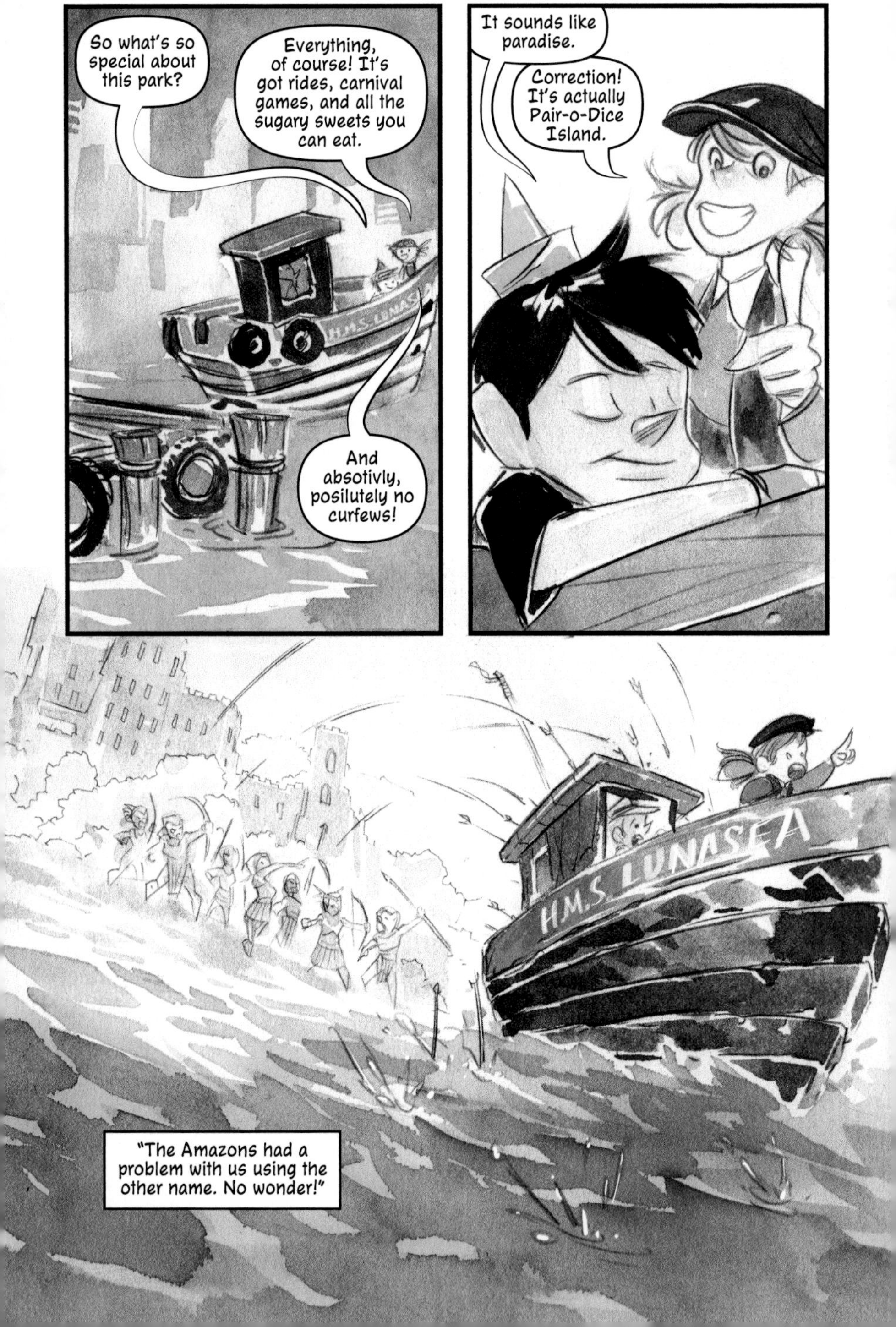
So what's so special about this park?
Everything, of course! It's got rides, carnival games, and all the sugary sweets you can eat.
H.M.S. LUNASEA
And absotivly, posilutely no curfews!
It sounds like paradise.
Correction! It's actually Pair-o-Dice Island.
H.M.S. LUNASEA
"The Amazons had a problem with us using the other name. No wonder!"

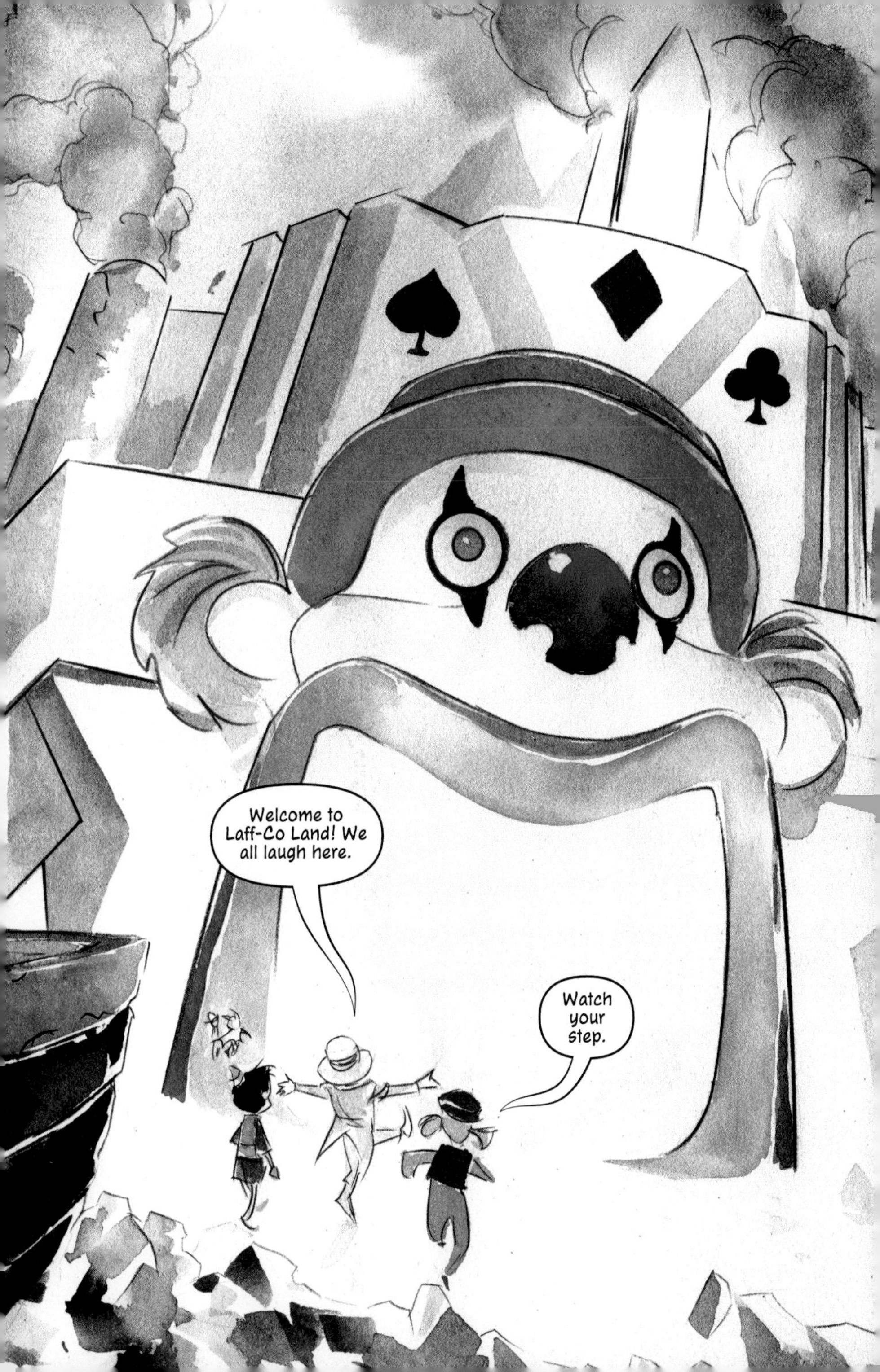
Welcome to Laff-Co Land! We all laugh here.
Watch your step.

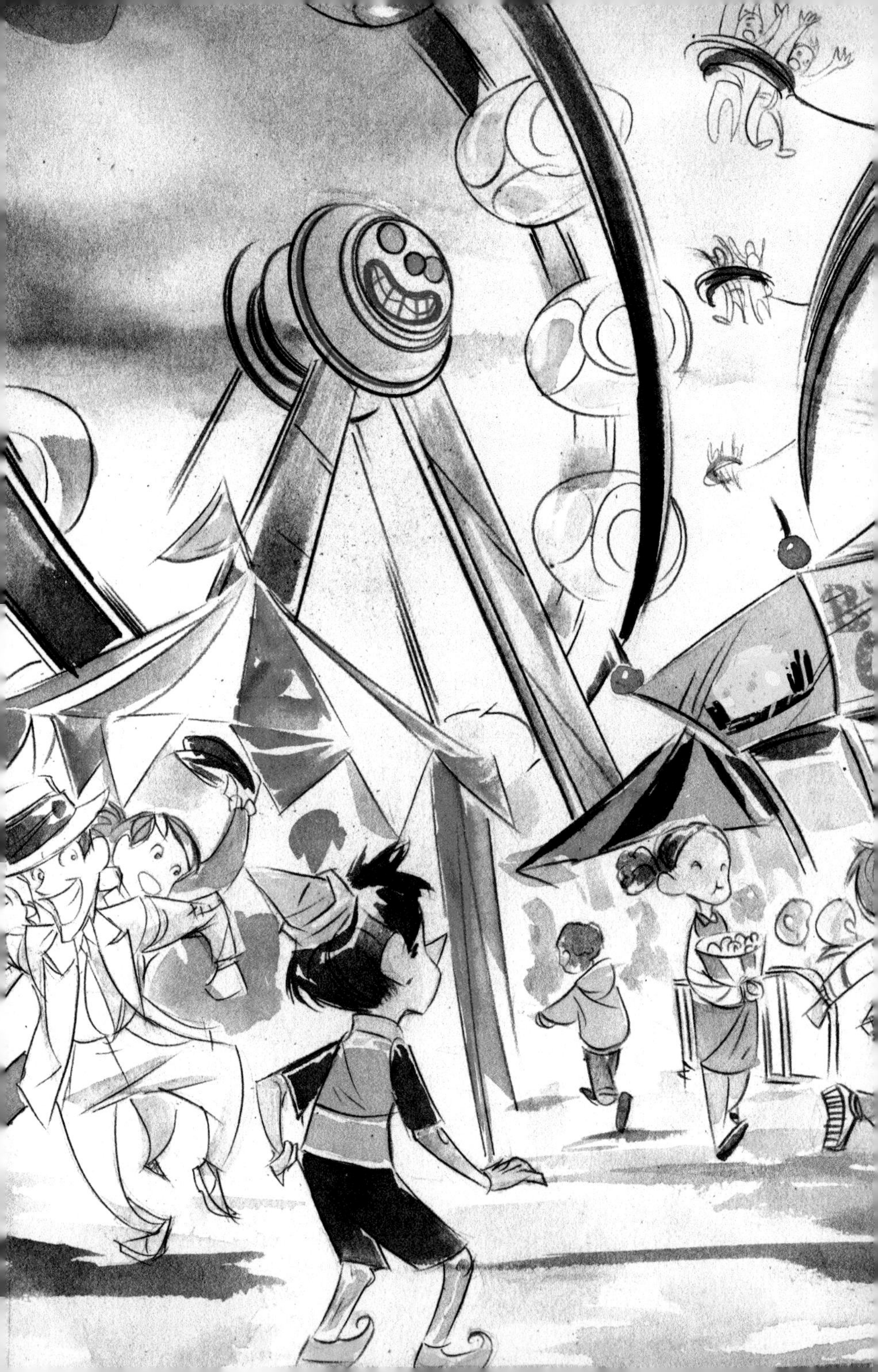

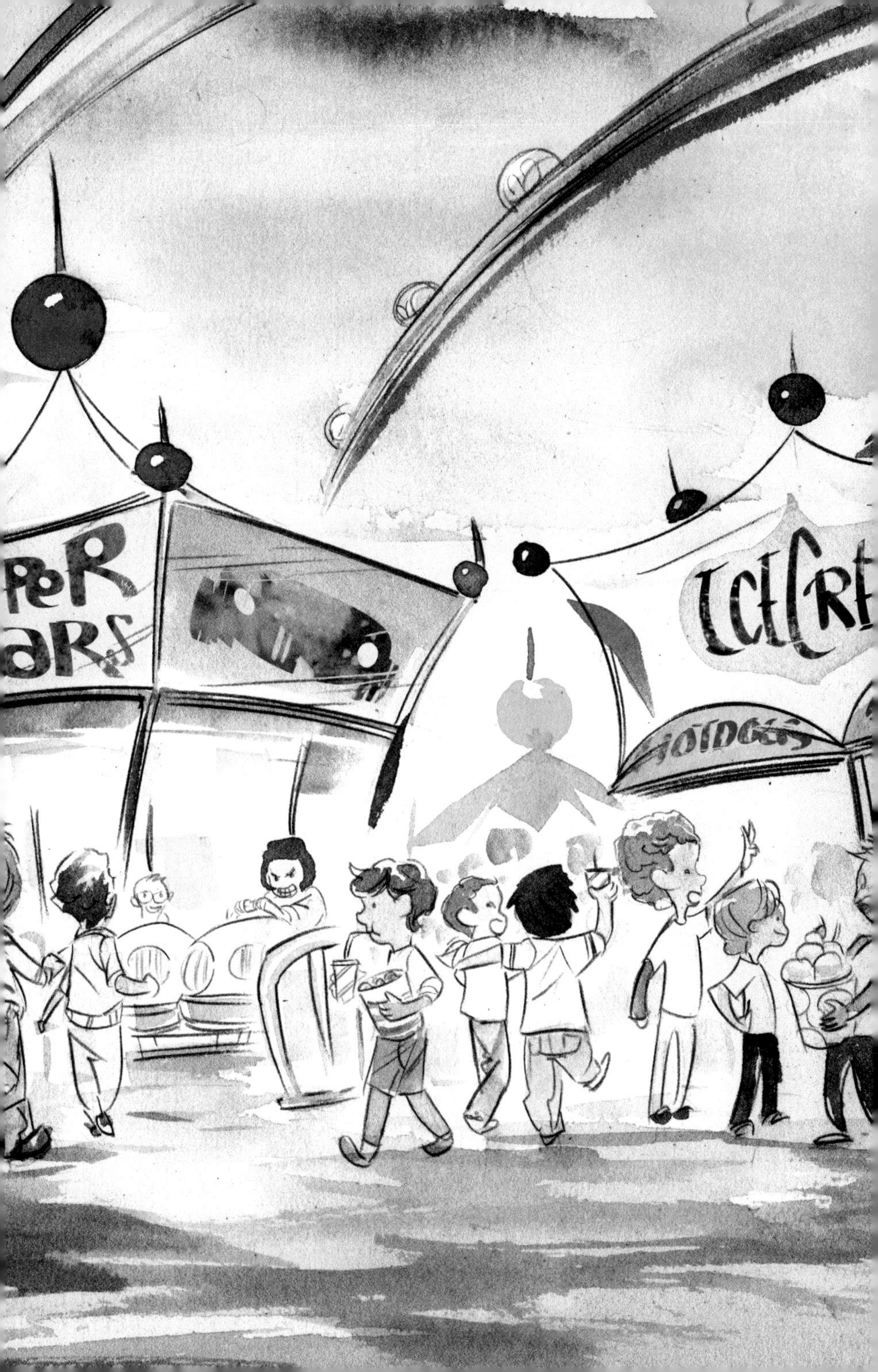

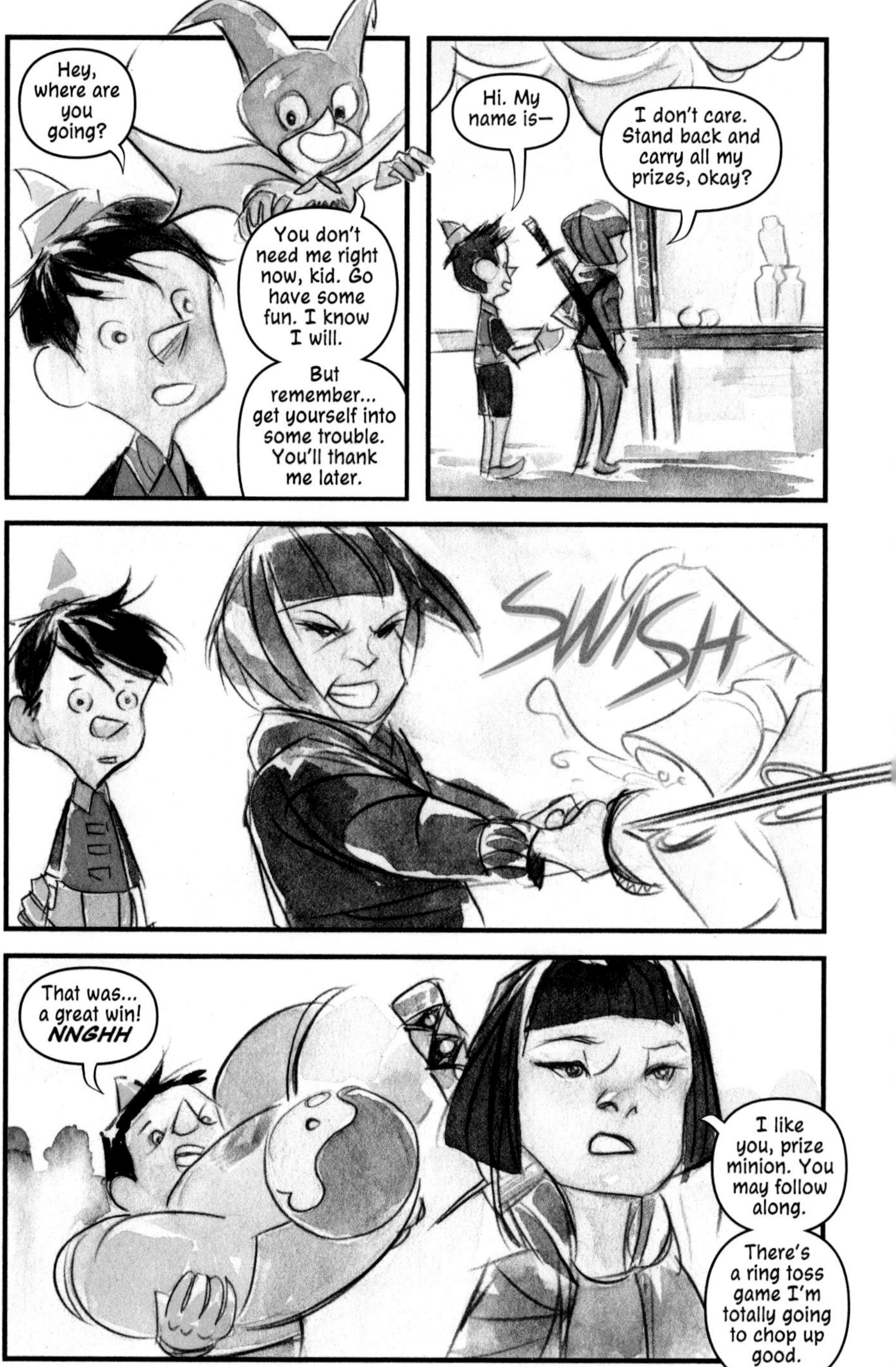

Hey, where are you going?
You don't need me right now, kid. Go have some fun. I know I will.
But remember... get yourself into some trouble. You'll thank me later.
Hi. My name is—
I don't care. Stand back and carry all my prizes, okay?
SWISH
That was... a great win! NNGHH
I like you, prize minion. You may follow along.
There's a ring toss game I'm totally going to chop up good.

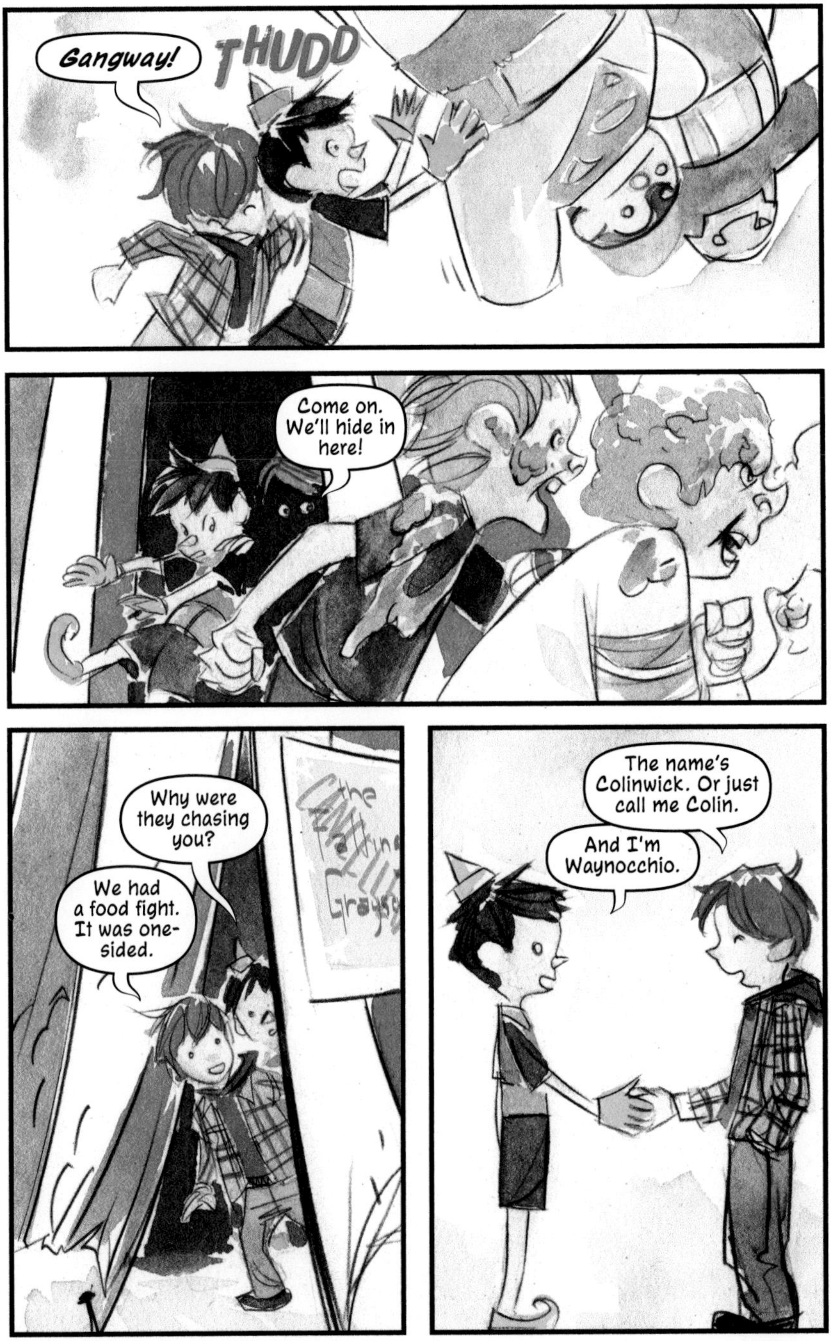
Gangway!
THUDD
Come on. We'll hide in here!
Why were they chasing you?
We had a food fight. It was one-sided.
The name's Colinwick. Or just call me Colin.
And I'm Waynocchio.

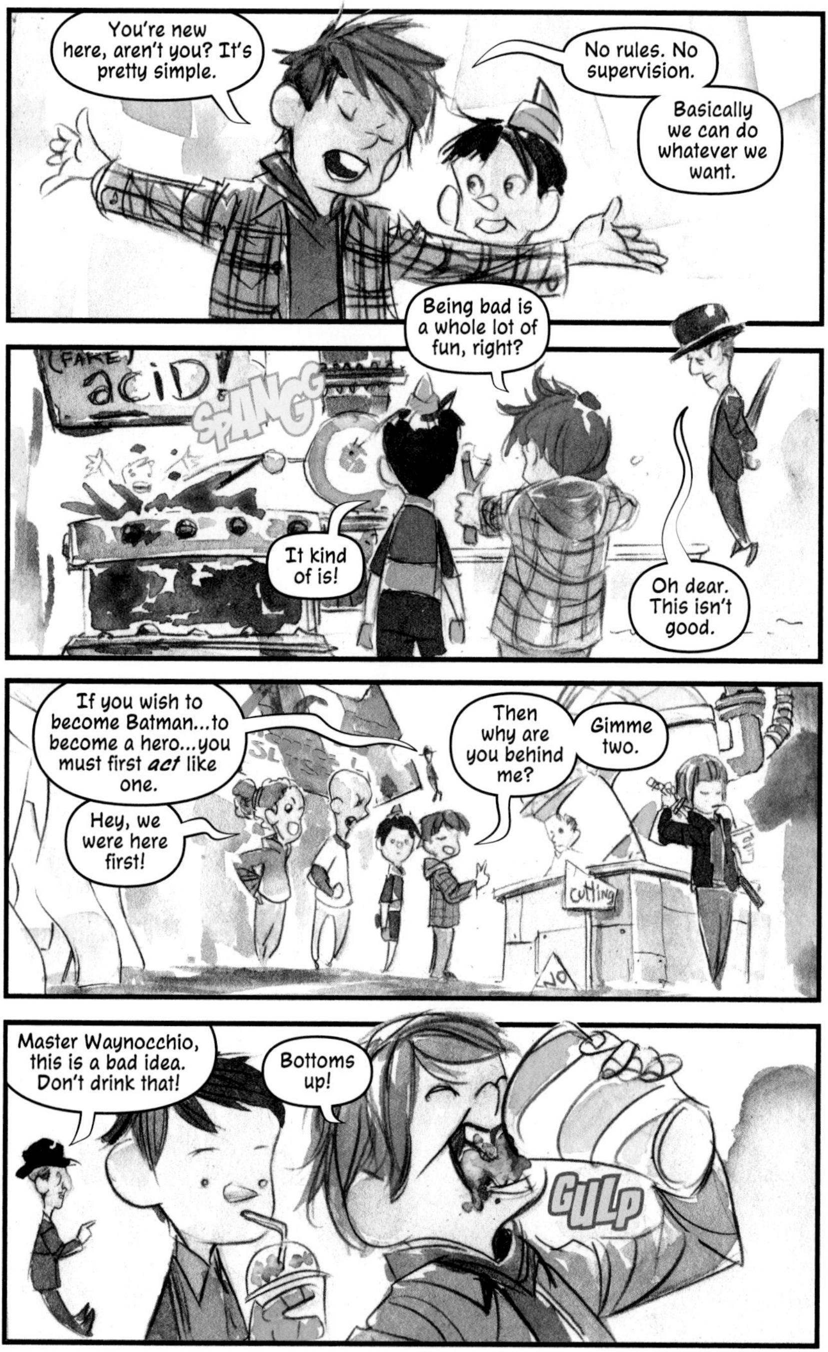
You're new here, aren't you? It's pretty simple.
No rules. No supervision.
Basically we can do whatever we want.
(FAKE) acid!
SPANGG
Being bad is a whole lot of fun, right?
It kind of is!
Oh dear. This isn't good.
If you wish to become Batman...to become a hero...you must first *act* like one.
Hey, we were here first!
Then why are you behind me?
Gimme two.
cutting
Master Waynocchio, this is a bad idea. Don't drink that!
Bottoms up!
GULP

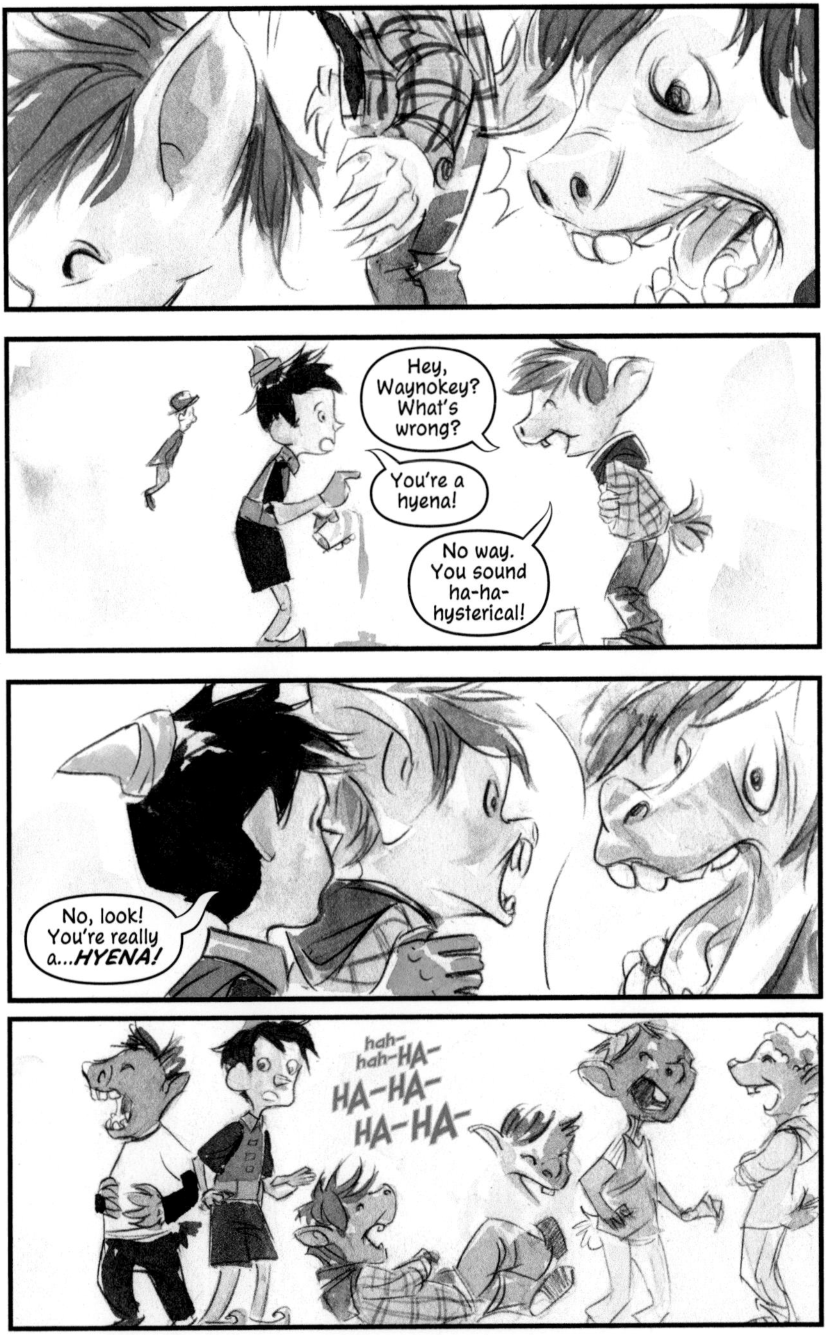
Hey, Waynokey? What's wrong?
You're a hyena!
No way. You sound ha-ha-hysterical!
No, look! You're really a...HYENA!
hah-hah-HA-HA-HA-HA-HA-

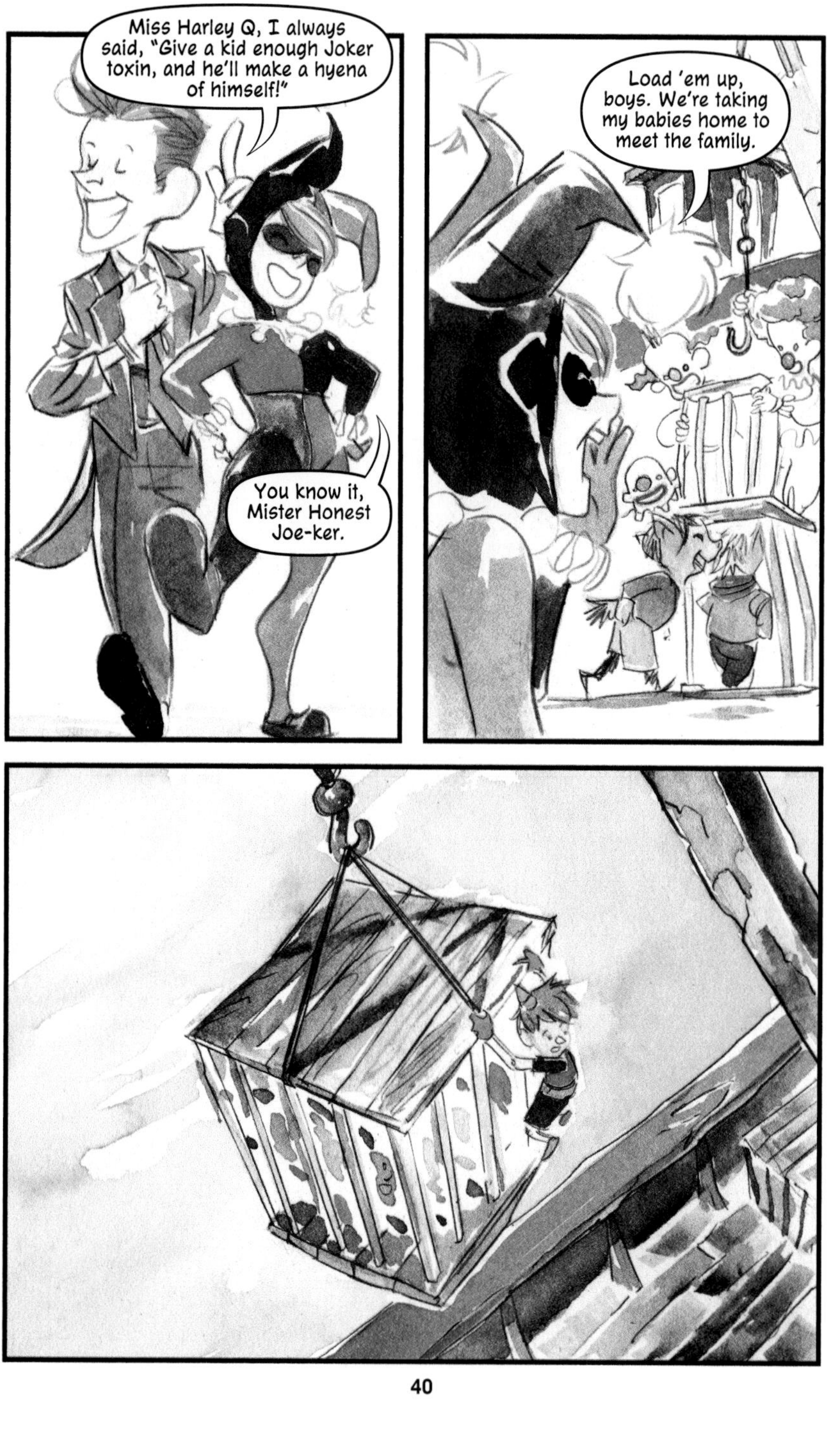
Miss Harley Q, I always said, "Give a kid enough Joker toxin, and he'll make a hyena of himself!"
You know it, Mister Honest Joe-ker.
Load 'em up, boys. We're taking my babies home to meet the family.

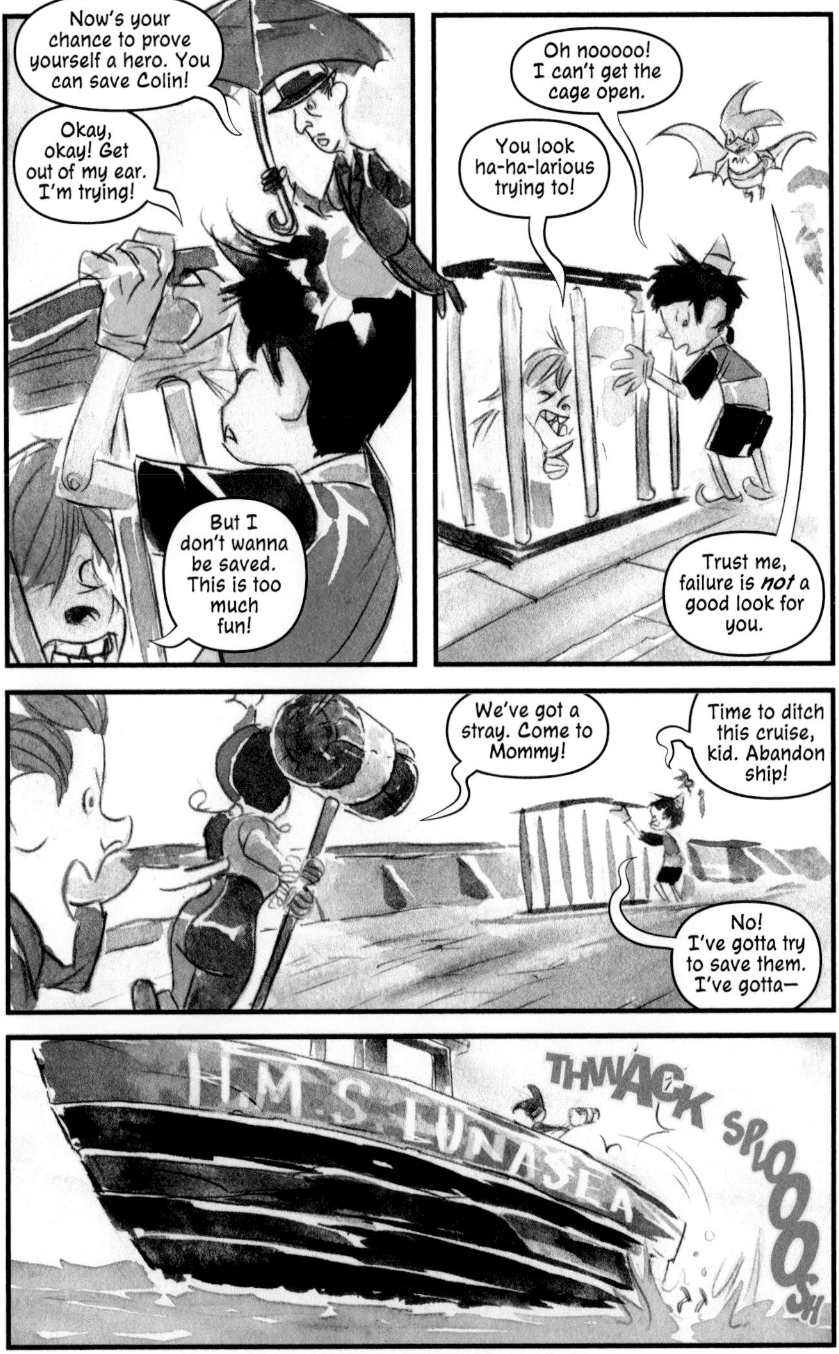
Now's your chance to prove yourself a hero. You can save Colin!
Okay, okay! Get out of my ear. I'm trying!
But I don't wanna be saved. This is too much fun!
Oh nooooo! I can't get the cage open.
You look ha-ha-larious trying to!
Trust me, failure is *not* a good look for you.
We've got a stray. Come to Mommy!
Time to ditch this cruise, kid. Abandon ship!
No! I've gotta try to save them. I've gotta—
H.M.S LUNASEA
THWACK
SPLOOOOSH

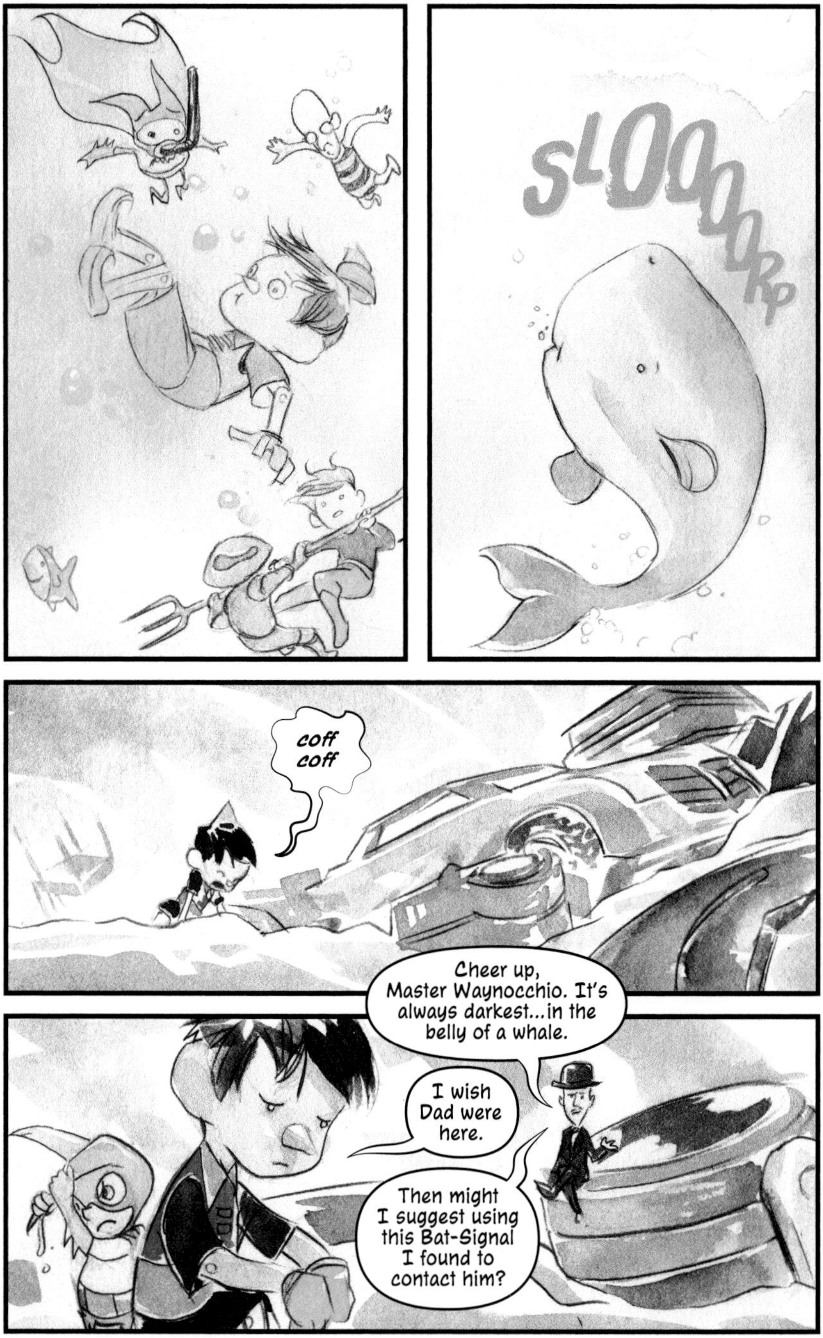
SLOOOORP
coff coff
Cheer up, Master Waynocchio. It's always darkest...in the belly of a whale.
I wish Dad were here.
Then might I suggest using this Bat-Signal I found to contact him?

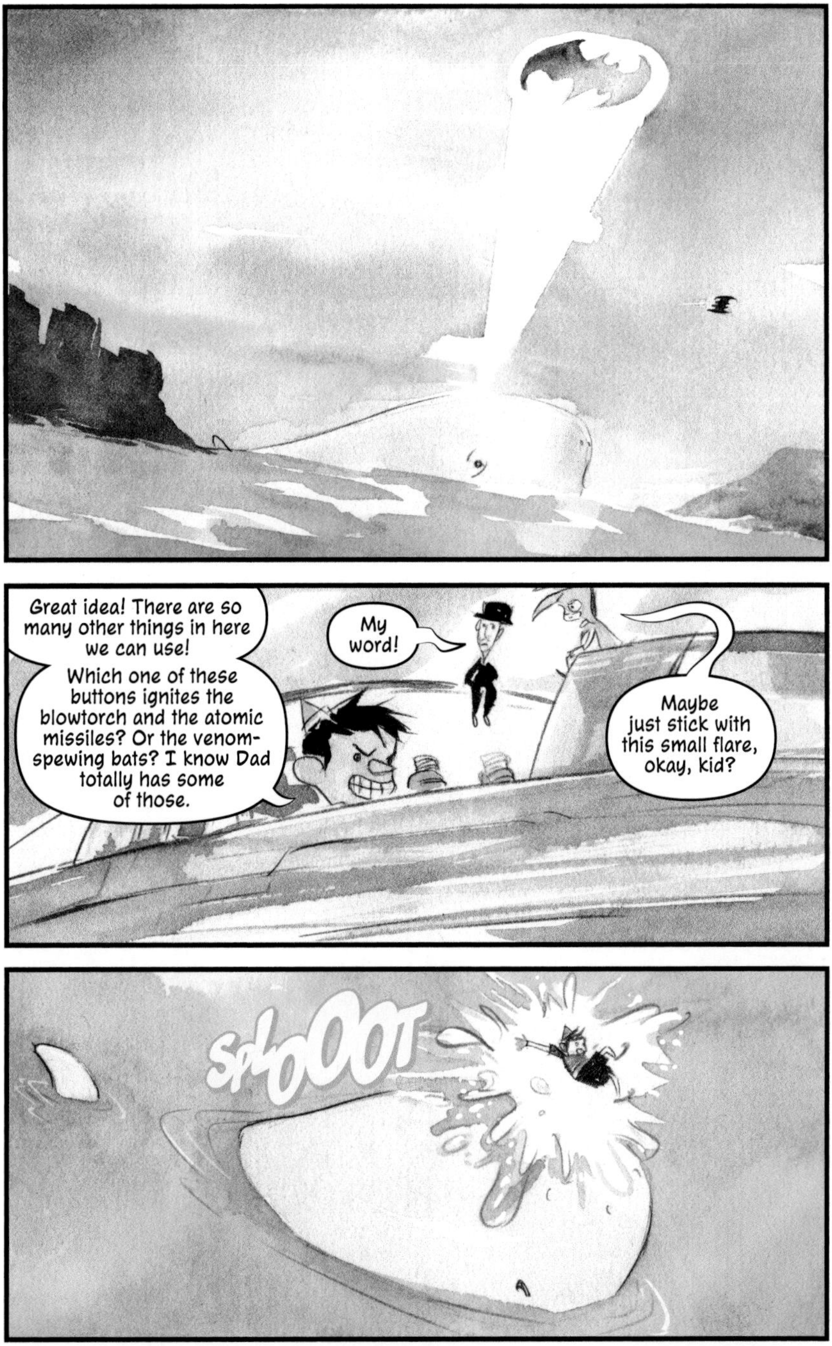
Great idea! There are so many other things in here we can use!
Which one of these buttons ignites the blowtorch and the atomic missiles? Or the venom-spewing bats? I know Dad totally has some of those.
My word!
Maybe just stick with this small flare, okay, kid?
SPLOOOT

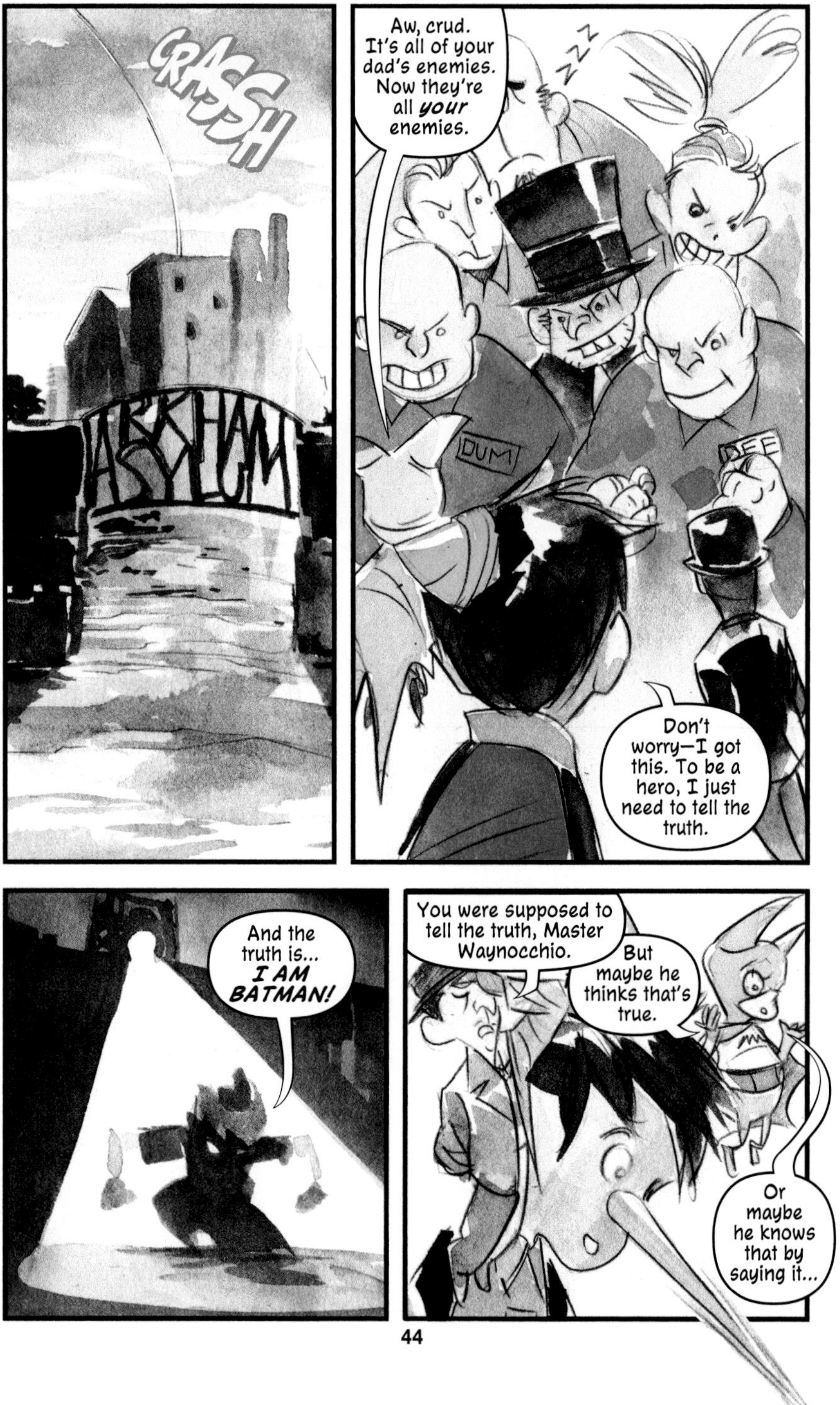
CRASSH
ARKHAM ASYLUM
Aw, crud. It's all of your dad's enemies. Now they're all ***your*** enemies.
ZZZ
DUM
DEE
Don't worry—I got this. To be a hero, I just need to tell the truth.
And the truth is... ***I AM BATMAN!***
You were supposed to tell the truth, Master Waynocchio.
But maybe he thinks that's true.
Or maybe he knows that by saying it...

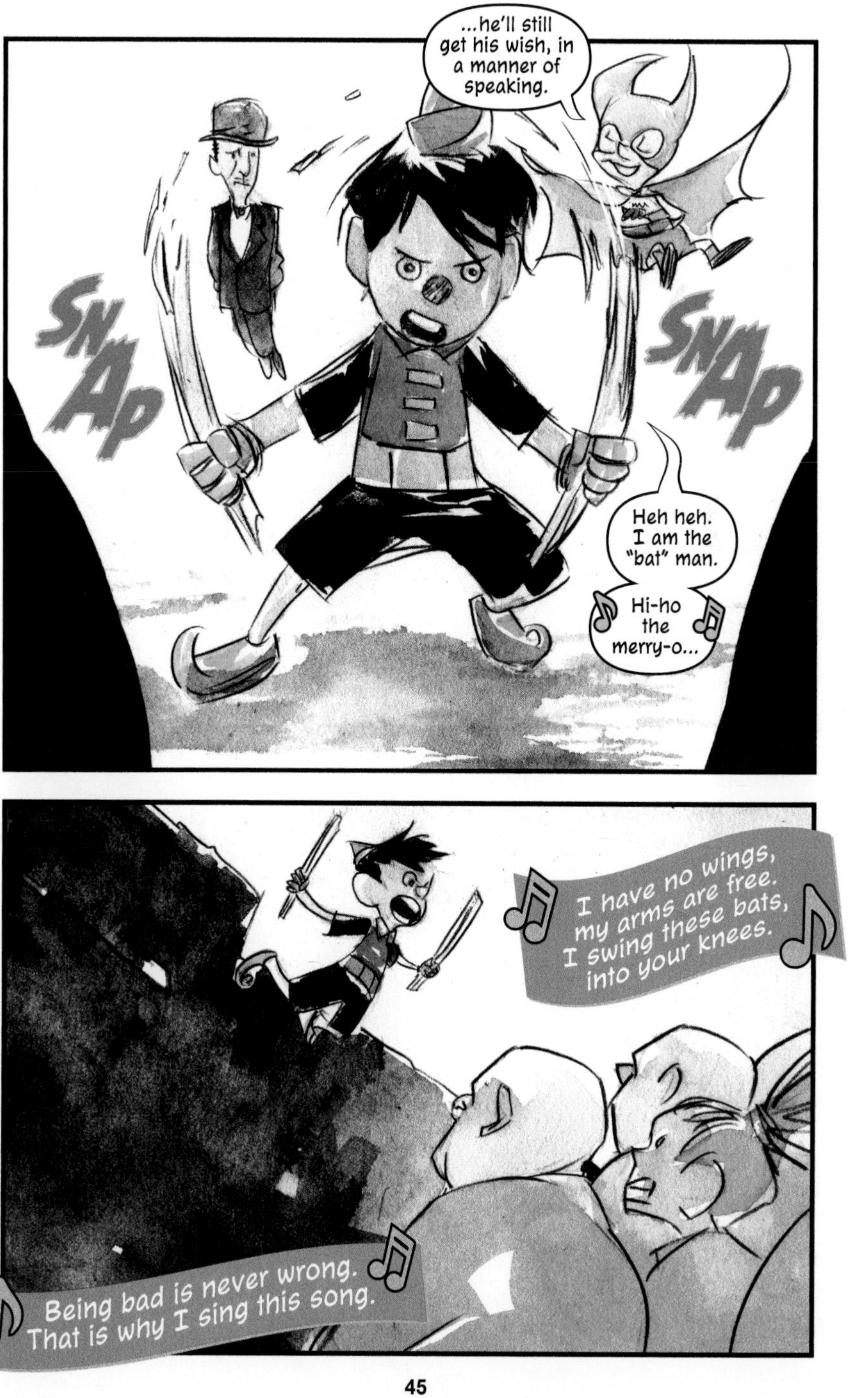
...he'll still get his wish, in a manner of speaking.
SNAP
SNAP
Heh heh. I am the "bat" man.
Hi-ho the merry-o...
I have no wings, my arms are free. I swing these bats, into your knees.
Being bad is never wrong. That is why I sing this song.

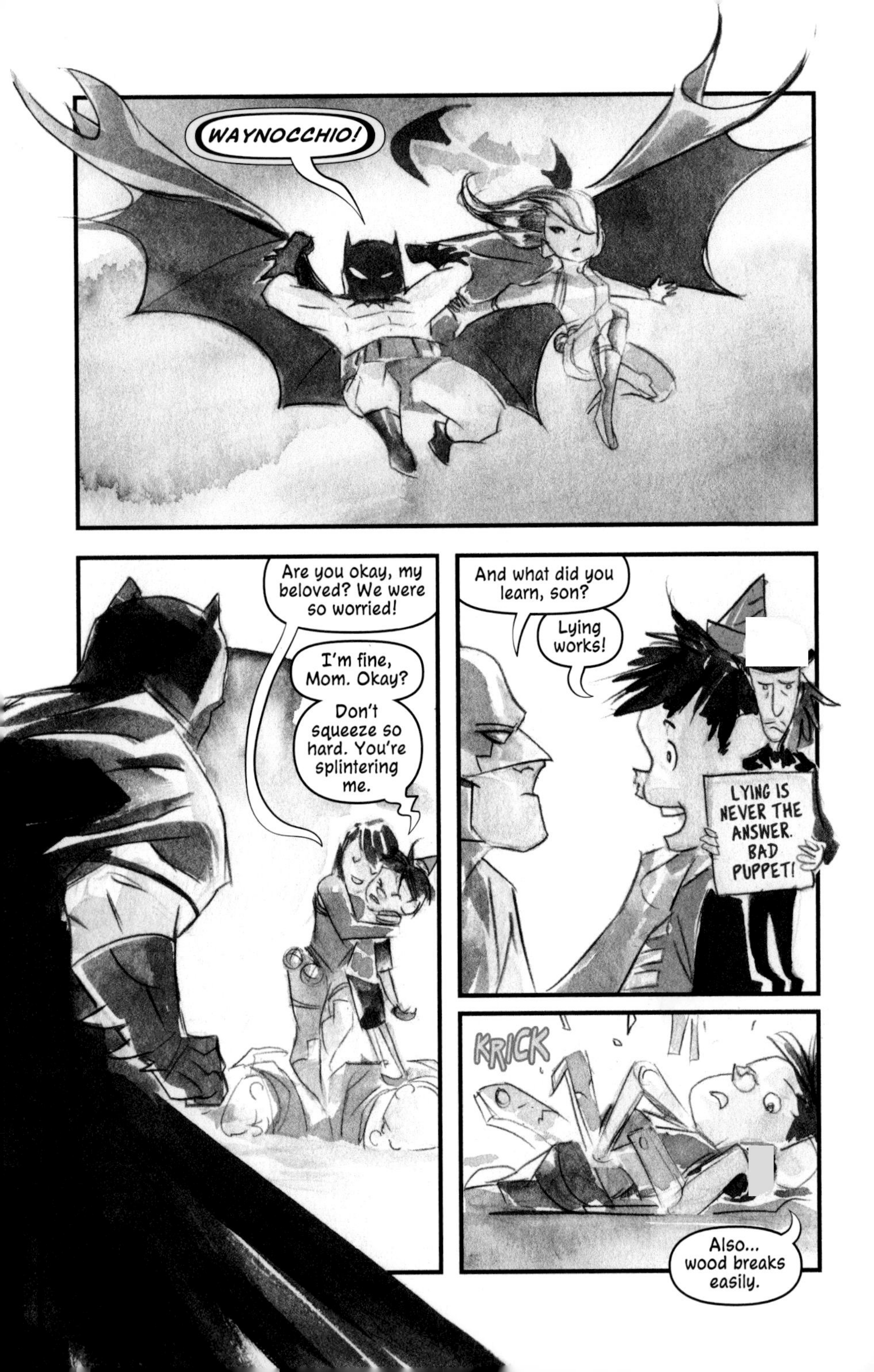
WAYNOCCHIO!
Are you okay, my beloved? We were so worried!
I'm fine, Mom. Okay?
Don't squeeze so hard. You're splintering me.
And what did you learn, son?
Lying works!
LYING IS NEVER THE ANSWER. BAD PUPPET!
KRICK
Also... wood breaks easily.

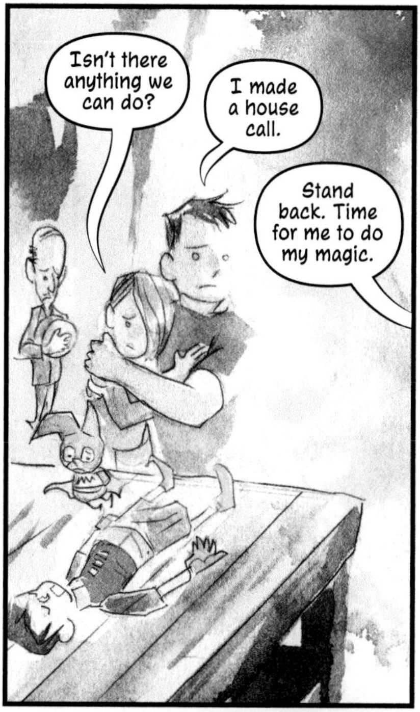
Isn't there anything we can do?
I made a house call.
Stand back. Time for me to do my magic.

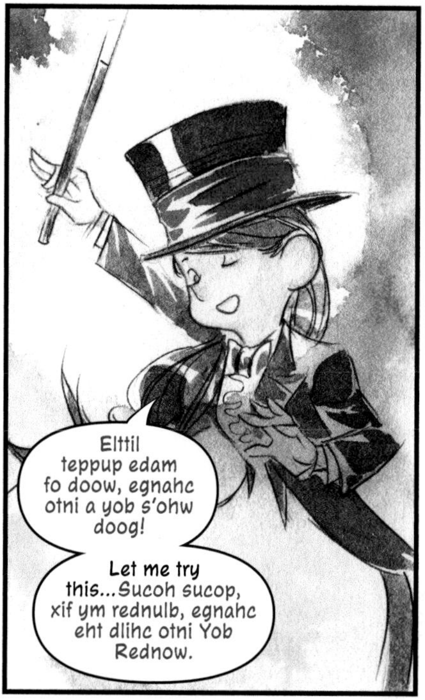
Elttil teppup edam fo doow, egnahc otni a yob s'ohw doog!
Let me try this...Sucoh sucop, xif ym rednulb, egnahc eht dlihc otni Yob Rednow.

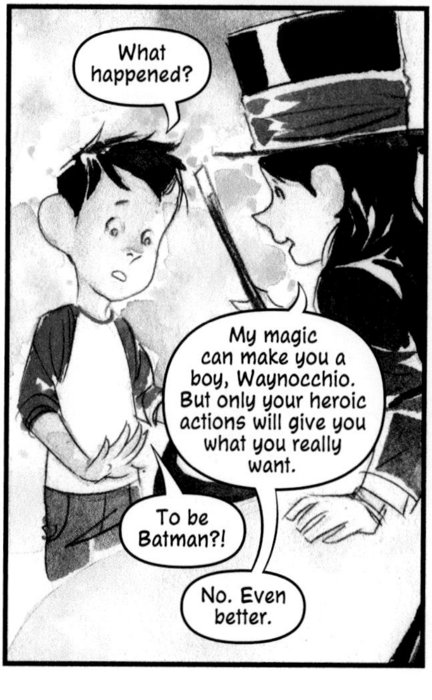
What happened?
My magic can make you a boy, Waynocchio. But only your heroic actions will give you what you really want.
To be Batman?!
No. Even better.

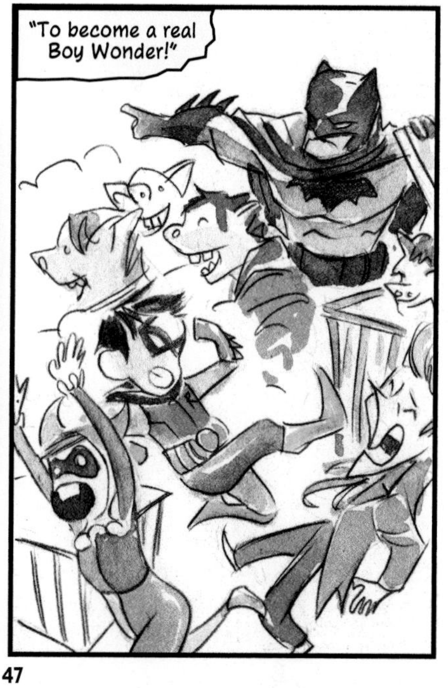
"To become a real Boy Wonder!"

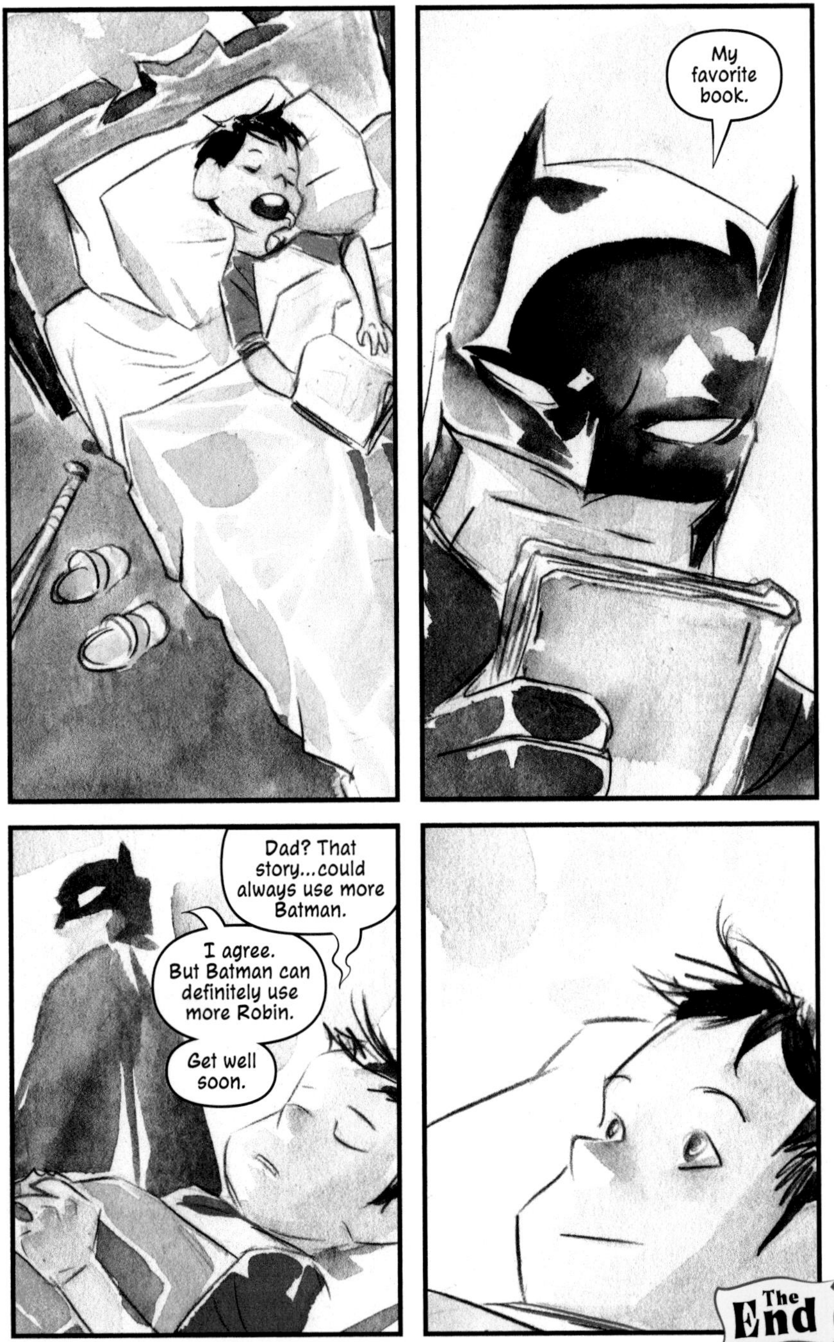
My favorite book.
Dad? That story...could always use more Batman.
I agree. But Batman can definitely use more Robin.
Get well soon.
The End

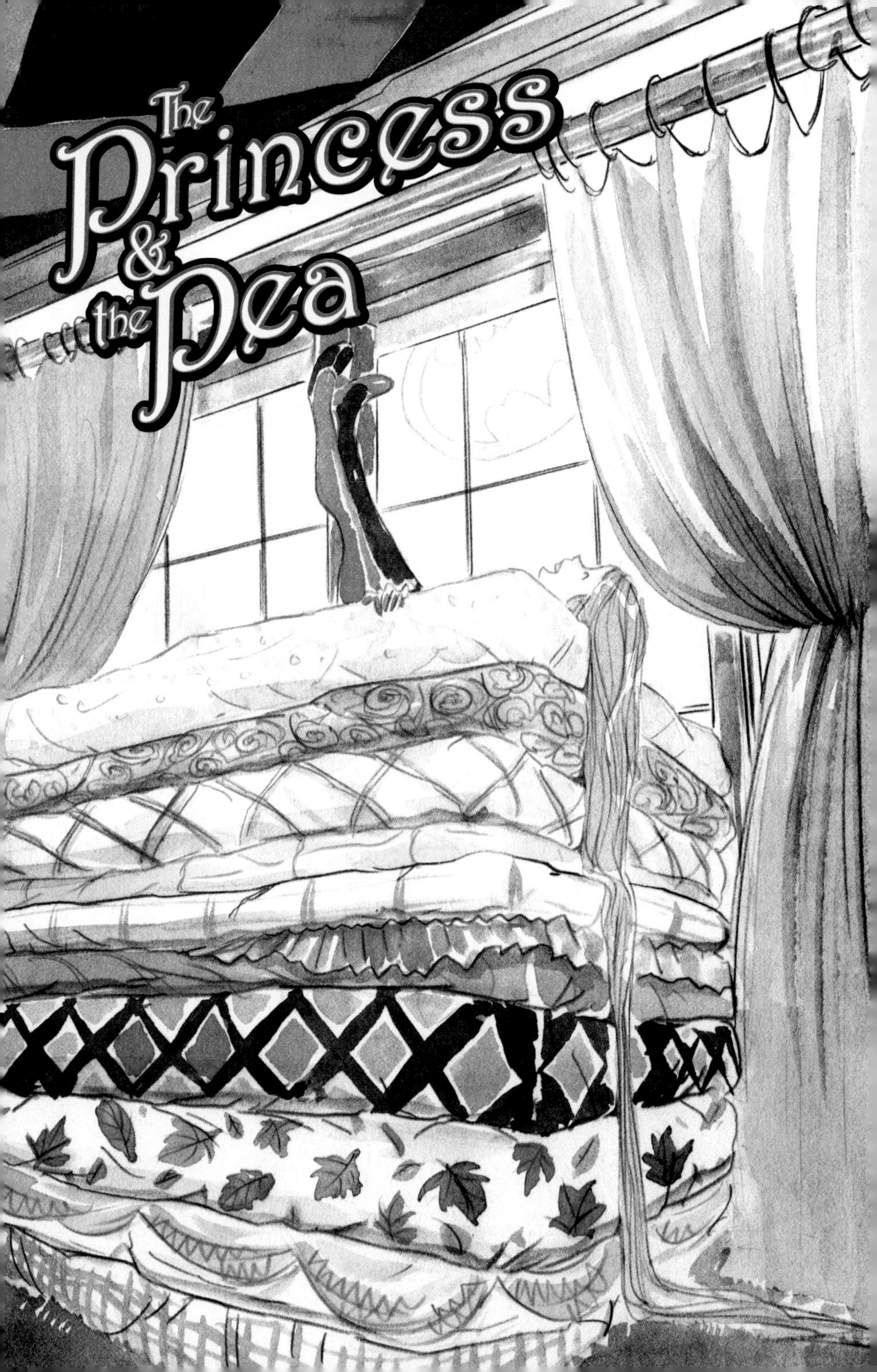
The Princess & the Pea

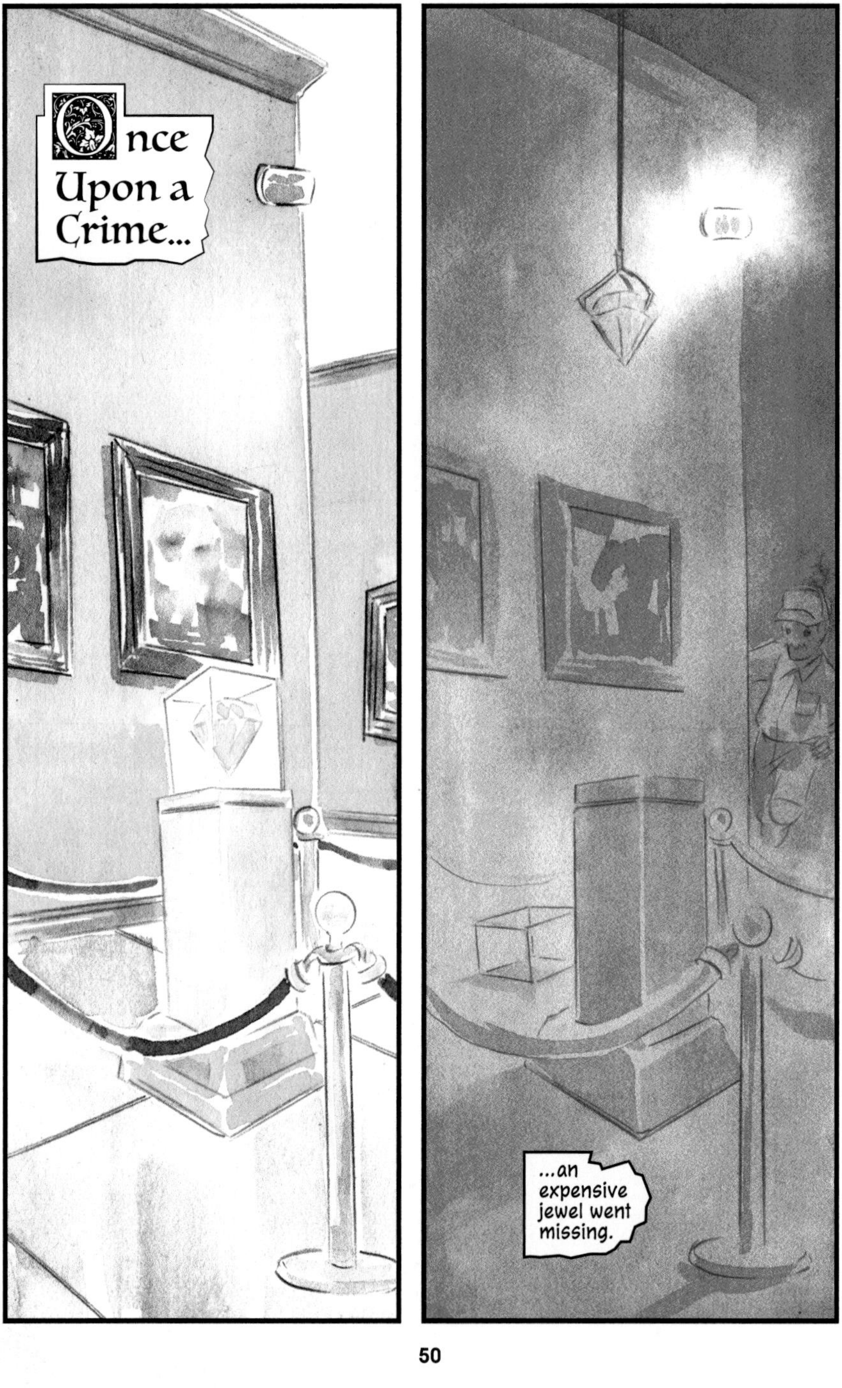
Once Upon a Crime...
...an expensive jewel went missing.

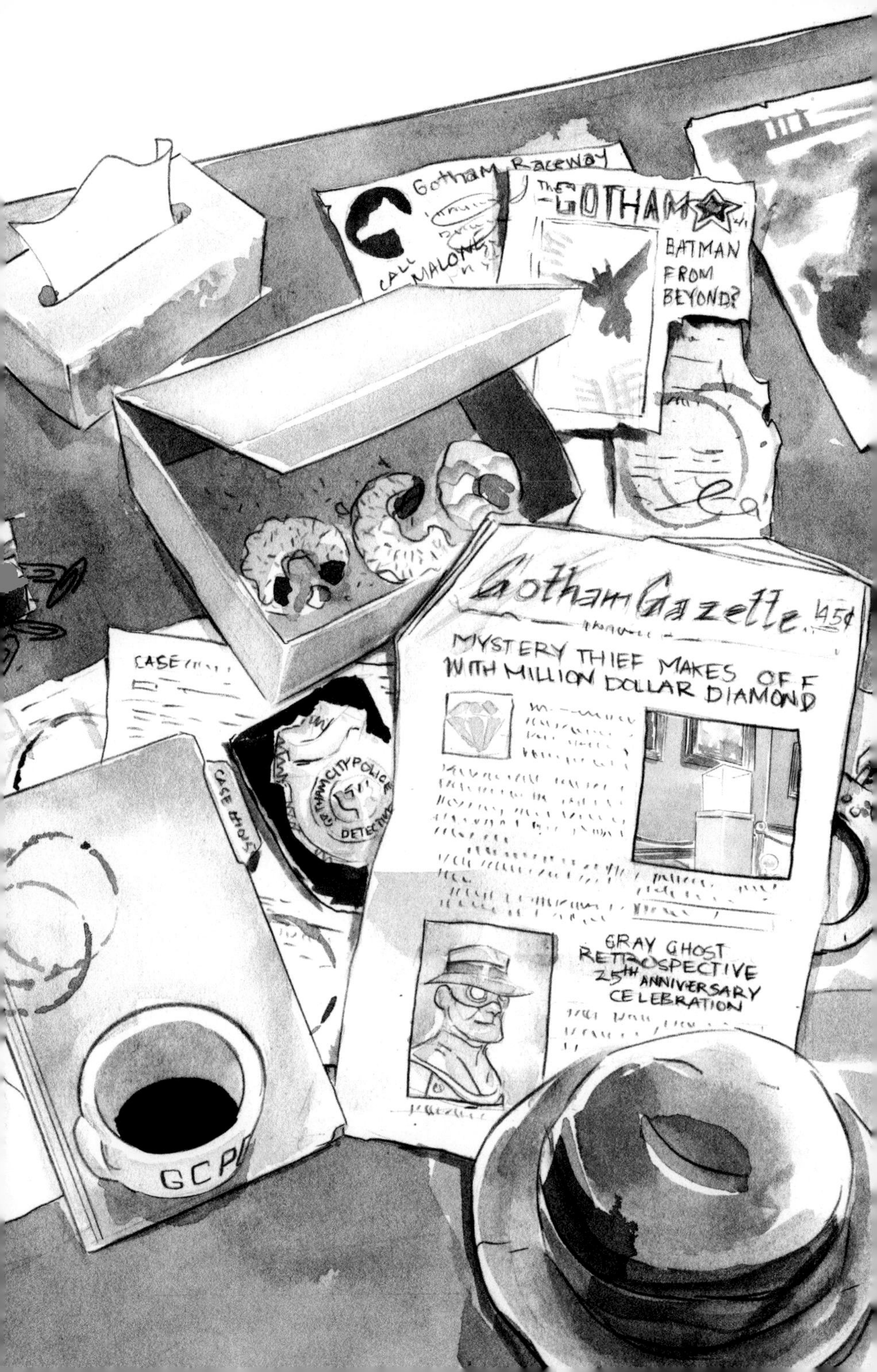
Gotham Raceway
MALONE
The GOTHAM
BATMAN FROM BEYOND?
CASE
CASE FILES
GOTHAM CITY POLICE DETECTIVE
Gotham Gazette 45¢
MYSTERY THIEF MAKES OFF WITH MILLION DOLLAR DIAMOND
GRAY GHOST RETROSPECTIVE 25TH ANNIVERSARY CELEBRATION
GCPD

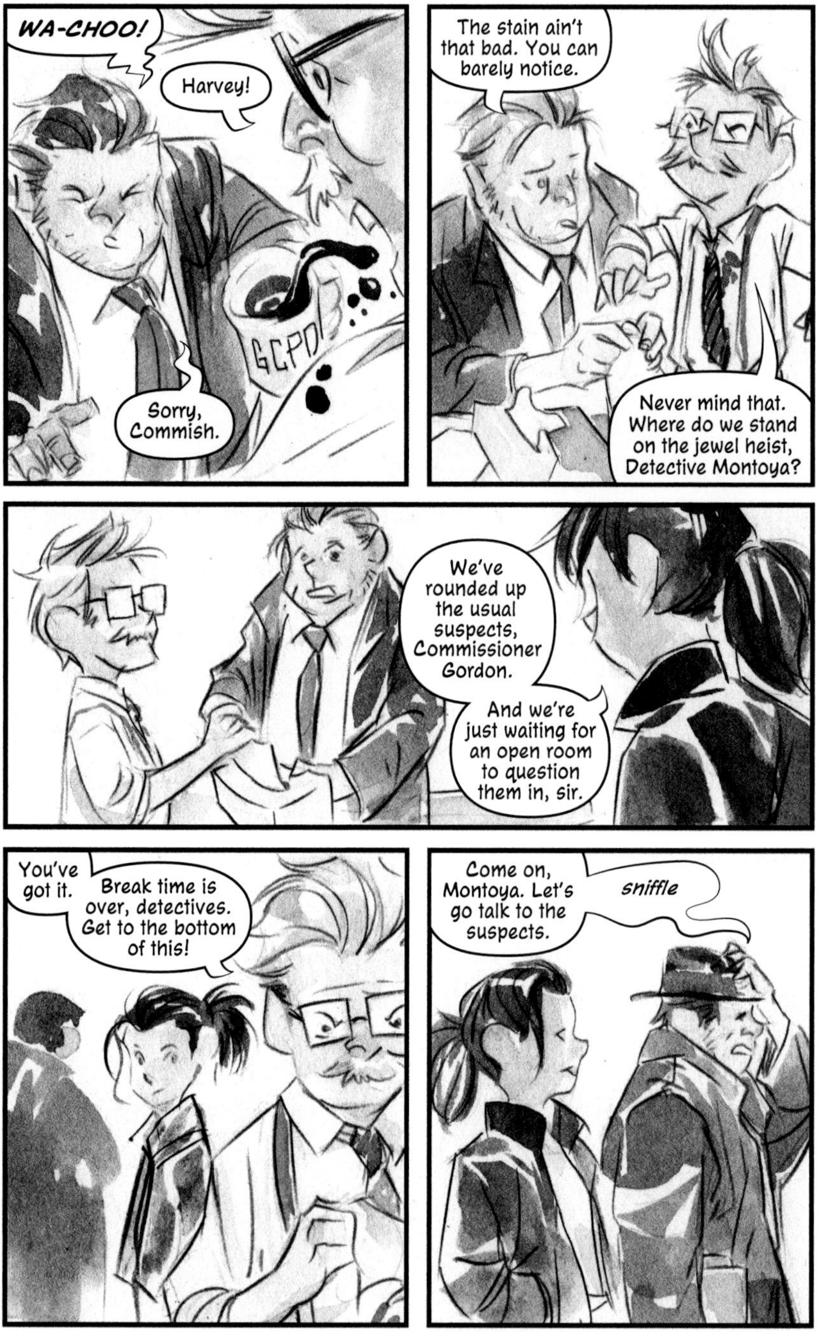
WA-CHOO!
Harvey!
Sorry, Commish.
The stain ain't that bad. You can barely notice.
Never mind that. Where do we stand on the jewel heist, Detective Montoya?
We've rounded up the usual suspects, Commissioner Gordon.
And we're just waiting for an open room to question them in, sir.
You've got it.
Break time is over, detectives. Get to the bottom of this!
Come on, Montoya. Let's go talk to the suspects.
sniffle

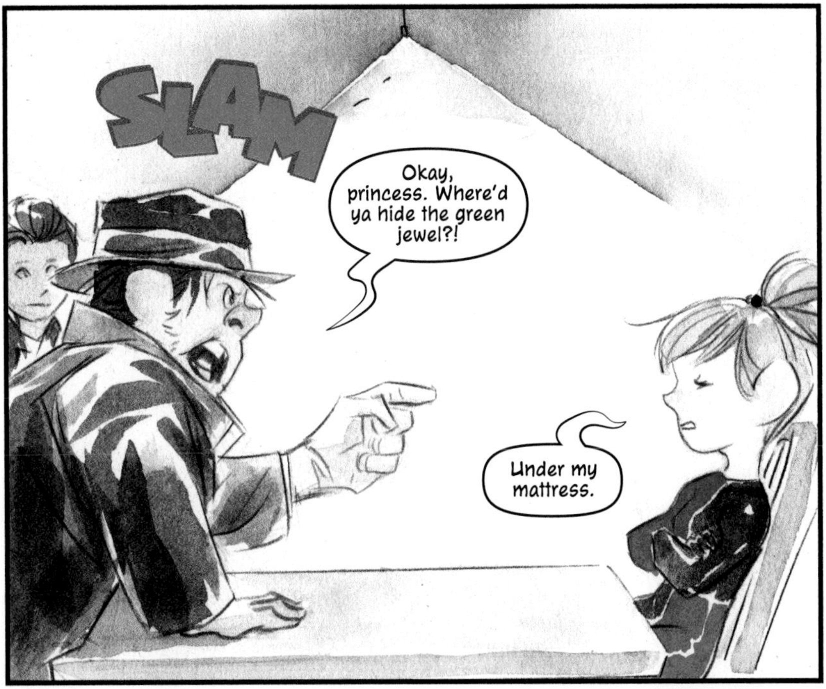
SLAM
Okay, princess. Where'd ya hide the green jewel?!
Under my mattress.

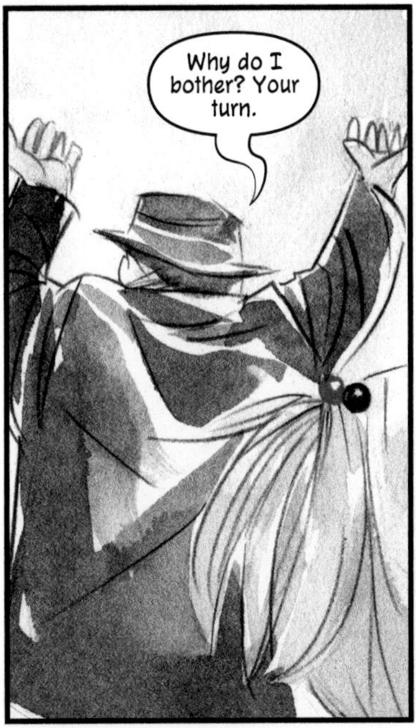
Why do I bother? Your turn.

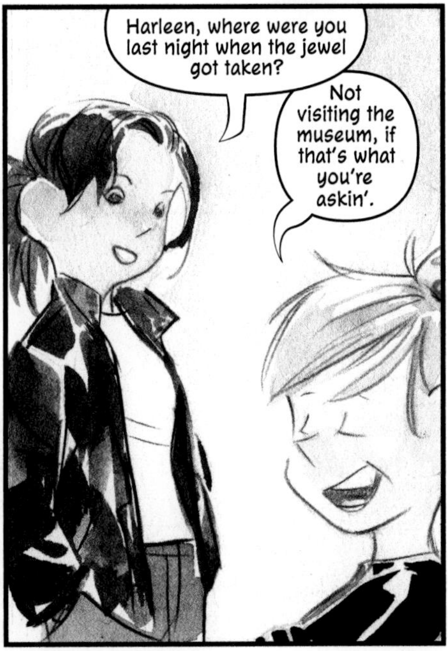
Harleen, where were you last night when the jewel got taken?
Not visiting the museum, if that's what you're askin'.

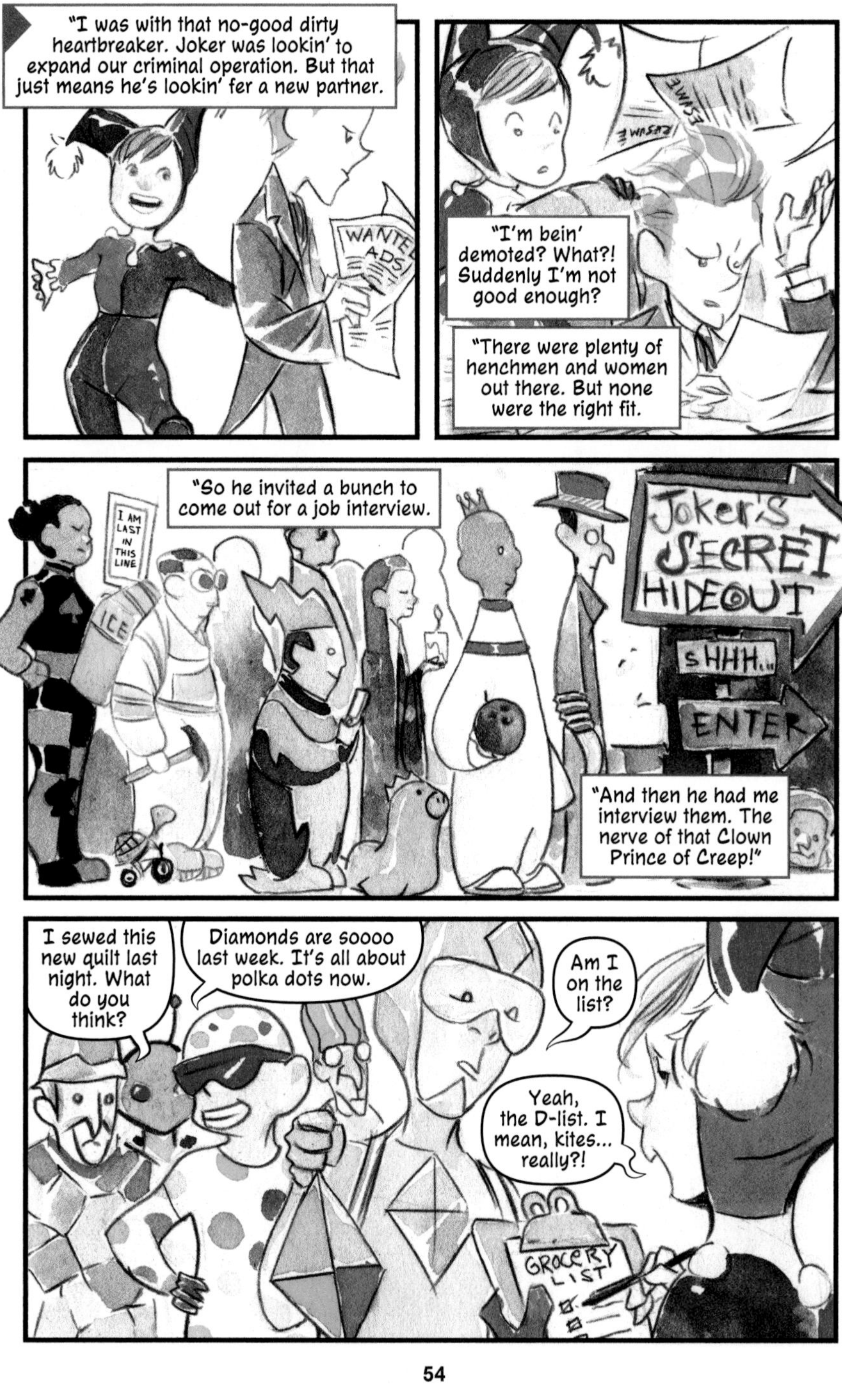
"I was with that no-good dirty heartbreaker. Joker was lookin' to expand our criminal operation. But that just means he's lookin' fer a new partner.
WANTED ADS
RESUME
RESUME
"I'm bein' demoted? What?! Suddenly I'm not good enough?
"There were plenty of henchmen and women out there. But none were the right fit.
"So he invited a bunch to come out for a job interview.
I AM LAST IN THIS LINE
ICE
JOKER'S SECRET HIDEOUT
SHHH...
ENTER
"And then he had me interview them. The nerve of that Clown Prince of Creep!"
I sewed this new quilt last night. What do you think?
Diamonds are soooo last week. It's all about polka dots now.
Am I on the list?
Yeah, the D-list. I mean, kites... really?!
GROCERY LIST

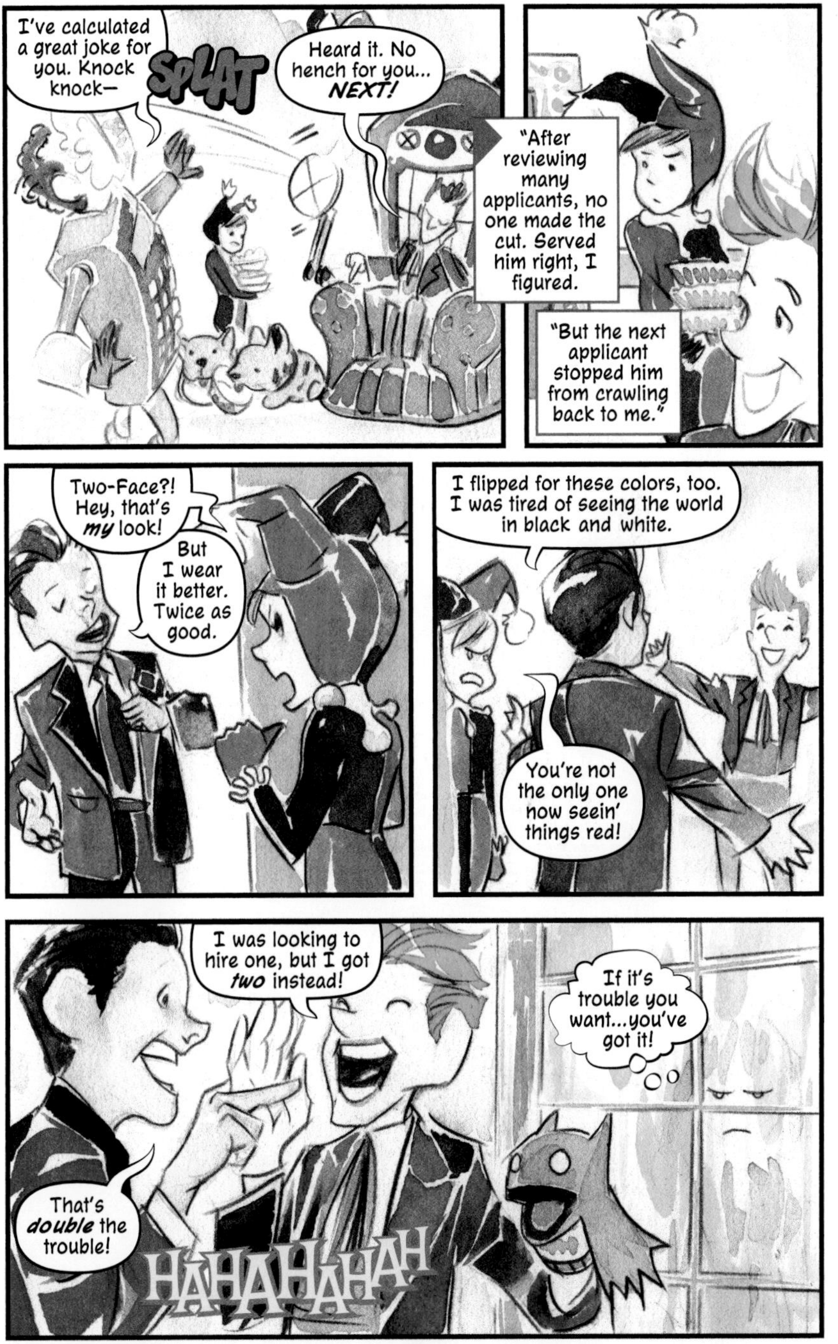
I've calculated a great joke for you. Knock knock—
SPLAT
Heard it. No hench for you... NEXT!
"After reviewing many applicants, no one made the cut. Served him right, I figured.
"But the next applicant stopped him from crawling back to me."
Two-Face?! Hey, that's my look!
But I wear it better. Twice as good.
I flipped for these colors, too. I was tired of seeing the world in black and white.
You're not the only one now seein' things red!
I was looking to hire one, but I got two instead!
If it's trouble you want...you've got it!
That's double the trouble!
HAHAHAHAH

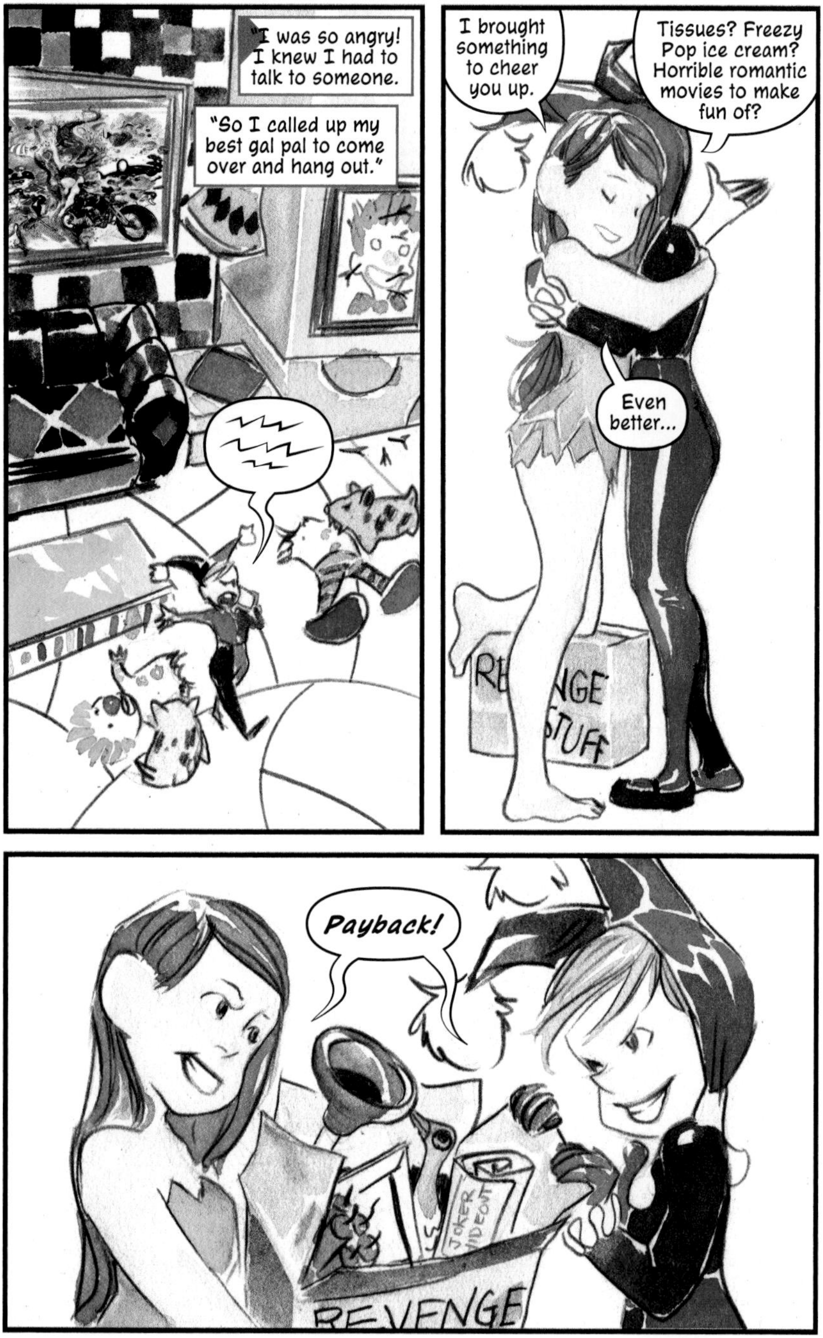
"I was so angry! I knew I had to talk to someone.
"So I called up my best gal pal to come over and hang out."
I brought something to cheer you up.
Tissues? Freezy Pop ice cream? Horrible romantic movies to make fun of?
Even better...
REVENGE STUFF
Payback!
JOKER VIDEOS
REVENGE

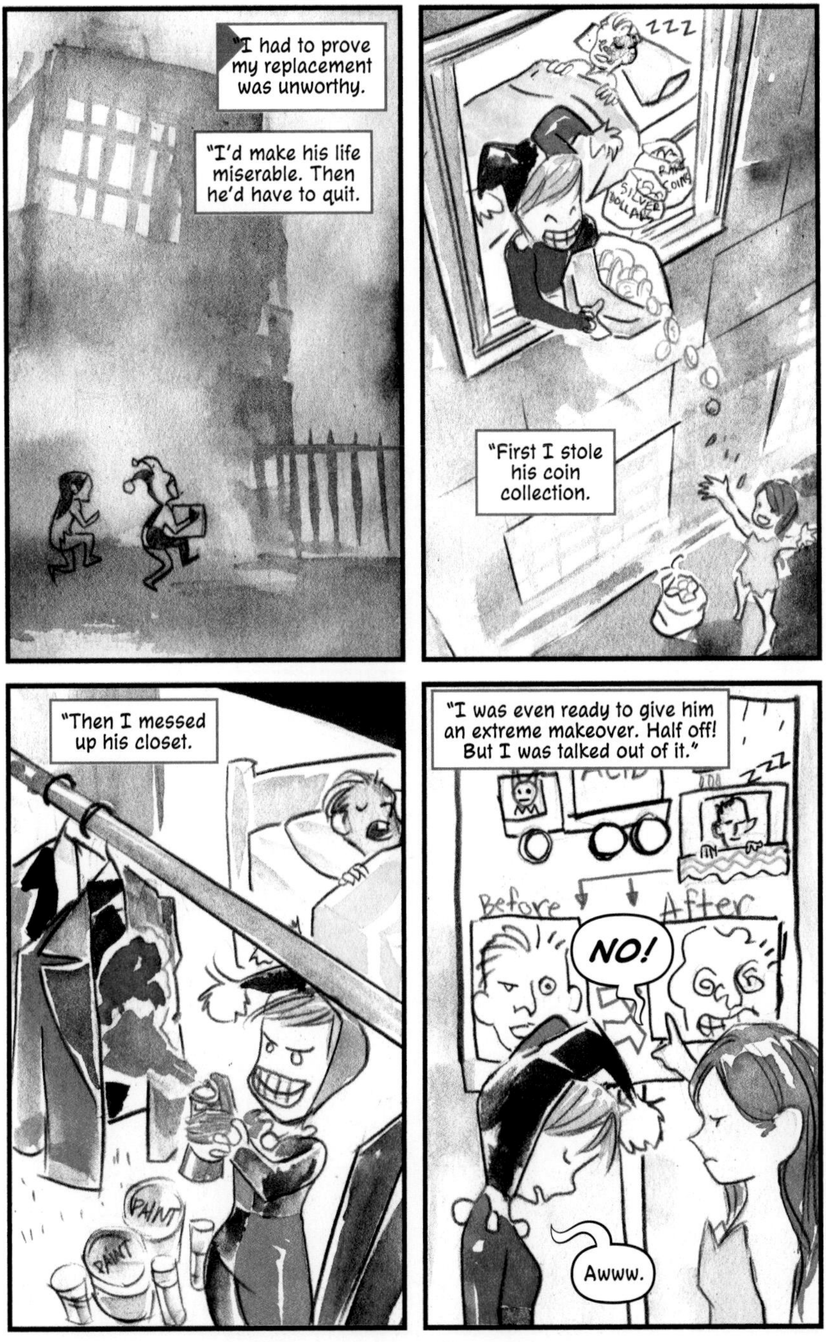
"I had to prove my replacement was unworthy.
"I'd make his life miserable. Then he'd have to quit.
ZZZ
"First I stole his coin collection.
"Then I messed up his closet.
PAINT
PAINT
"I was even ready to give him an extreme makeover. Half off! But I was talked out of it."
ZZZ
Before
After
NO!
Awww.

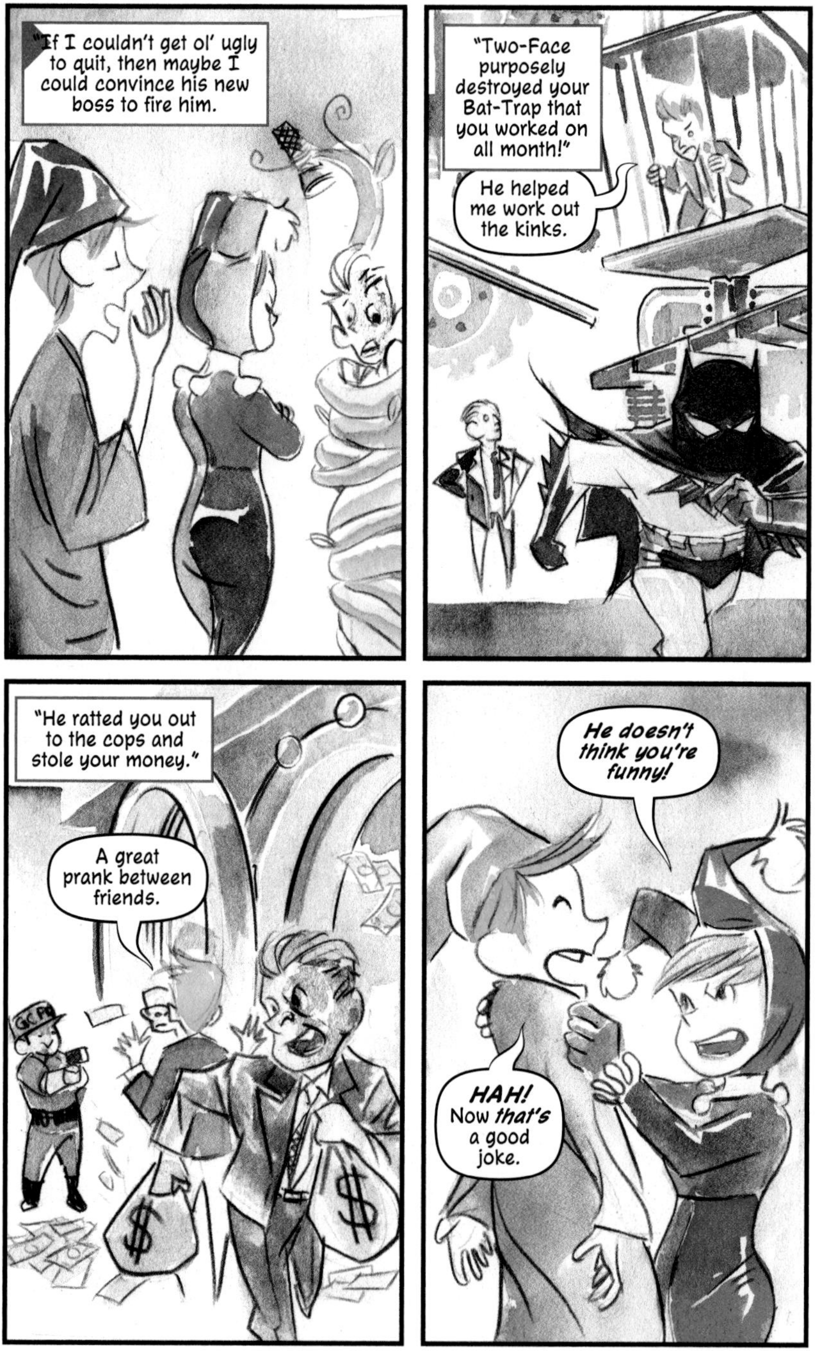
"If I couldn't get ol' ugly to quit, then maybe I could convince his new boss to fire him.
"Two-Face purposely destroyed your Bat-Trap that you worked on all month!"
He helped me work out the kinks.
"He ratted you out to the cops and stole your money."
A great prank between friends.
GCPD
He doesn't think you're funny!
HAH! Now that's a good joke.

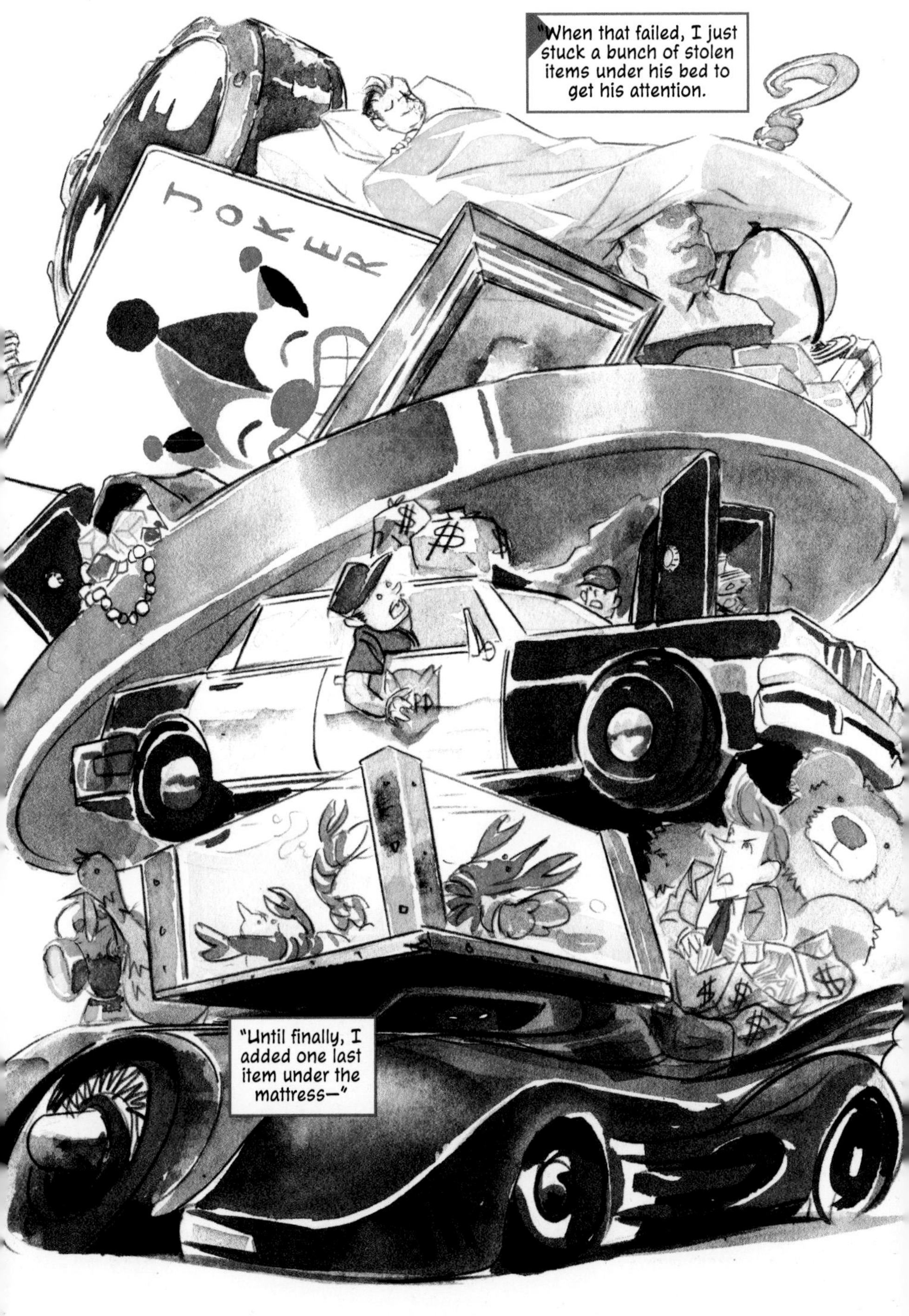
"When that failed, I just stuck a bunch of stolen items under his bed to get his attention.
JOKER
"Until finally, I added one last item under the mattress—"

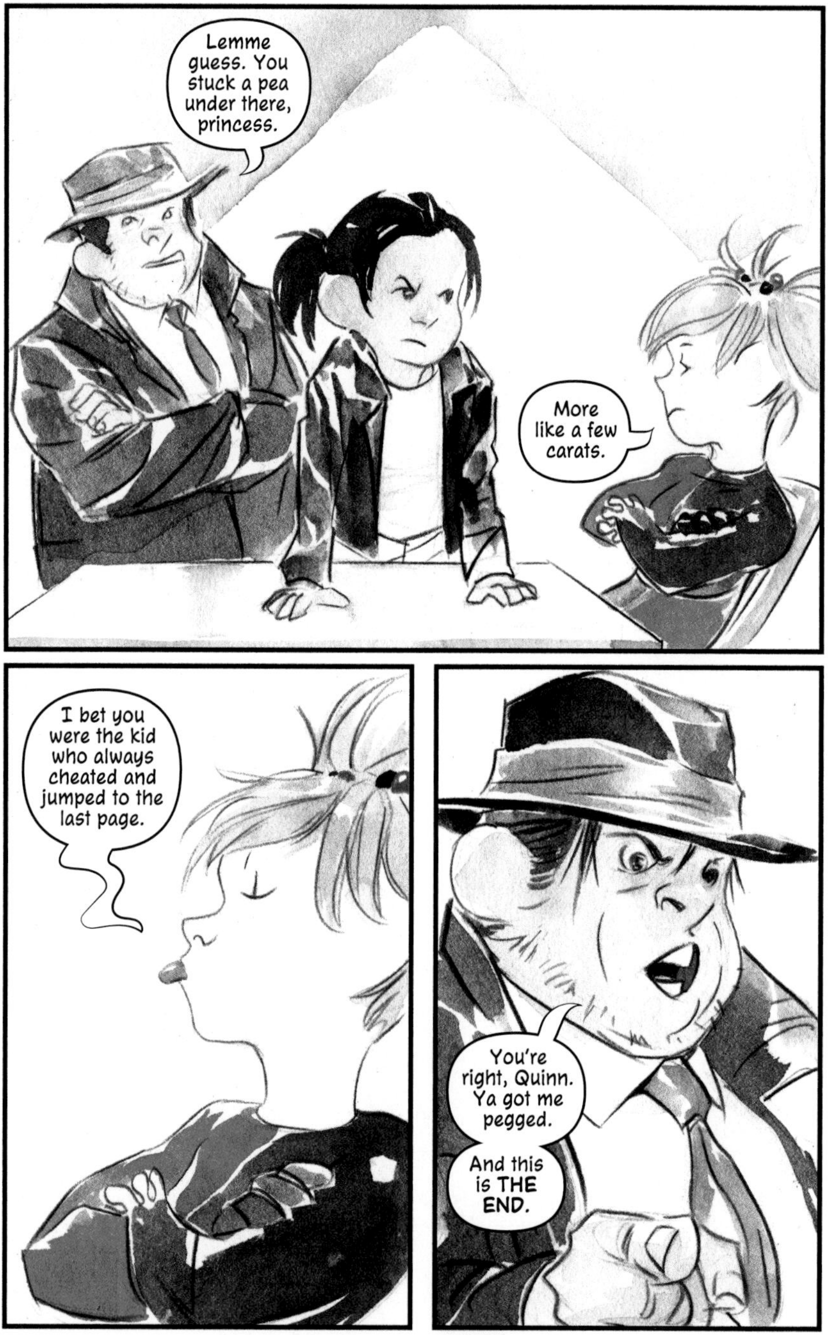

Lemme guess. You stuck a pea under there, princess.
More like a few carats.
I bet you were the kid who always cheated and jumped to the last page.
You're right, Quinn. Ya got me pegged.
And this is THE END.

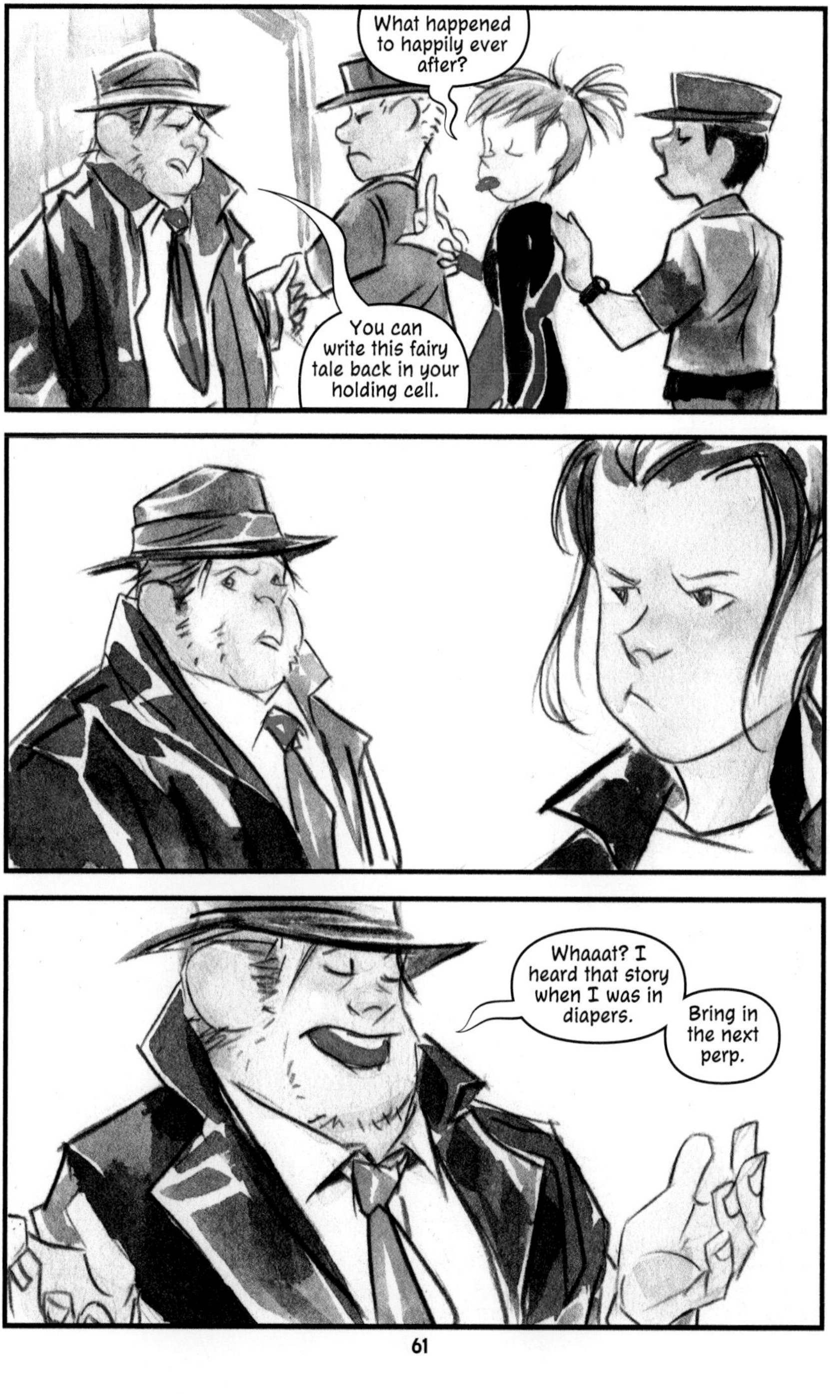
What happened to happily ever after?
You can write this fairy tale back in your holding cell.
Whaaat? I heard that story when I was in diapers.
Bring in the next perp.

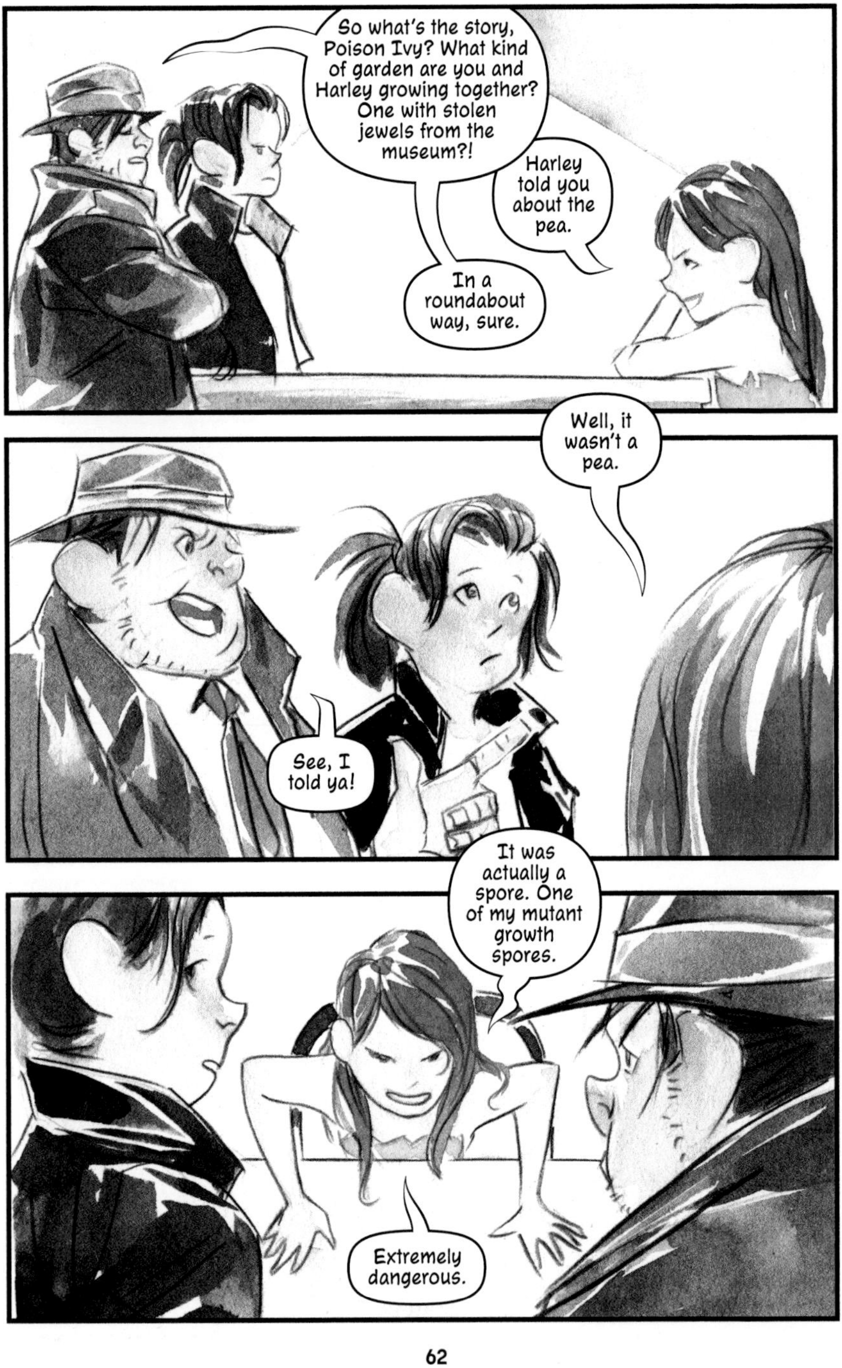
So what's the story, Poison Ivy? What kind of garden are you and Harley growing together? One with stolen jewels from the museum?!
Harley told you about the pea.
In a roundabout way, sure.
Well, it wasn't a pea.
See, I told ya!
It was actually a spore. One of my mutant growth spores.
Extremely dangerous.

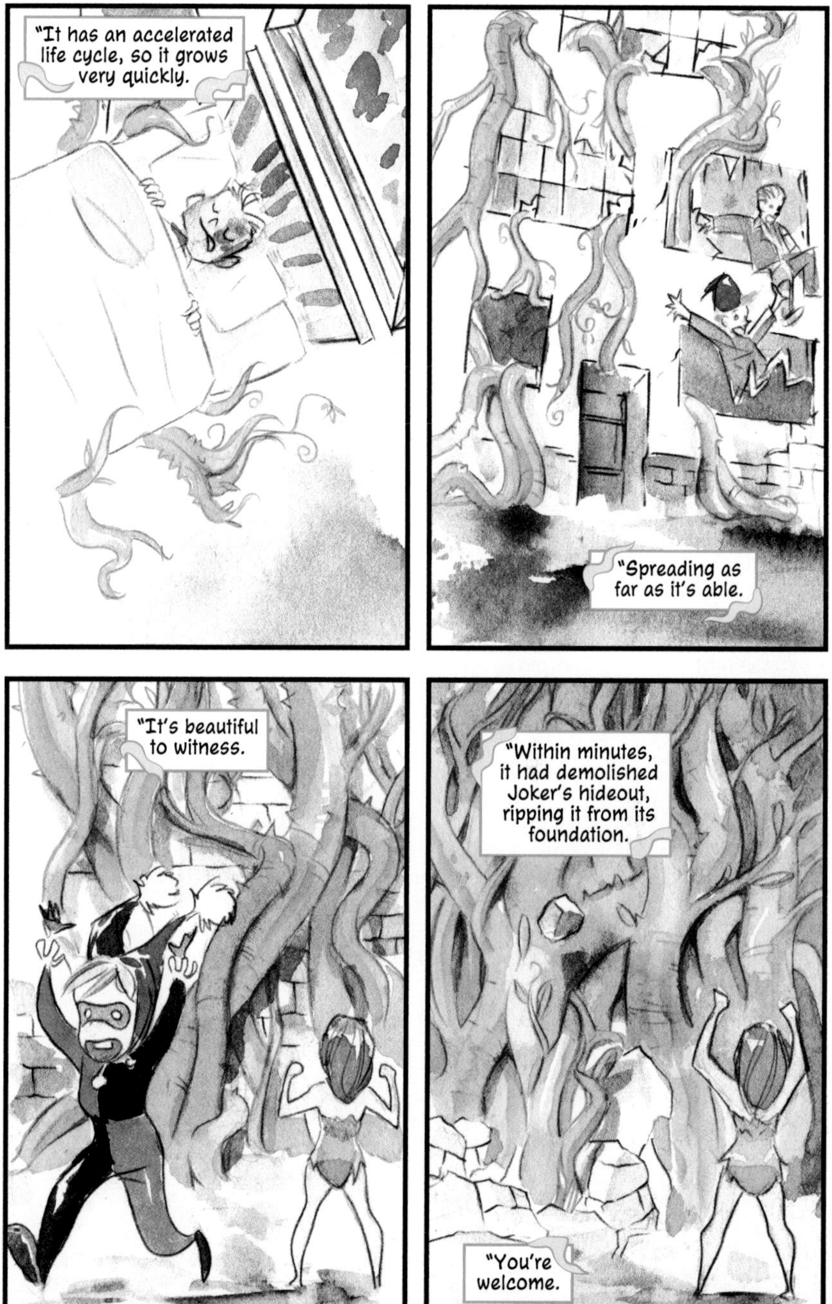
"It has an accelerated life cycle, so it grows very quickly.
"Spreading as far as it's able.
"It's beautiful to witness.
"Within minutes, it had demolished Joker's hideout, ripping it from its foundation.
"You're welcome.

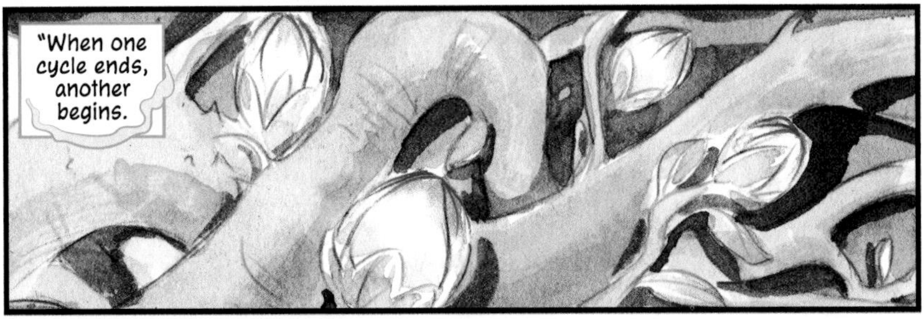
"When one cycle ends, another begins.

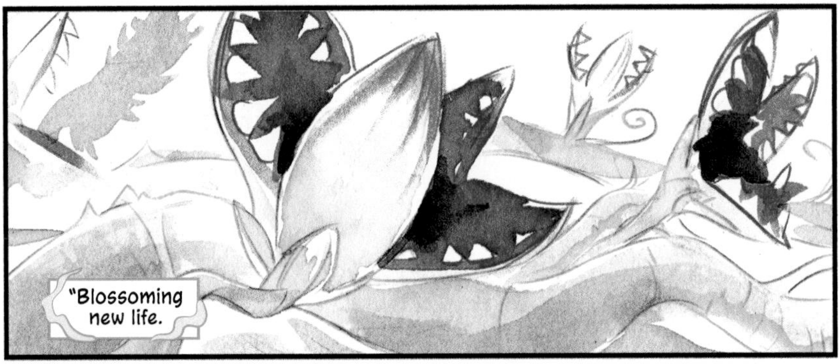
"Blossoming new life.

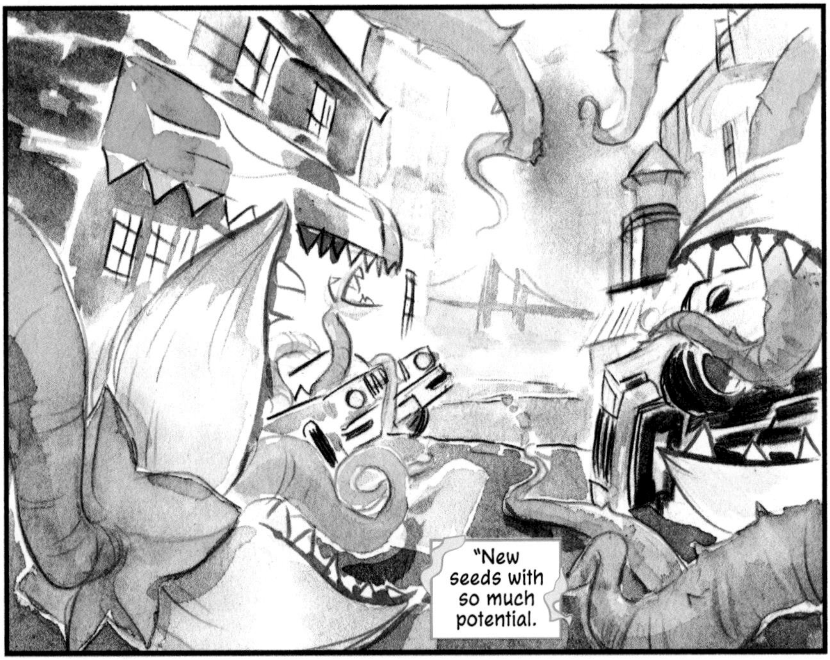
"New seeds with so much potential.

"But this world hates and attacks anything that is beautiful.

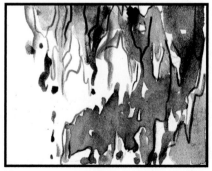

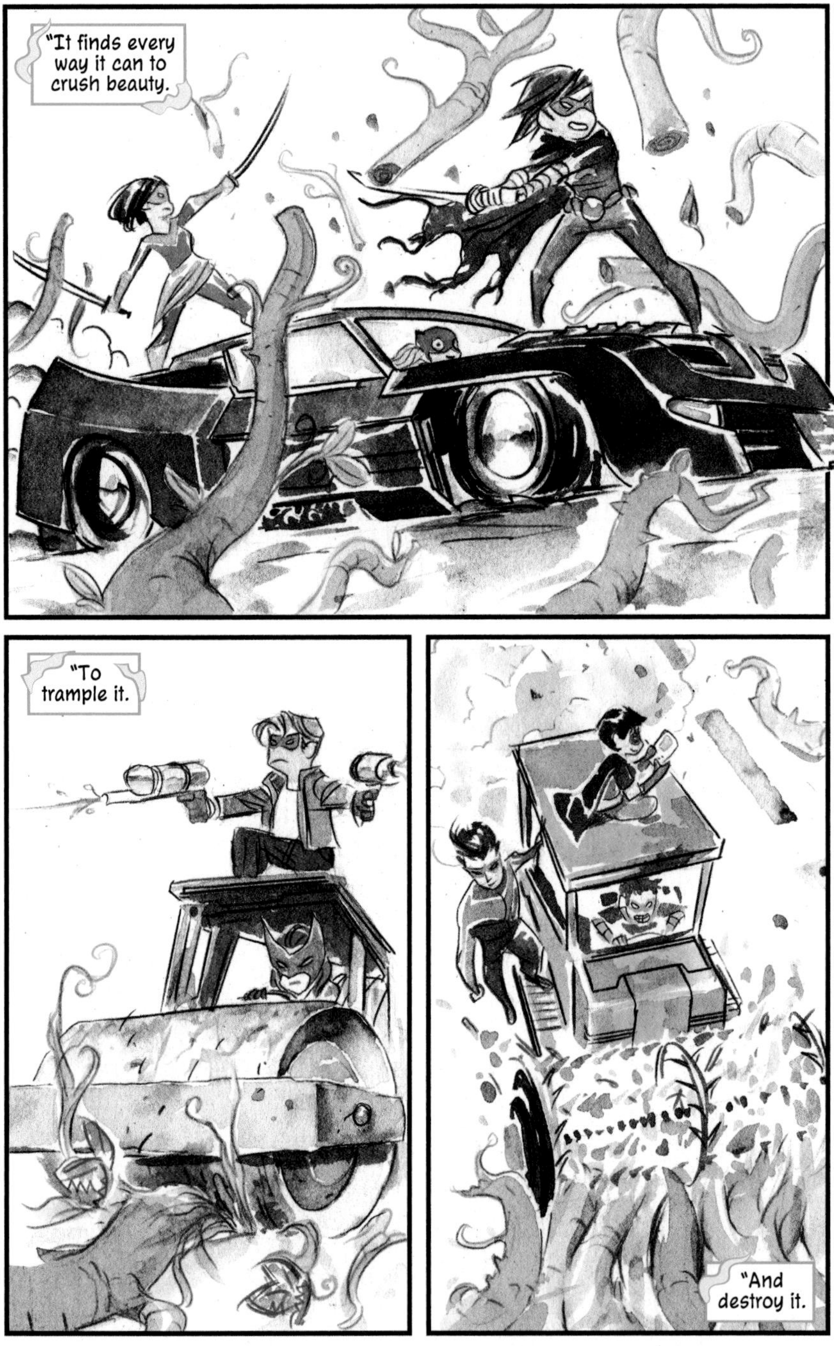
"It finds every way it can to crush beauty.
"To trample it.
"And destroy it.

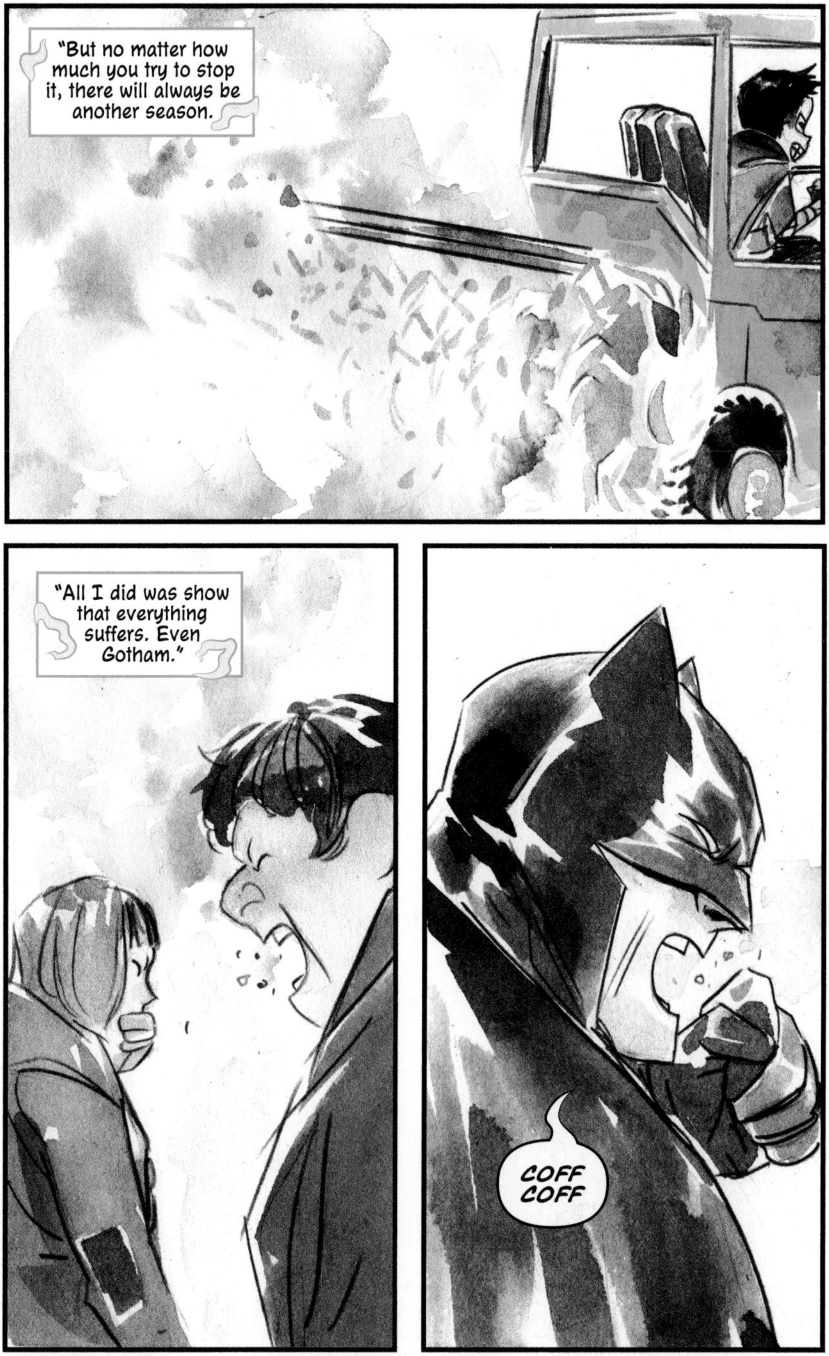
"But no matter how much you try to stop it, there will always be another season.
"All I did was show that everything suffers. Even Gotham."
COFF COFF

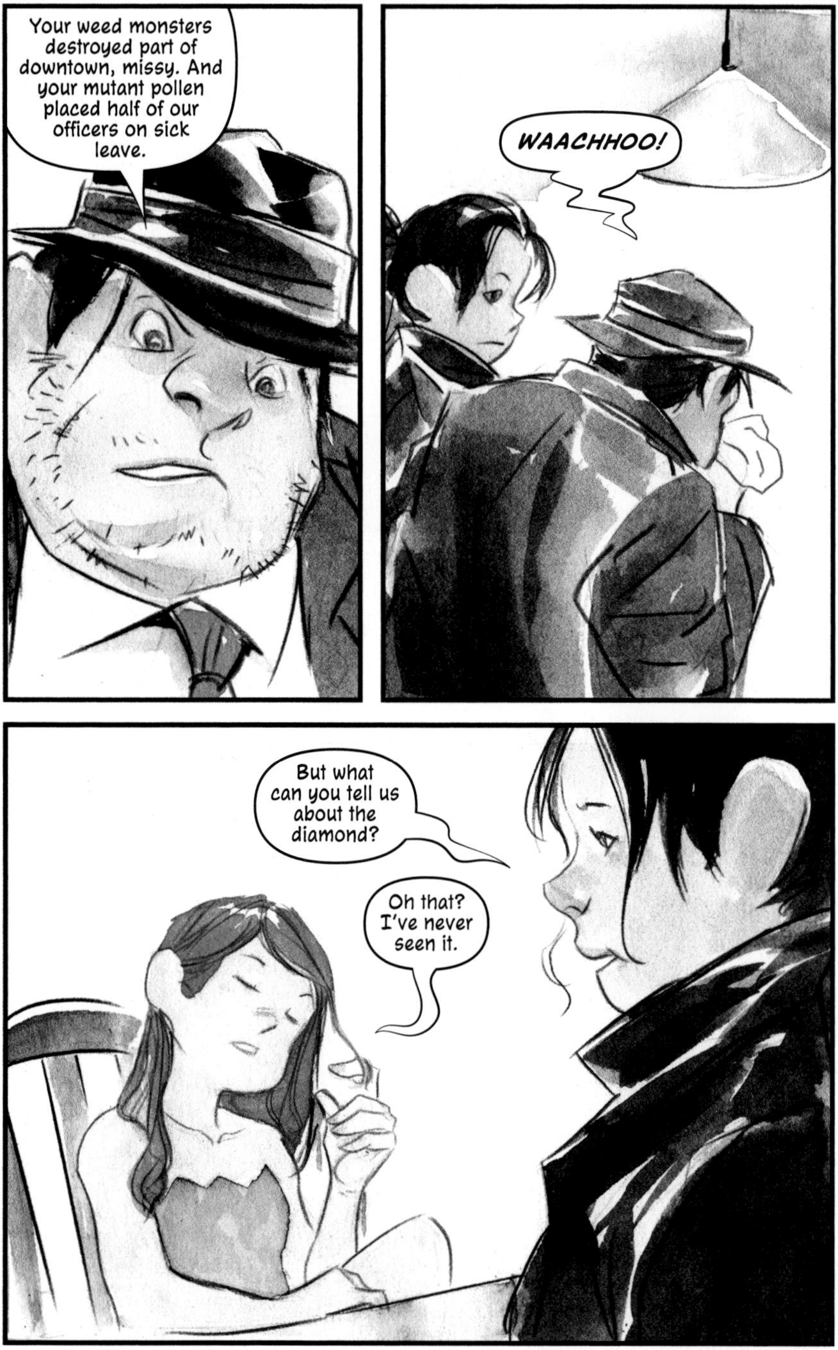
Your weed monsters destroyed part of downtown, missy. And your mutant pollen placed half of our officers on sick leave.
WAACHHOO!
But what can you tell us about the diamond?
Oh that? I've never seen it.

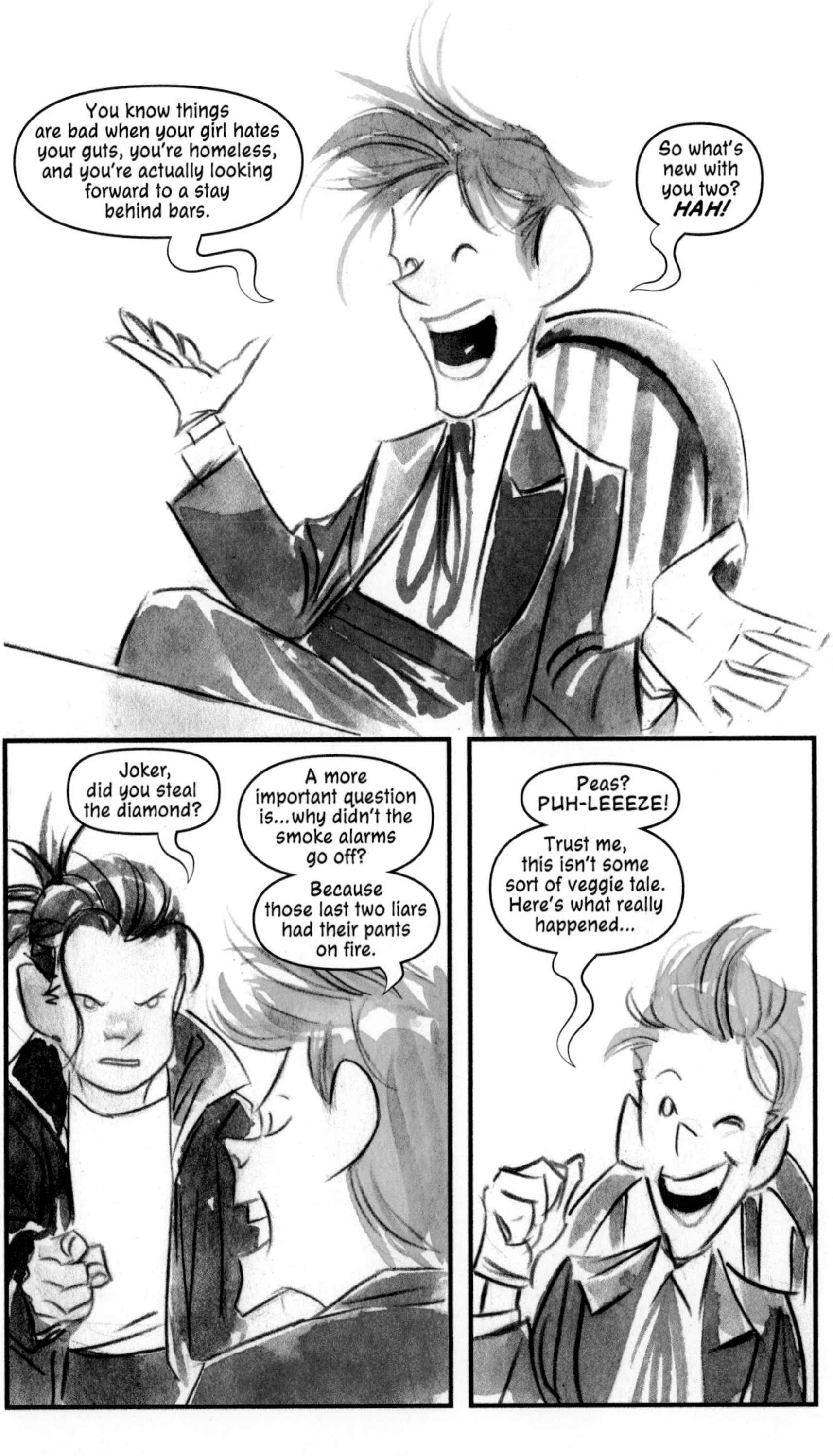
You know things are bad when your girl hates your guts, you're homeless, and you're actually looking forward to a stay behind bars.
So what's new with you two? HAH!
Joker, did you steal the diamond?
A more important question is...why didn't the smoke alarms go off?
Because those last two liars had their pants on fire.
Peas? PUH-LEEEZE!
Trust me, this isn't some sort of veggie tale. Here's what really happened...

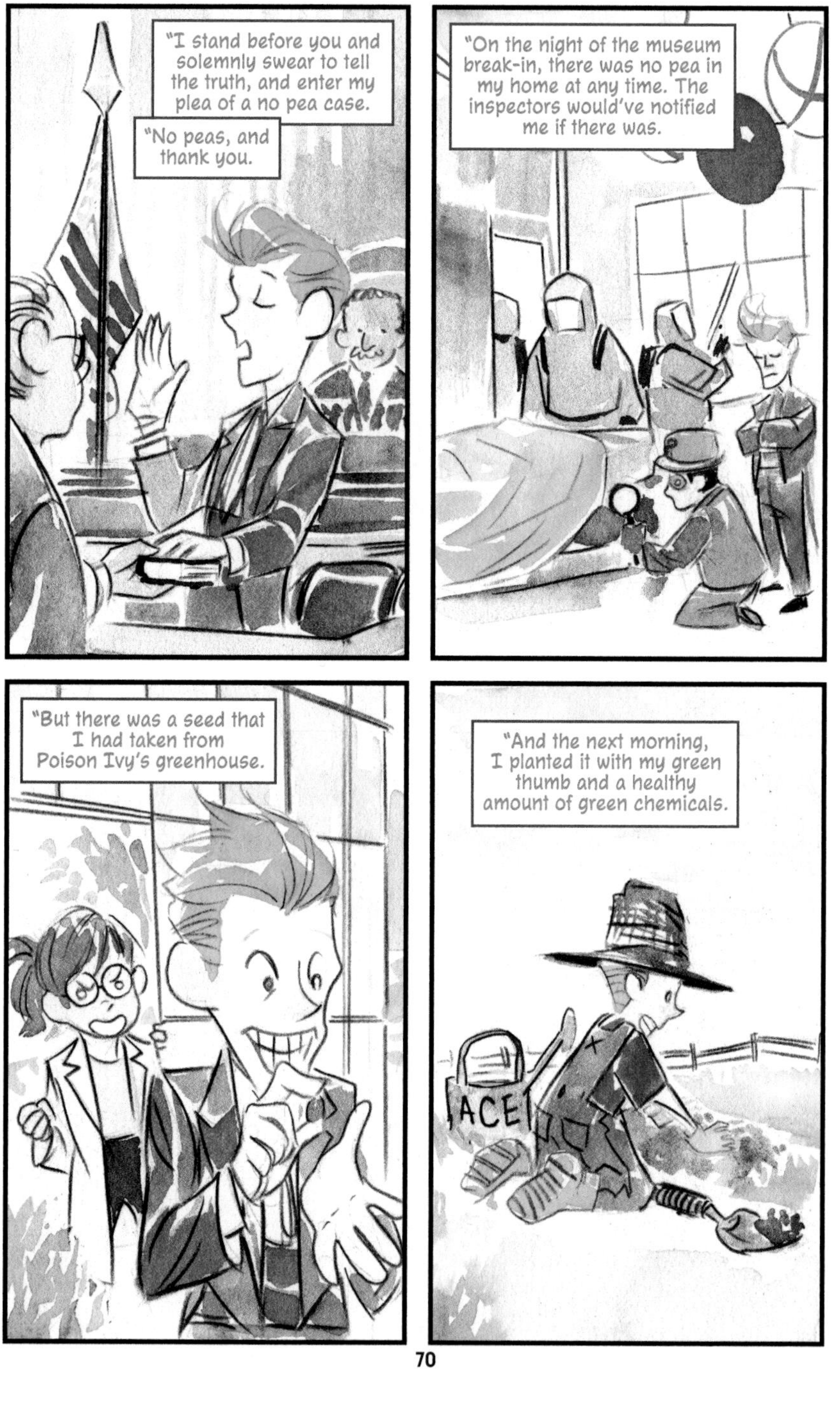
"I stand before you and solemnly swear to tell the truth, and enter my plea of a no pea case.
"No peas, and thank you.
"On the night of the museum break-in, there was no pea in my home at any time. The inspectors would've notified me if there was.
"But there was a seed that I had taken from Poison Ivy's greenhouse.
"And the next morning, I planted it with my green thumb and a healthy amount of green chemicals.
ACE

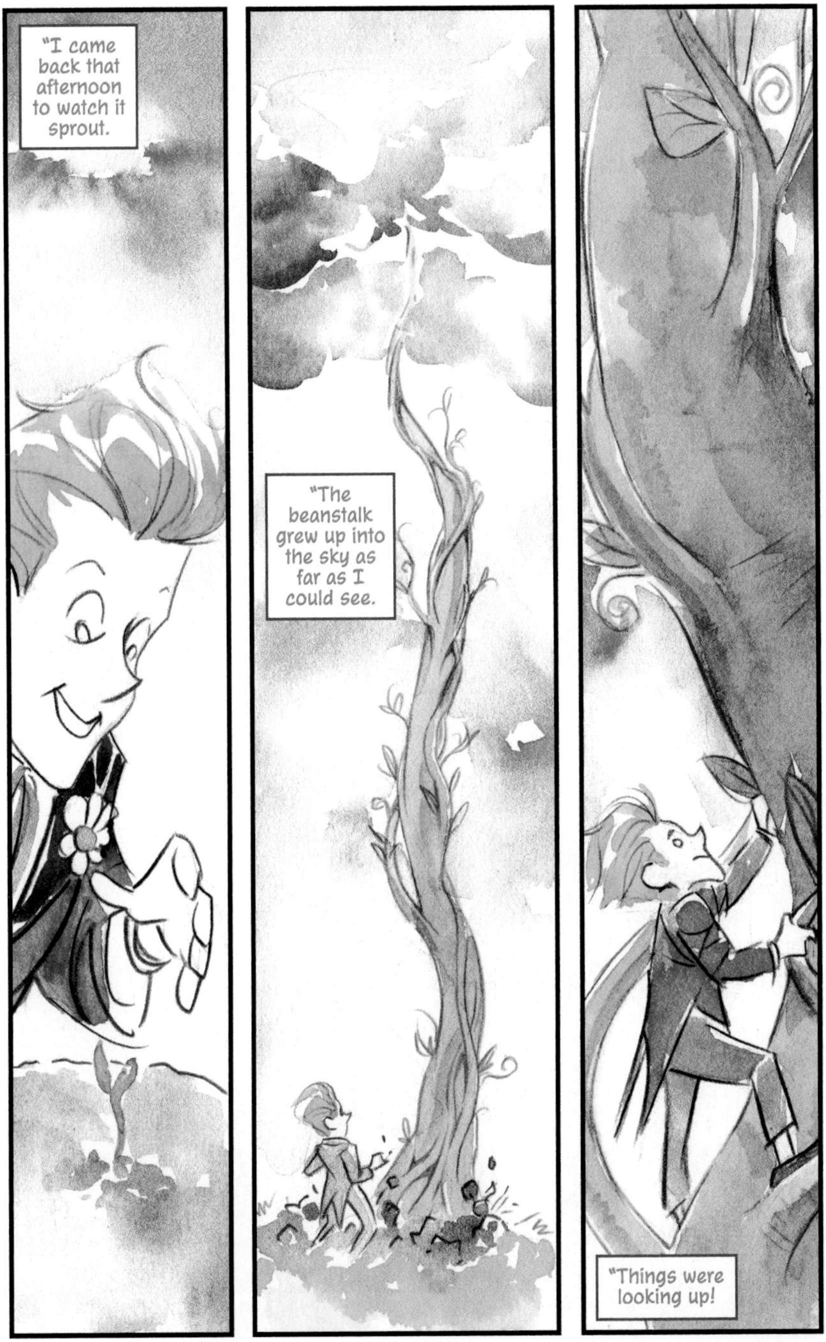
"I came back that afternoon to watch it sprout.
"The beanstalk grew up into the sky as far as I could see.
"Things were looking up!

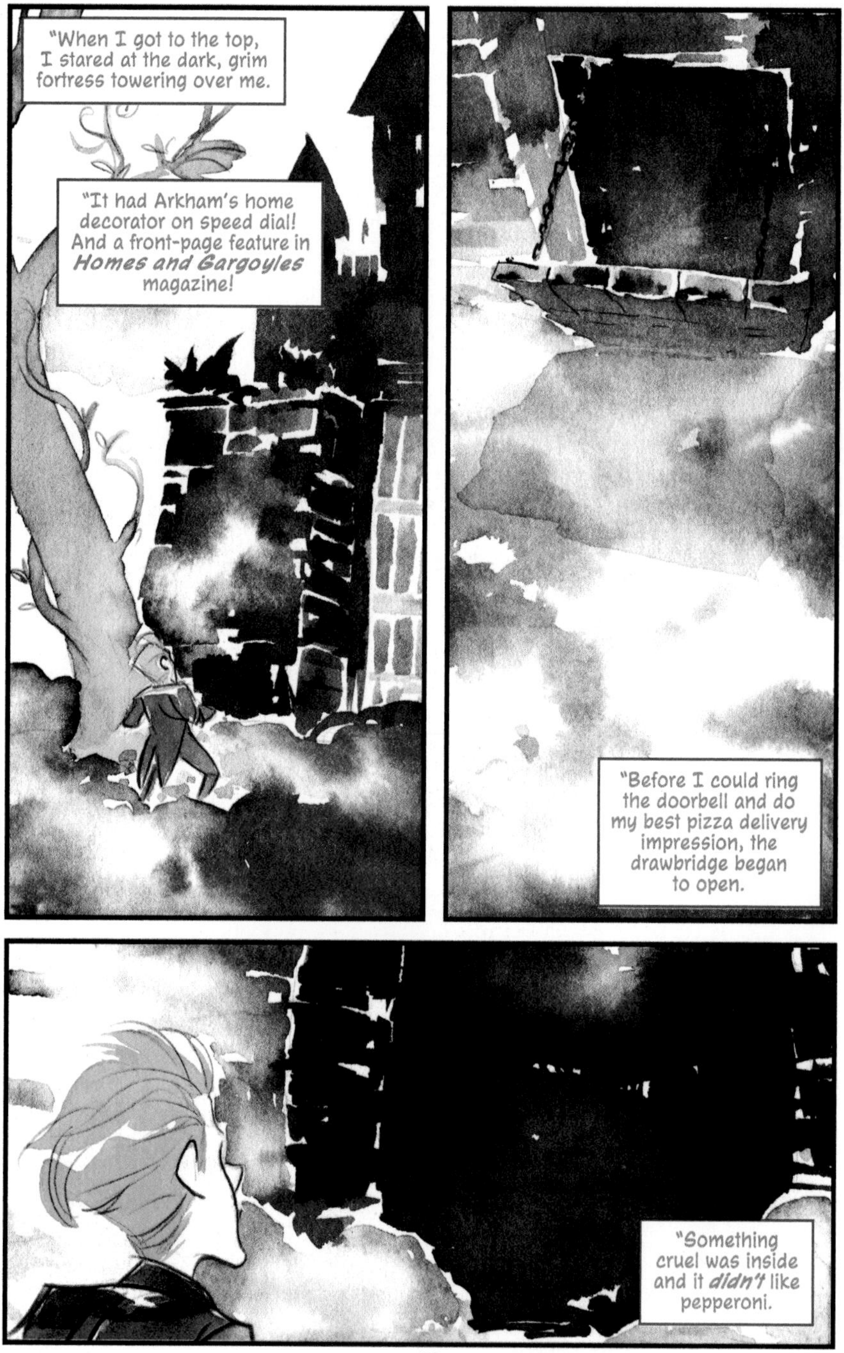
"When I got to the top, I stared at the dark, grim fortress towering over me.
"It had Arkham's home decorator on speed dial! And a front-page feature in *Homes and Gargoyles* magazine!
"Before I could ring the doorbell and do my best pizza delivery impression, the drawbridge began to open.
"Something cruel was inside and it *didn't* like pepperoni.

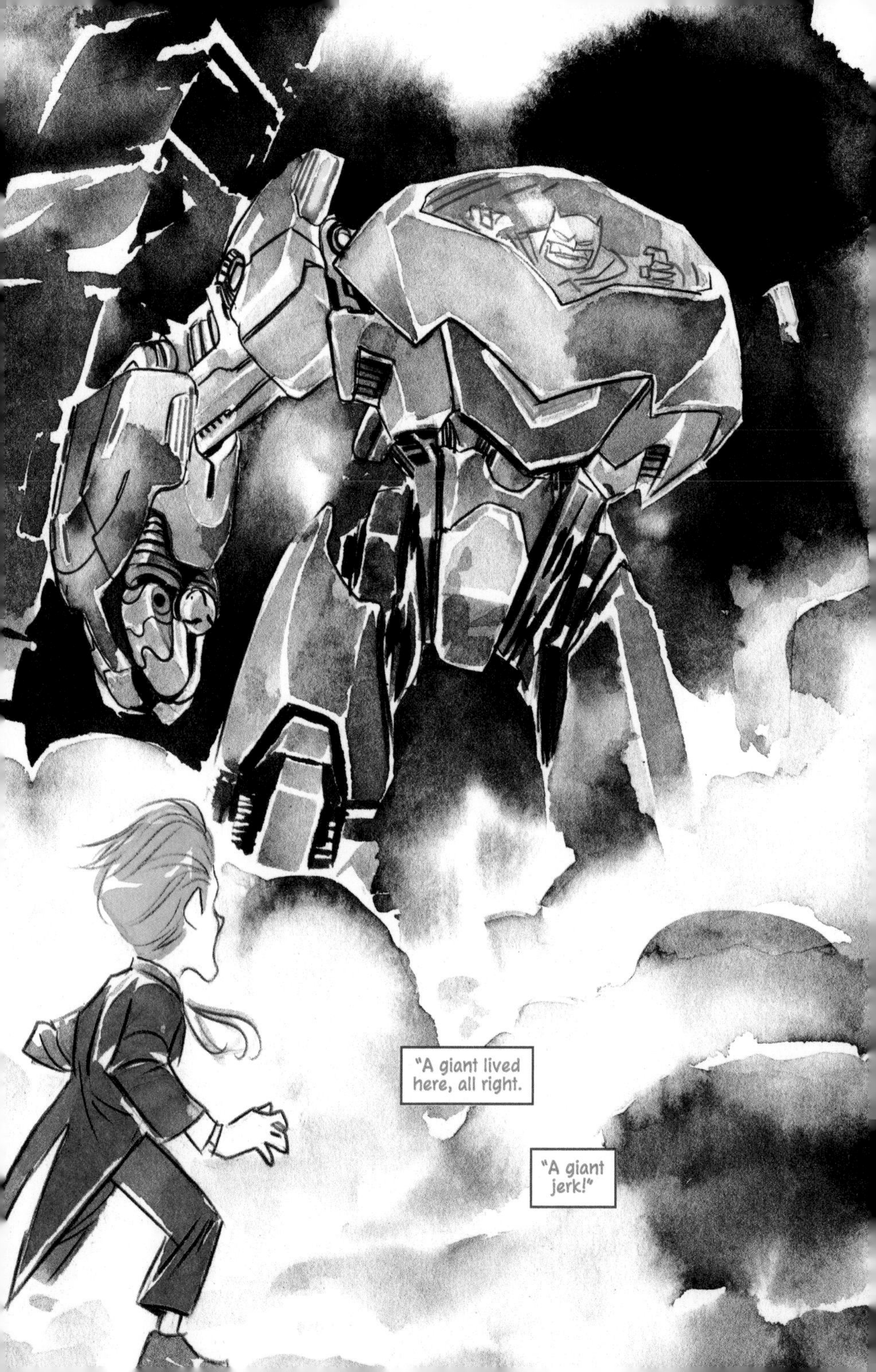
"A giant lived here, all right.
"A giant jerk!"

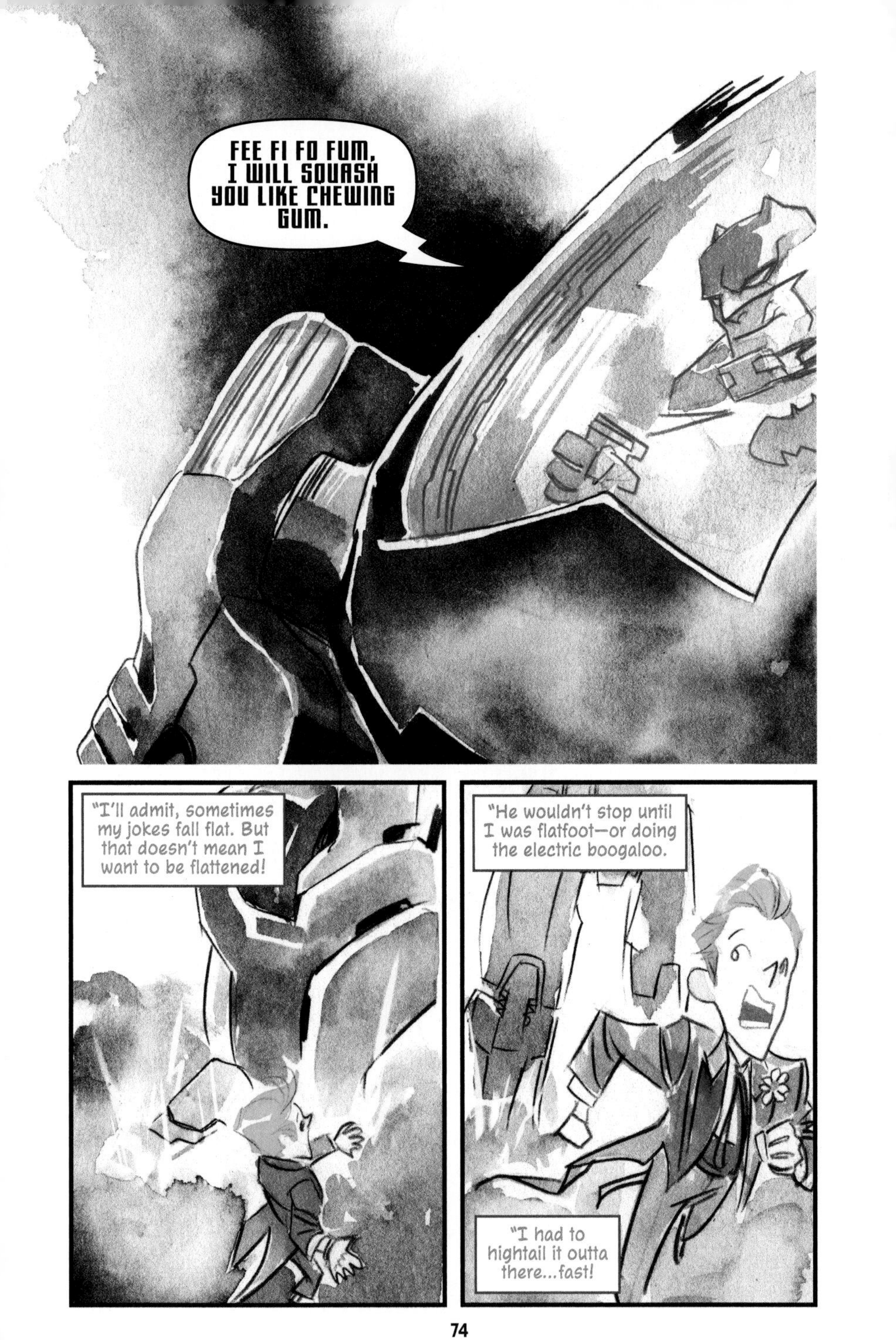
FEE FI FO FUM, I WILL SQUASH YOU LIKE CHEWING GUM.
"I'll admit, sometimes my jokes fall flat. But that doesn't mean I want to be flattened!
"He wouldn't stop until I was flatfoot—or doing the electric boogaloo.
"I had to hightail it outta there...fast!

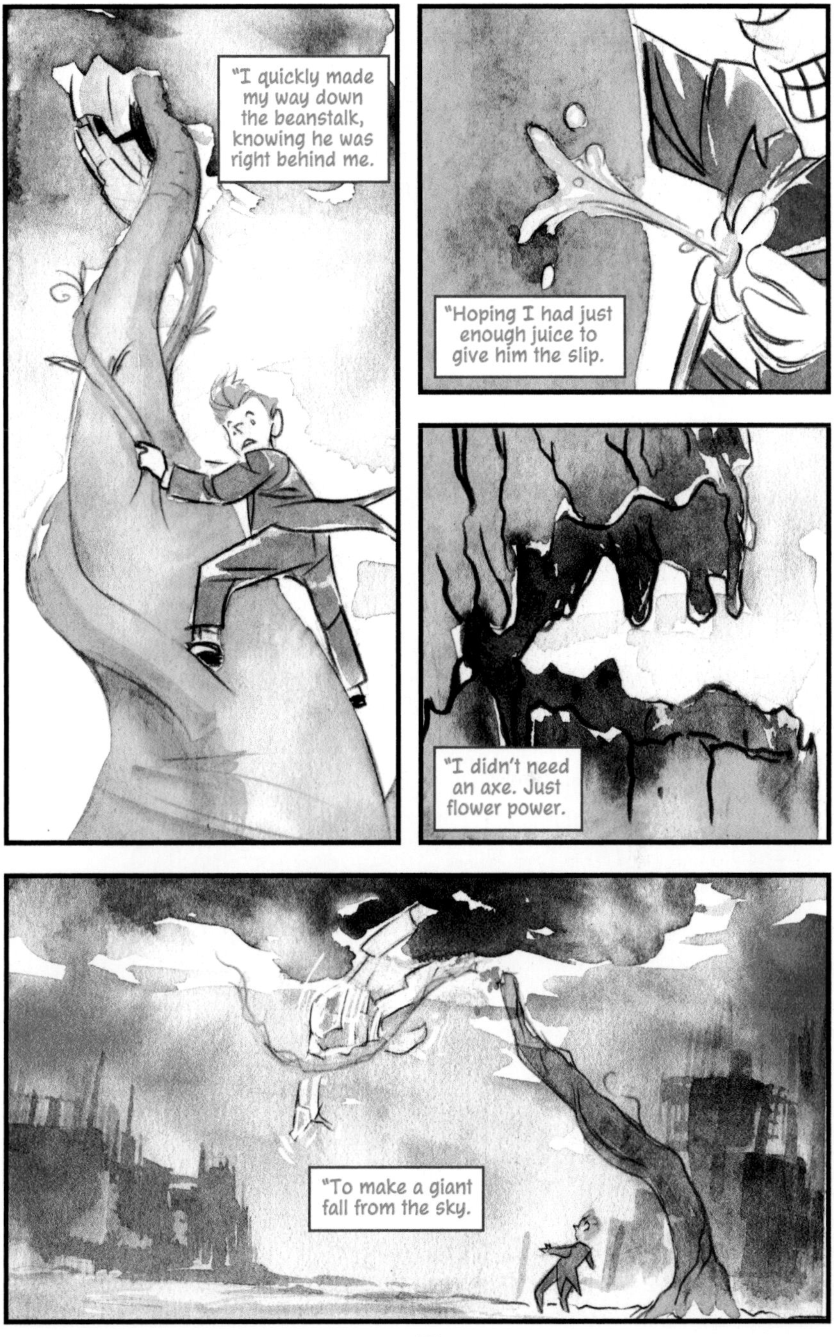
"I quickly made my way down the beanstalk, knowing he was right behind me.
"Hoping I had just enough juice to give him the slip.
"I didn't need an axe. Just flower power.
"To make a giant fall from the sky.

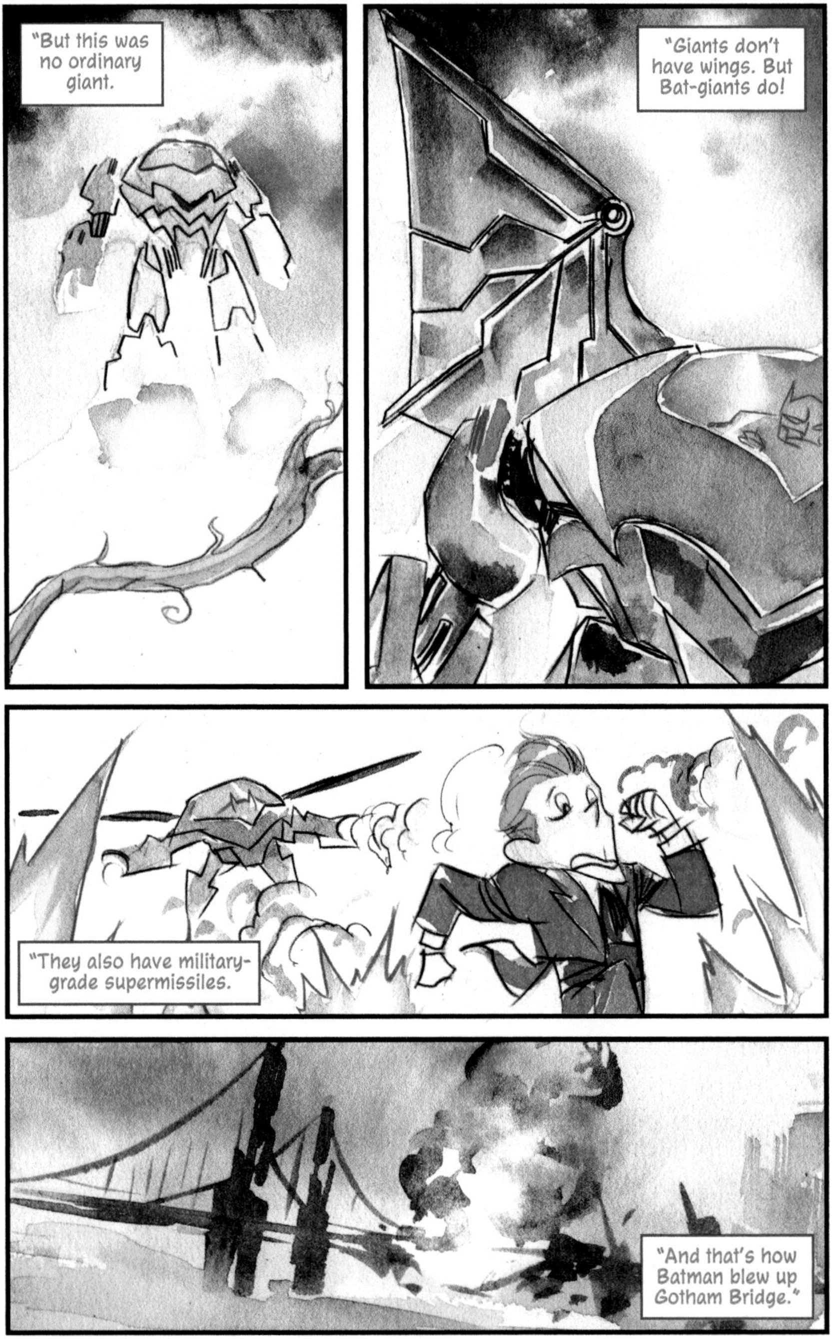
"But this was no ordinary giant.
"Giants don't have wings. But Bat-giants do!
"They also have military-grade supermissiles.
"And that's how Batman blew up Gotham Bridge."

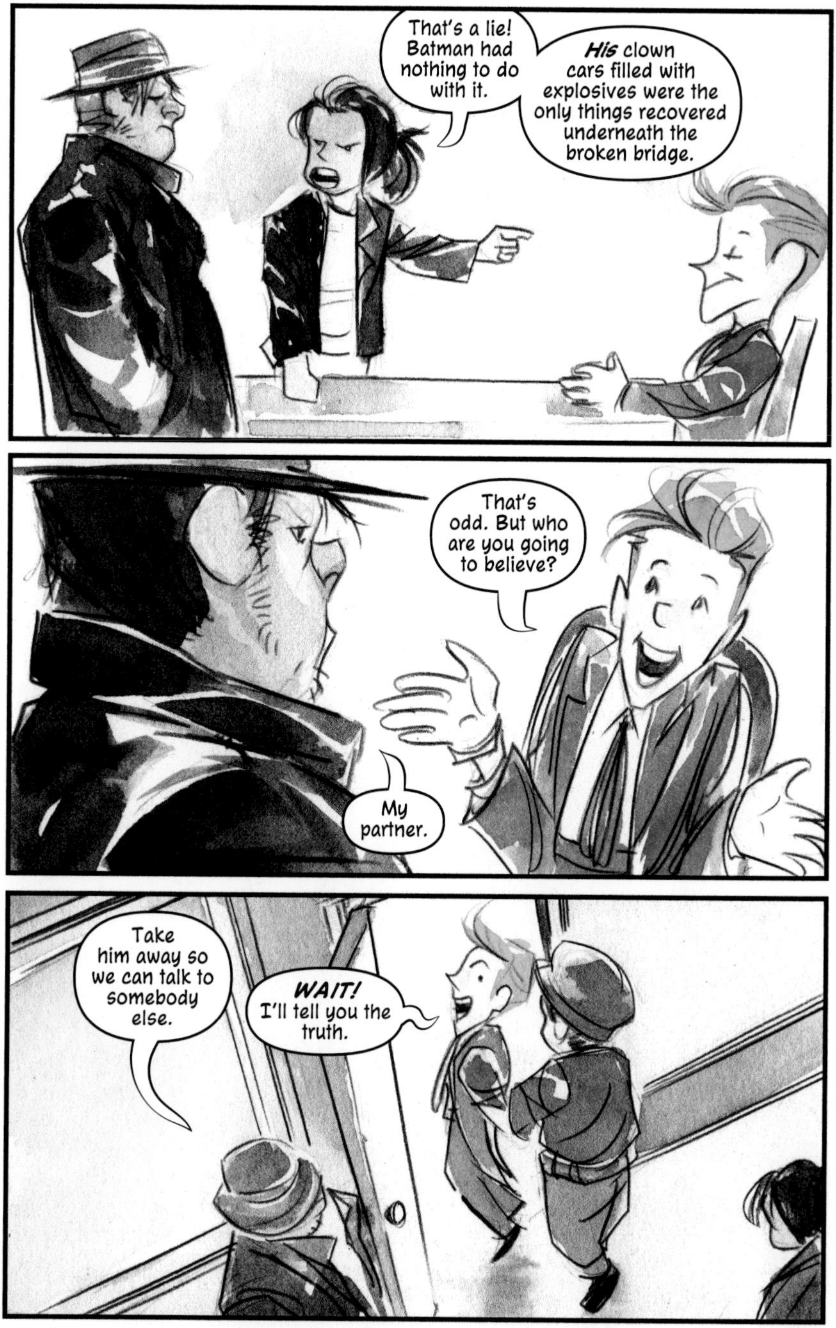
That's a lie! Batman had nothing to do with it.
His clown cars filled with explosives were the only things recovered underneath the broken bridge.
That's odd. But who are you going to believe?
My partner.
Take him away so we can talk to somebody else.
WAIT! I'll tell you the truth.

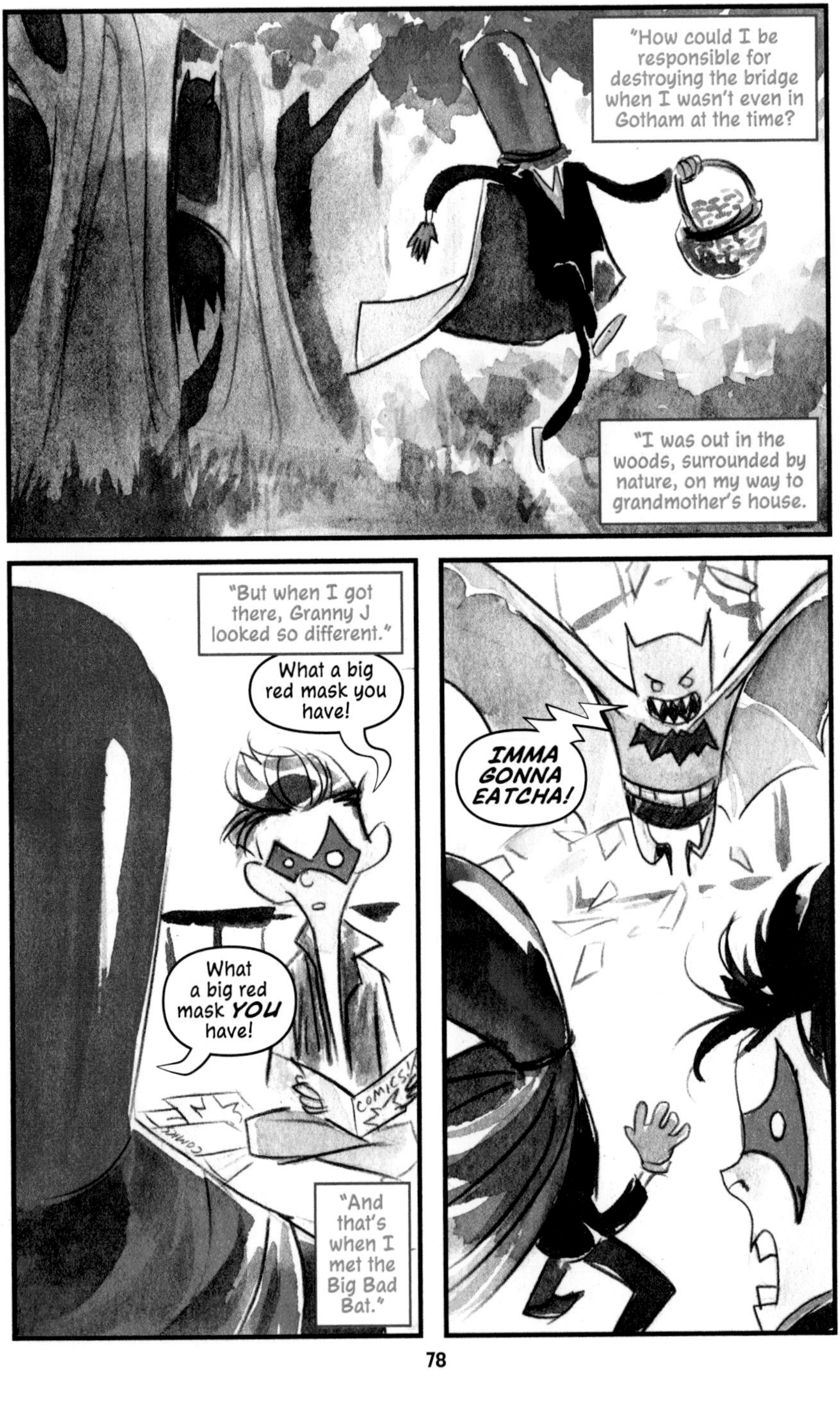
"How could I be responsible for destroying the bridge when I wasn't even in Gotham at the time?
"I was out in the woods, surrounded by nature, on my way to grandmother's house.
"But when I got there, Granny J looked so different."
What a big red mask you have!
What a big red mask **YOU** have!
COMICS!
"And that's when I met the Big Bad Bat."
IMMA GONNA EATCHA!

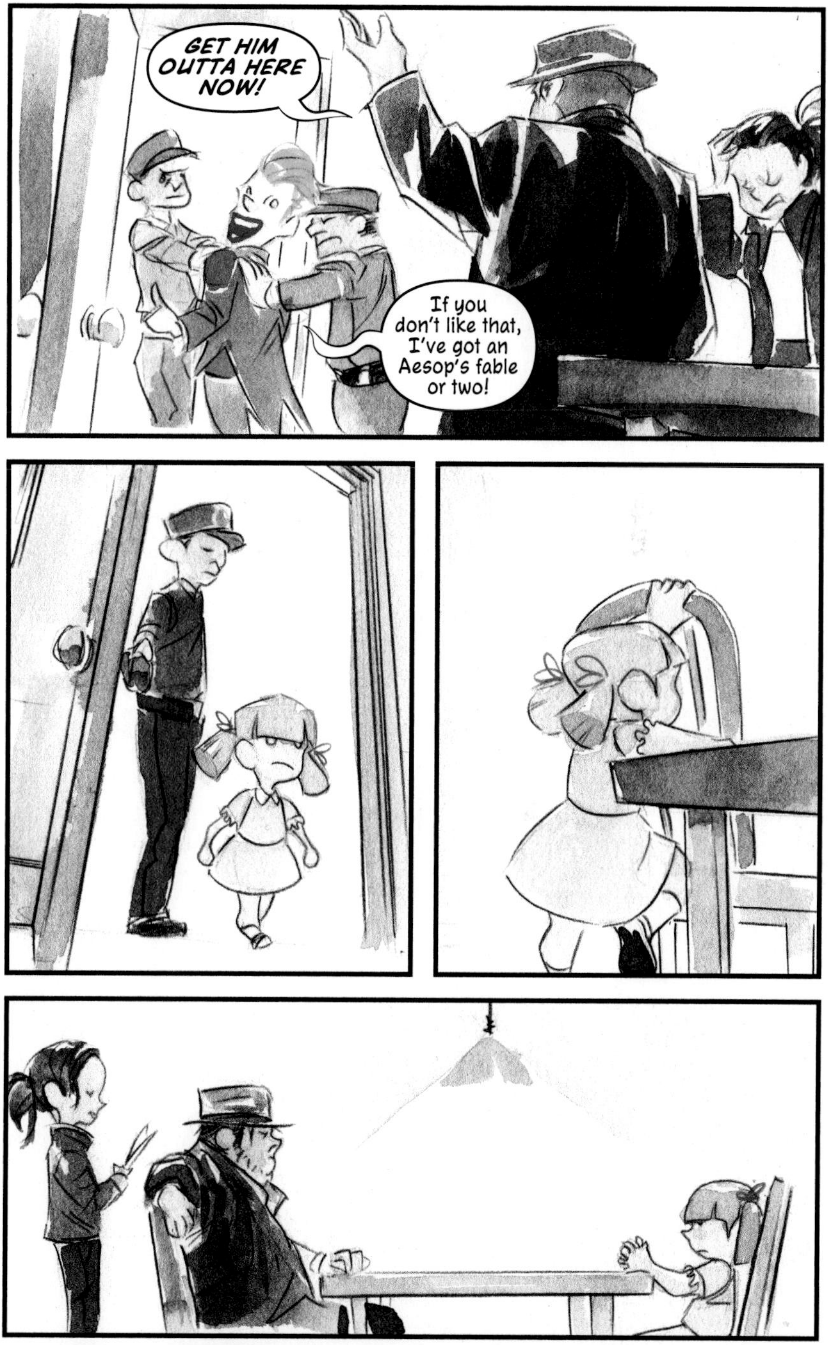
GET HIM OUTTA HERE NOW!
If you don't like that, I've got an Aesop's fable or two!

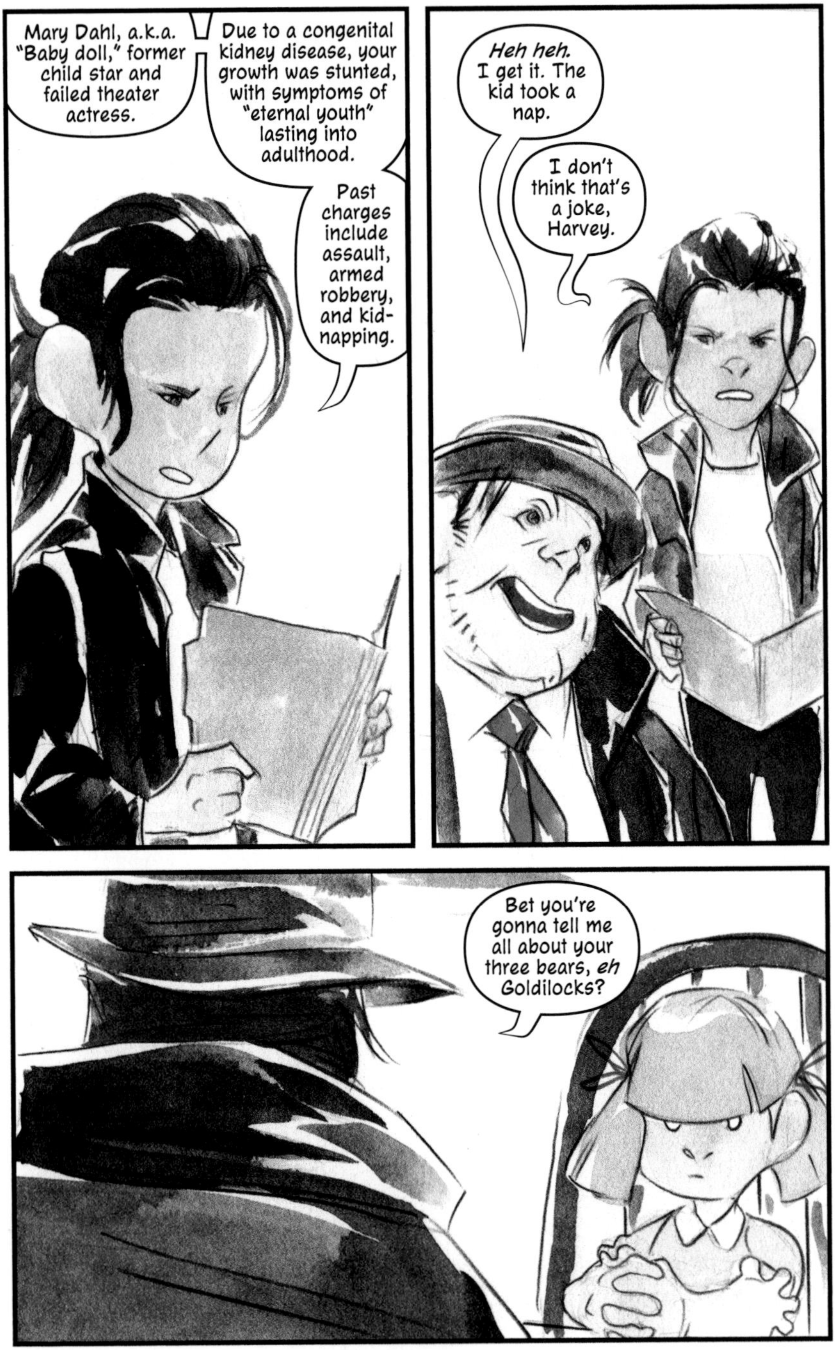
Mary Dahl, a.k.a. "Baby doll," former child star and failed theater actress.
Due to a congenital kidney disease, your growth was stunted, with symptoms of "eternal youth" lasting into adulthood.
Past charges include assault, armed robbery, and kid-napping.
Heh heh. I get it. The kid took a nap.
I don't think that's a joke, Harvey.
Bet you're gonna tell me all about your three bears, *eh* Goldilocks?

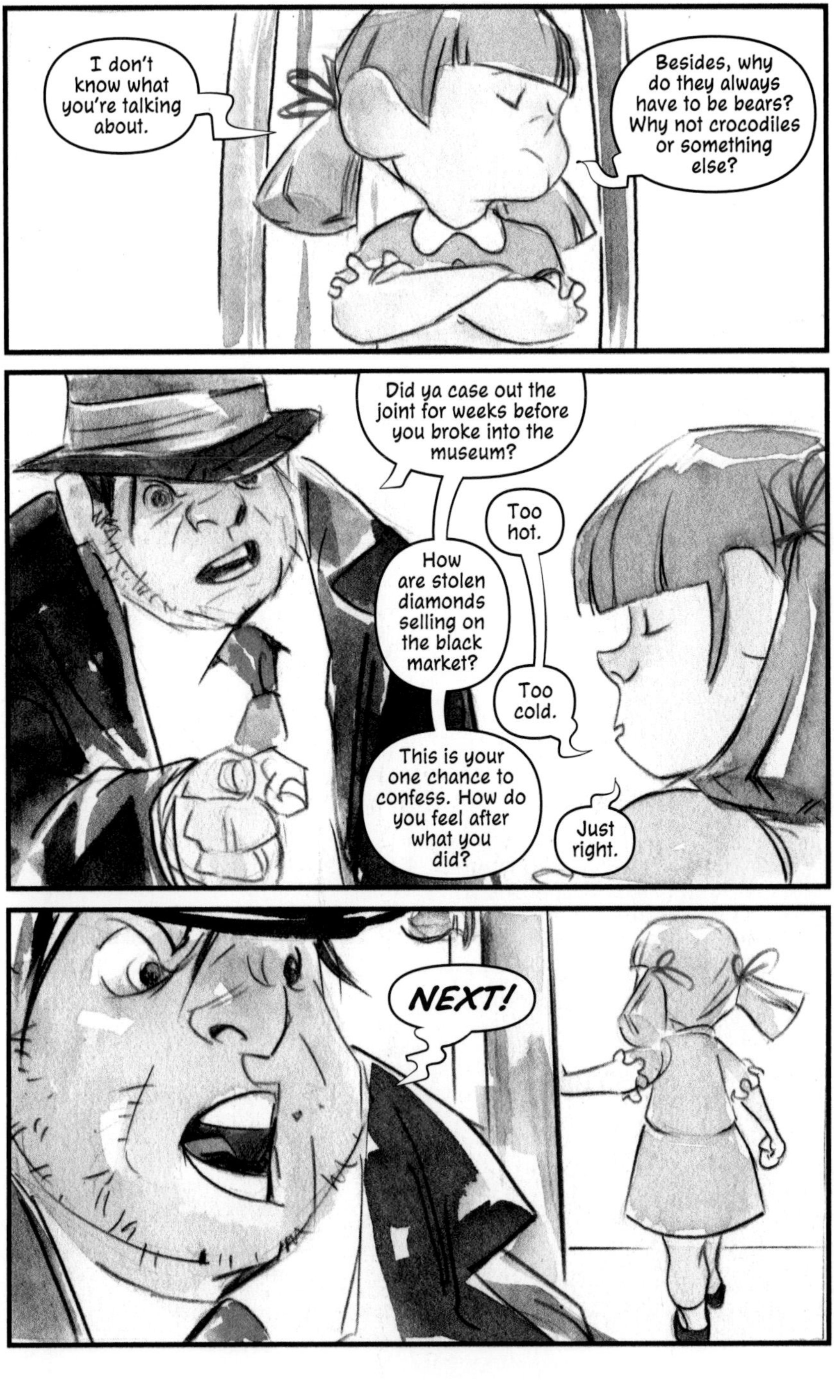
I don't know what you're talking about.
Besides, why do they always have to be bears? Why not crocodiles or something else?
Did ya case out the joint for weeks before you broke into the museum?
Too hot.
How are stolen diamonds selling on the black market?
Too cold.
This is your one chance to confess. How do you feel after what you did?
Just right.
NEXT!

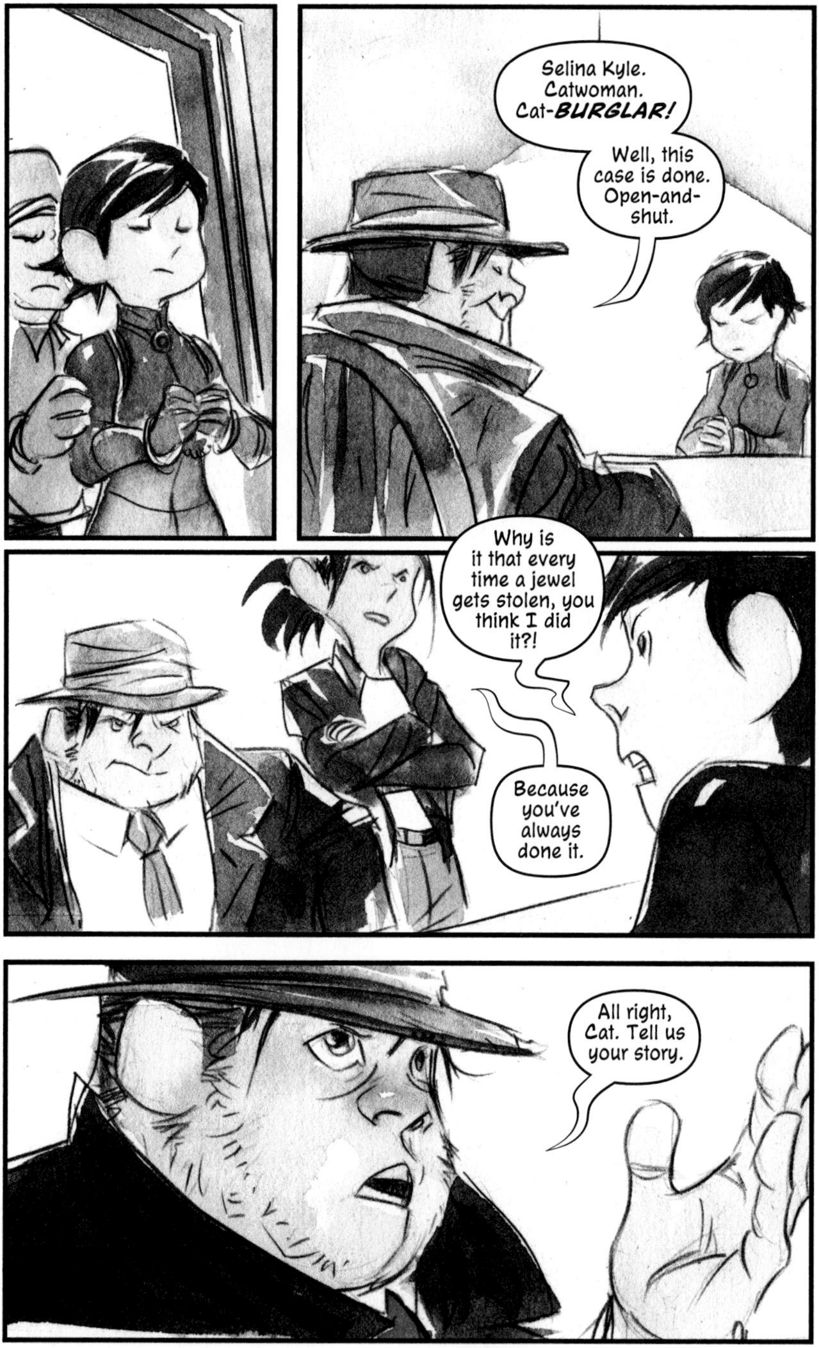
Selina Kyle. Catwoman. Cat-BURGLAR!
Well, this case is done. Open-and-shut.
Why is it that every time a jewel gets stolen, you think I did it?!
Because you've always done it.
All right, Cat. Tell us your story.

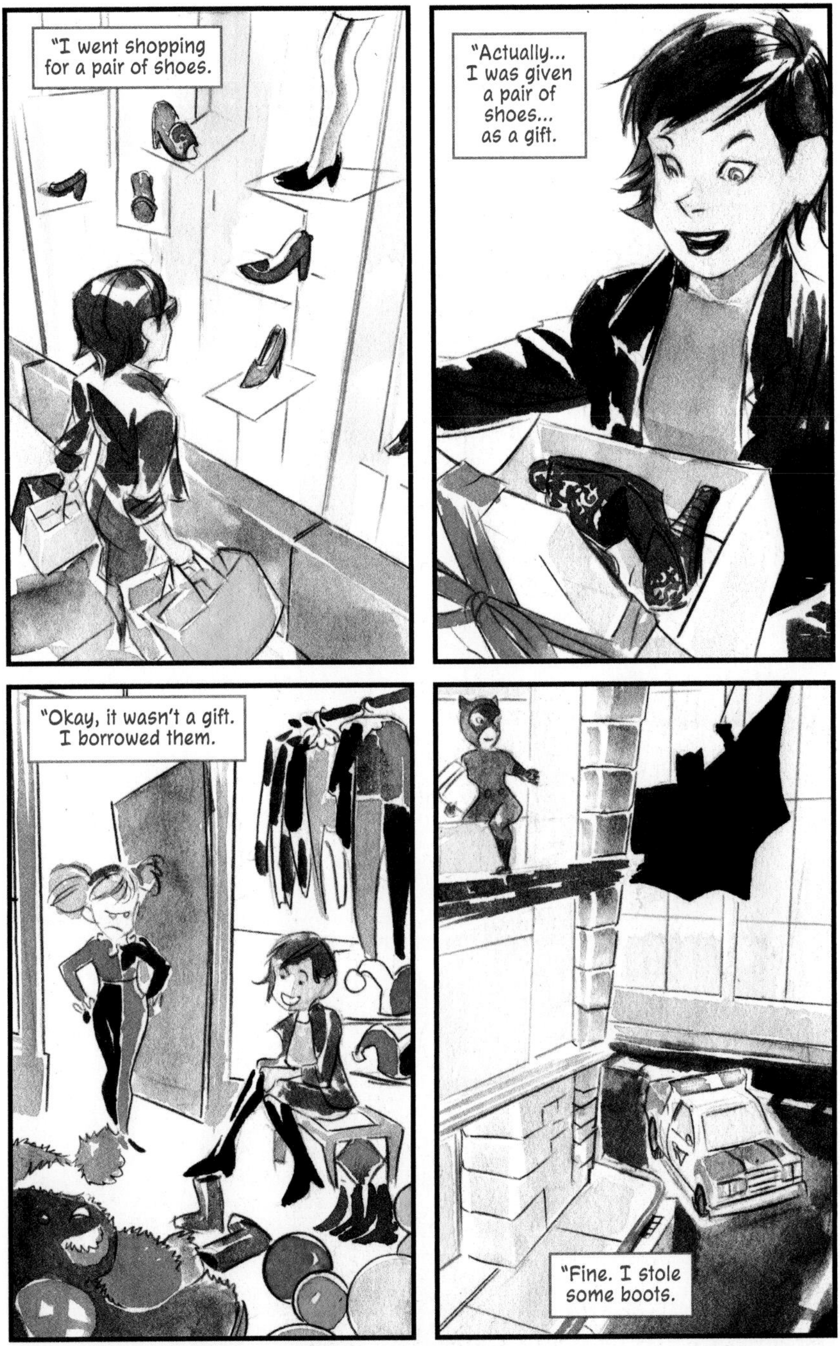
"I went shopping for a pair of shoes.
"Actually... I was given a pair of shoes... as a gift.
"Okay, it wasn't a gift. I borrowed them.
"Fine. I stole some boots.

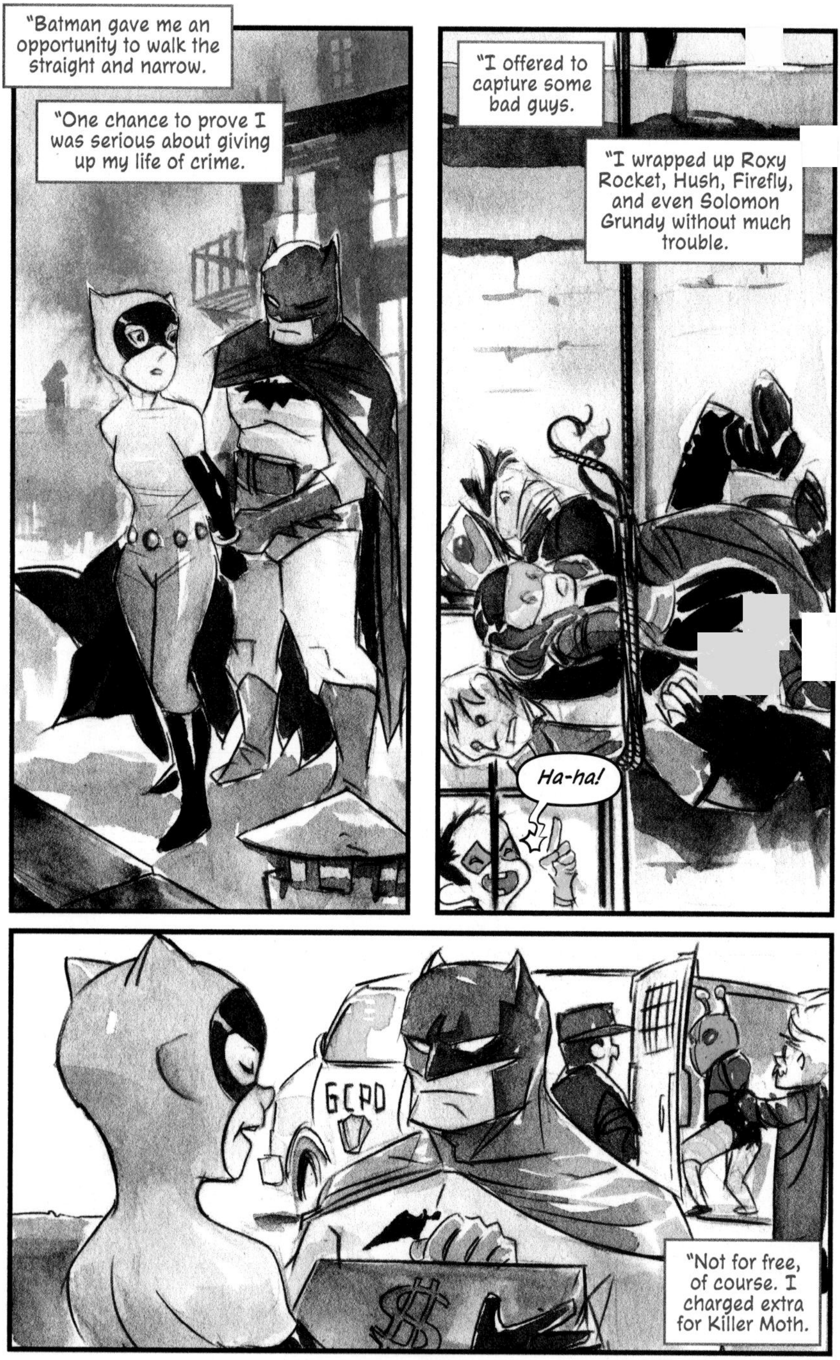
"Batman gave me an opportunity to walk the straight and narrow.
"One chance to prove I was serious about giving up my life of crime.
"I offered to capture some bad guys.
"I wrapped up Roxy Rocket, Hush, Firefly, and even Solomon Grundy without much trouble.
Ha-ha!
GCPD
"Not for free, of course. I charged extra for Killer Moth.

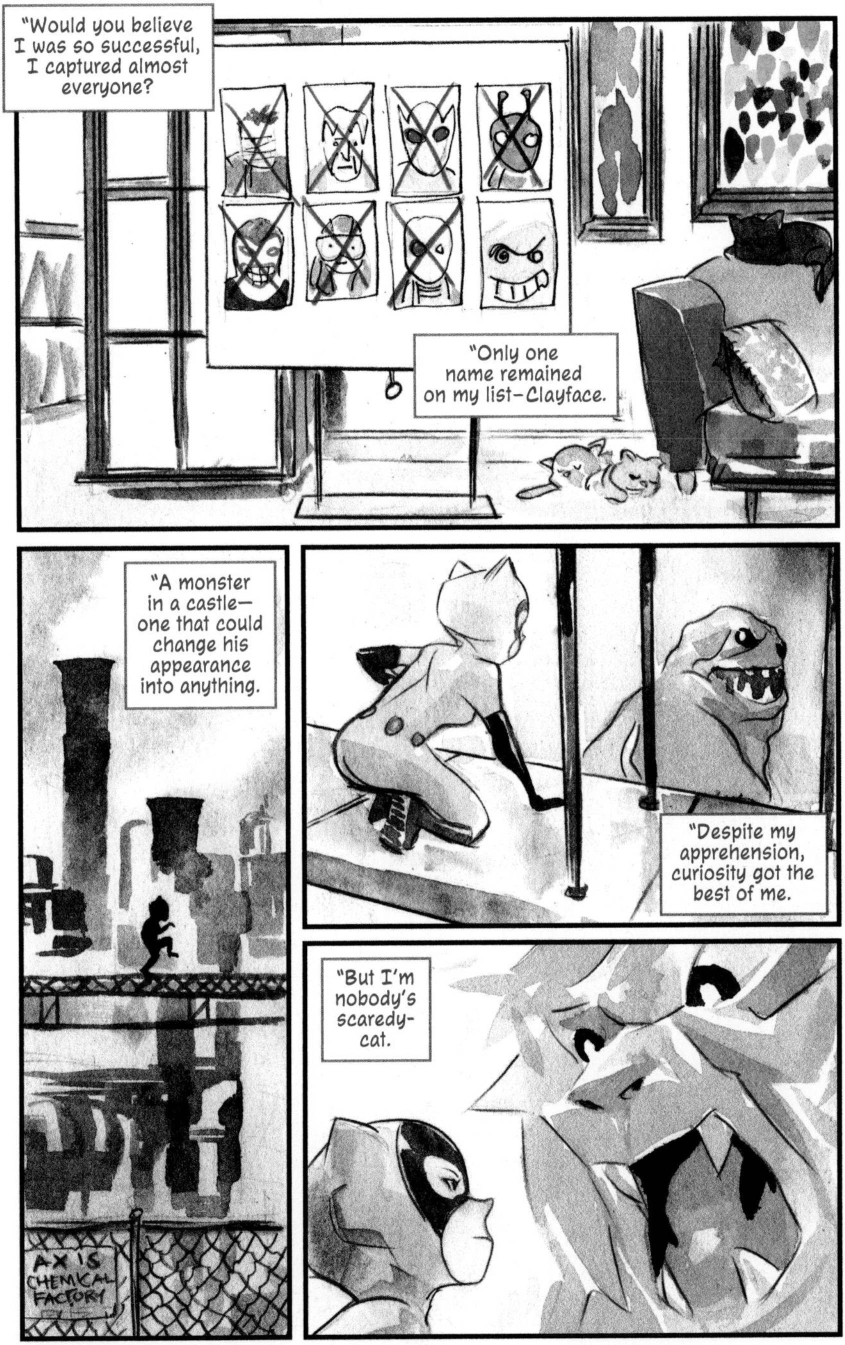
"Would you believe I was so successful, I captured almost everyone?
"Only one name remained on my list–Clayface.
"A monster in a castle– one that could change his appearance into anything.
AXIS CHEMICAL FACTORY
"Despite my apprehension, curiosity got the best of me.
"But I'm nobody's scaredy-cat.

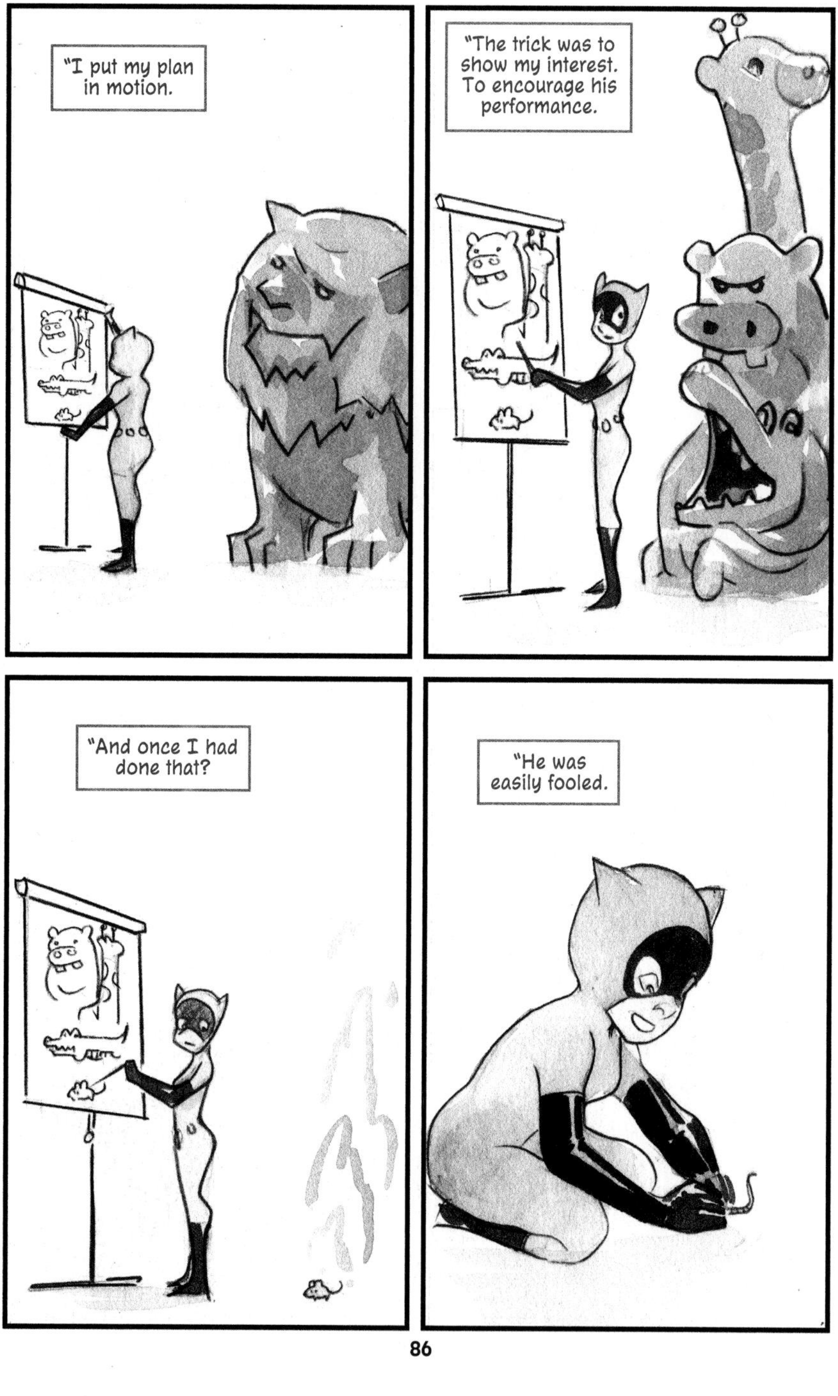
"I put my plan in motion.
"The trick was to show my interest. To encourage his performance.
"And once I had done that?
"He was easily fooled.

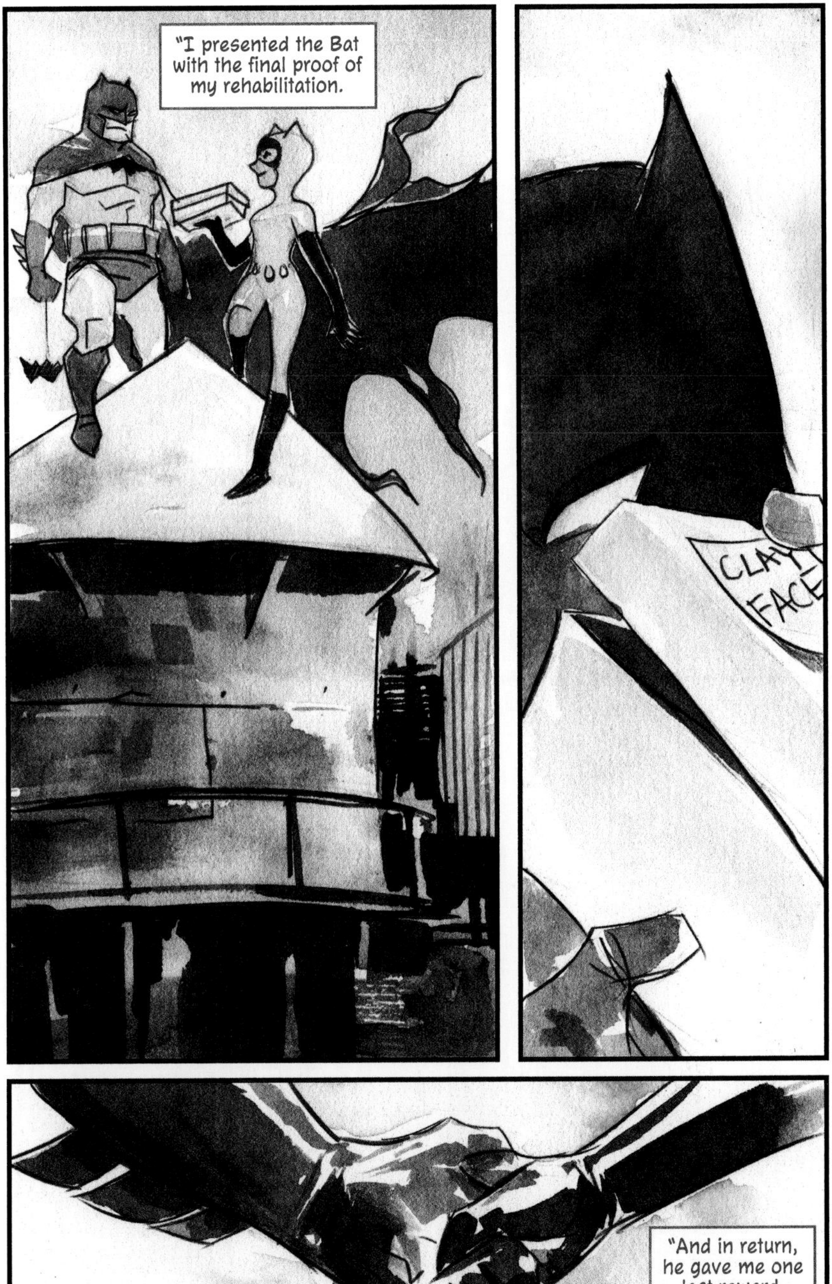
"I presented the Bat with the final proof of my rehabilitation.
"And in return, he gave me one last reward.

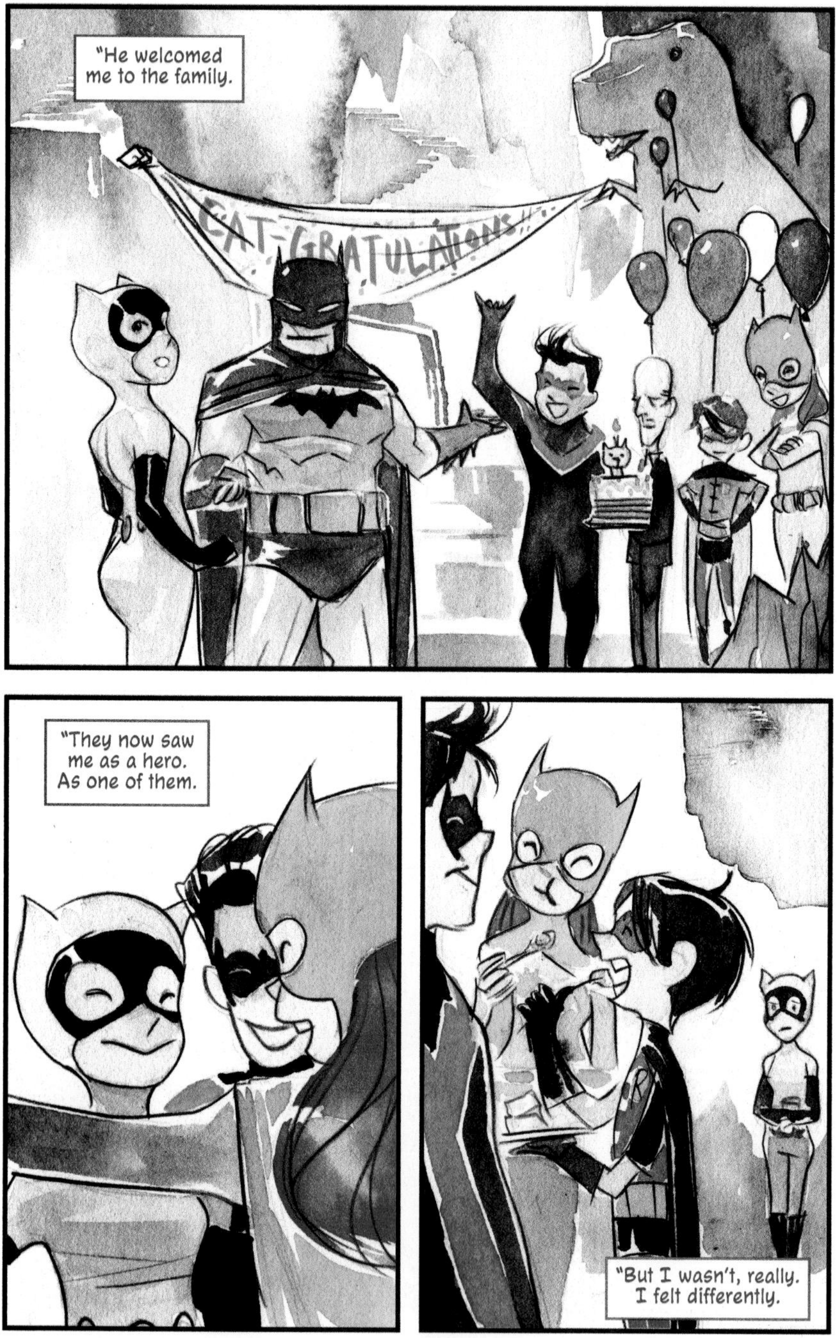
"He welcomed me to the family.
CAT-GRATULATIONS!!!
"They now saw me as a hero. As one of them.
"But I wasn't, really. I felt differently.

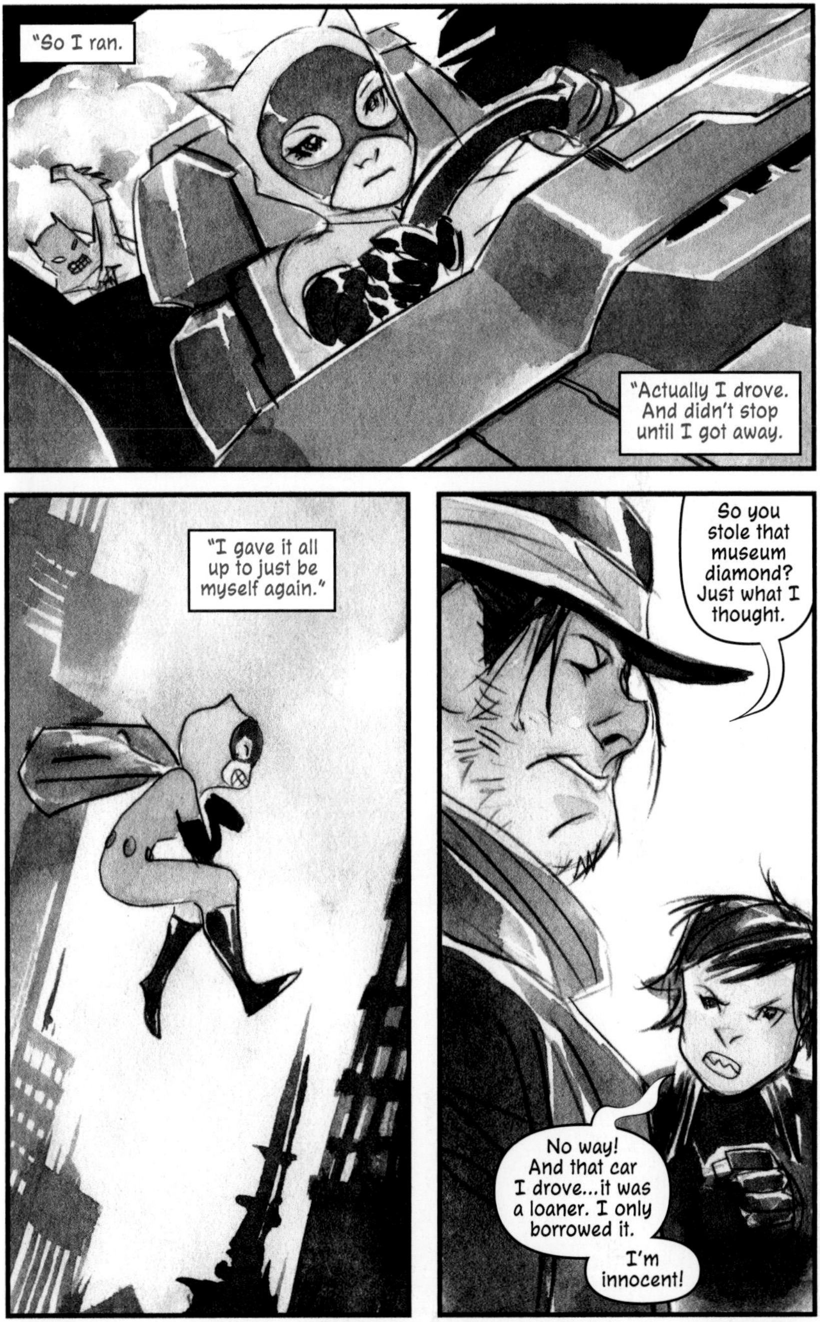
"So I ran.
"Actually I drove. And didn't stop until I got away.
"I gave it all up to just be myself again."
So you stole that museum diamond? Just what I thought.
No way! And that car I drove...it was a loaner. I only borrowed it.
I'm innocent!

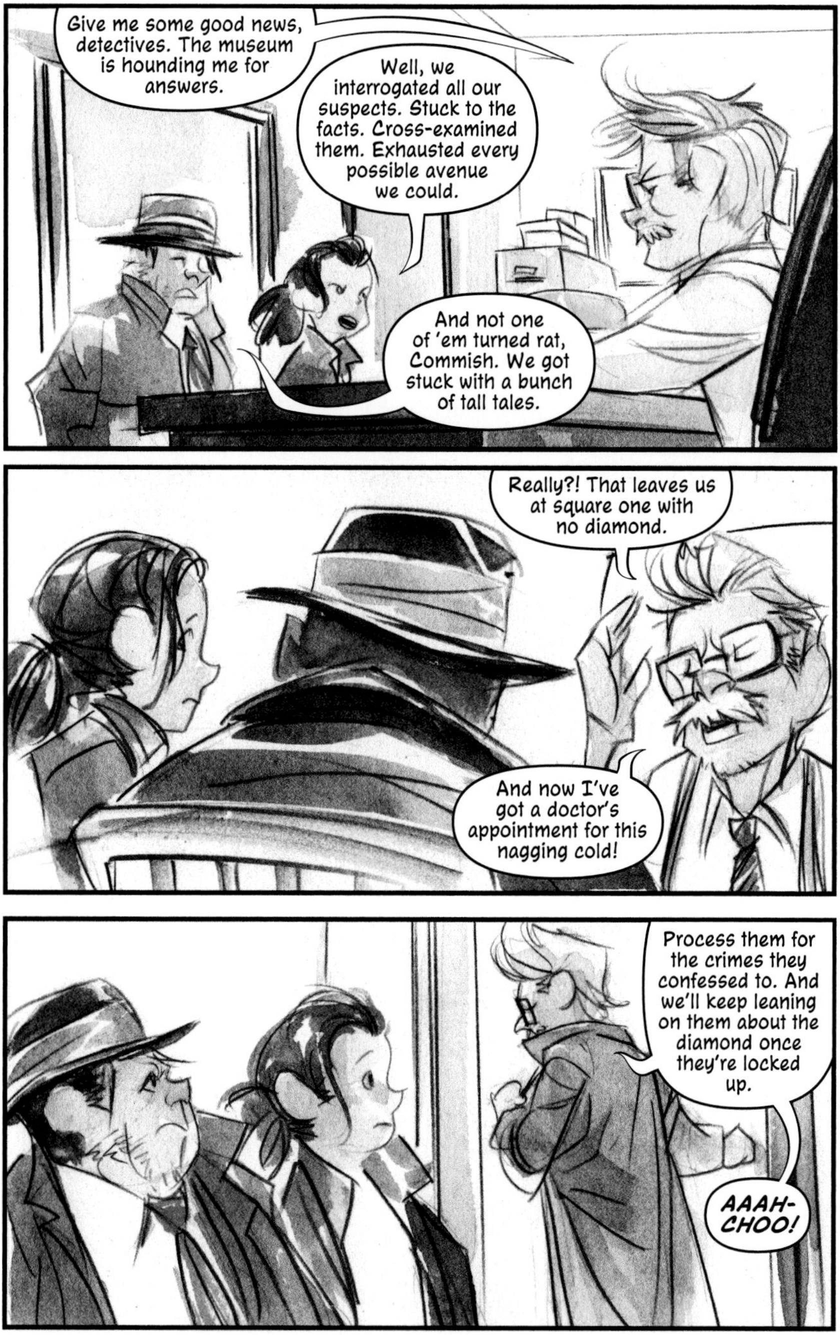
Give me some good news, detectives. The museum is hounding me for answers.
Well, we interrogated all our suspects. Stuck to the facts. Cross-examined them. Exhausted every possible avenue we could.
And not one of 'em turned rat, Commish. We got stuck with a bunch of tall tales.
Really?! That leaves us at square one with no diamond.
And now I've got a doctor's appointment for this nagging cold!
Process them for the crimes they confessed to. And we'll keep leaning on them about the diamond once they're locked up.
AAAH-CHOO!

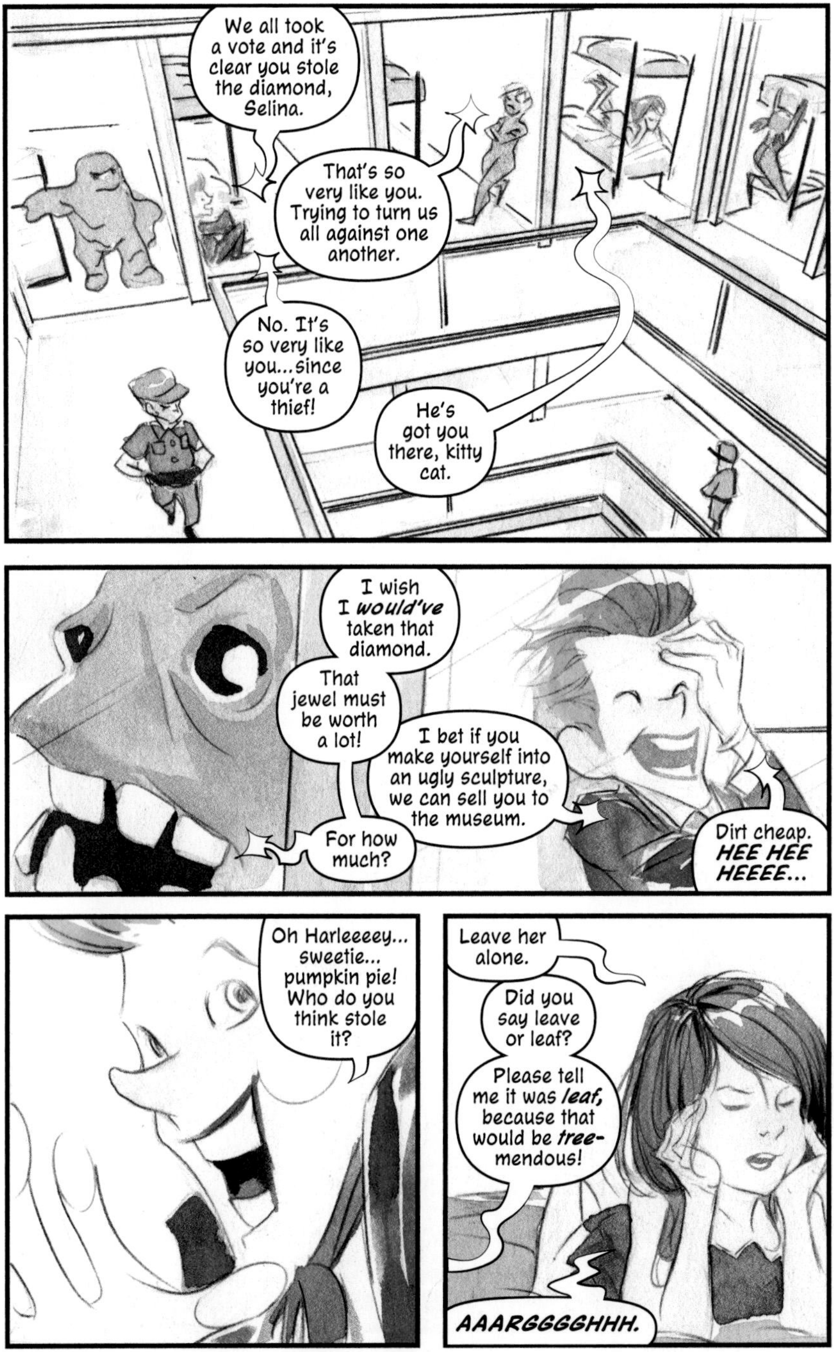
We all took a vote and it's clear you stole the diamond, Selina.
That's so very like you. Trying to turn us all against one another.
No. It's so very like you...since you're a thief!
He's got you there, kitty cat.
I wish I *would've* taken that diamond.
That jewel must be worth a lot!
I bet if you make yourself into an ugly sculpture, we can sell you to the museum.
For how much?
Dirt cheap. ***HEE HEE HEEEE...***
Oh Harleeeey... sweetie... pumpkin pie! Who do you think stole it?
Leave her alone.
Did you say leave or leaf?
Please tell me it was *leaf,* because that would be *tree-*mendous!
AAARGGGGHHH.

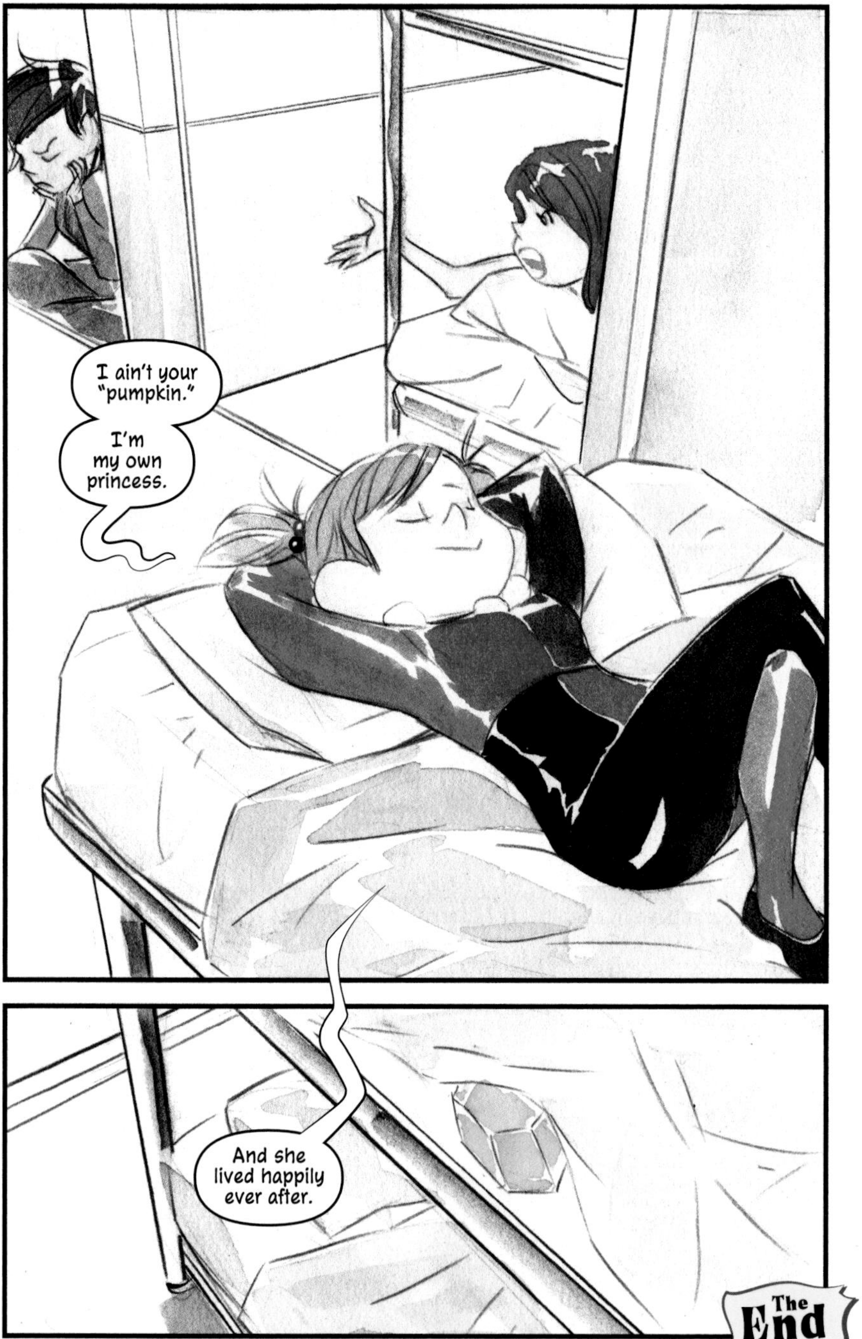
I ain't your "pumpkin."
I'm my own princess.
And she lived happily ever after.
The End

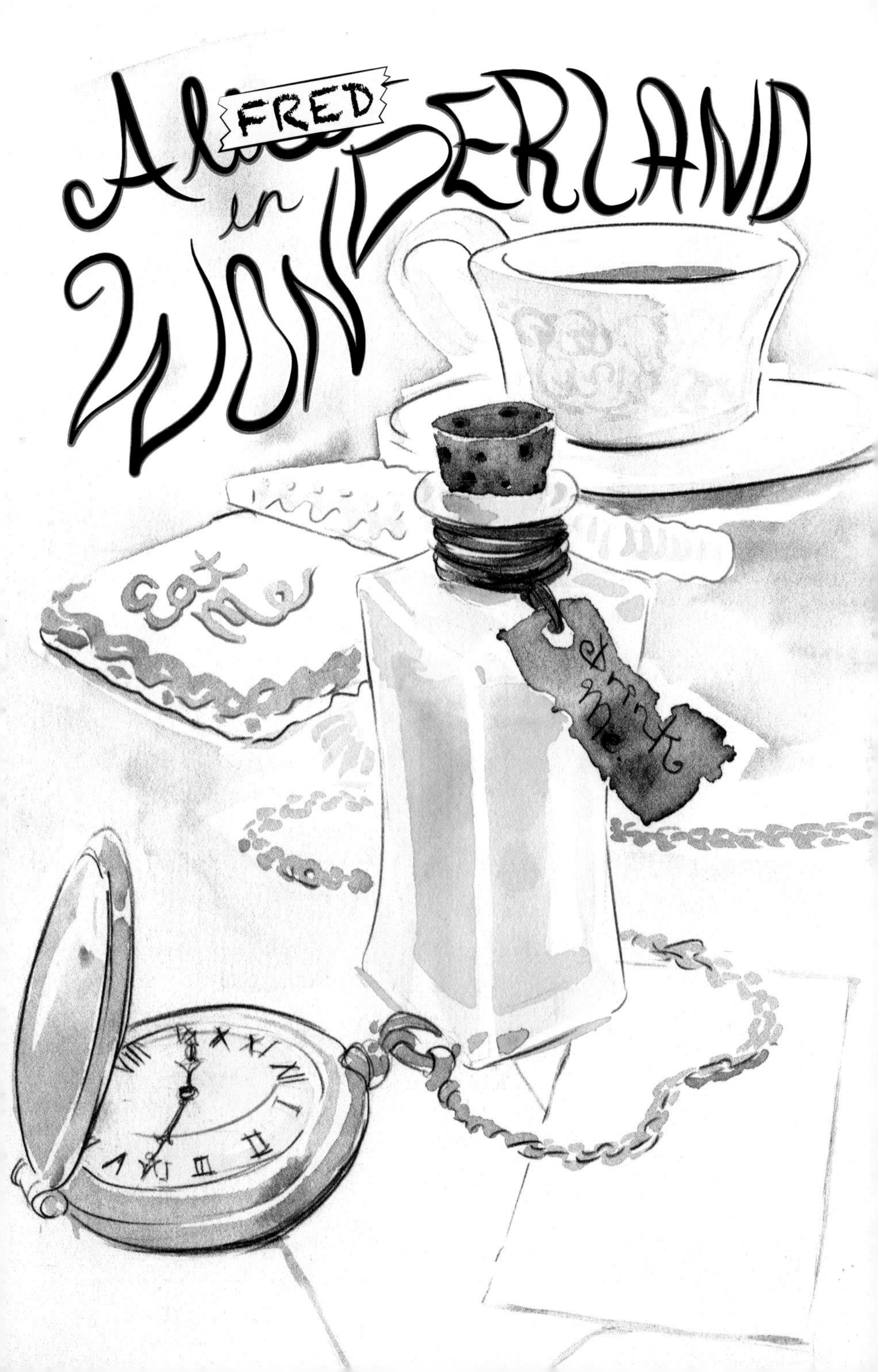

Alice FRED in WONDERLAND
eat me
drink me

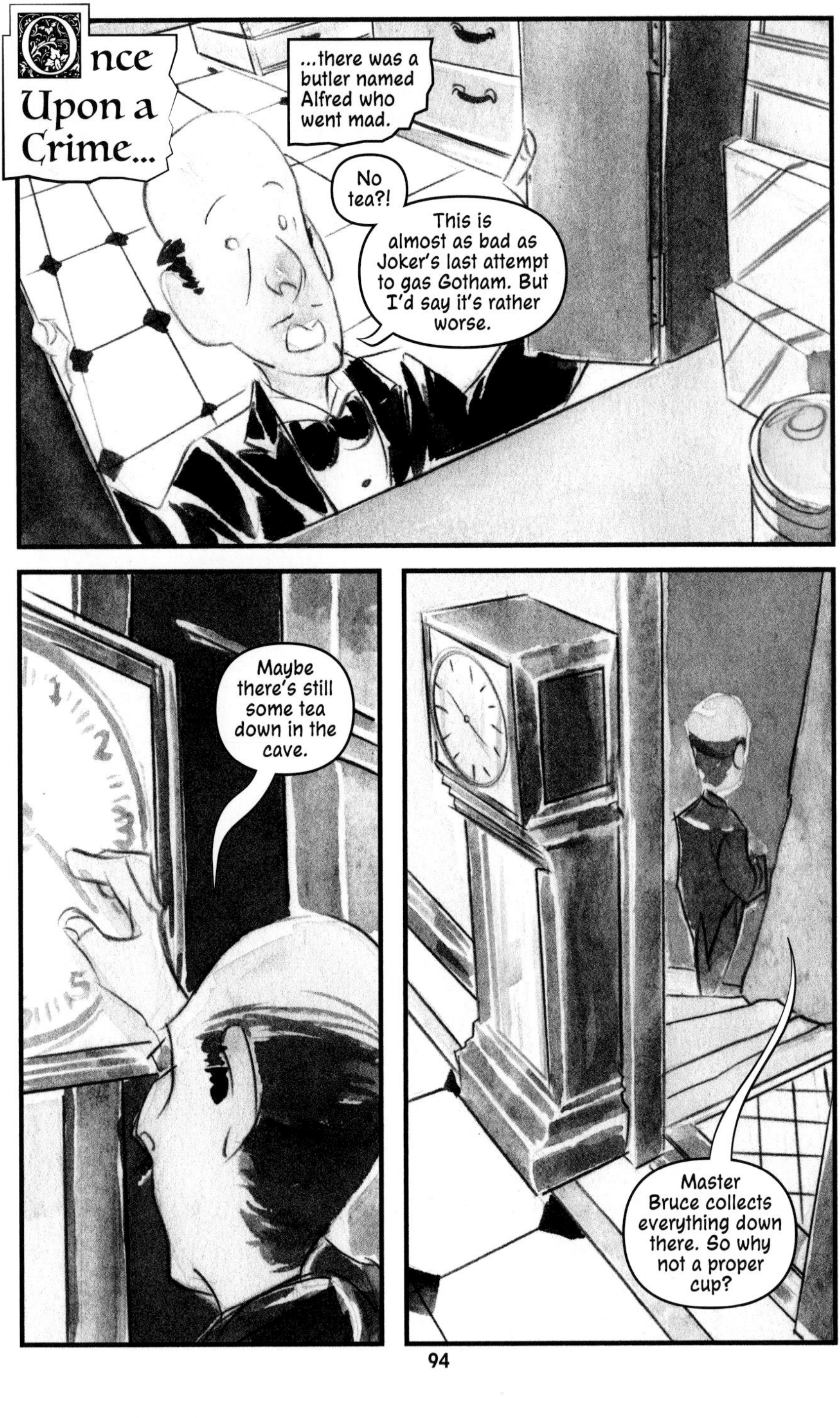
Once Upon a Crime...
...there was a butler named Alfred who went mad.
No tea?!
This is almost as bad as Joker's last attempt to gas Gotham. But I'd say it's rather worse.
Maybe there's still some tea down in the cave.
Master Bruce collects everything down there. So why not a proper cup?

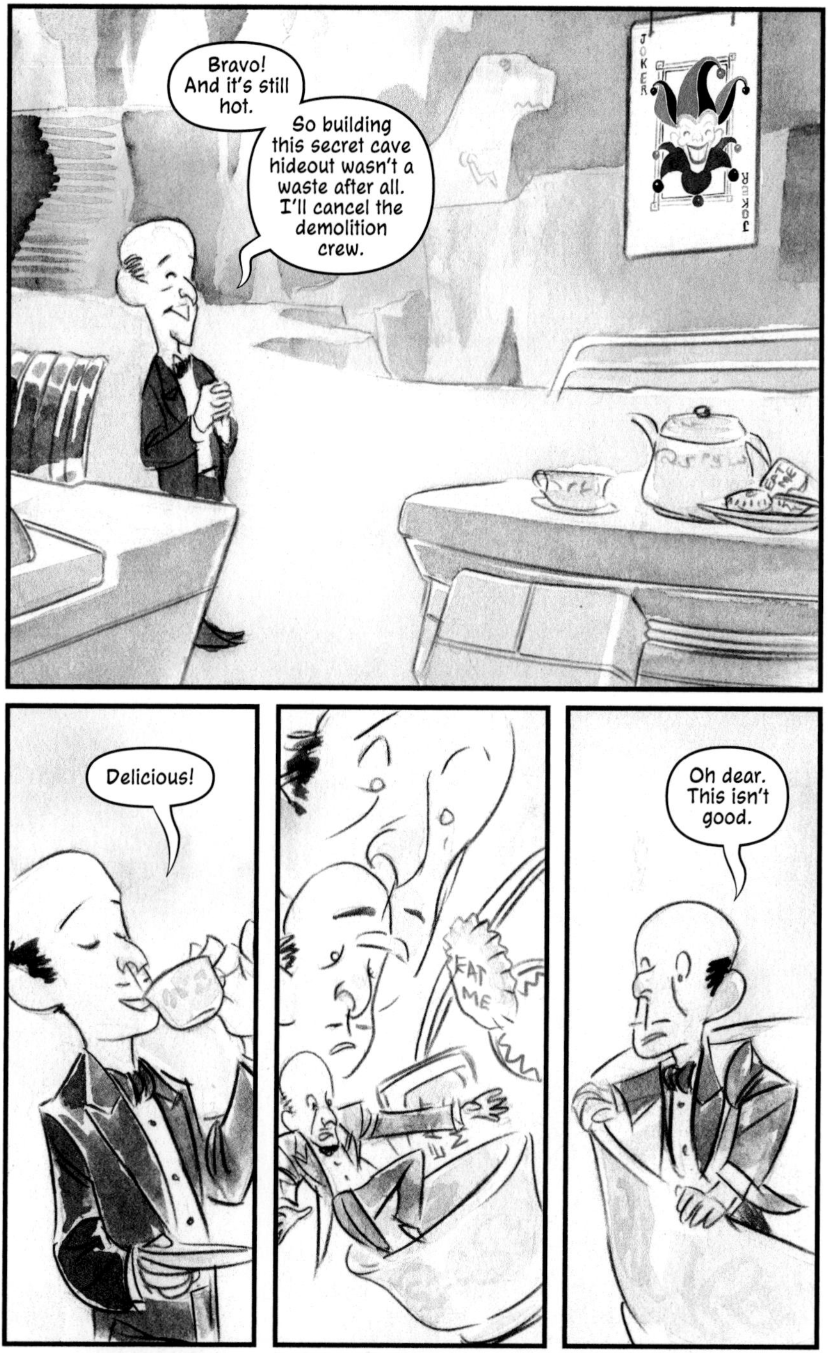
JOKER
JOKER
Bravo! And it's still hot.
So building this secret cave hideout wasn't a waste after all. I'll cancel the demolition crew.
EAT ME
Delicious!
EAT ME
Oh dear. This isn't good.

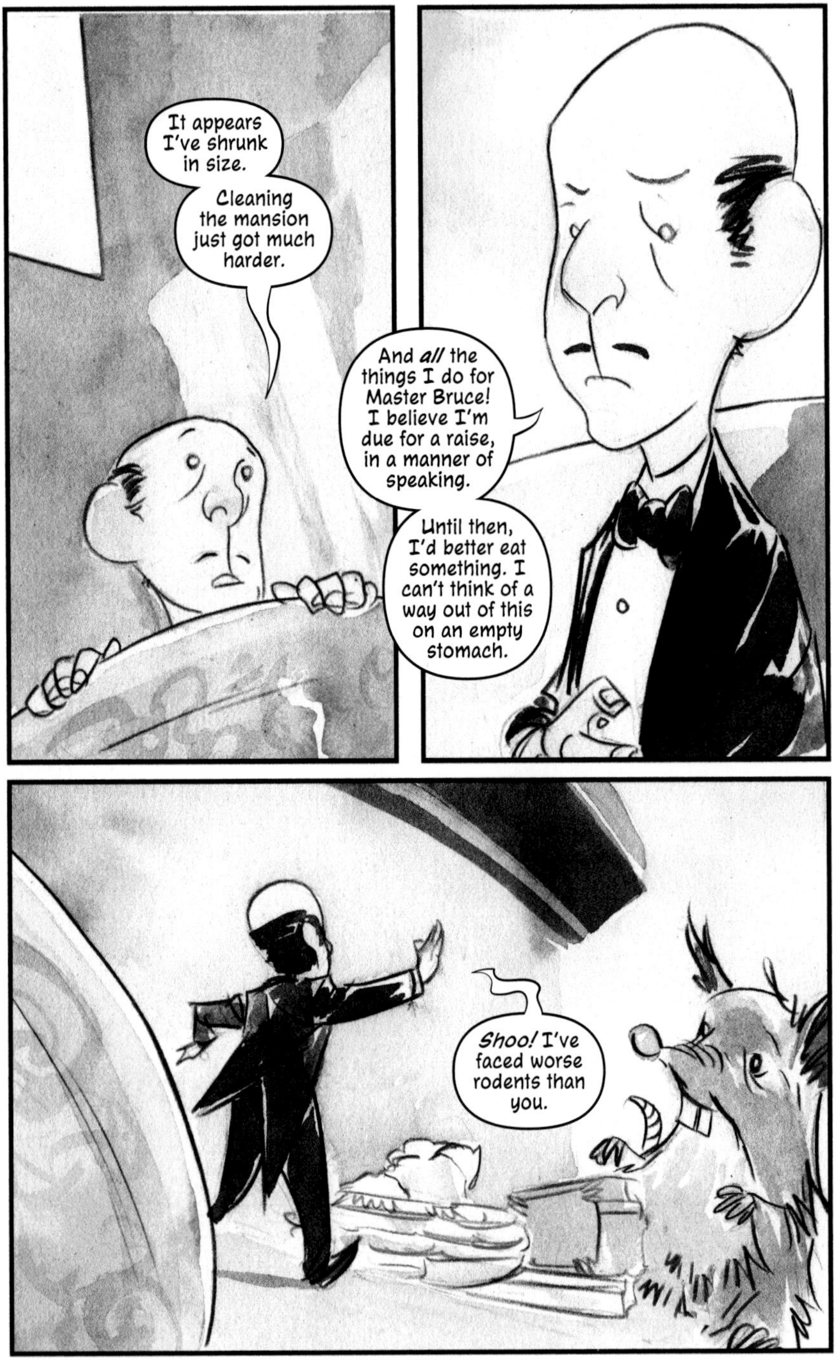

It appears I've shrunk in size.
Cleaning the mansion just got much harder.
And *all* the things I do for Master Bruce! I believe I'm due for a raise, in a manner of speaking.
Until then, I'd better eat something. I can't think of a way out of this on an empty stomach.
Shoo! I've faced worse rodents than you.

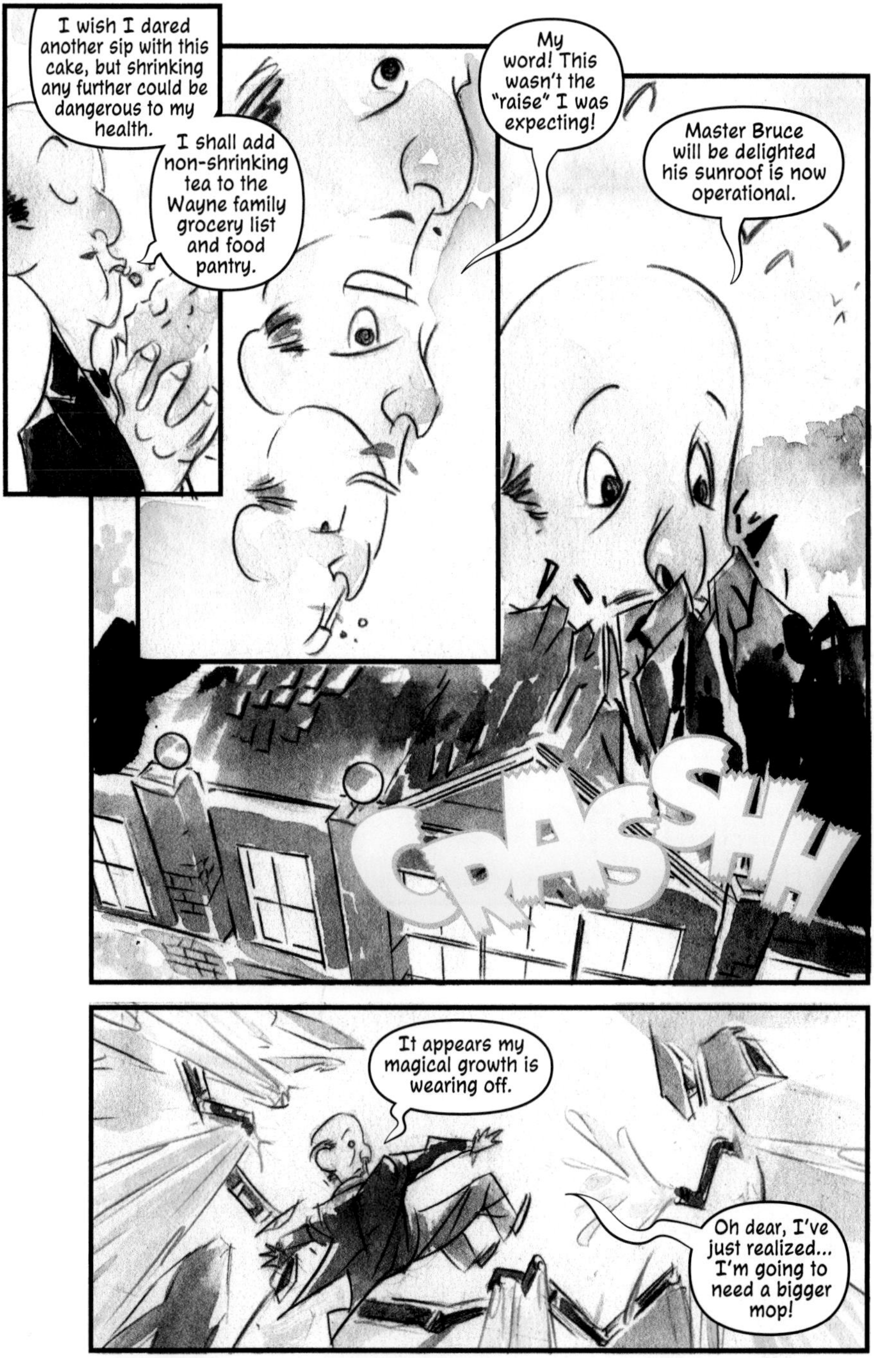
I wish I dared another sip with this cake, but shrinking any further could be dangerous to my health.
I shall add non-shrinking tea to the Wayne family grocery list and food pantry.
My word! This wasn't the "raise" I was expecting!
Master Bruce will be delighted his sunroof is now operational.
CRASSHH
It appears my magical growth is wearing off.
Oh dear, I've just realized... I'm going to need a bigger mop!

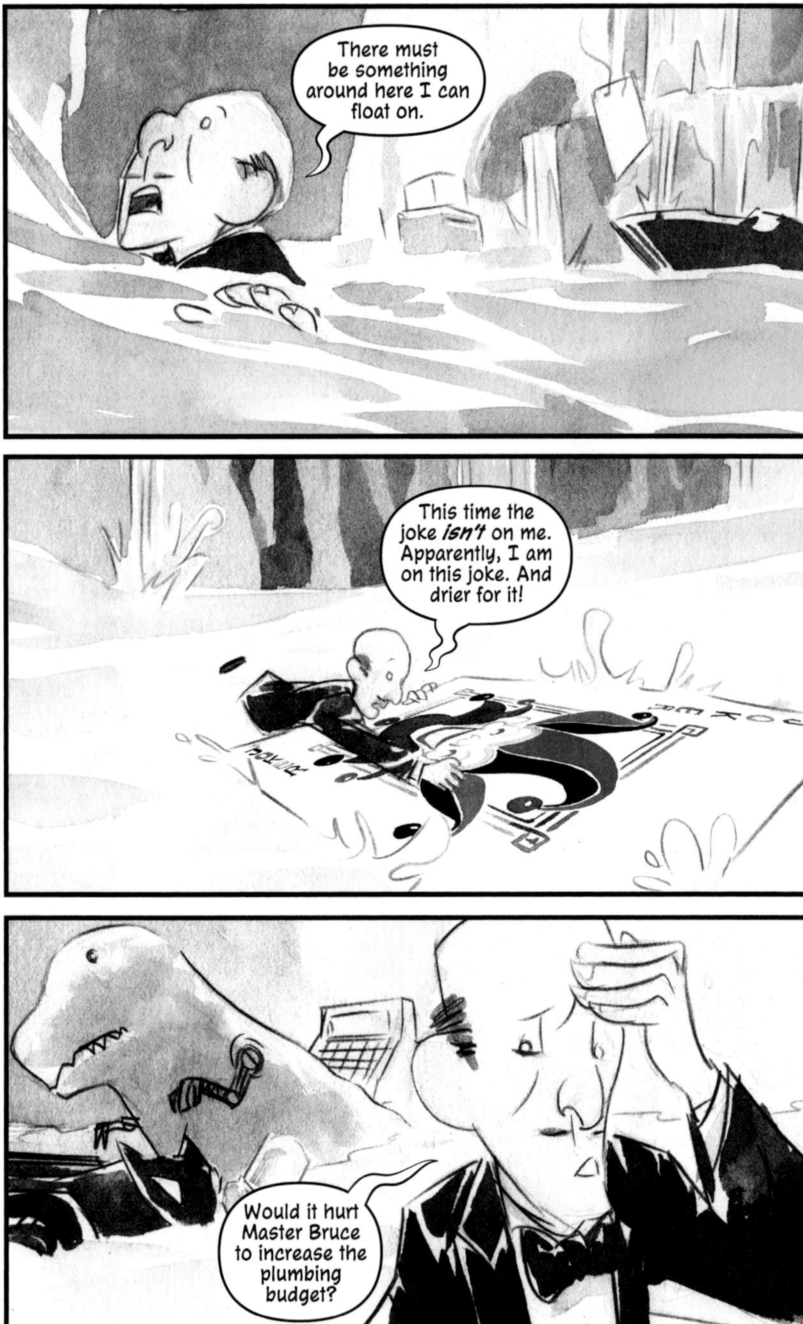
There must be something around here I can float on.
This time the joke *isn't* on me. Apparently, I am on this joke. And drier for it!
Would it hurt Master Bruce to increase the plumbing budget?

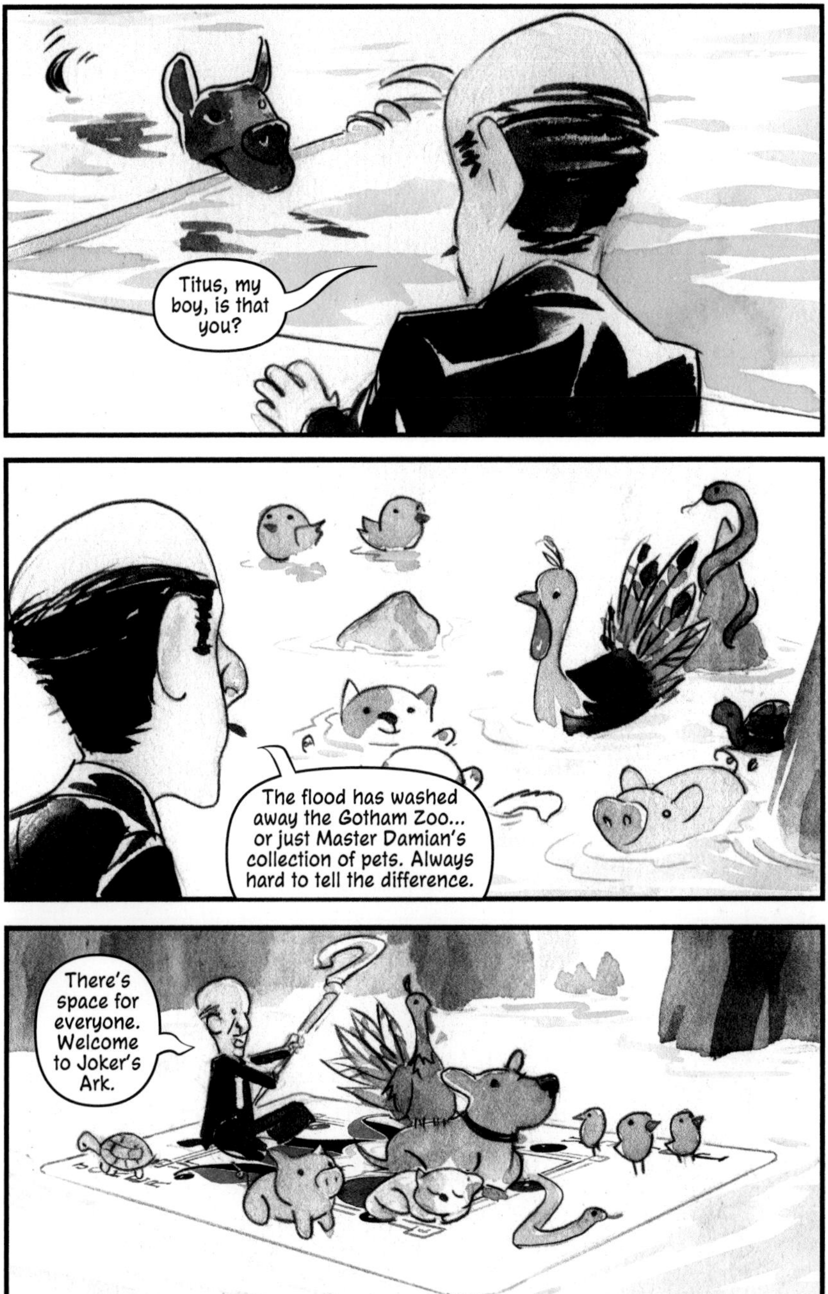
Titus, my boy, is that you?
The flood has washed away the Gotham Zoo... or just Master Damian's collection of pets. Always hard to tell the difference.
There's space for everyone. Welcome to Joker's Ark.

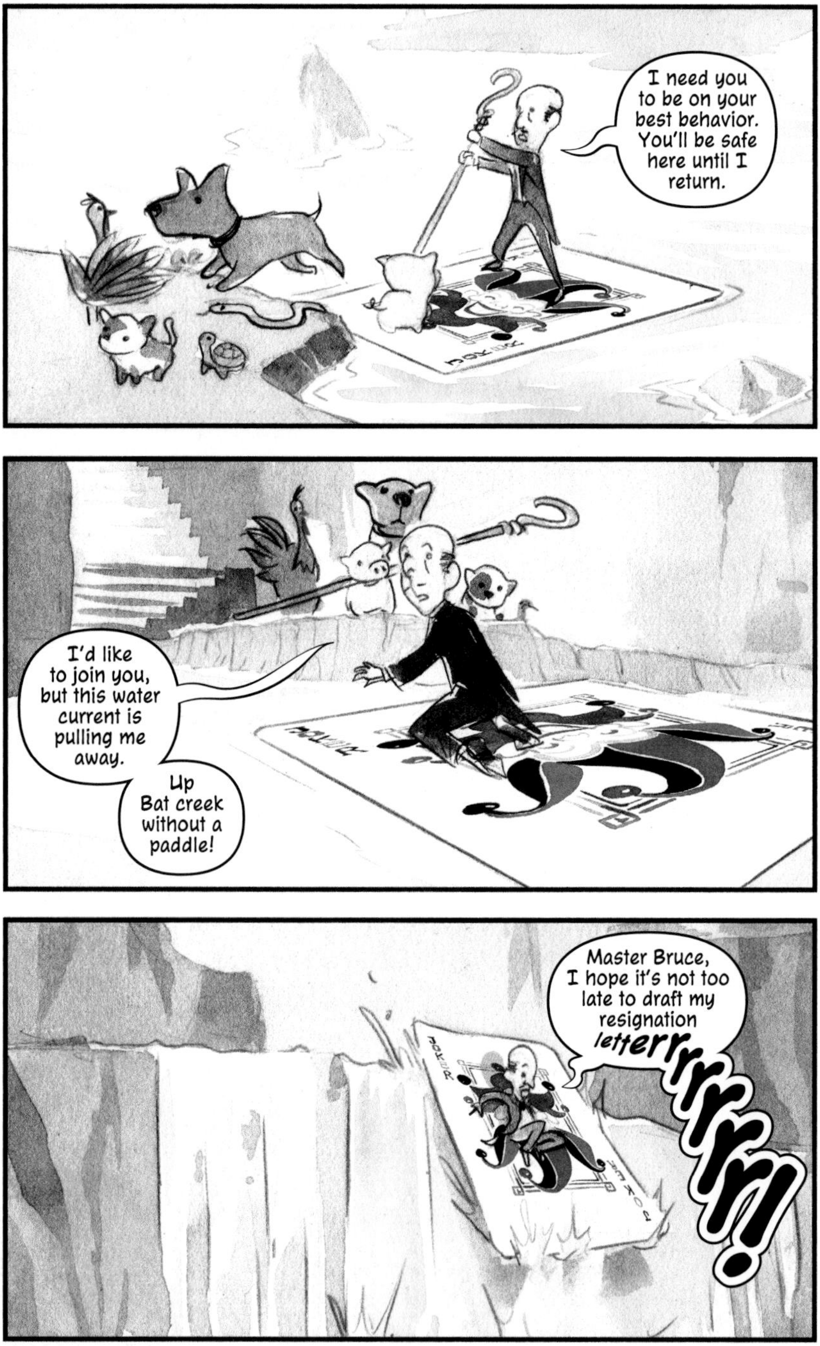
I need you to be on your best behavior. You'll be safe here until I return.
I'd like to join you, but this water current is pulling me away.
Up Bat creek without a paddle!
Master Bruce, I hope it's not too late to draft my resignation letterrrrrrr!

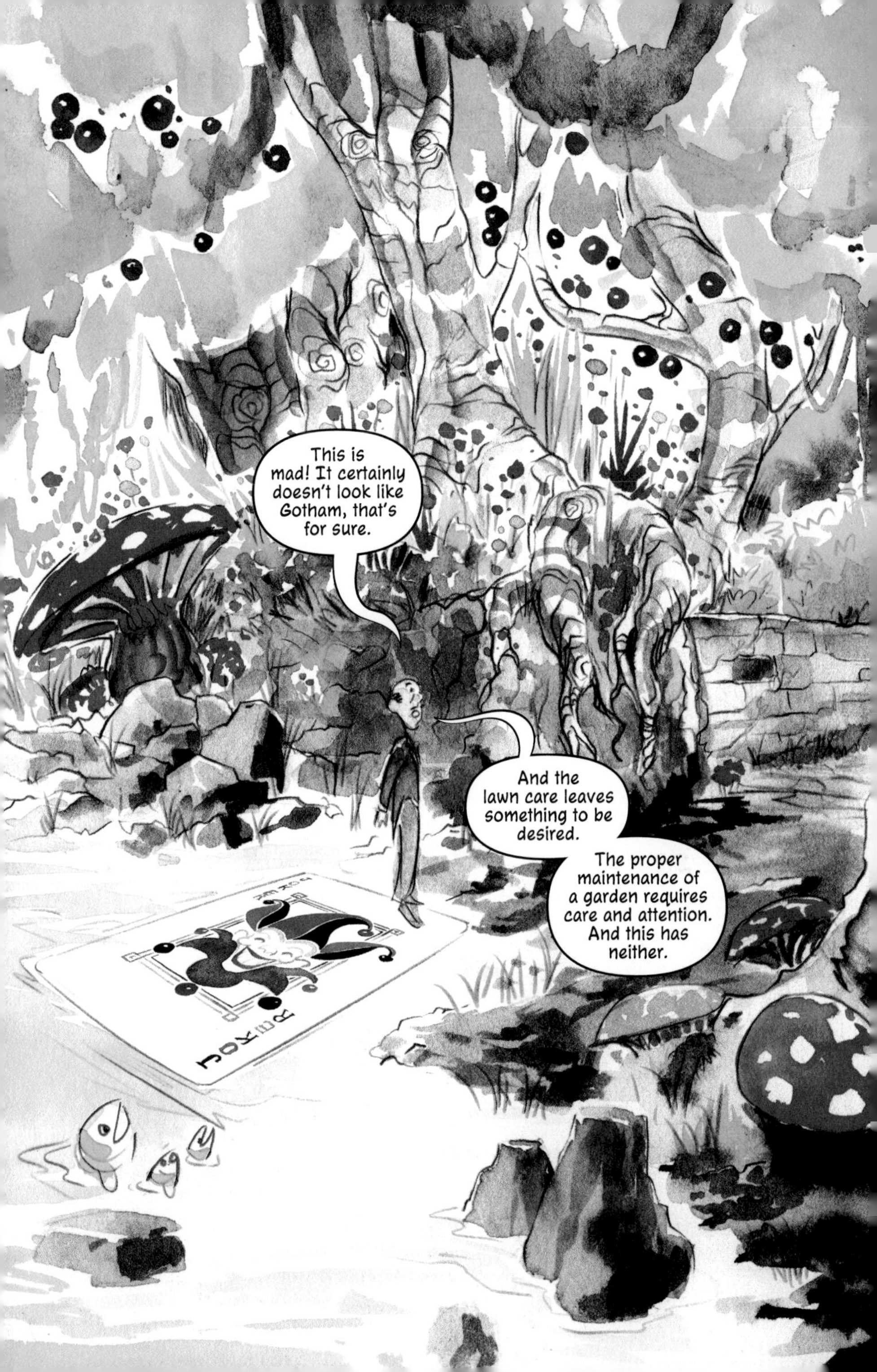
This is mad! It certainly doesn't look like Gotham, that's for sure.
And the lawn care leaves something to be desired.
The proper maintenance of a garden requires care and attention. And this has neither.
JOKER

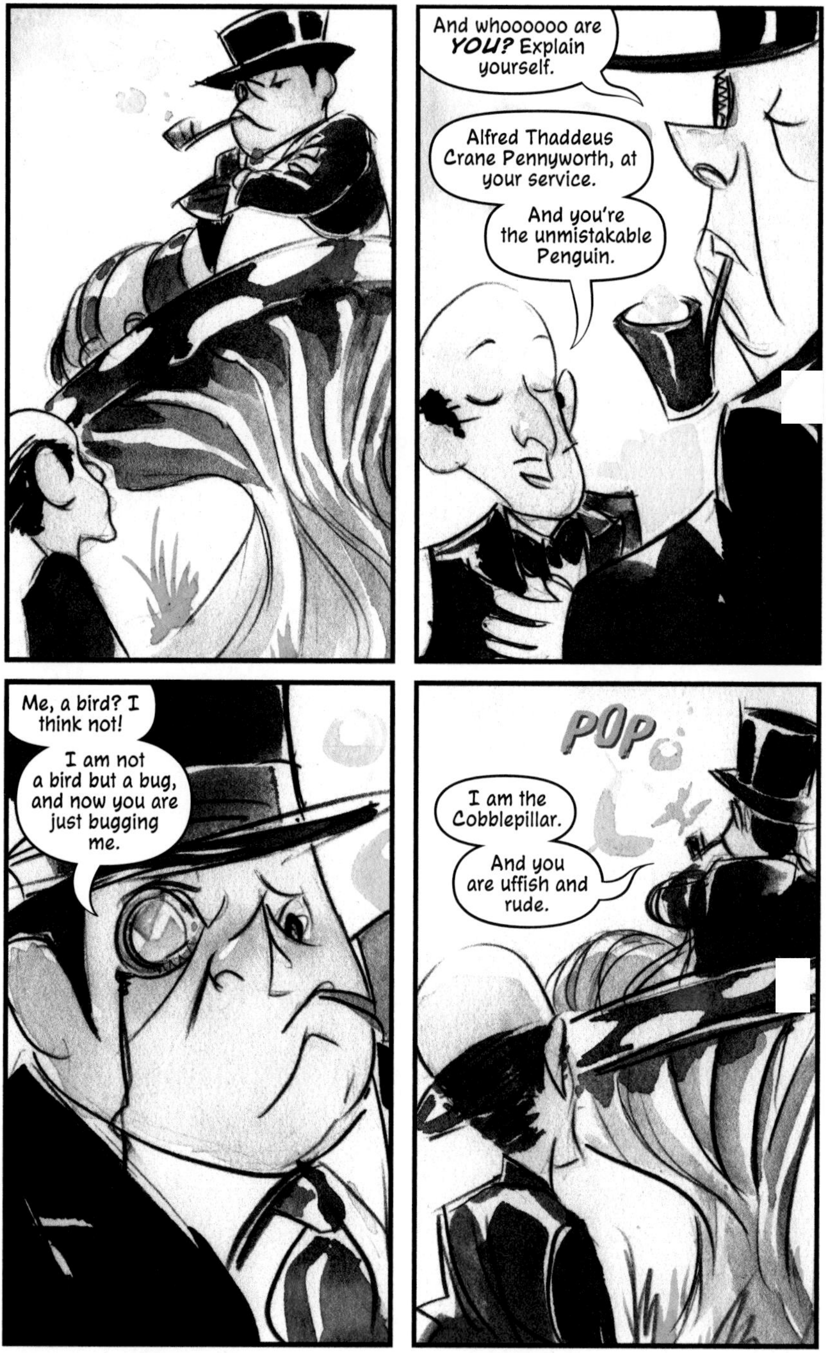
And whoooooo are *YOU?* Explain yourself.
Alfred Thaddeus Crane Pennyworth, at your service.
And you're the unmistakable Penguin.
Me, a bird? I think not!
I am not a bird but a bug, and now you are just bugging me.
POP
I am the Cobblepillar.
And you are uffish and rude.

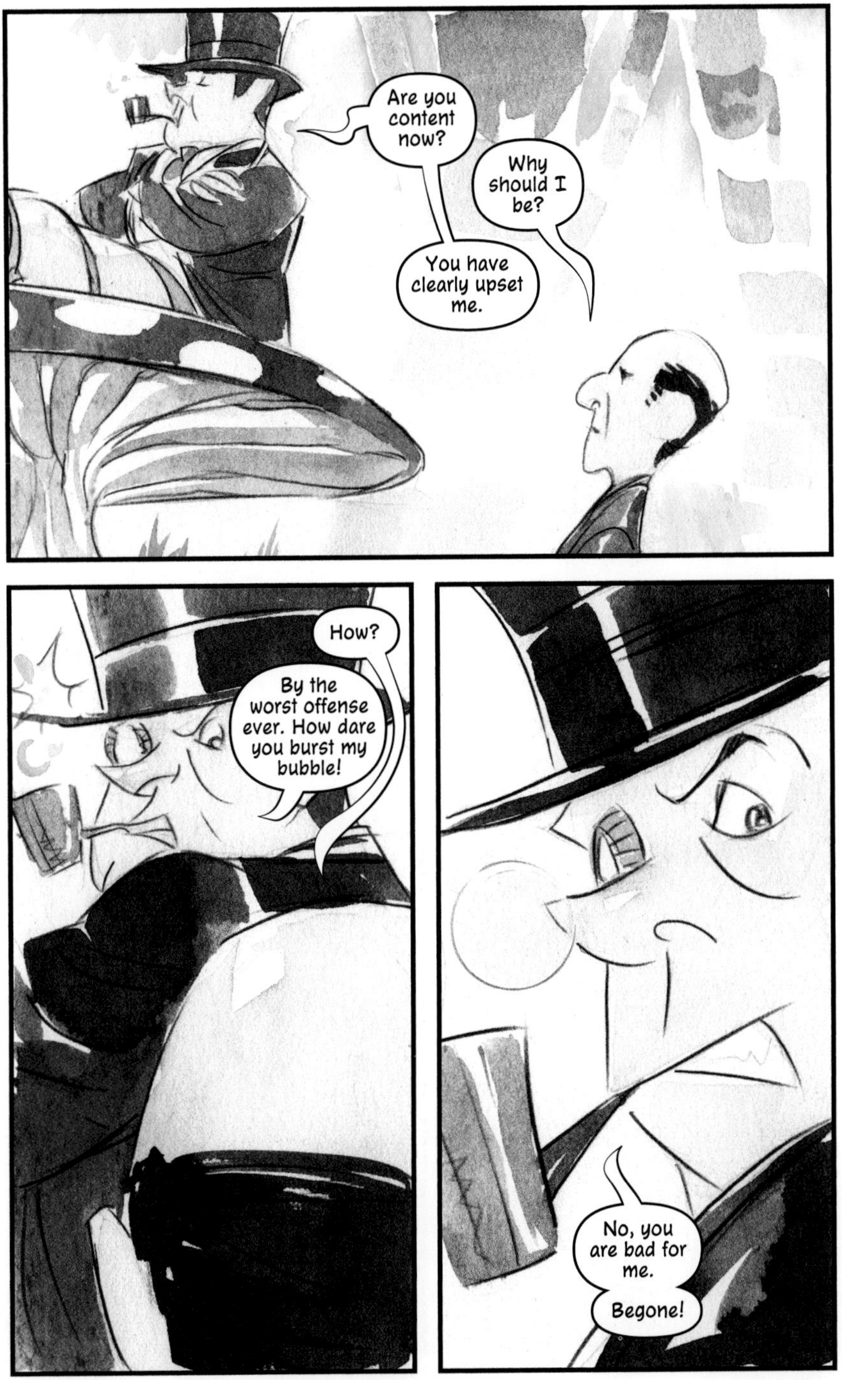
Are you content now?
Why should I be?
You have clearly upset me.
How?
By the worst offense ever. How dare you burst my bubble!
No, you are bad for me.
Begone!

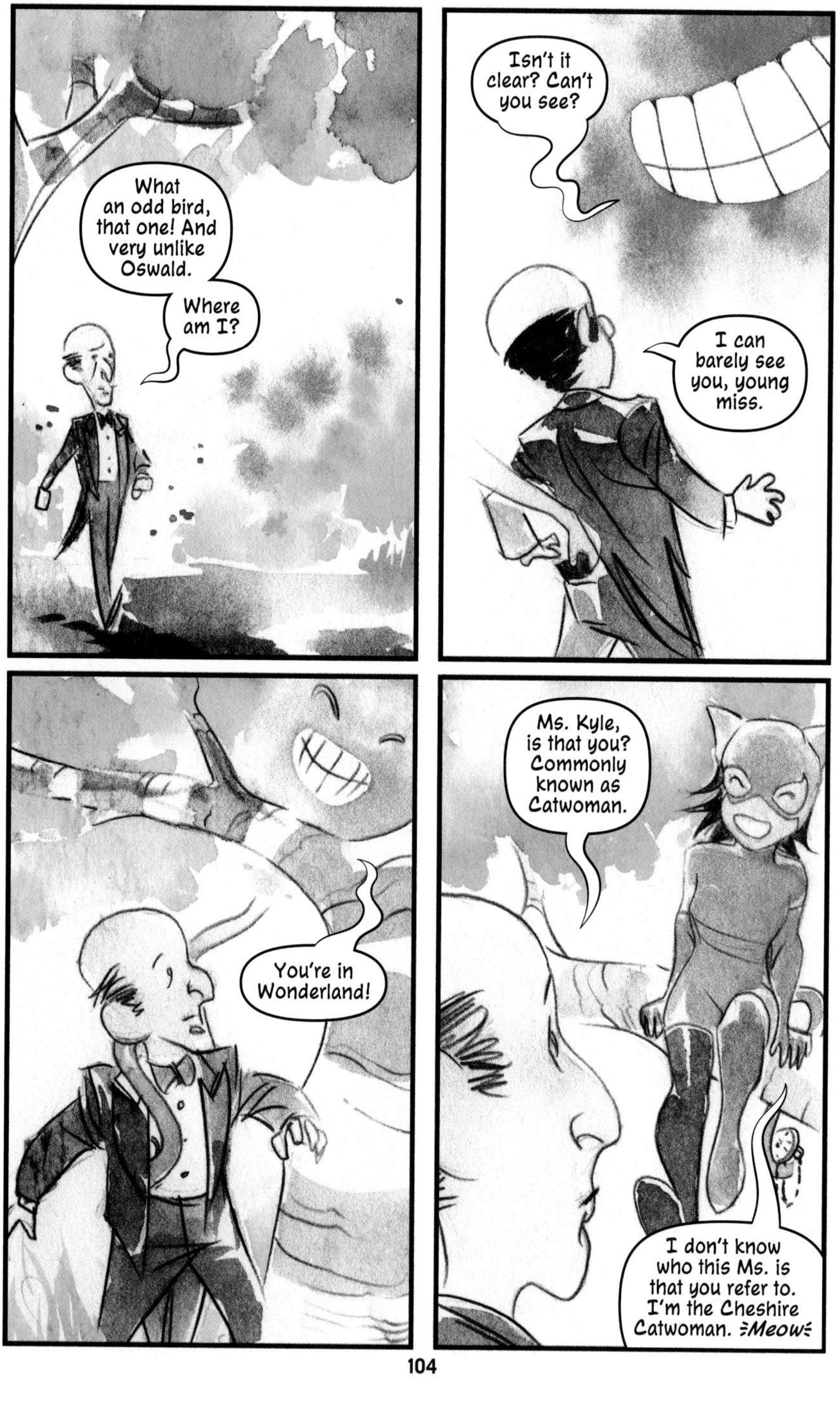
What an odd bird, that one! And very unlike Oswald.
Where am I?
Isn't it clear? Can't you see?
I can barely see you, young miss.
You're in Wonderland!
Ms. Kyle, is that you? Commonly known as Catwoman.
I don't know who this Ms. is that you refer to. I'm the Cheshire Catwoman. Meow

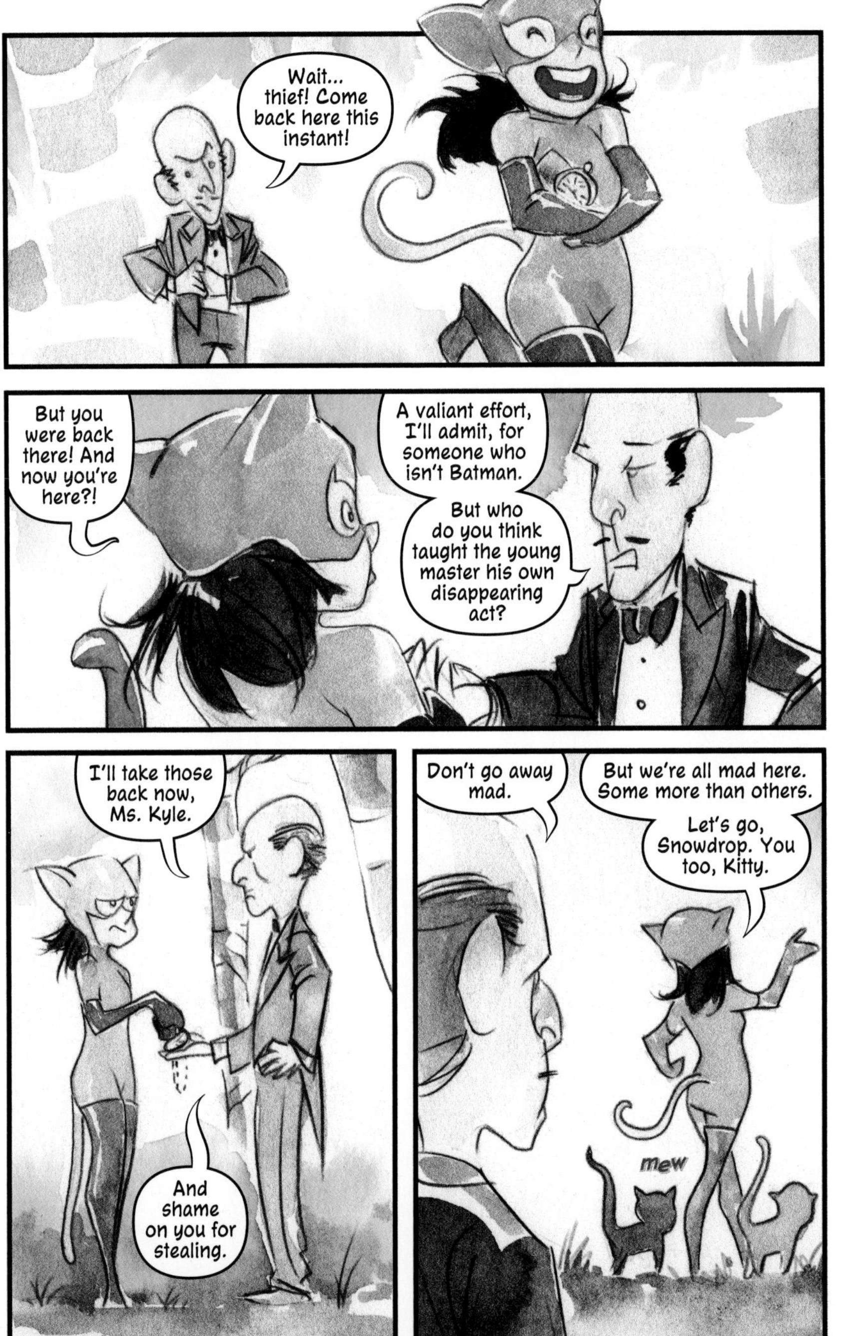
Wait... thief! Come back here this instant!
But you were back there! And now you're here?!
A valiant effort, I'll admit, for someone who isn't Batman.
But who do you think taught the young master his own disappearing act?
I'll take those back now, Ms. Kyle.
And shame on you for stealing.
Don't go away mad.
But we're all mad here. Some more than others.
Let's go, Snowdrop. You too, Kitty.
mew

I say, that doesn't look like a safe place to sit.

Happy unbirthday to me! Happy unbirthday to me!

If you'll excuse me, did I hear you correctly?

There is no such thing as an unbirthday. A birthday is to be celebrated only once a year.

And an *UN*-birthday can be celebrated the rest of the year.

When I use a word, it means what I choose it to mean.

And I mean... *happy unbirthday to me!*

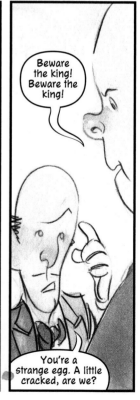

Beware the king! Beware the king!

You're a strange egg. A little cracked, are we?

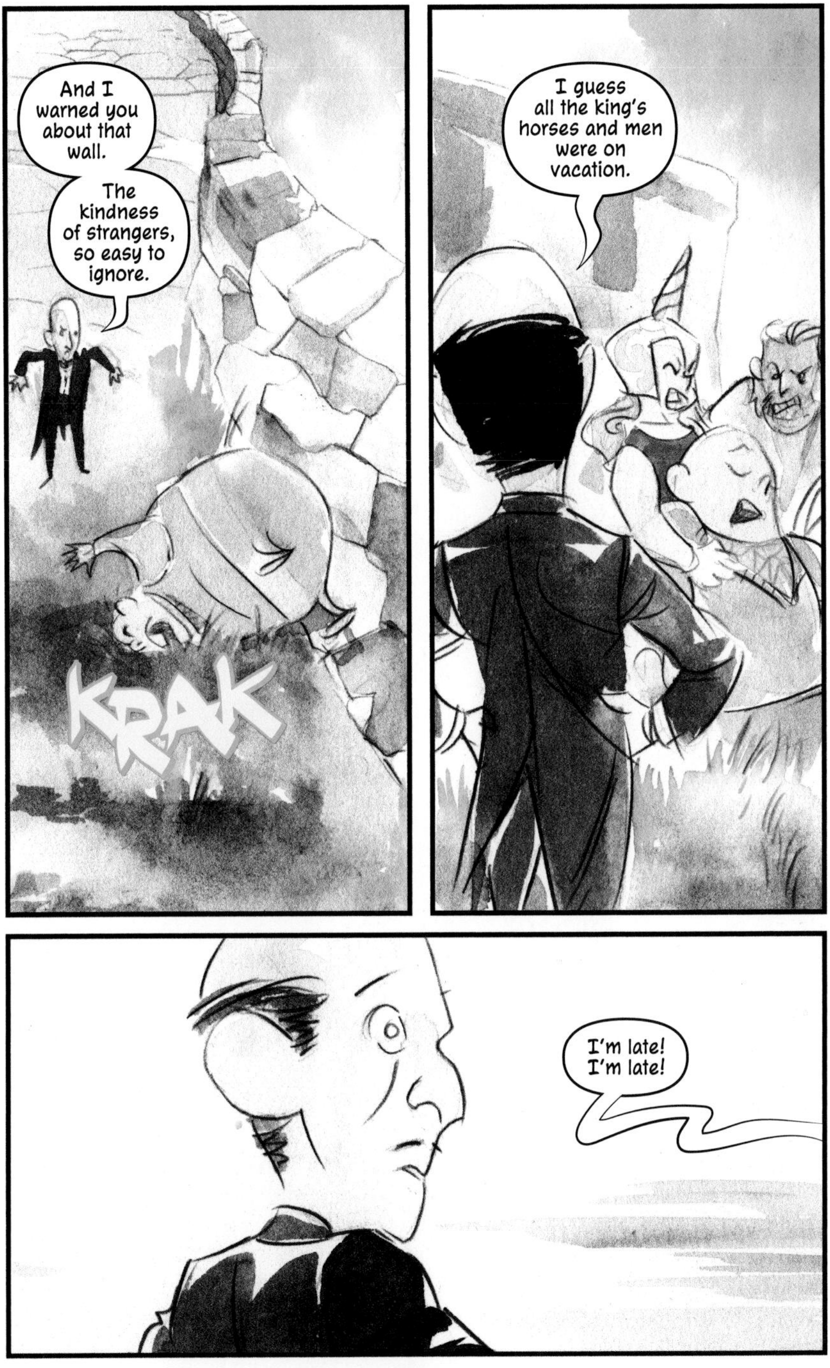
And I warned you about that wall.
The kindness of strangers, so easy to ignore.
KRAK
I guess all the king's horses and men were on vacation.
I'm late! I'm late!

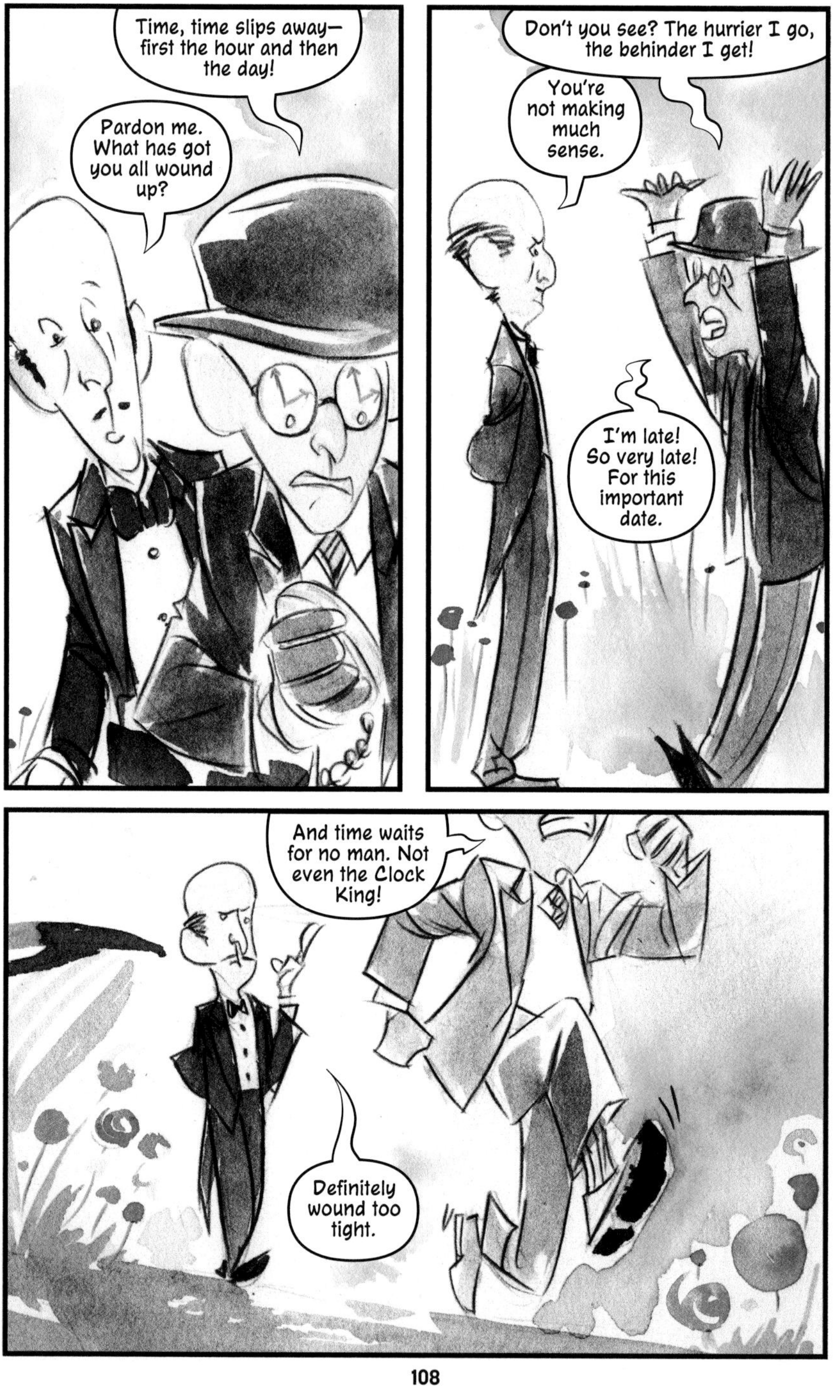
Time, time slips away—first the hour and then the day!
Pardon me. What has got you all wound up?
Don't you see? The hurrier I go, the behinder I get!
You're not making much sense.
I'm late! So very late! For this important date.
And time waits for no man. Not even the Clock King!
Definitely wound too tight.

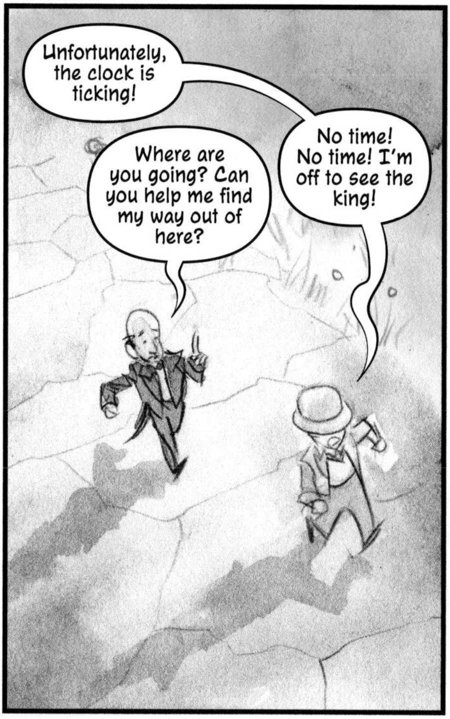
Unfortunately, the clock is ticking!
Where are you going? Can you help me find my way out of here?
No time! No time! I'm off to see the king!
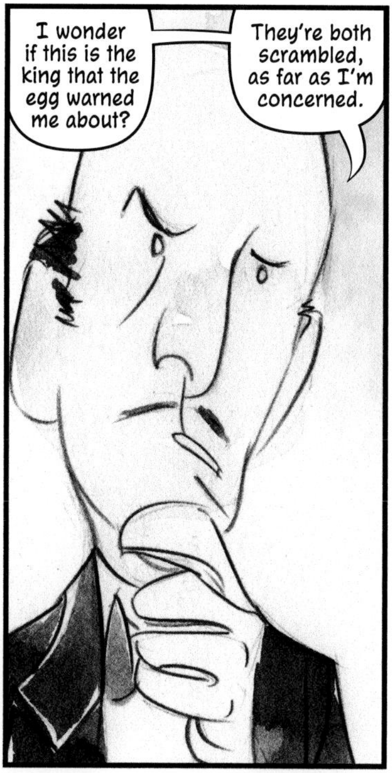
I wonder if this is the king that the egg warned me about?
They're both scrambled, as far as I'm concerned.
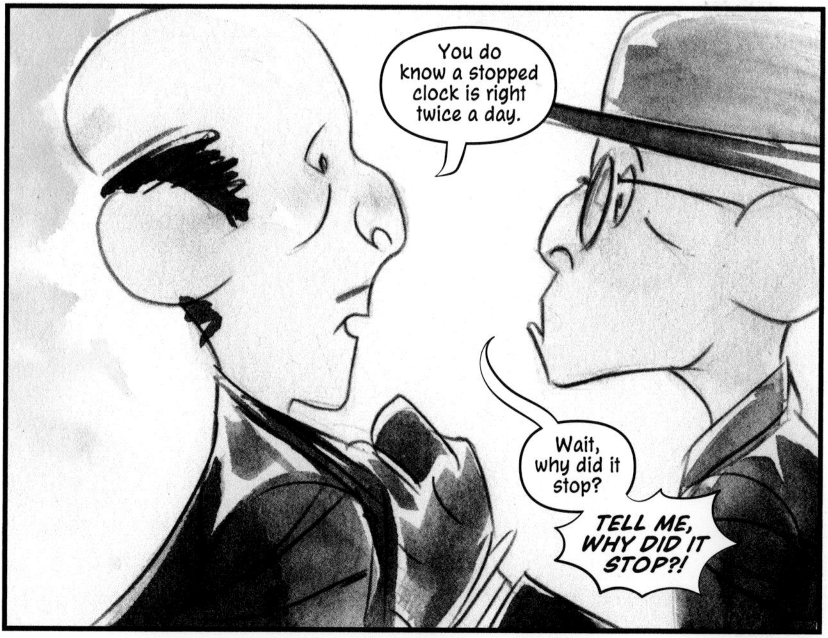
You do know a stopped clock is right twice a day.
Wait, why did it stop?
TELL ME, WHY DID IT STOP?!

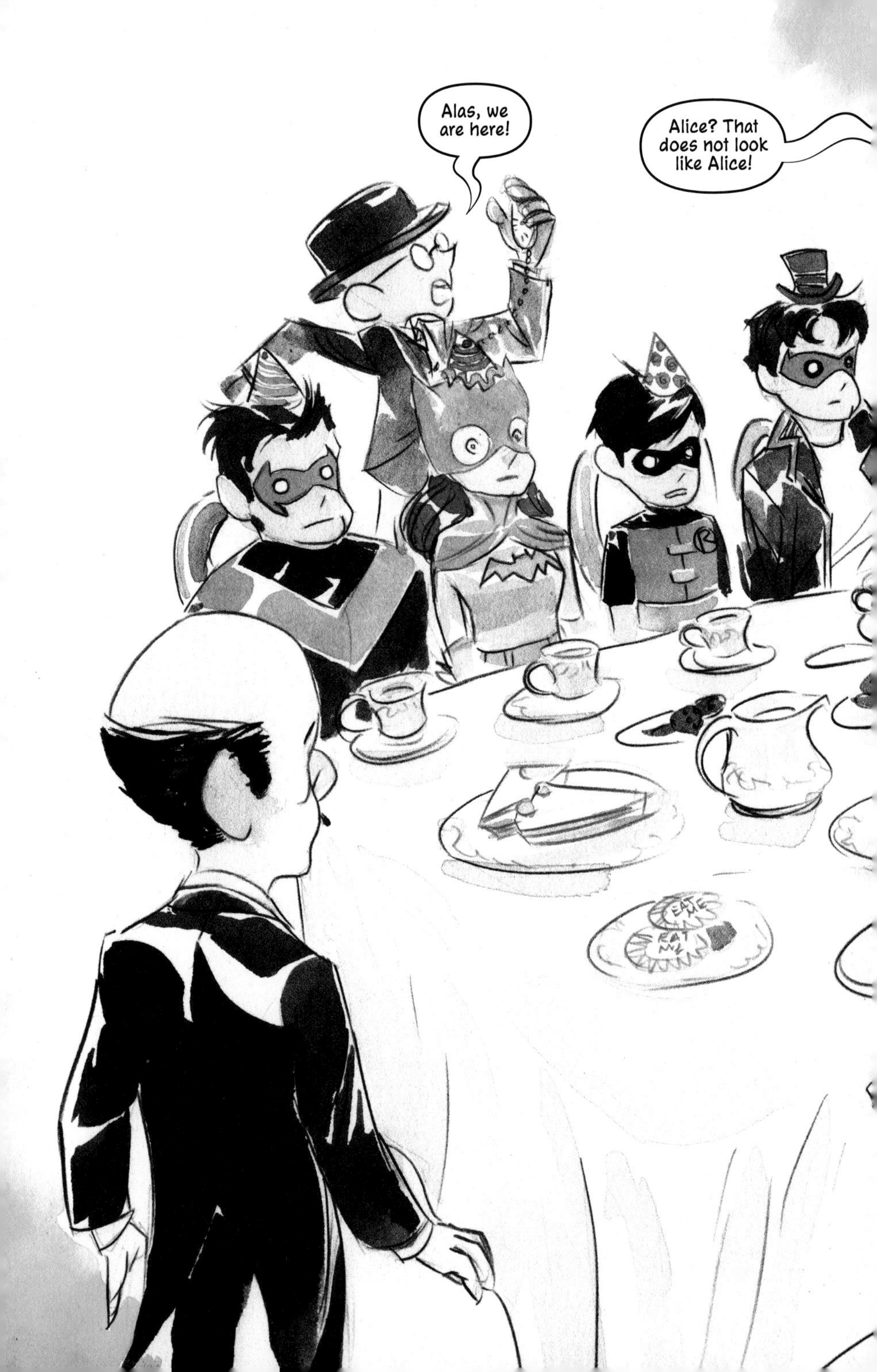
Alas, we are here!
Alice? That does not look like Alice!
EAT ME
EAT ME

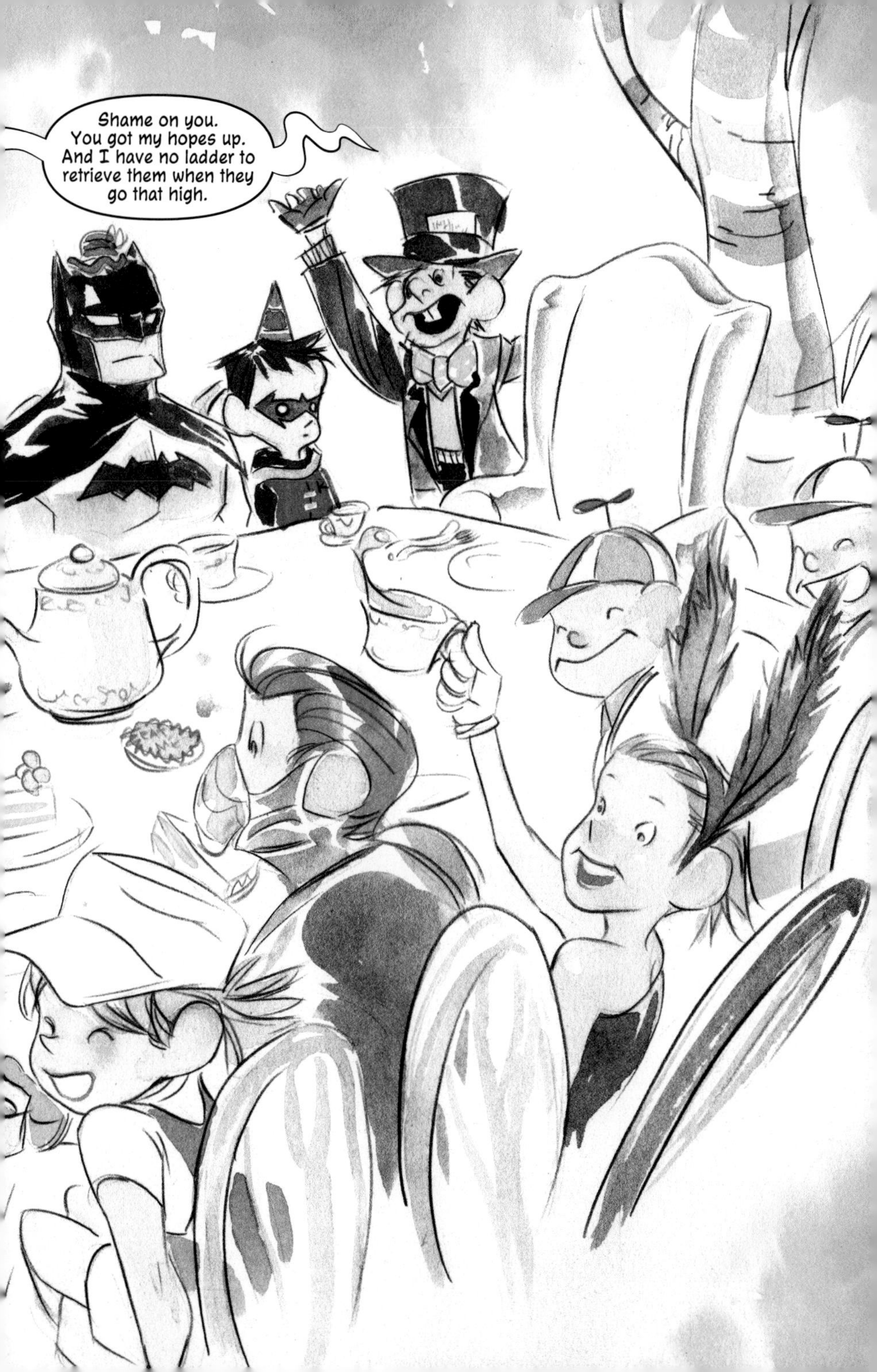
Shame on you. You got my hopes up. And I have no ladder to retrieve them when they go that high.

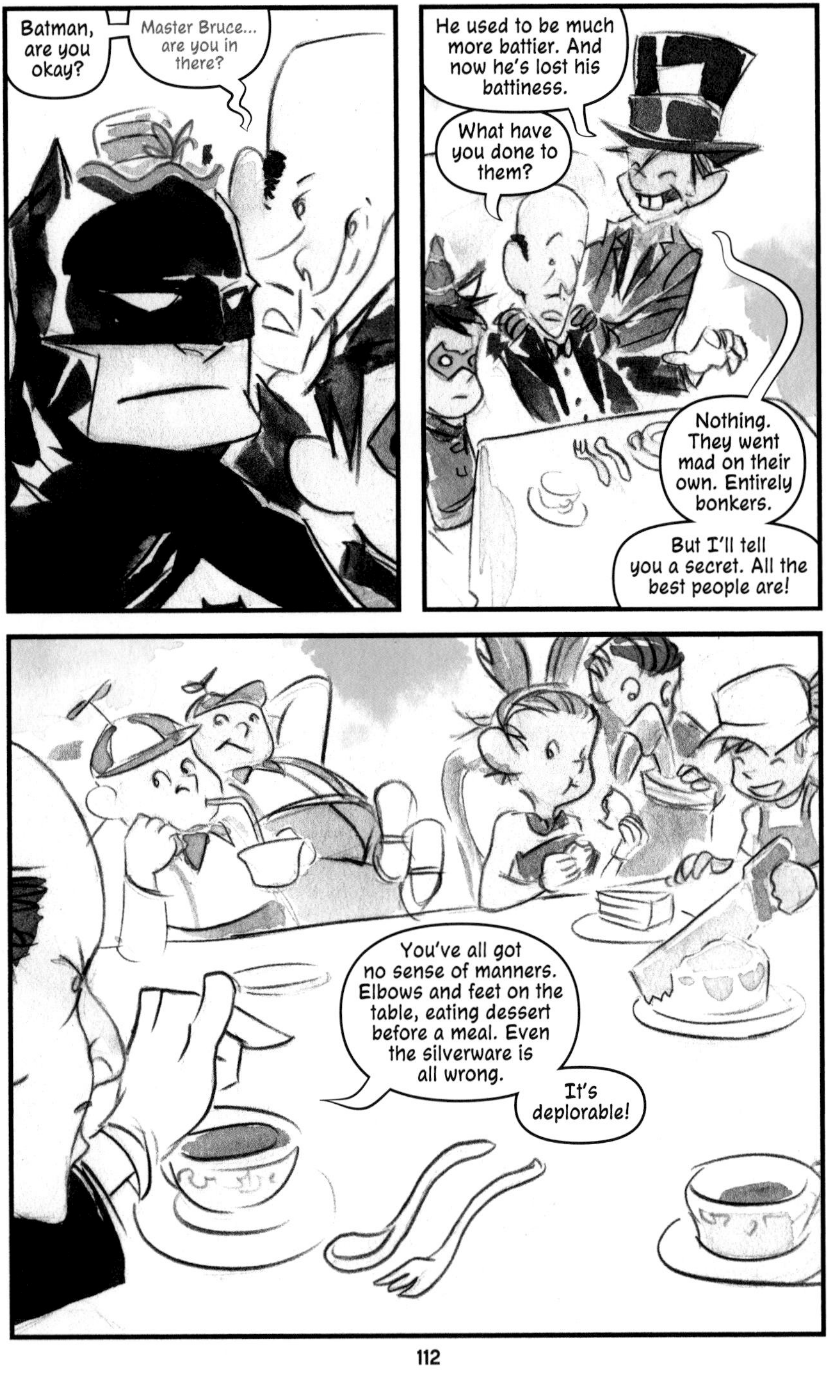
Batman, are you okay?
Master Bruce... are you in there?
He used to be much more battier. And now he's lost his battiness.
What have you done to them?
Nothing. They went mad on their own. Entirely bonkers.
But I'll tell you a secret. All the best people are!
You've all got no sense of manners. Elbows and feet on the table, eating dessert before a meal. Even the silverware is all wrong.
It's deplorable!

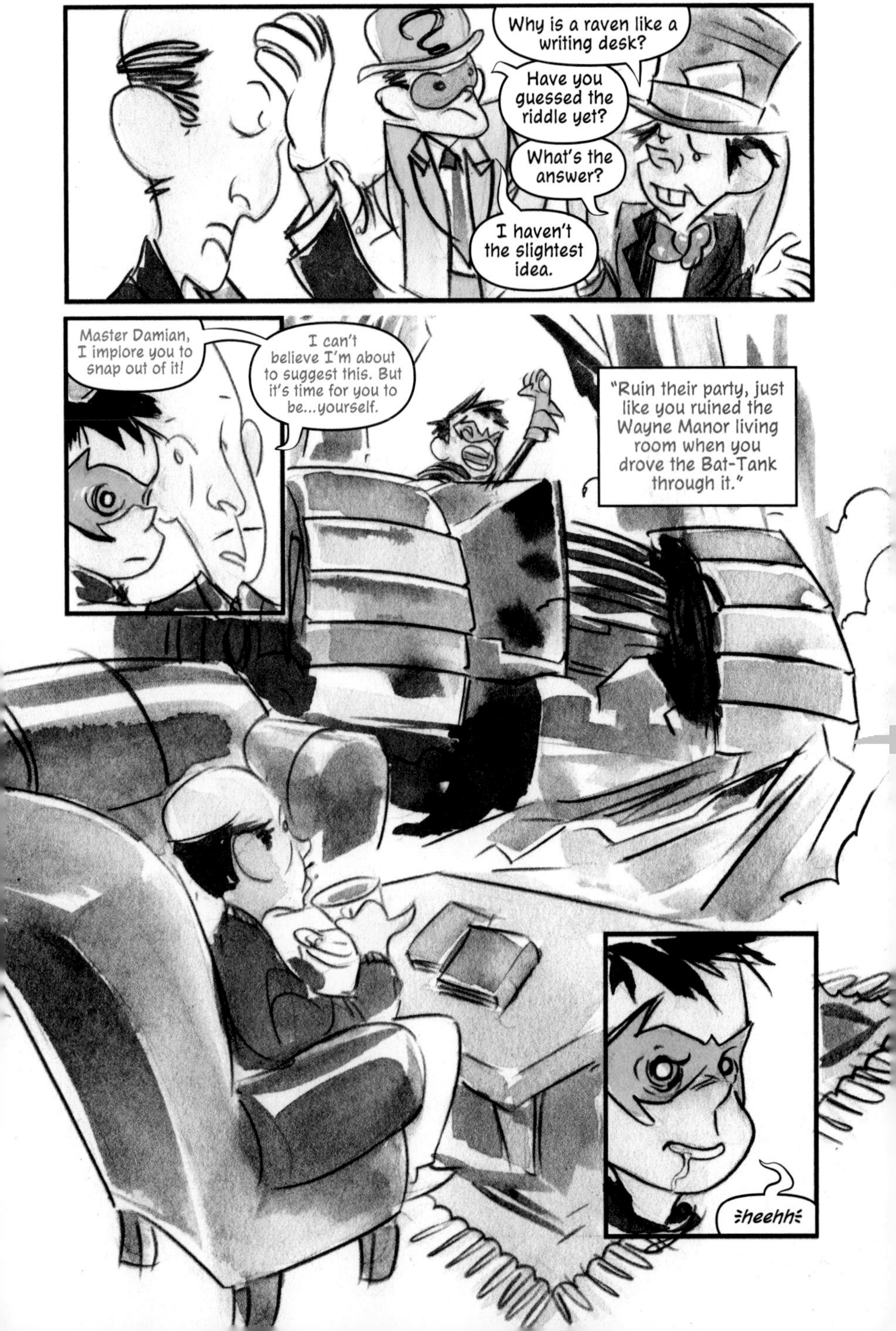
Why is a raven like a writing desk?
Have you guessed the riddle yet?
What's the answer?
I haven't the slightest idea.
Master Damian, I implore you to snap out of it!
I can't believe I'm about to suggest this. But it's time for you to be...yourself.
"Ruin their party, just like you ruined the Wayne Manor living room when you drove the Bat-Tank through it."
heehh

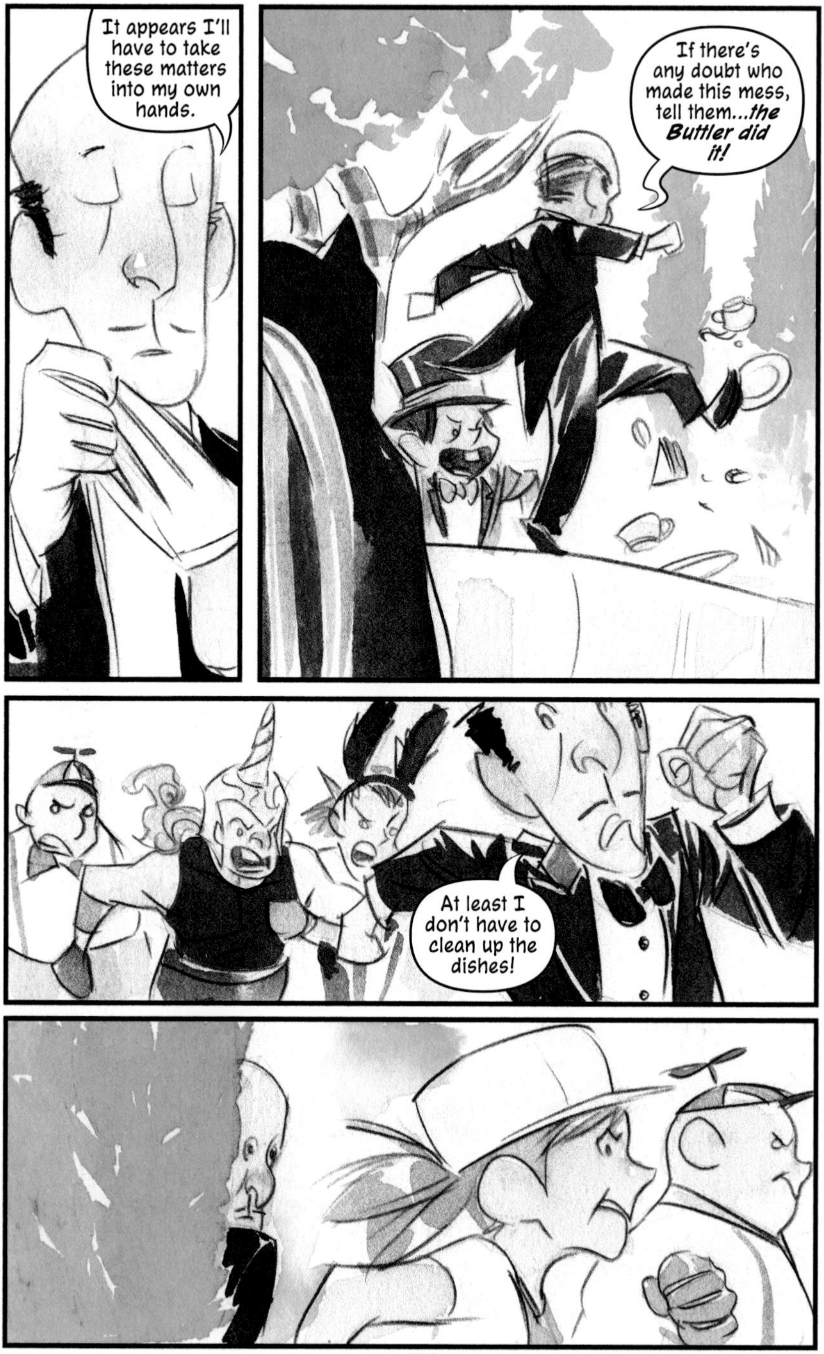
It appears I'll have to take these matters into my own hands.
If there's any doubt who made this mess, tell them...*the Butler did it!*
At least I don't have to clean up the dishes!

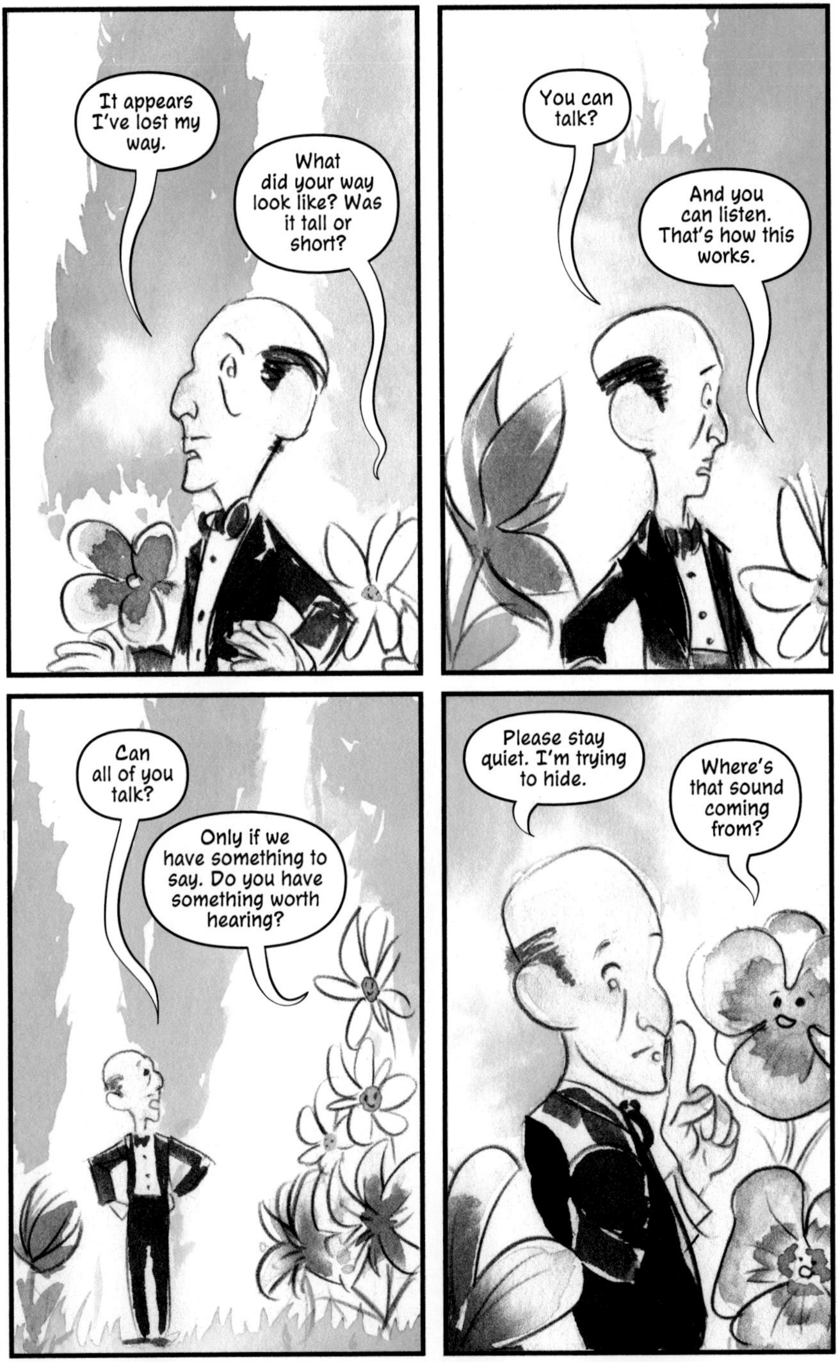
It appears I've lost my way.
What did your way look like? Was it tall or short?
You can talk?
And you can listen. That's how this works.
Can all of you talk?
Only if we have something to say. Do you have something worth hearing?
Please stay quiet. I'm trying to hide.
Where's that sound coming from?

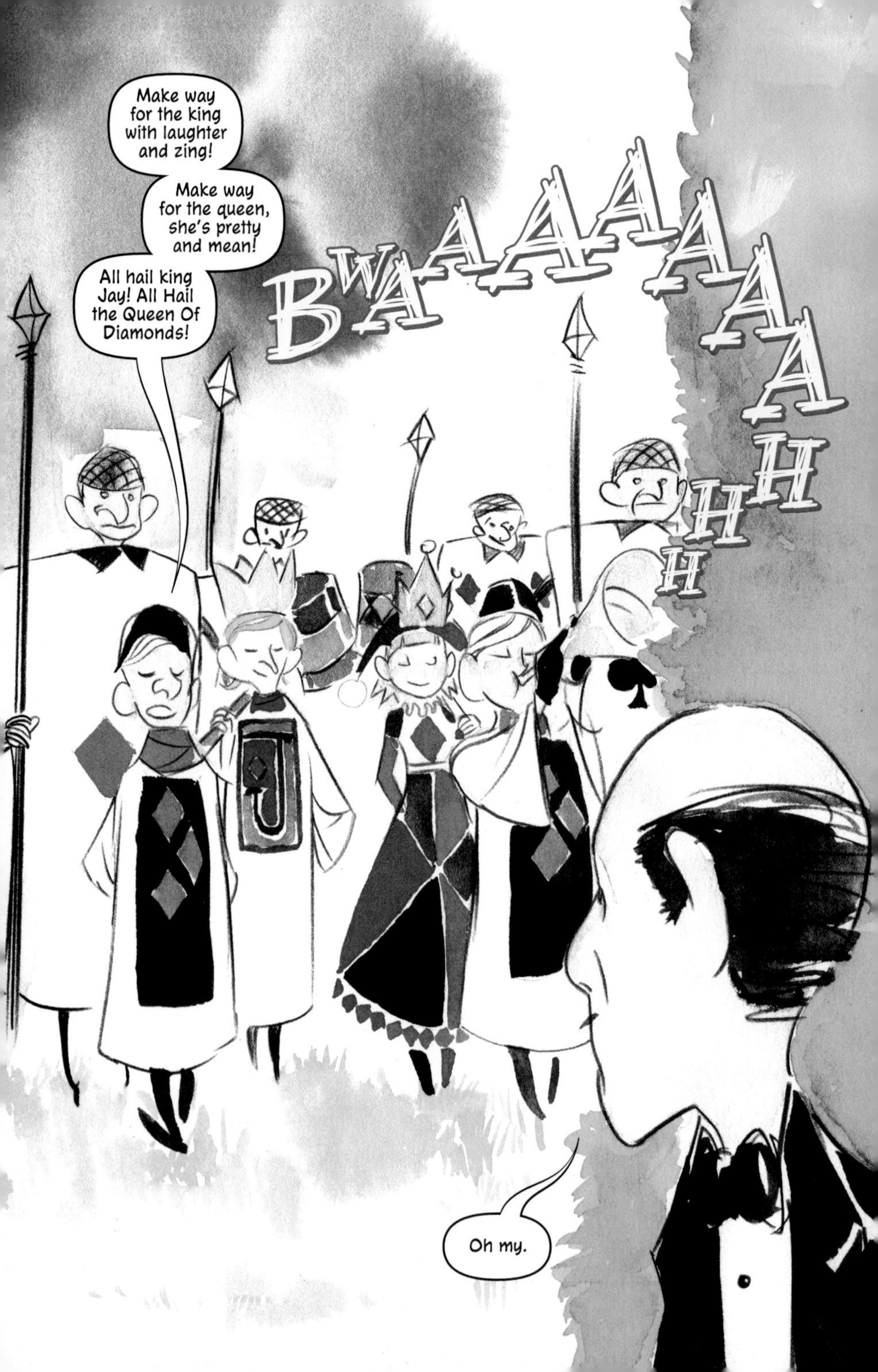
Make way for the king with laughter and zing!
Make way for the queen, she's pretty and mean!
All hail king Jay! All Hail the Queen Of Diamonds!
BWAAAAAAAAAAHHHH
Oh my.

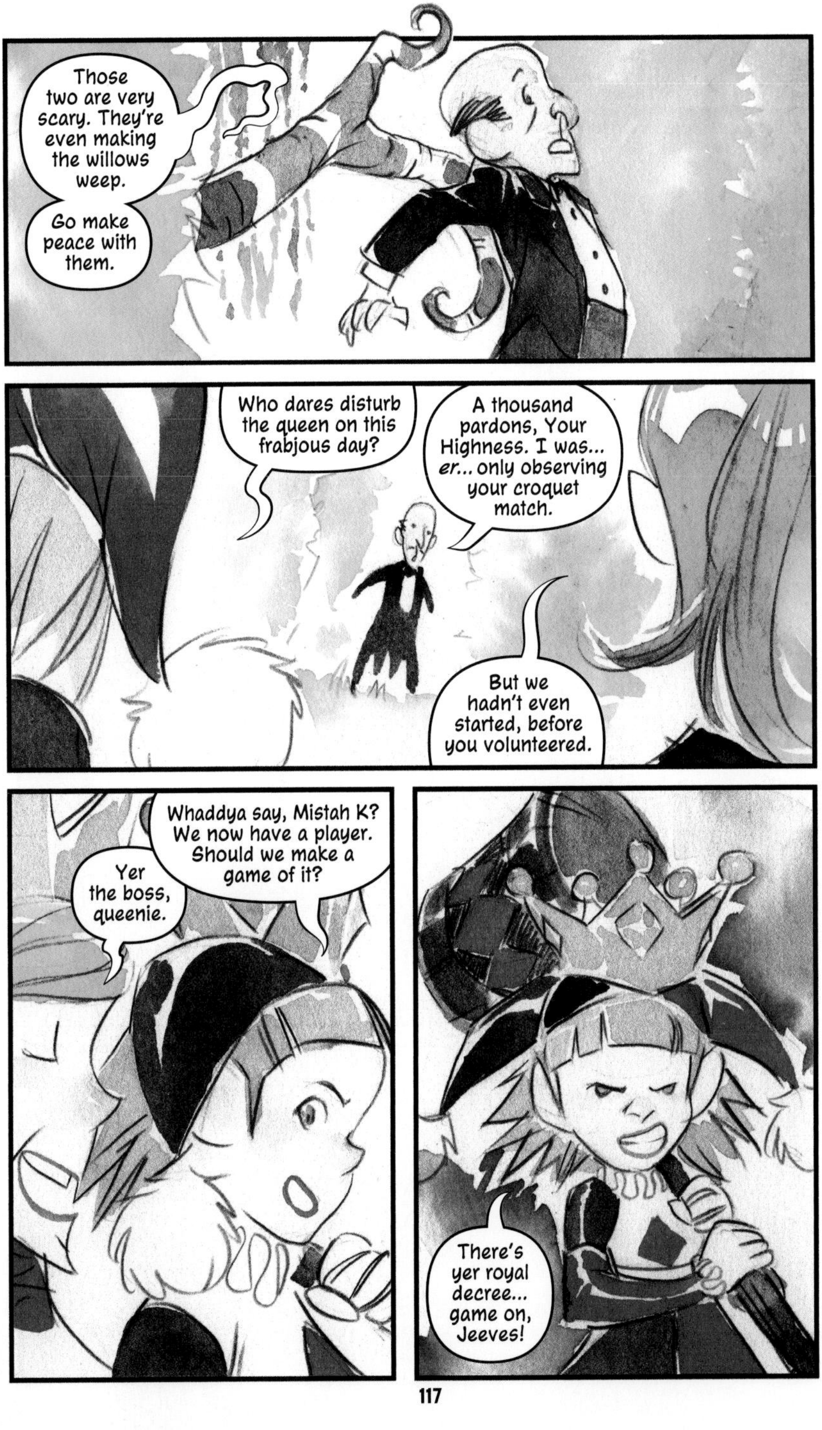
Those two are very scary. They're even making the willows weep.
Go make peace with them.
Who dares disturb the queen on this frabjous day?
A thousand pardons, Your Highness. I was... er... only observing your croquet match.
But we hadn't even started, before you volunteered.
Whaddya say, Mistah K? We now have a player. Should we make a game of it?
Yer the boss, queenie.
There's yer royal decree... game on, Jeeves!

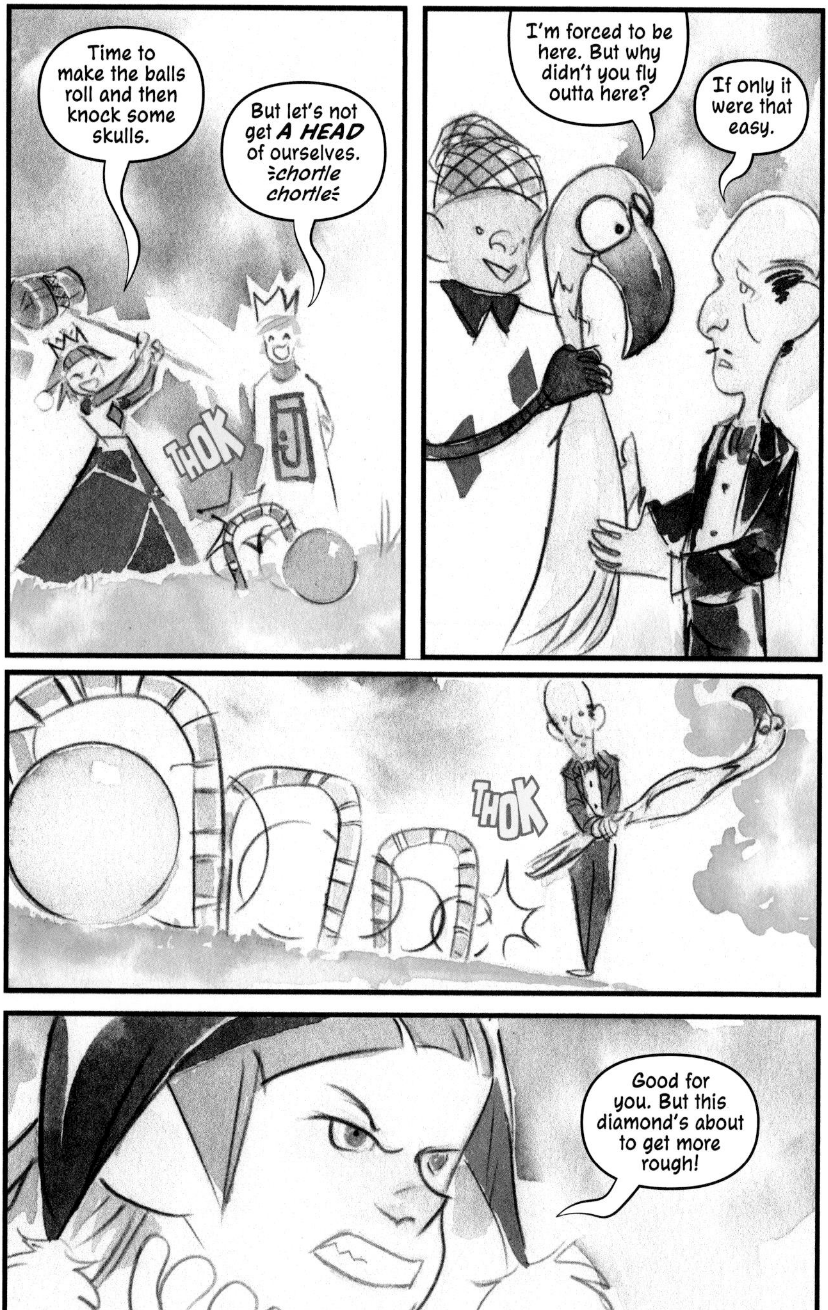
Time to make the balls roll and then knock some skulls.
But let's not get A HEAD of ourselves. chortle chortle
THOK
I'm forced to be here. But why didn't you fly outta here?
If only it were that easy.
THOK
Good for you. But this diamond's about to get more rough!

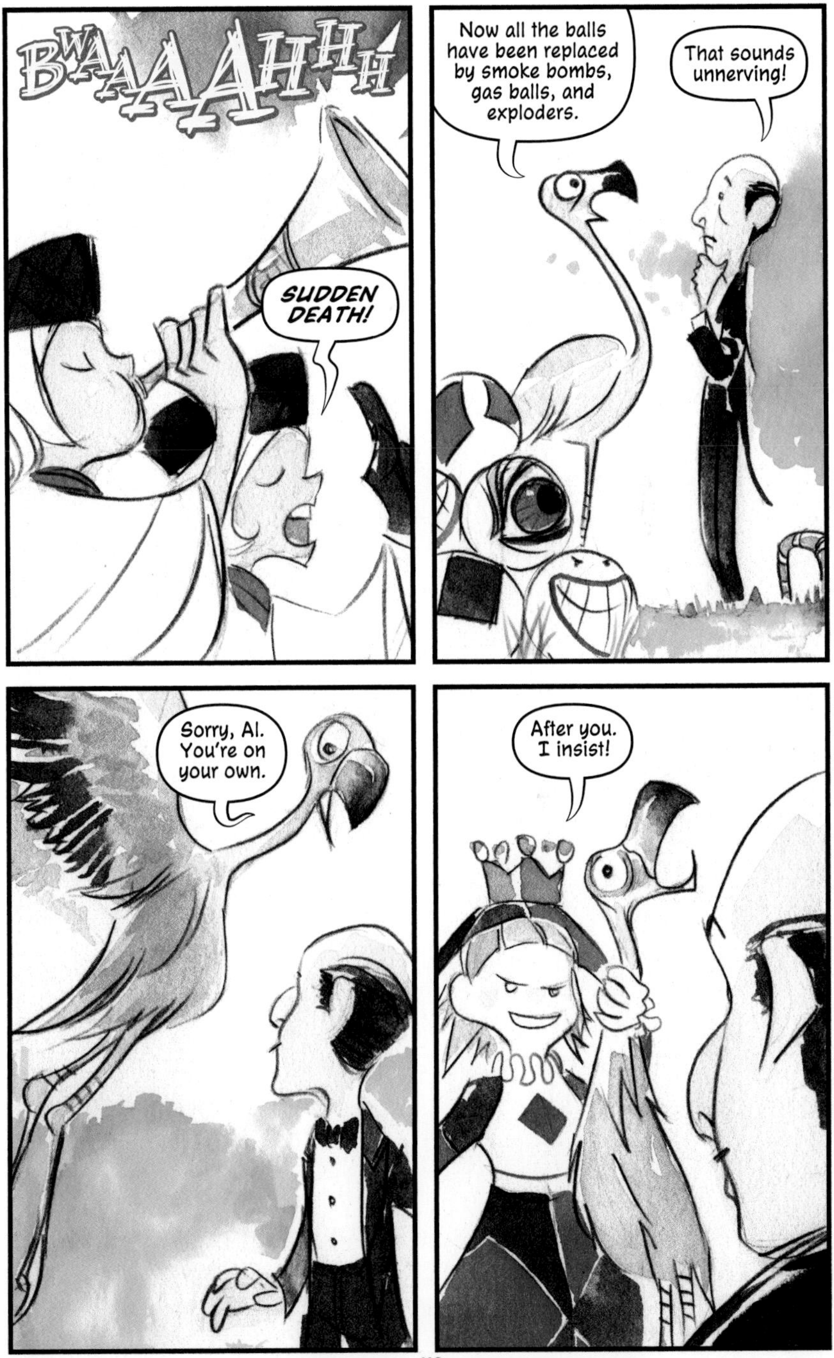
BWAAAAHHHH
SUDDEN DEATH!
Now all the balls have been replaced by smoke bombs, gas balls, and exploders.
That sounds unnerving!
Sorry, Al. You're on your own.
After you. I insist!

gulp
POOF POOF
Is this game almost over? I thought it was halftime.
Half for me and none for you.
Oh who am I kidding... it's all for me!
I'm so frumious! Royal Flush Gang...
...BRING ME BOTH THEIR HEADS!

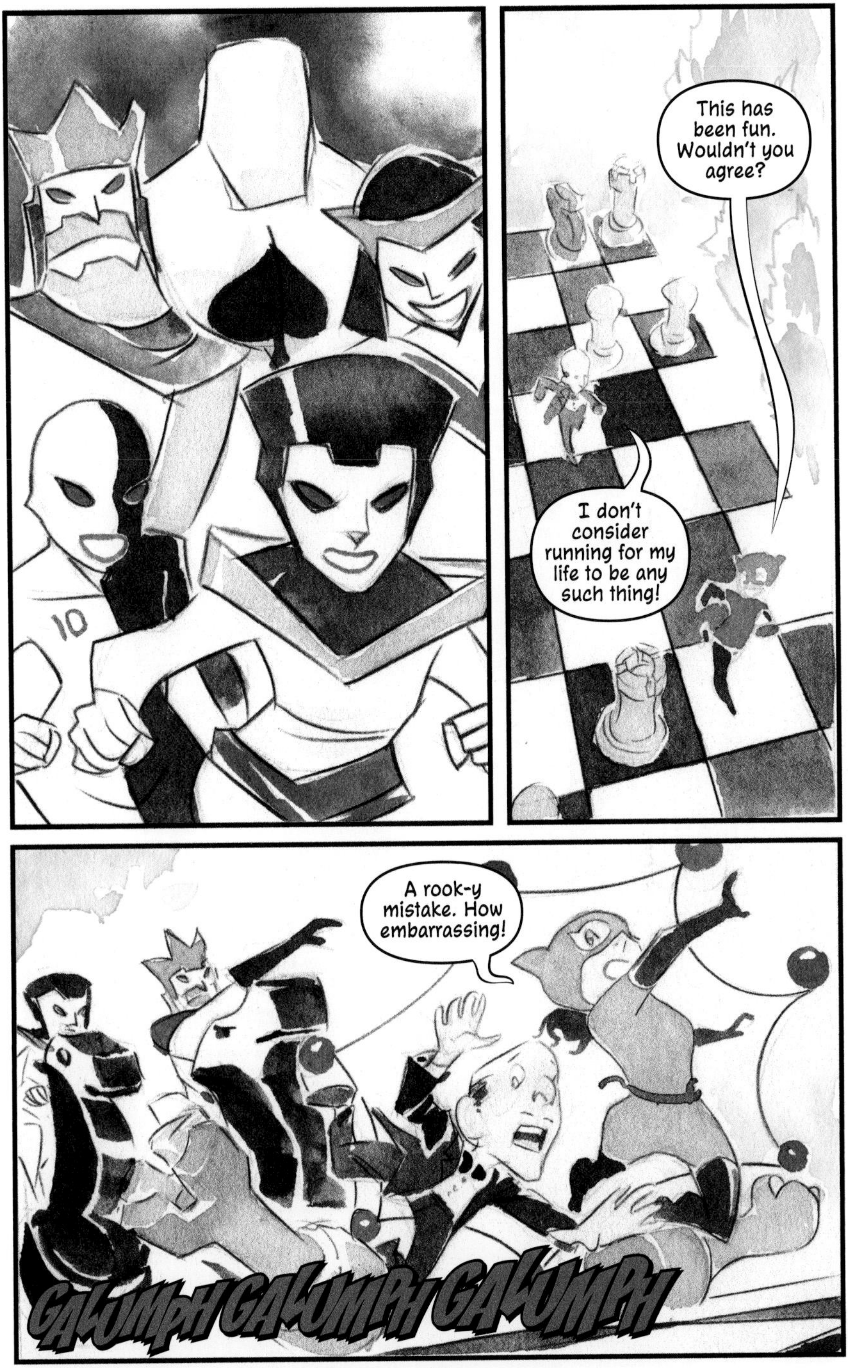
This has been fun. Wouldn't you agree?
I don't consider running for my life to be any such thing!
A rook-y mistake. How embarrassing!
GALUMPH GALUMPH GALUMPH

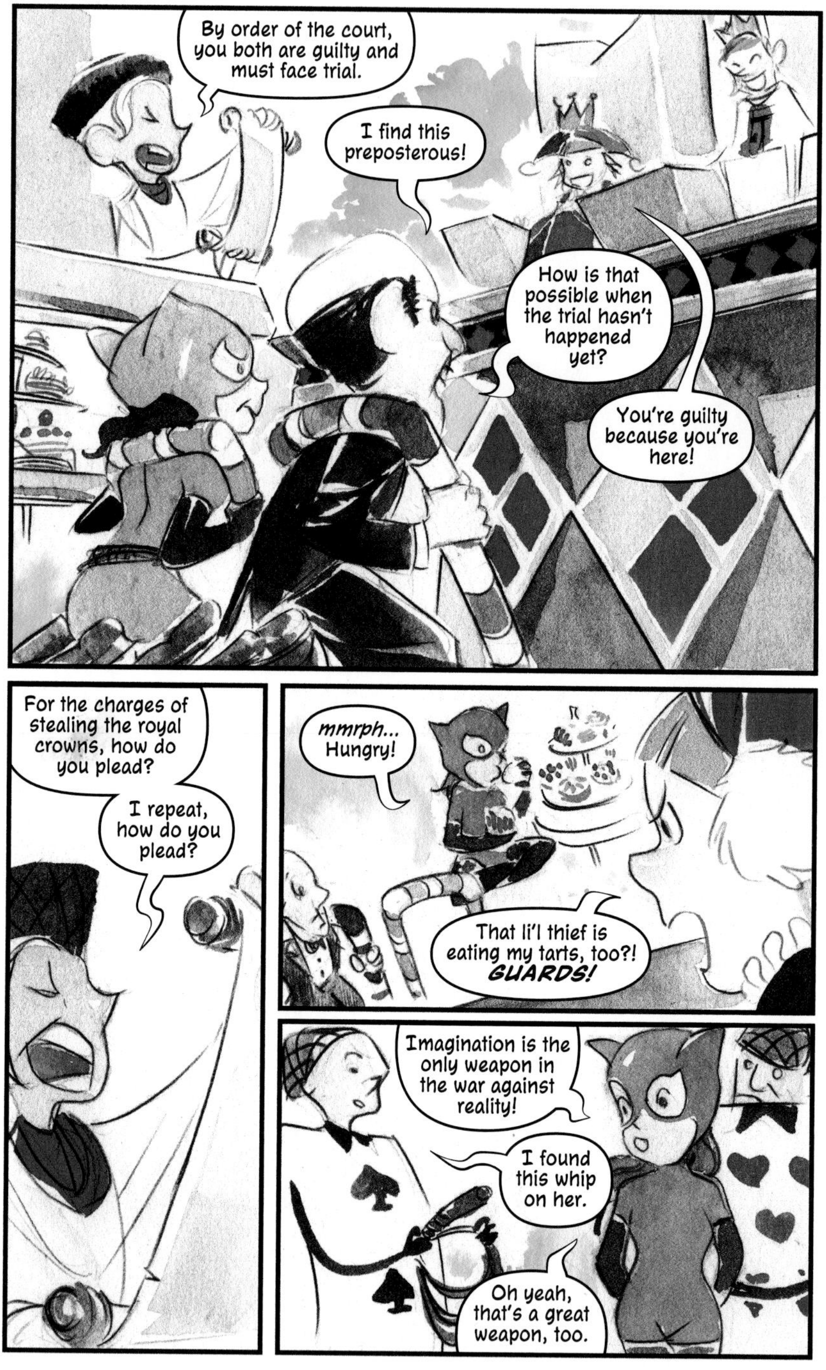
By order of the court, you both are guilty and must face trial.
I find this preposterous!
How is that possible when the trial hasn't happened yet?
You're guilty because you're here!
For the charges of stealing the royal crowns, how do you plead?
I repeat, how do you plead?
mmrph... Hungry!
That li'l thief is eating my tarts, too?! GUARDS!
Imagination is the only weapon in the war against reality!
I found this whip on her.
Oh yeah, that's a great weapon, too.

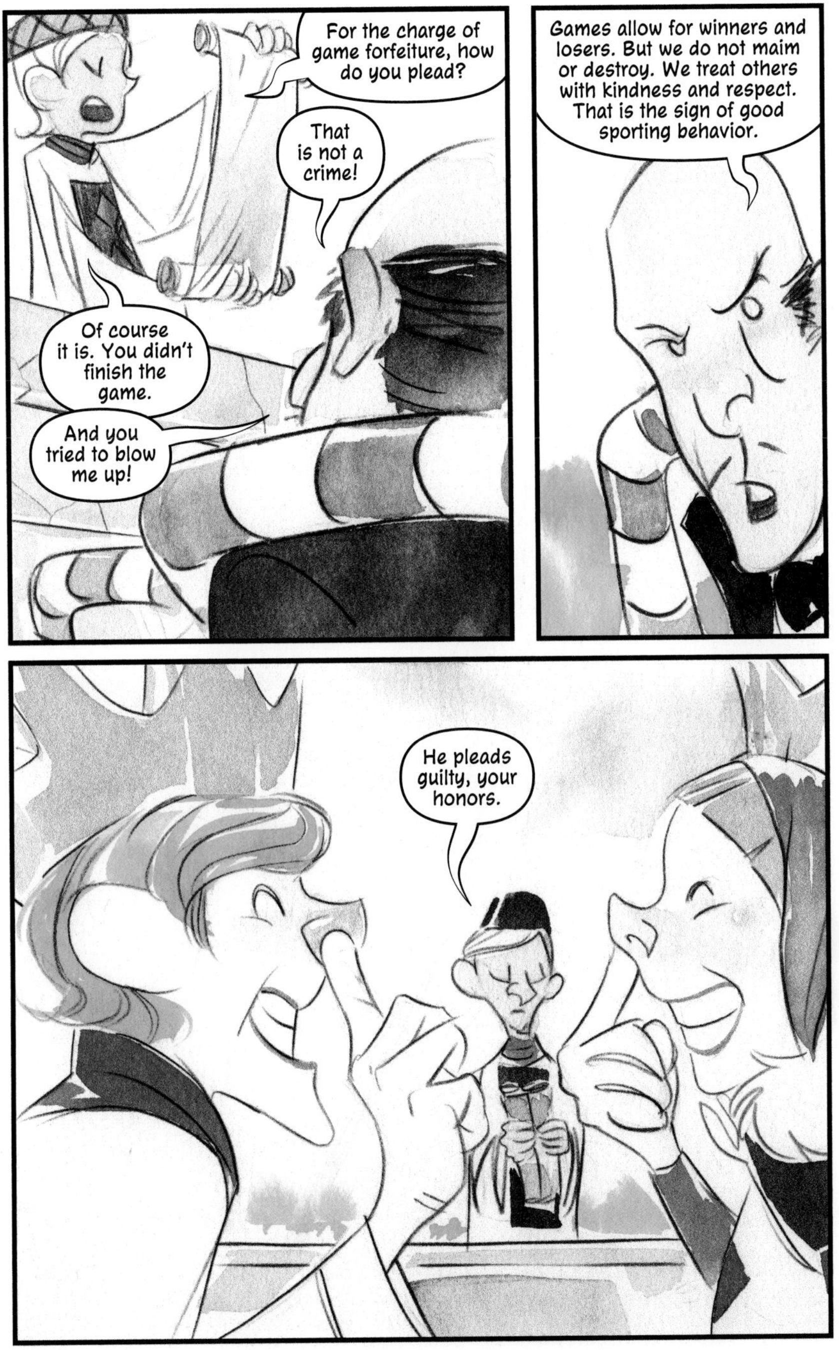
For the charge of game forfeiture, how do you plead?
That is not a crime!
Of course it is. You didn't finish the game.
And you tried to blow me up!
Games allow for winners and losers. But we do not maim or destroy. We treat others with kindness and respect. That is the sign of good sporting behavior.
He pleads guilty, your honors.

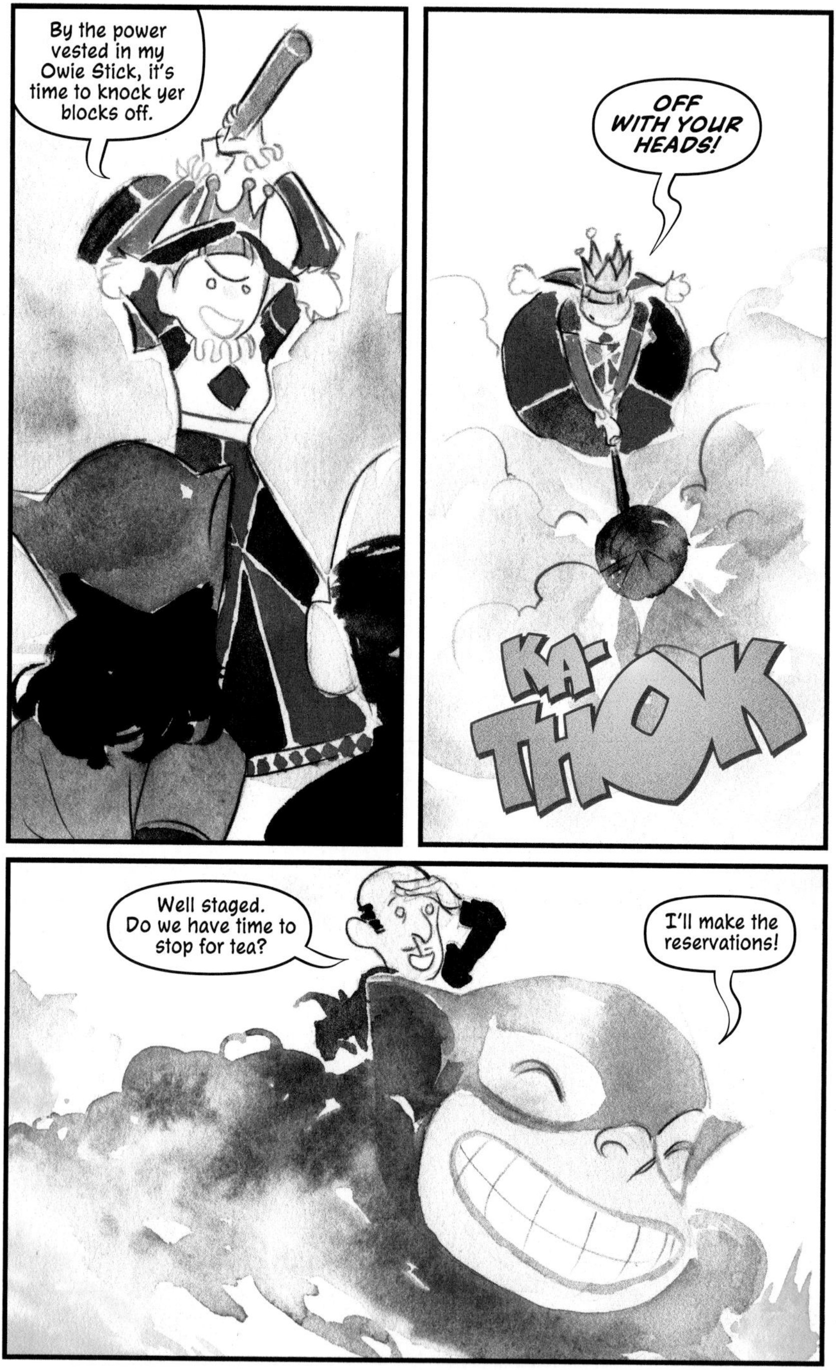
By the power vested in my Owie Stick, it's time to knock yer blocks off.
OFF WITH YOUR HEADS!
KA-THOK
Well staged. Do we have time to stop for tea?
I'll make the reservations!

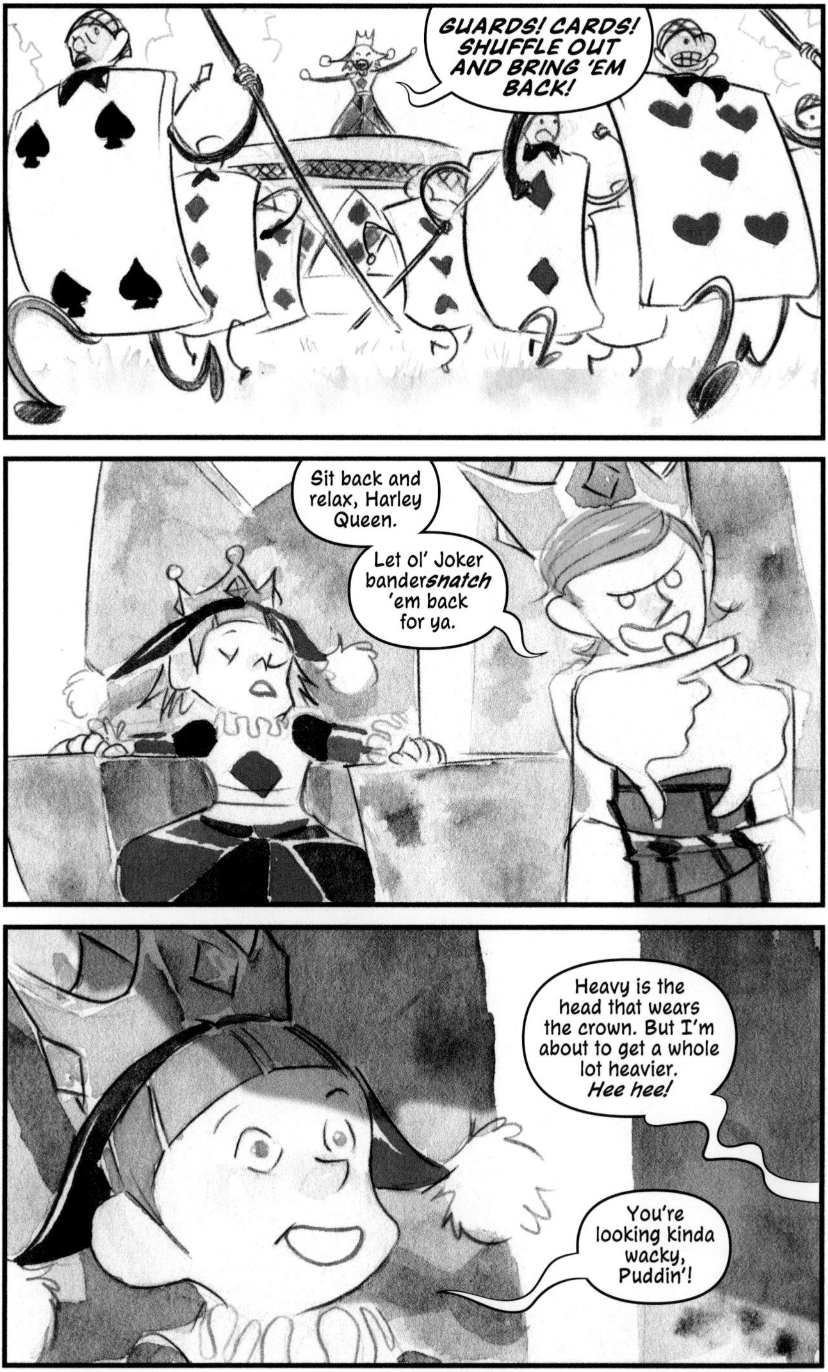
GUARDS! CARDS! SHUFFLE OUT AND BRING 'EM BACK!
Sit back and relax, Harley Queen.
Let ol' Joker bander*snatch* 'em back for ya.
Heavy is the head that wears the crown. But I'm about to get a whole lot heavier. *Hee hee!*
You're looking kinda wacky, Puddin'!

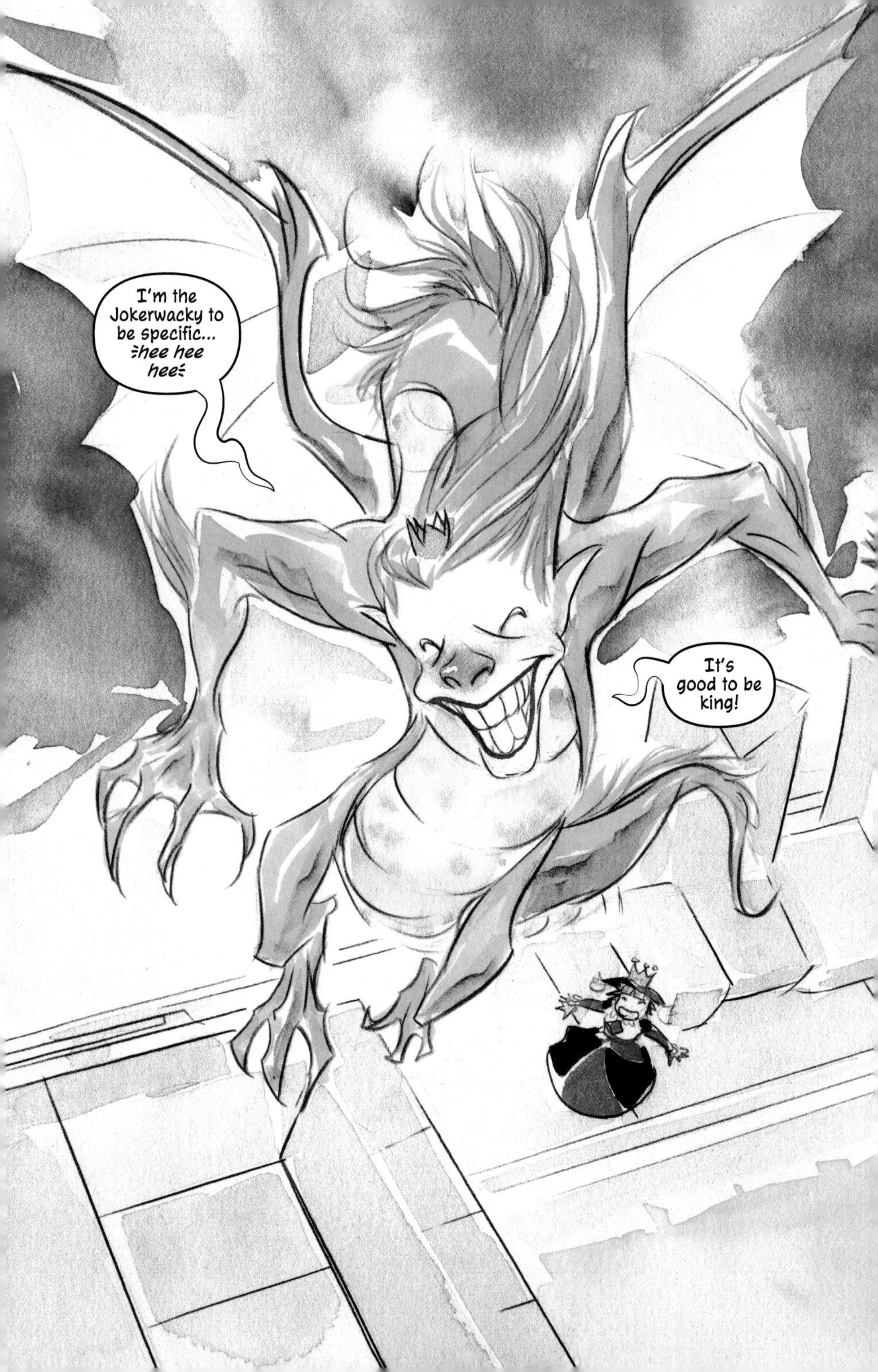
I'm the Jokerwacky to be specific... hee hee hee
It's good to be king!

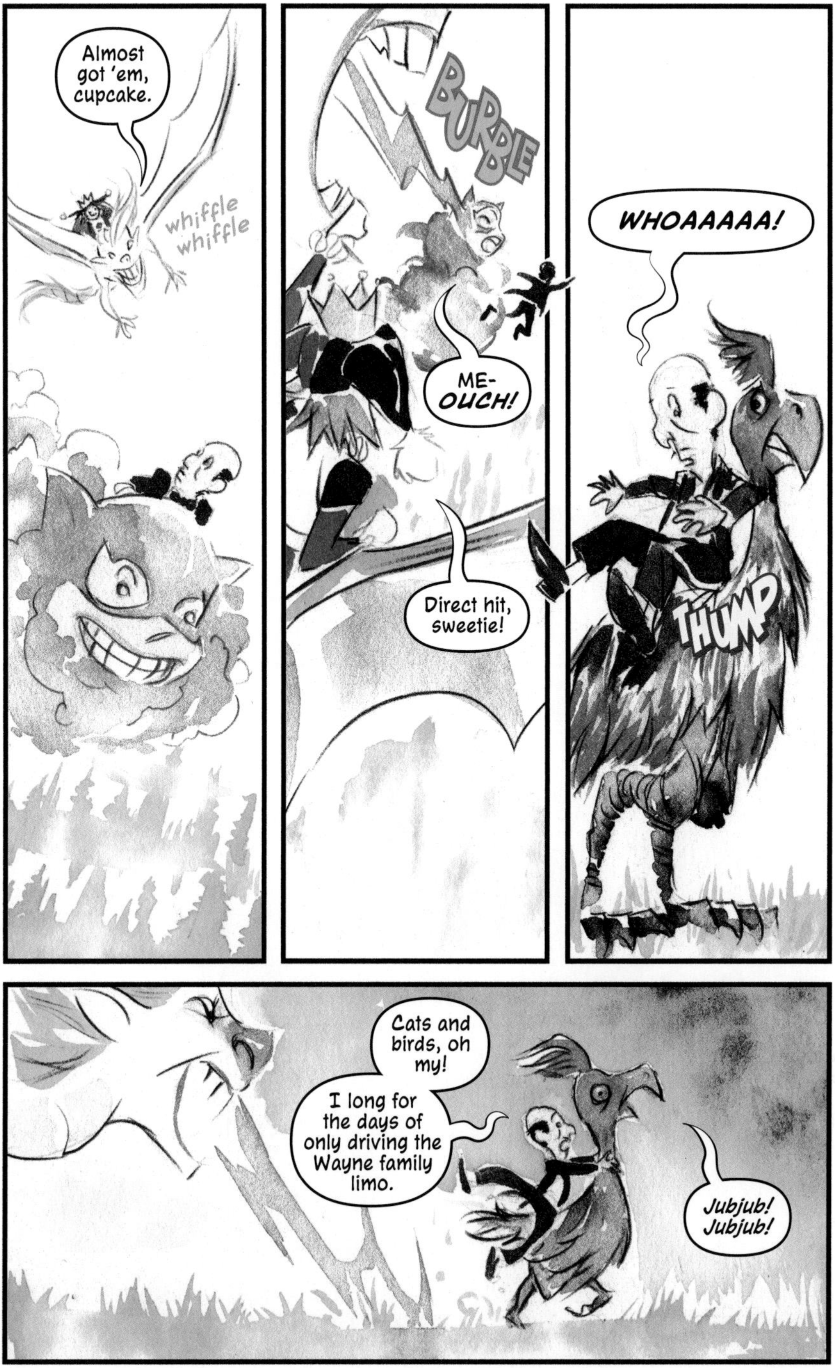
Almost got 'em, cupcake.
whiffle whiffle
BURBLE
ME-OUCH!
Direct hit, sweetie!
WHOAAAAA!
THUMP
Cats and birds, oh my!
I long for the days of only driving the Wayne family limo.
Jubjub! Jubjub!

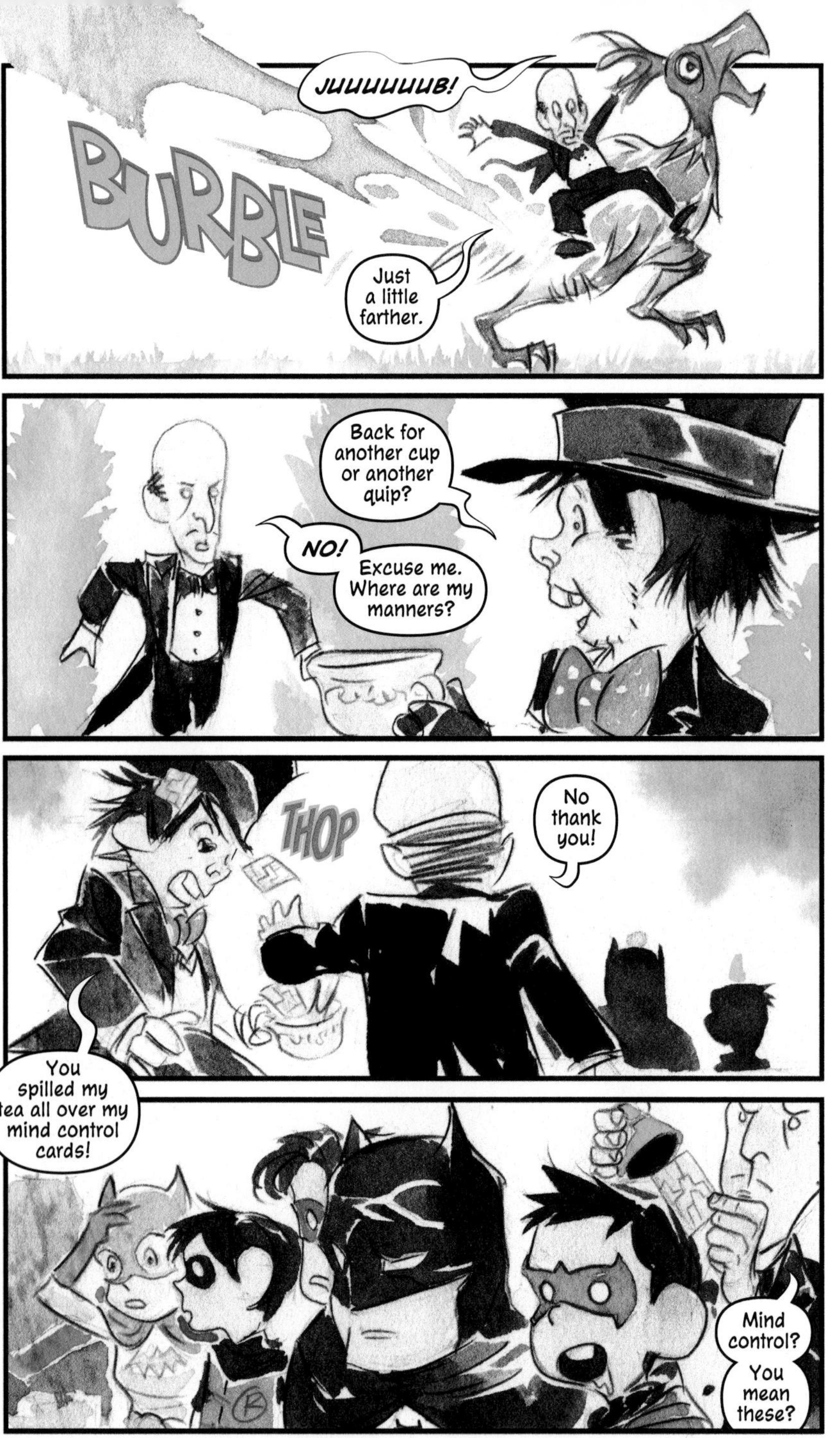
JUUUUUUB!
BURBLE
Just a little farther.
Back for another cup or another quip?
NO!
Excuse me. Where are my manners?
THOP
No thank you!
You spilled my tea all over my mind control cards!
Mind control?
You mean these?

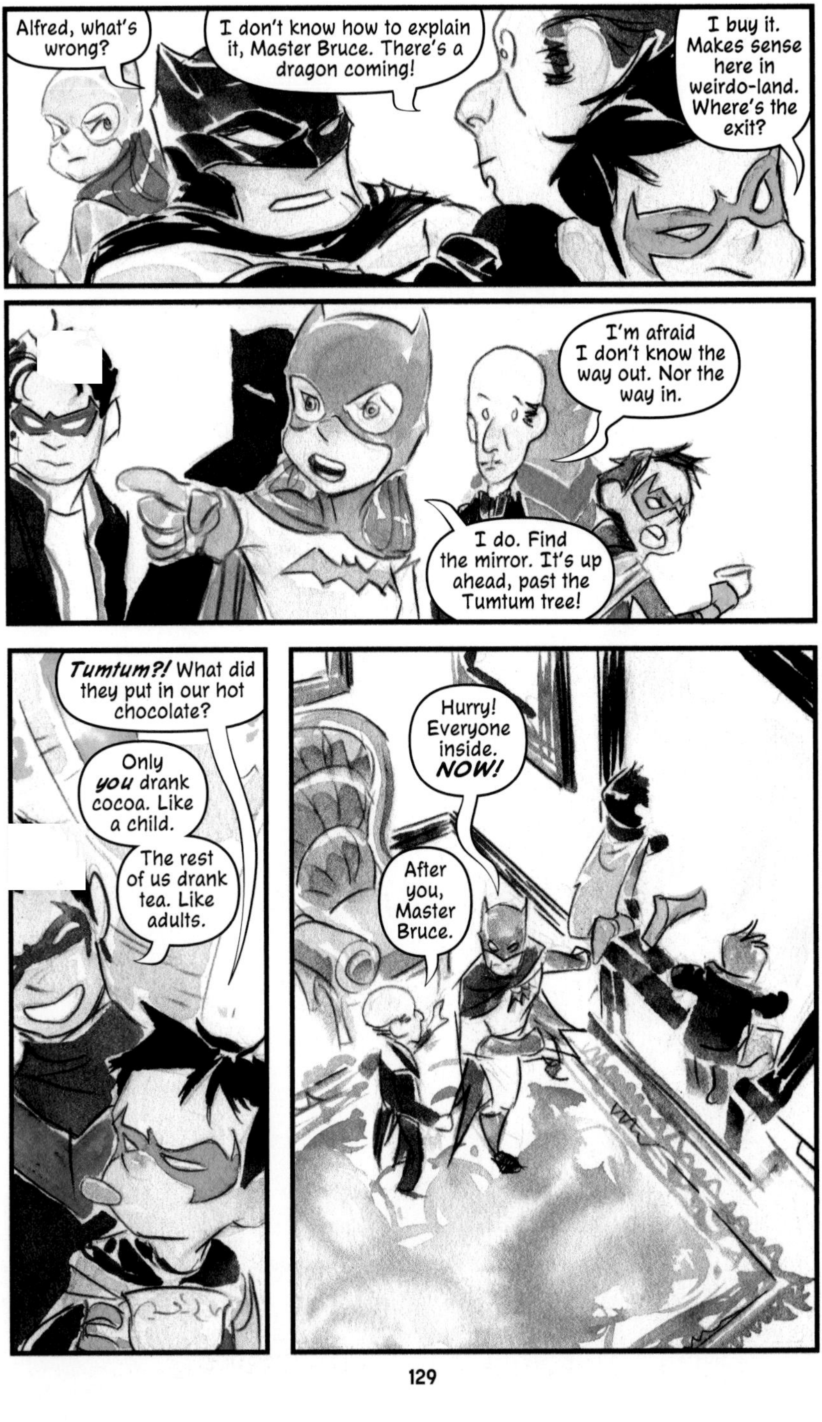
Alfred, what's wrong?
I don't know how to explain it, Master Bruce. There's a dragon coming!
I buy it. Makes sense here in weirdo-land. Where's the exit?
I'm afraid I don't know the way out. Nor the way in.
I do. Find the mirror. It's up ahead, past the Tumtum tree!
Tumtum?! What did they put in our hot chocolate?
Only ***you*** drank cocoa. Like a child.
The rest of us drank tea. Like adults.
Hurry! Everyone inside. ***NOW!***
After you, Master Bruce.

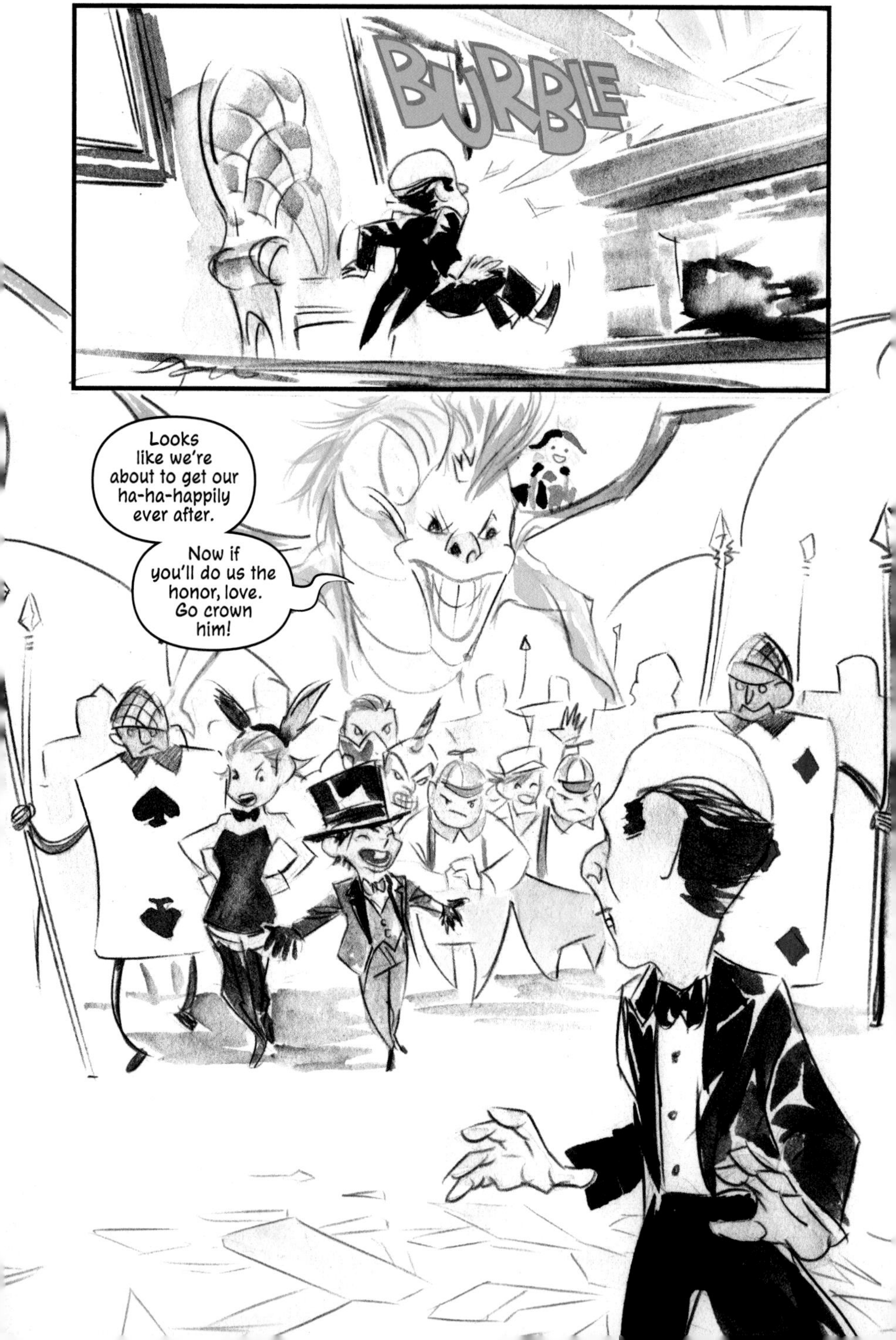
BURBLE
Looks like we're about to get our ha-ha-happily ever after.
Now if you'll do us the honor, love. Go crown him!

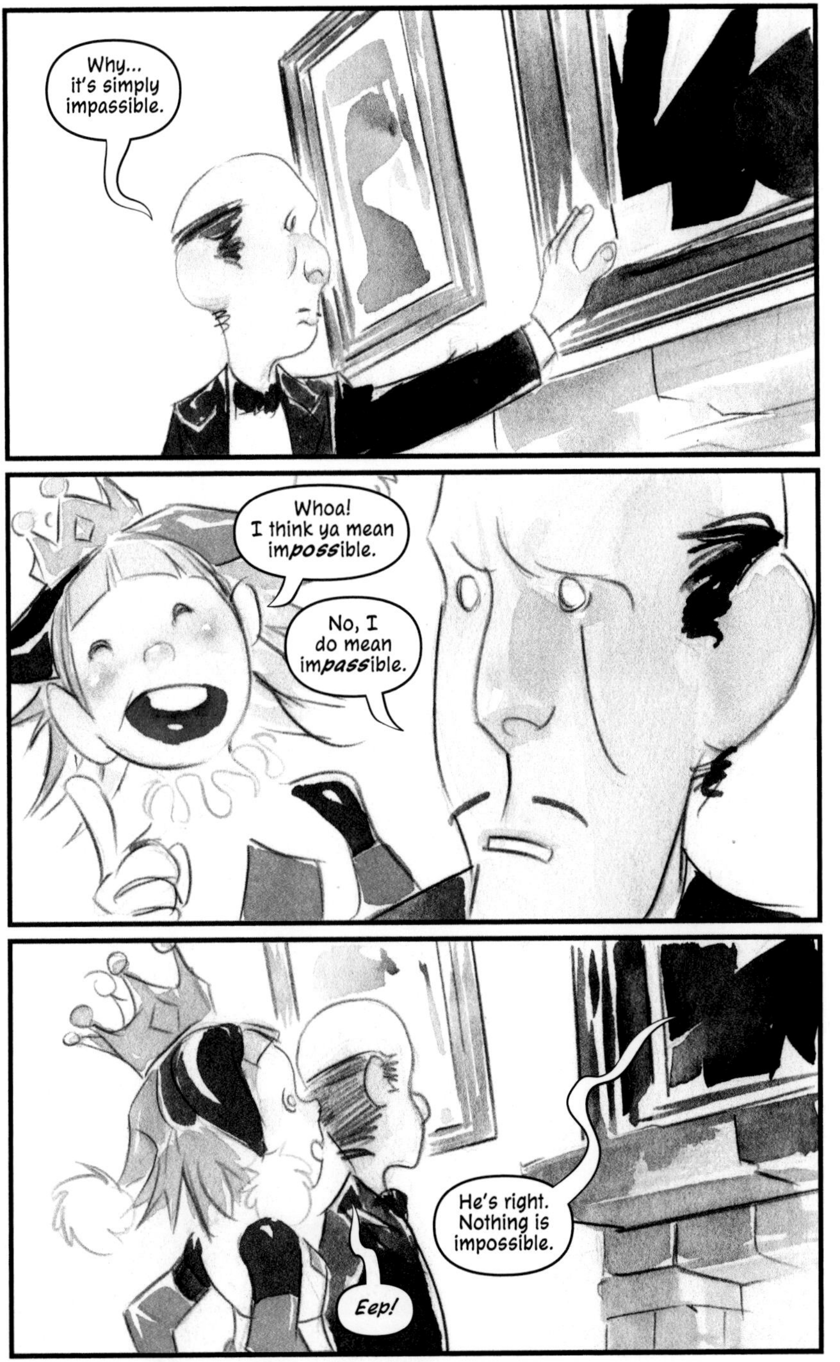
Why... it's simply impassible.
Whoa! I think ya mean im*poss*ible.
No, I do mean im*pass*ible.
He's right. Nothing is impossible.
Eep!

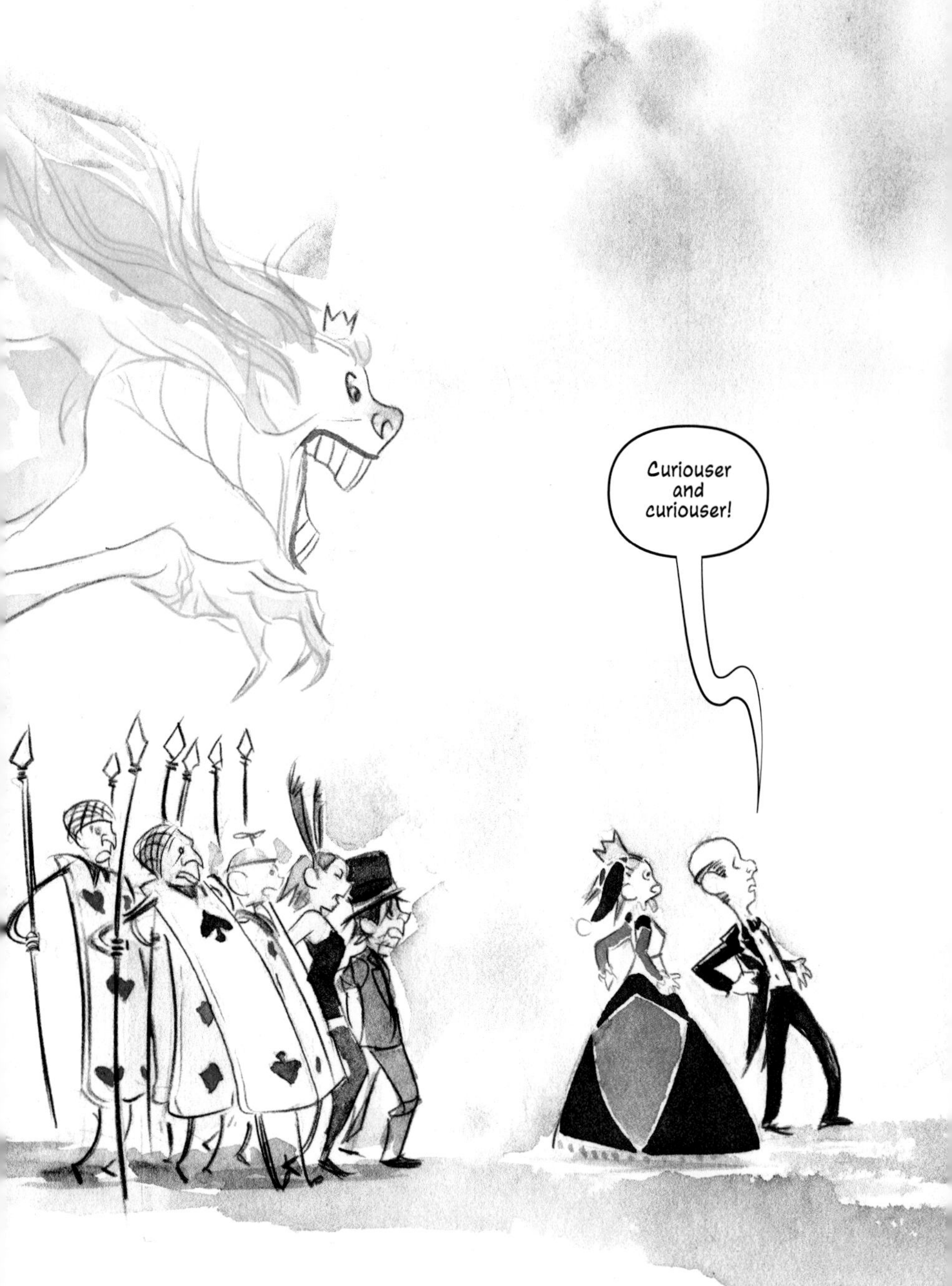
Curiouser and curiouser!

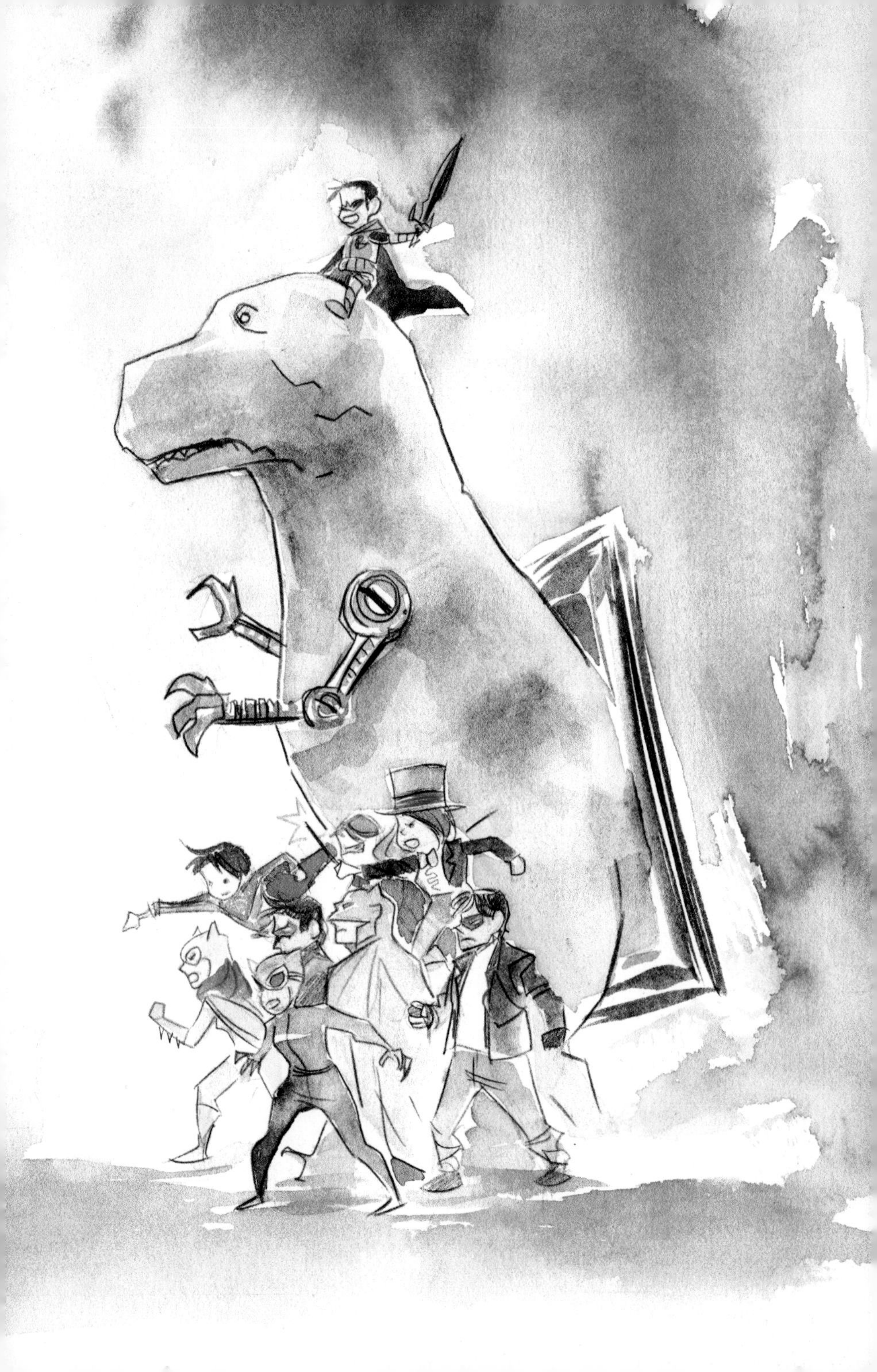

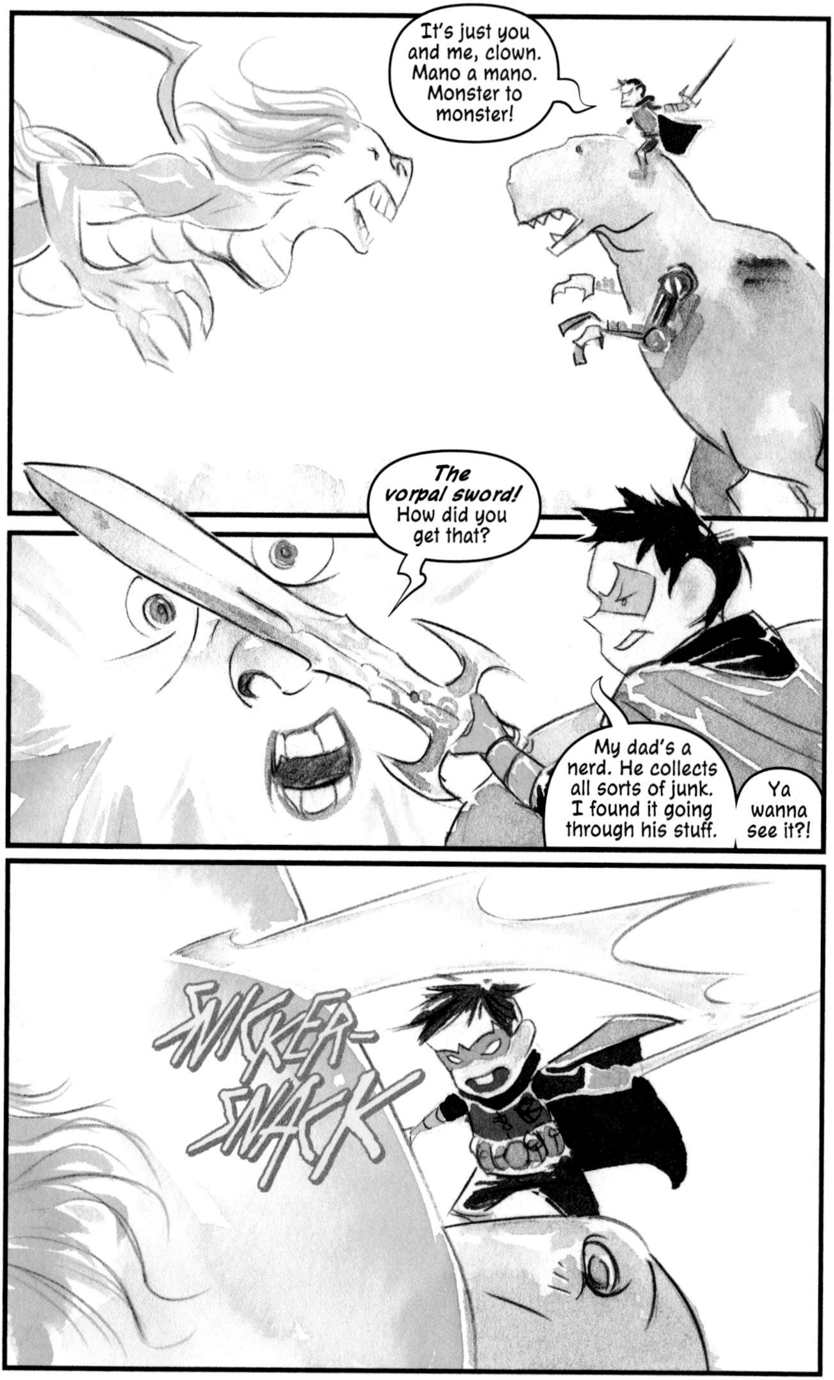
It's just you and me, clown. Mano a mano. Monster to monster!
The vorpal sword! How did you get that?
My dad's a nerd. He collects all sorts of junk. I found it going through his stuff.
Ya wanna see it?!
SNICKER-SNACK

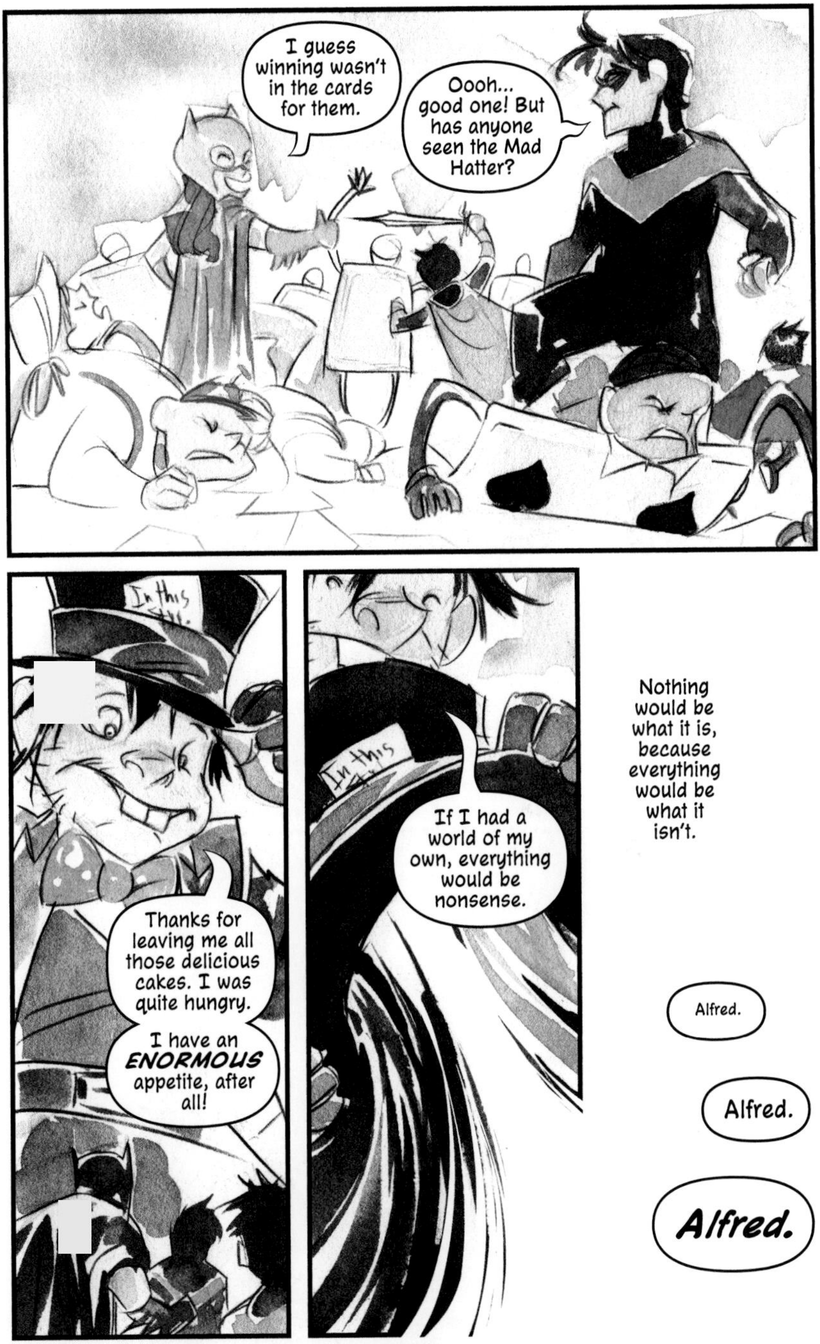
I guess winning wasn't in the cards for them.
Oooh... good one! But has anyone seen the Mad Hatter?
Thanks for leaving me all those delicious cakes. I was quite hungry.
I have an ENORMOUS appetite, after all!
If I had a world of my own, everything would be nonsense.
Nothing would be what it is, because everything would be what it isn't.
Alfred.
Alfred.
Alfred.

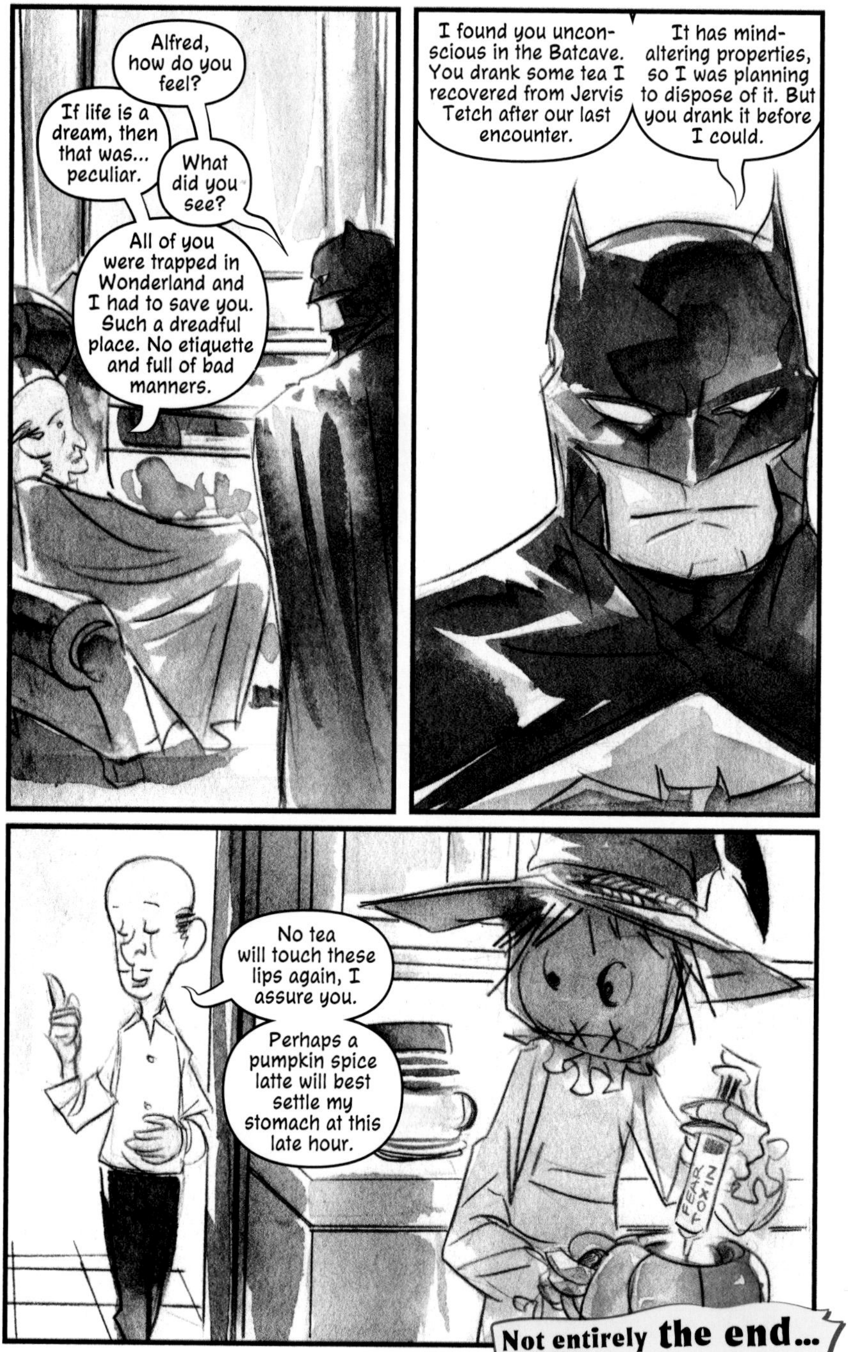
Alfred, how do you feel?
If life is a dream, then that was... peculiar.
What did you see?
All of you were trapped in Wonderland and I had to save you. Such a dreadful place. No etiquette and full of bad manners.
I found you unconscious in the Batcave. You drank some tea I recovered from Jervis Tetch after our last encounter.
It has mind-altering properties, so I was planning to dispose of it. But you drank it before I could.
No tea will touch these lips again, I assure you.
Perhaps a pumpkin spice latte will best settle my stomach at this late hour.
FEAR TOXIN
Not entirely the end...

THE SNOW QUEEN

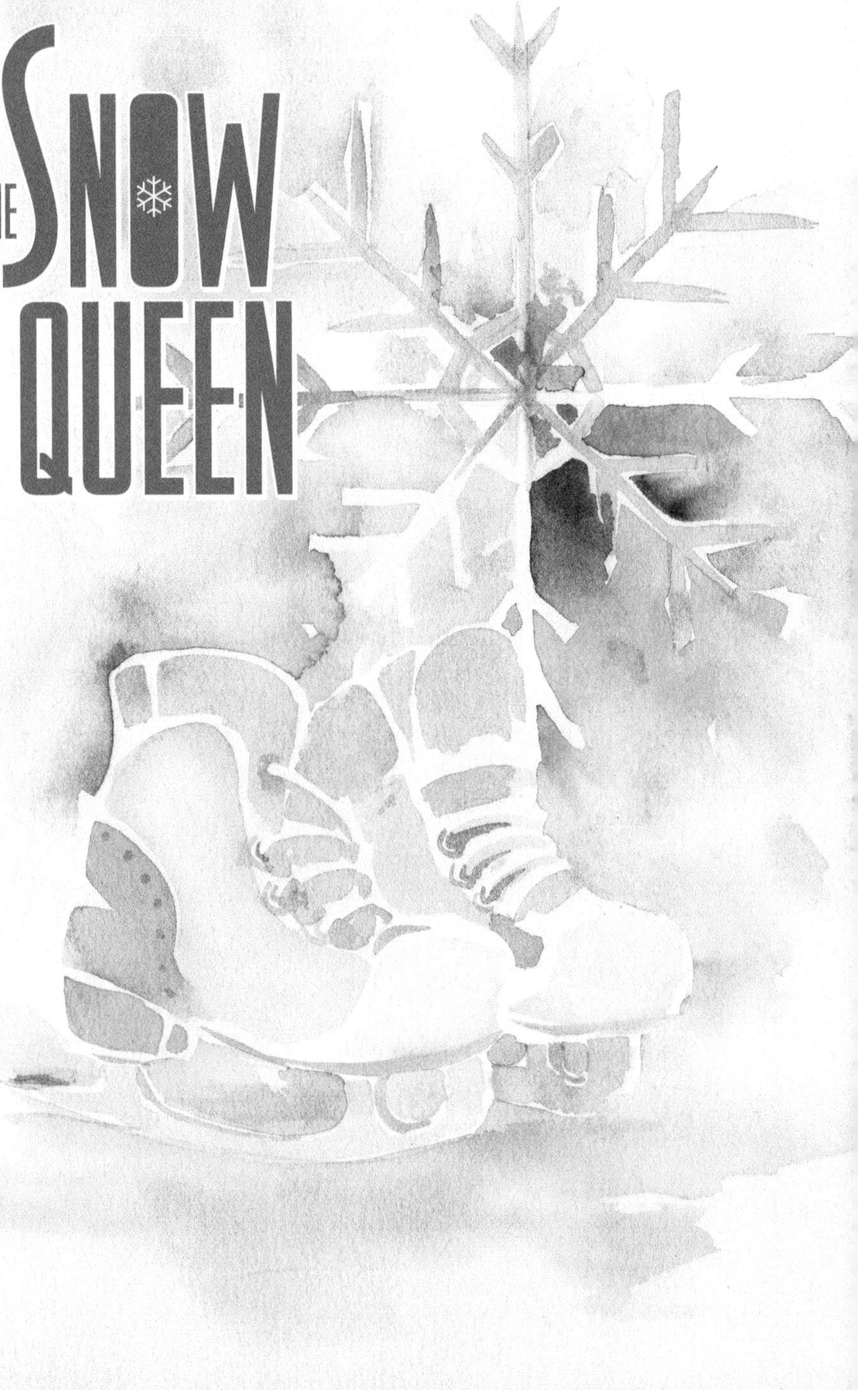

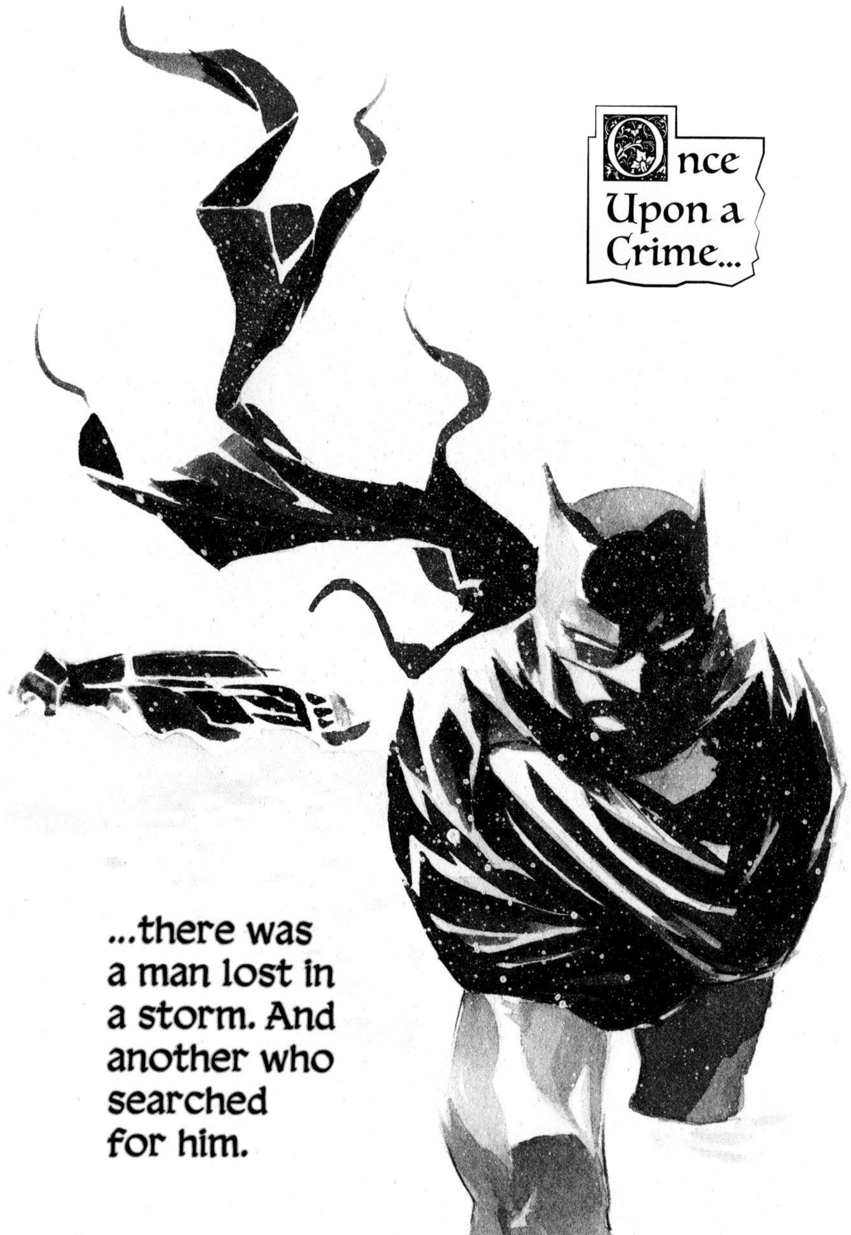
Once Upon a Crime...
...there was a man lost in a storm. And another who searched for him.

Each step became a burden.
Each inch forward, a promise.

The Batman would
continue for as long
as he could hold out.

But nature was relentless.
And she was winning.

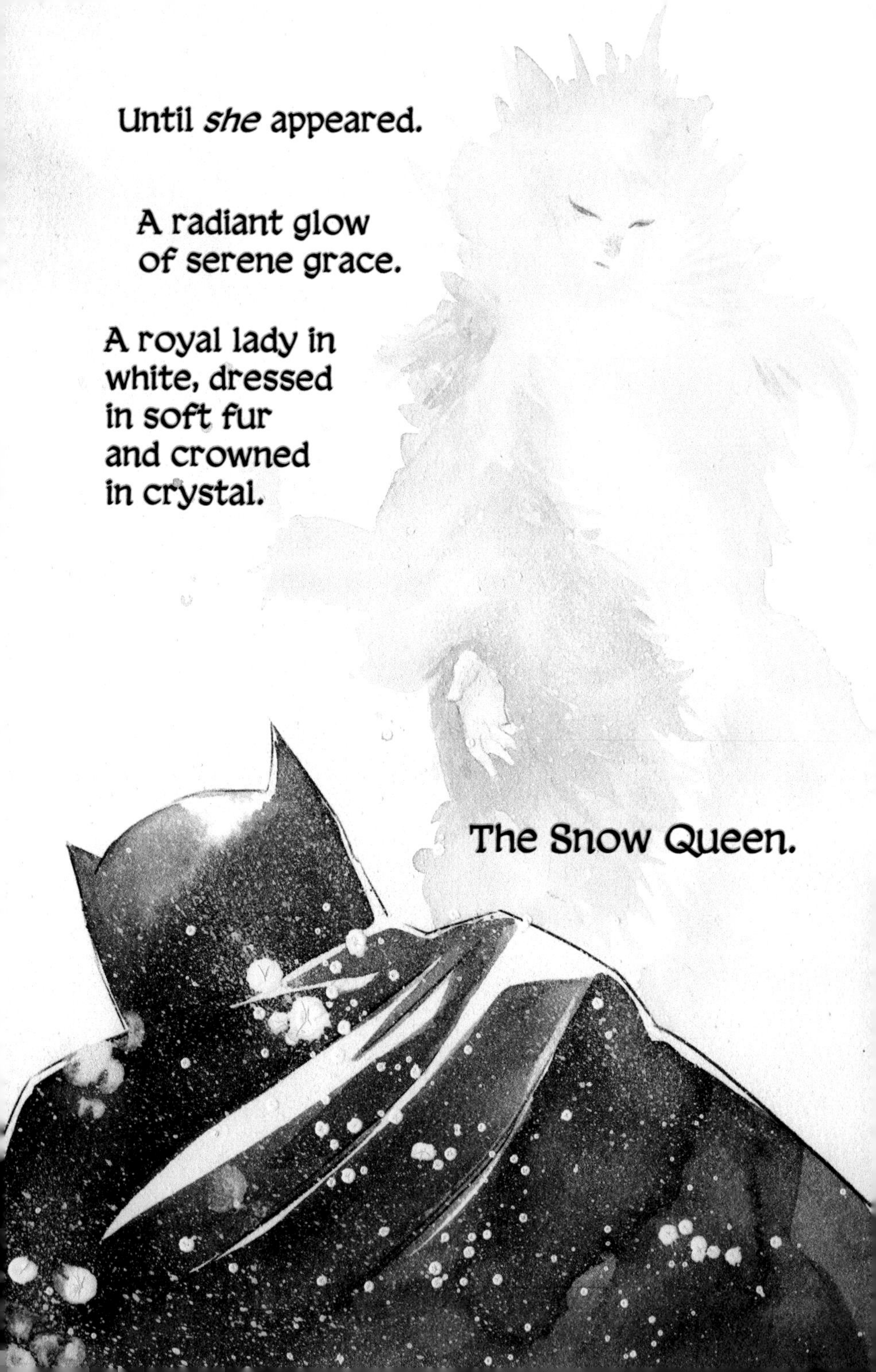

Until *she* appeared.
A radiant glow of serene grace.
A royal lady in white, dressed in soft fur and crowned in crystal.
The Snow Queen.

As she approached,
the white surface
remained undisturbed.

She helped him
to her carriage.

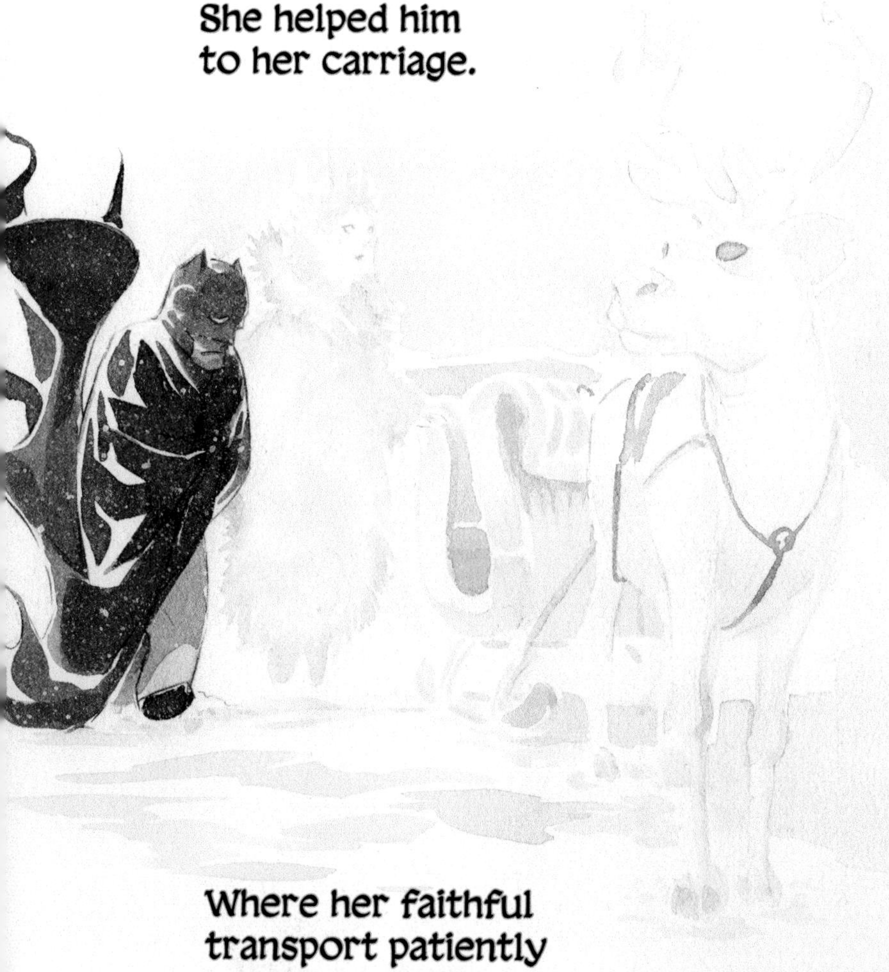

Where her faithful
transport patiently
waited to depart.

As he trembled, she smiled.
Not uncaring, but with kindness.

The cold air chilled him.
His breathing became more labored.

Unable to continue, he exhaled,
allowing his breath to escape.

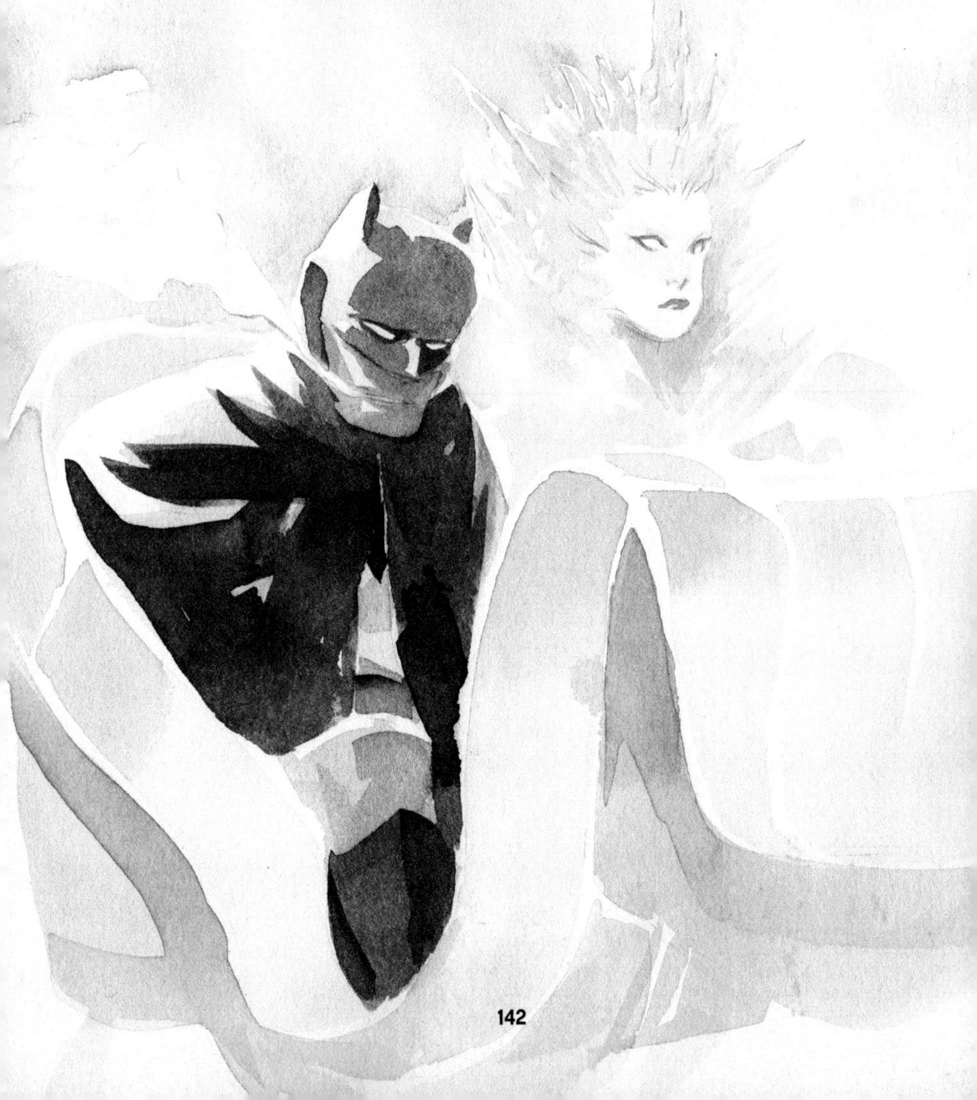

But swiftly, she retrieved it
with a delicate touch.

Offering it back to him,
warm and in full.

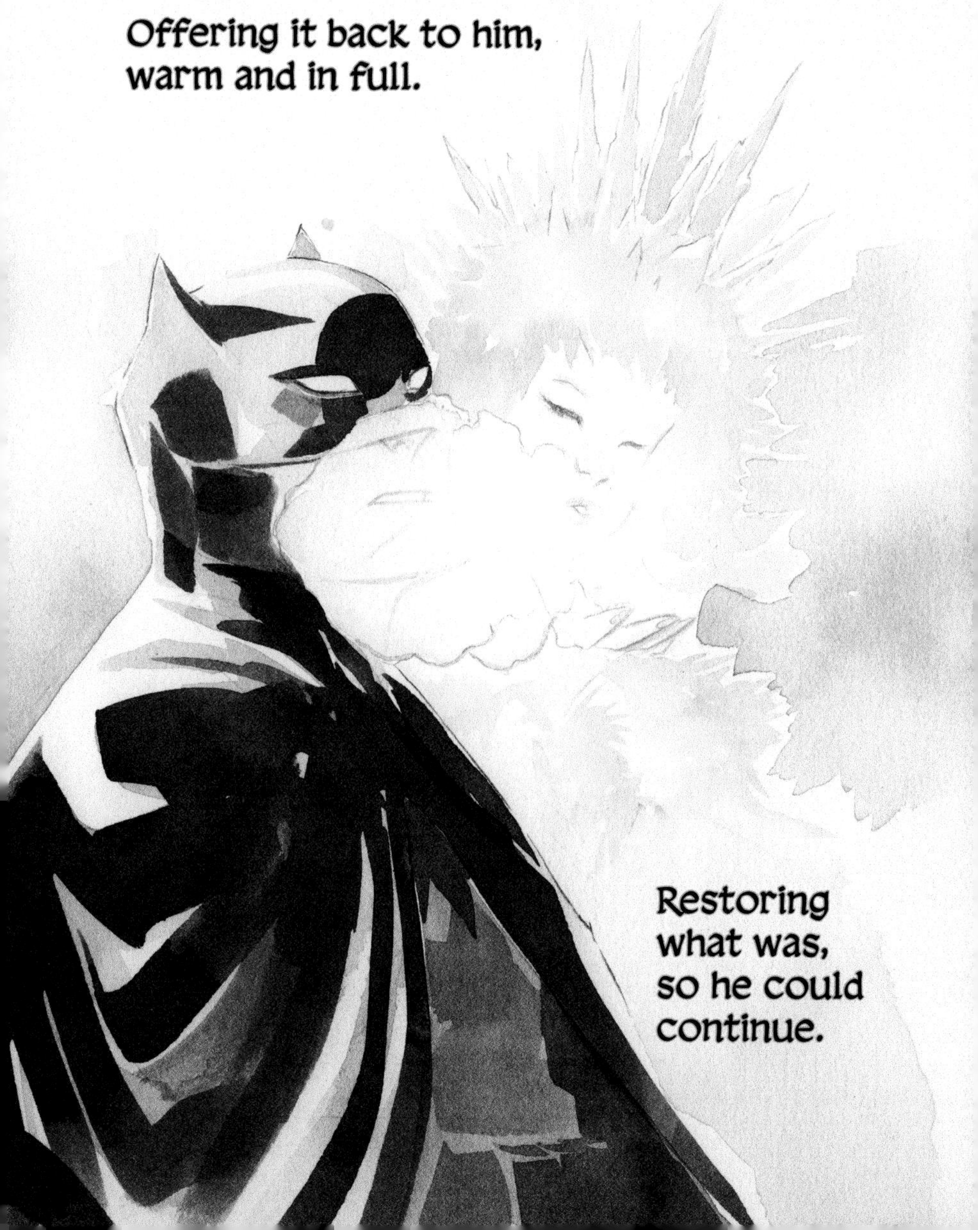
Restoring what was, so he could continue.

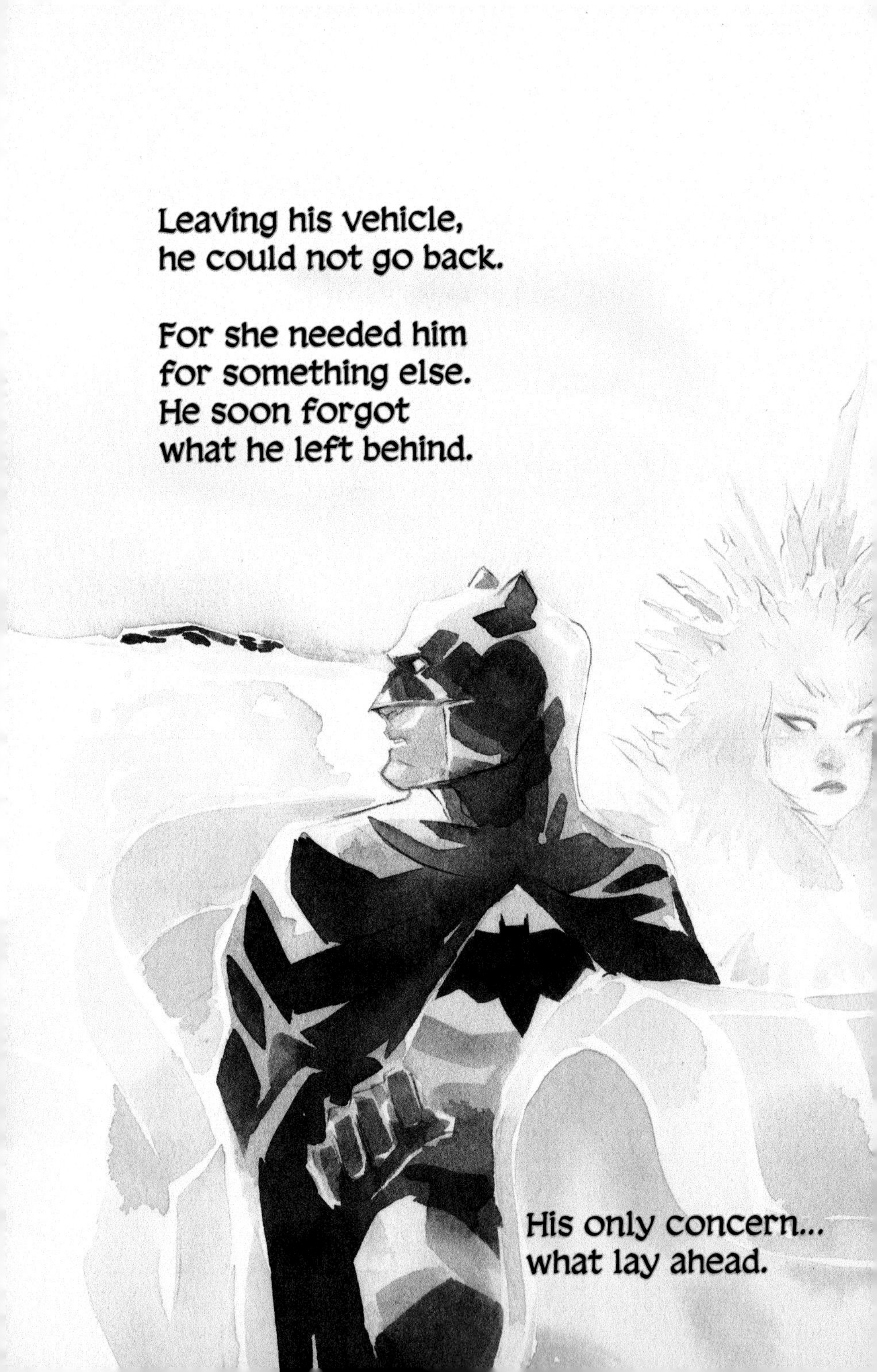
Leaving his vehicle,
he could not go back.
For she needed him
for something else.
He soon forgot
what he left behind.
His only concern...
what lay ahead.

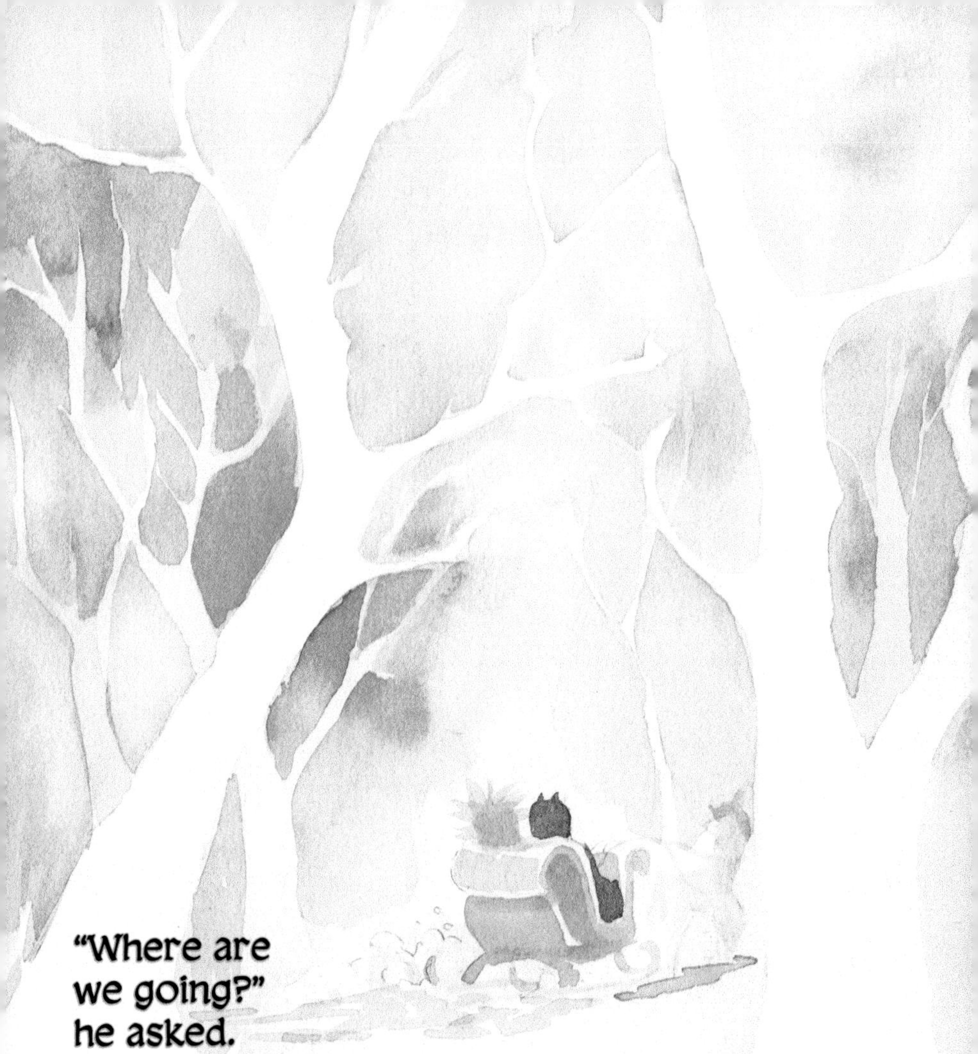

"Where are
we going?"
he asked.

"We are searching,"
she answered.

"For what?"
he wondered.

And she replied, "A
cold hand to hold."

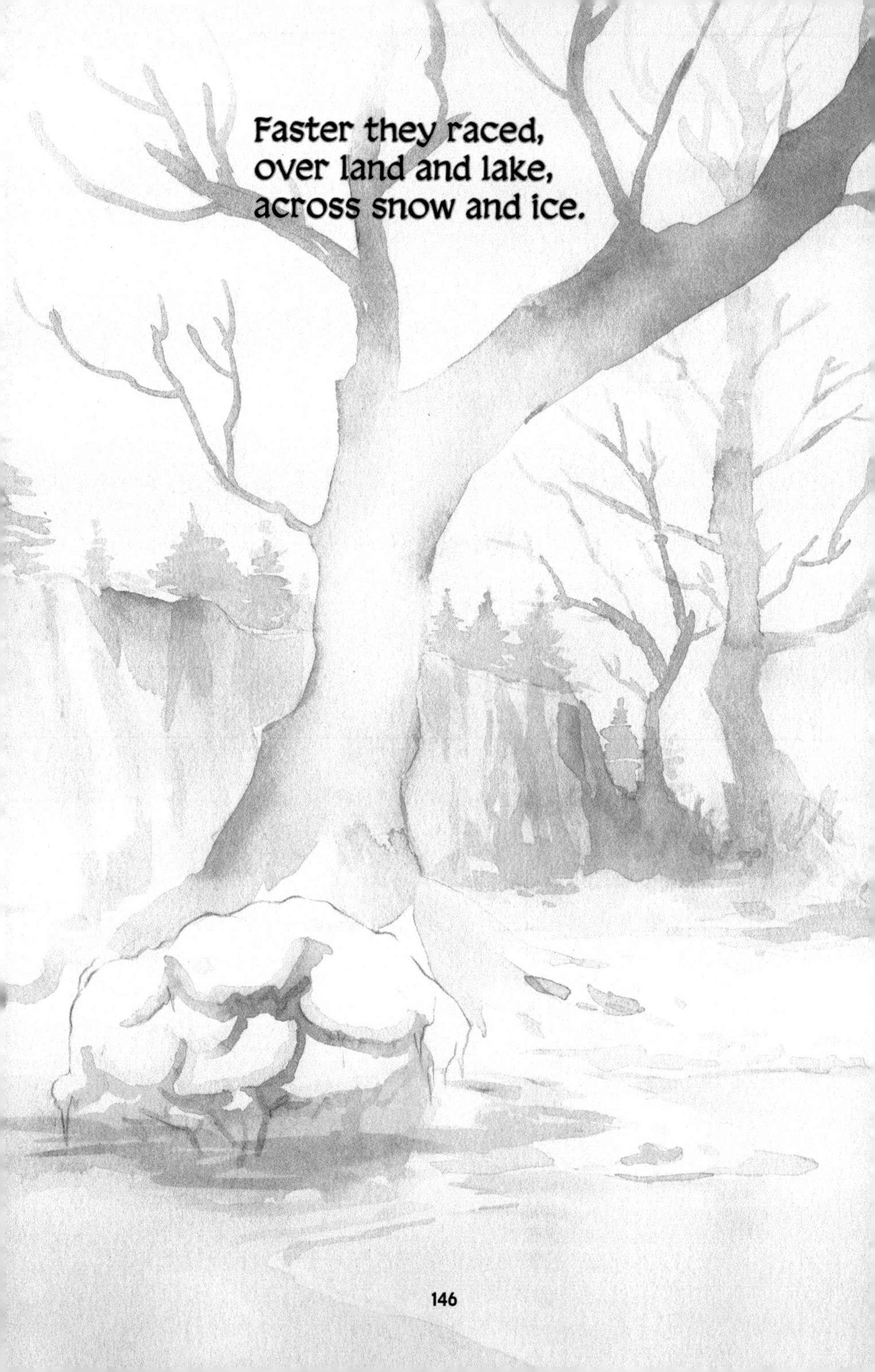

Faster they raced,
over land and lake,
across snow and ice.

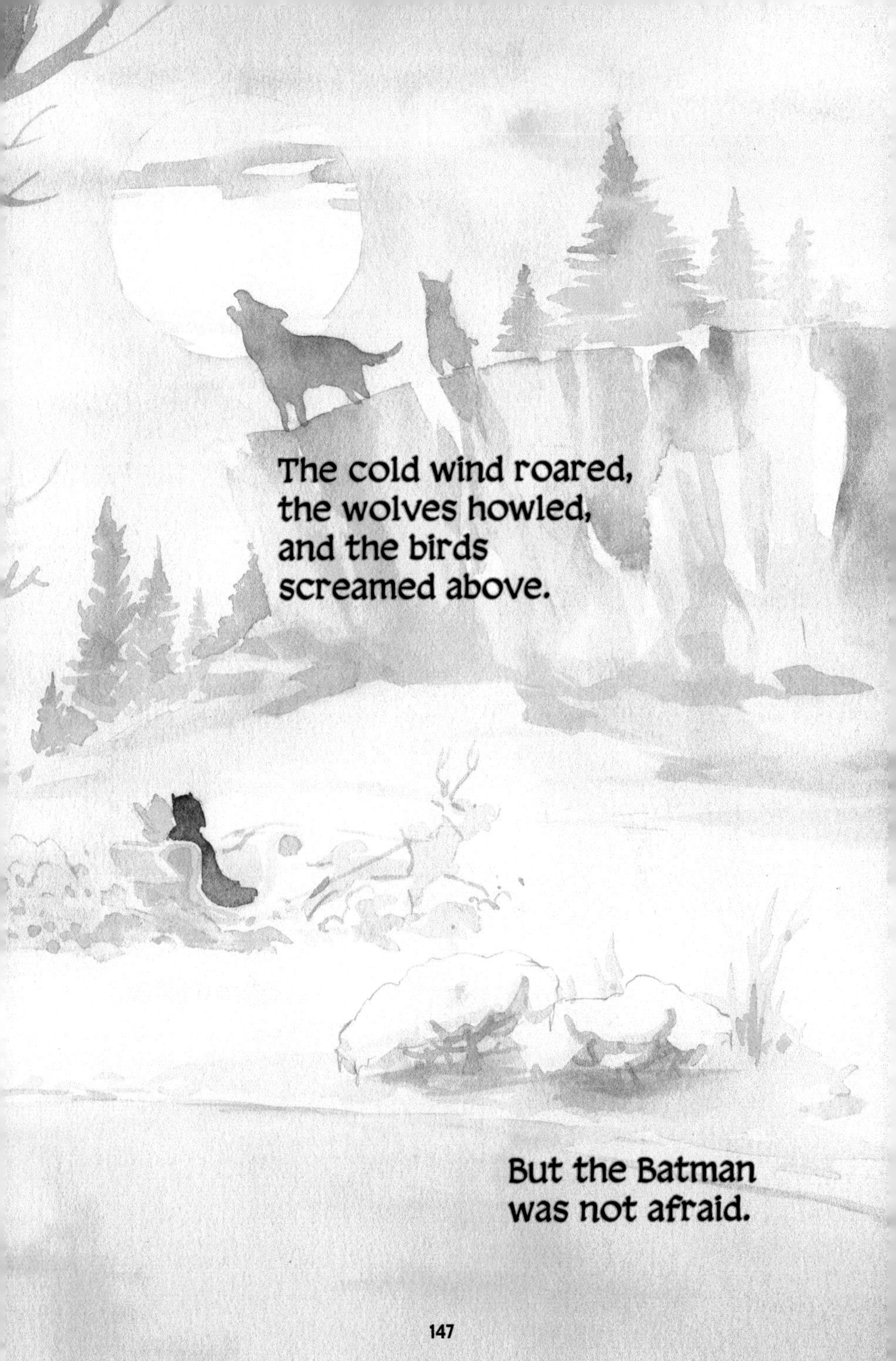

The cold wind roared,
the wolves howled,
and the birds
screamed above.

But the Batman
was not afraid.

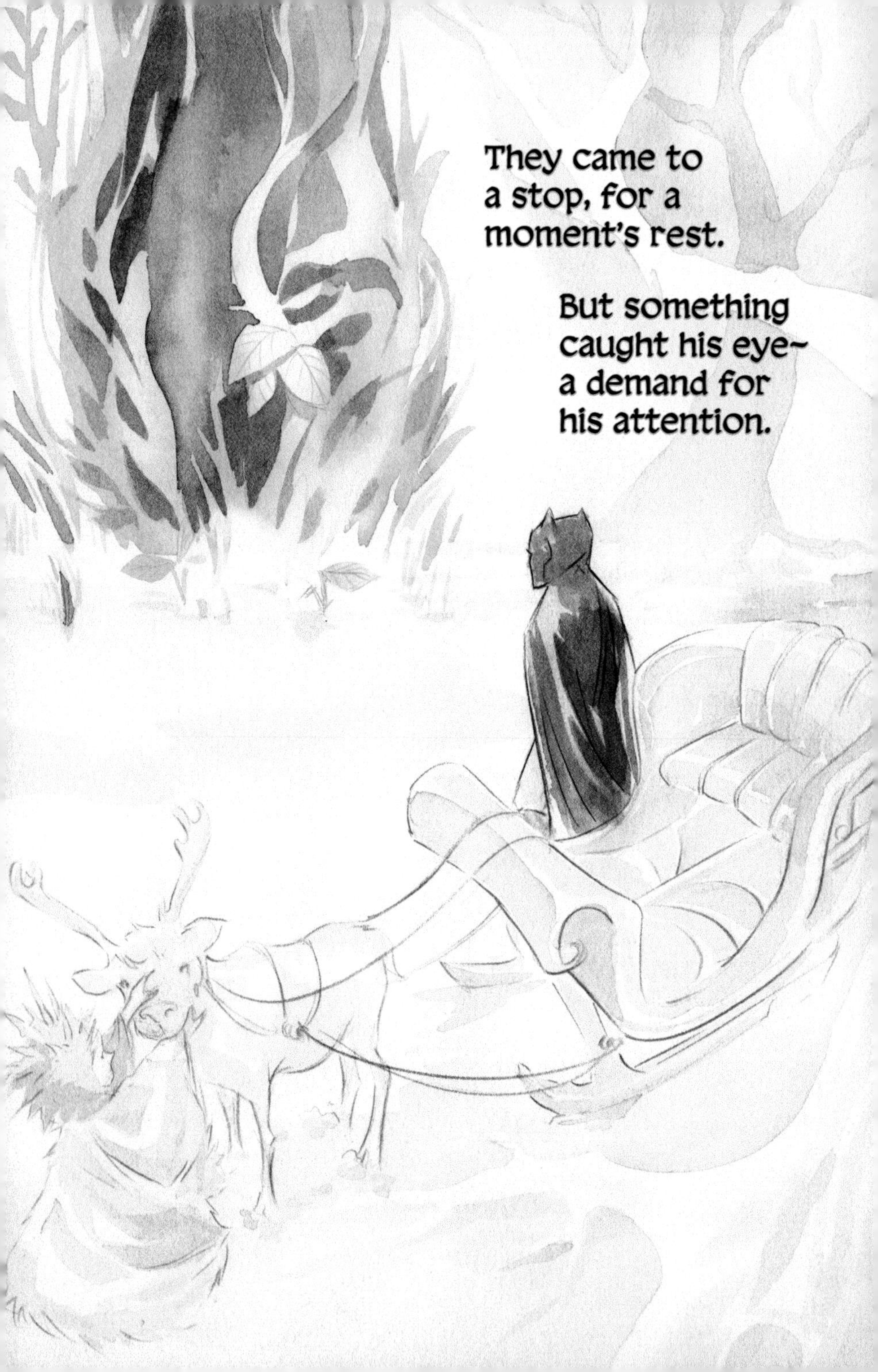
They came to a stop, for a moment's rest.
But something caught his eye~ a demand for his attention.

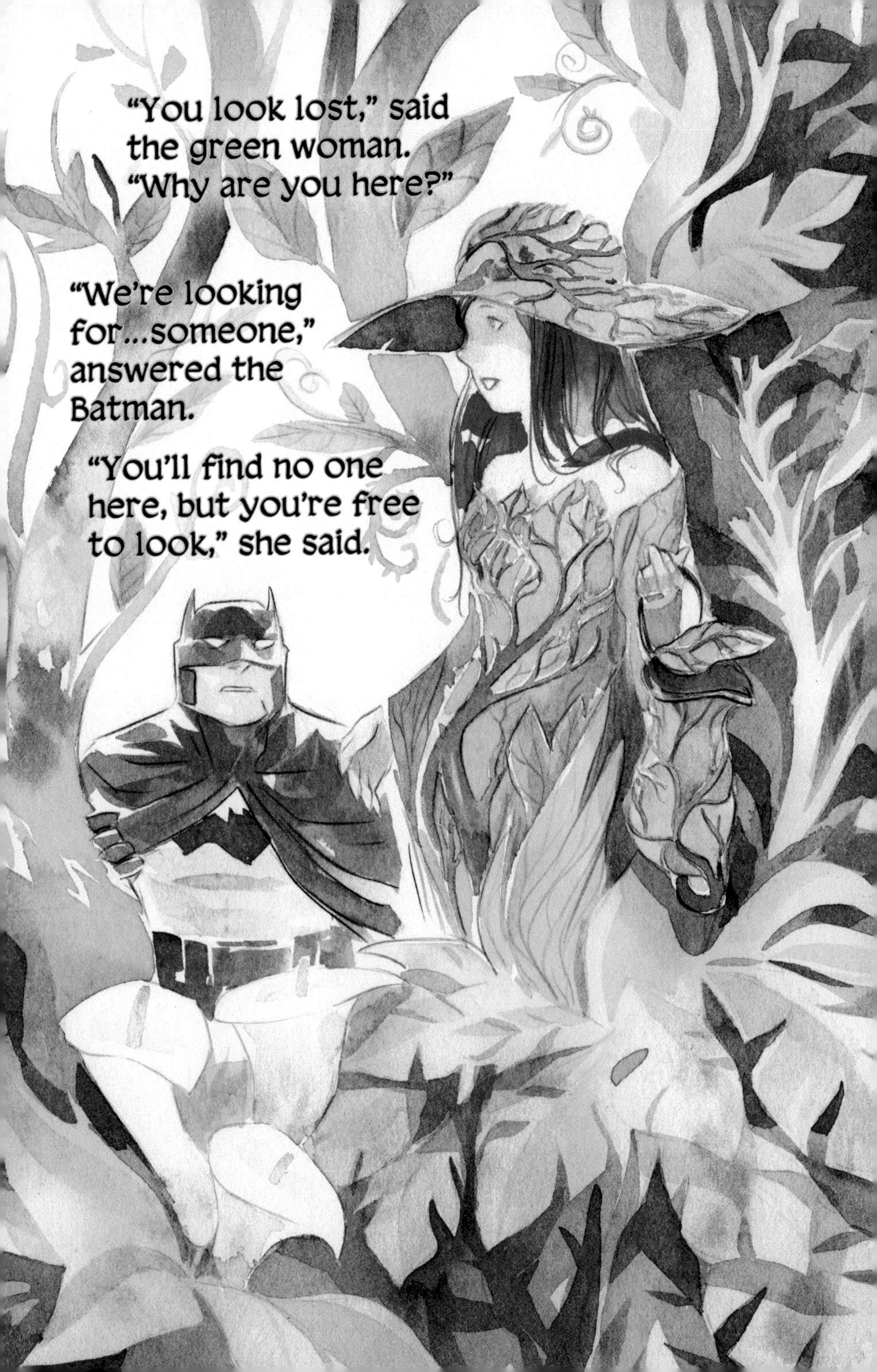
"You look lost," said the green woman. "Why are you here?"
"We're looking for...someone," answered the Batman.
"You'll find no one here, but you're free to look," she said.

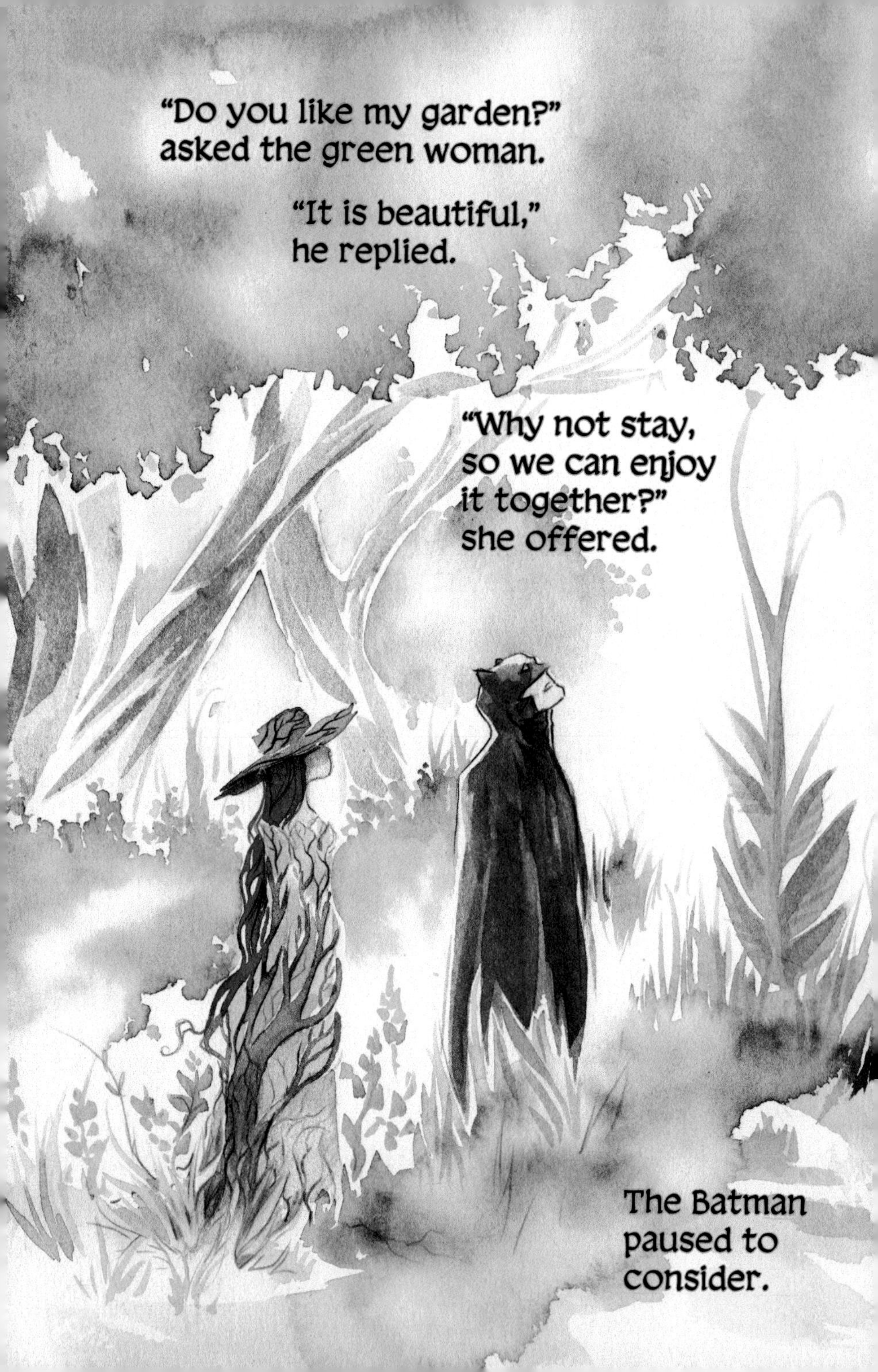
"Do you like my garden?" asked the green woman.
"It is beautiful," he replied.
"Why not stay, so we can enjoy it together?" she offered.
The Batman paused to consider.

The garden was enchanting.
A calming peace washed over him.
And yet something felt off.

"I sense you are troubled."

"Something is missing from
your garden," he responded.
"Or perhaps...concealed."

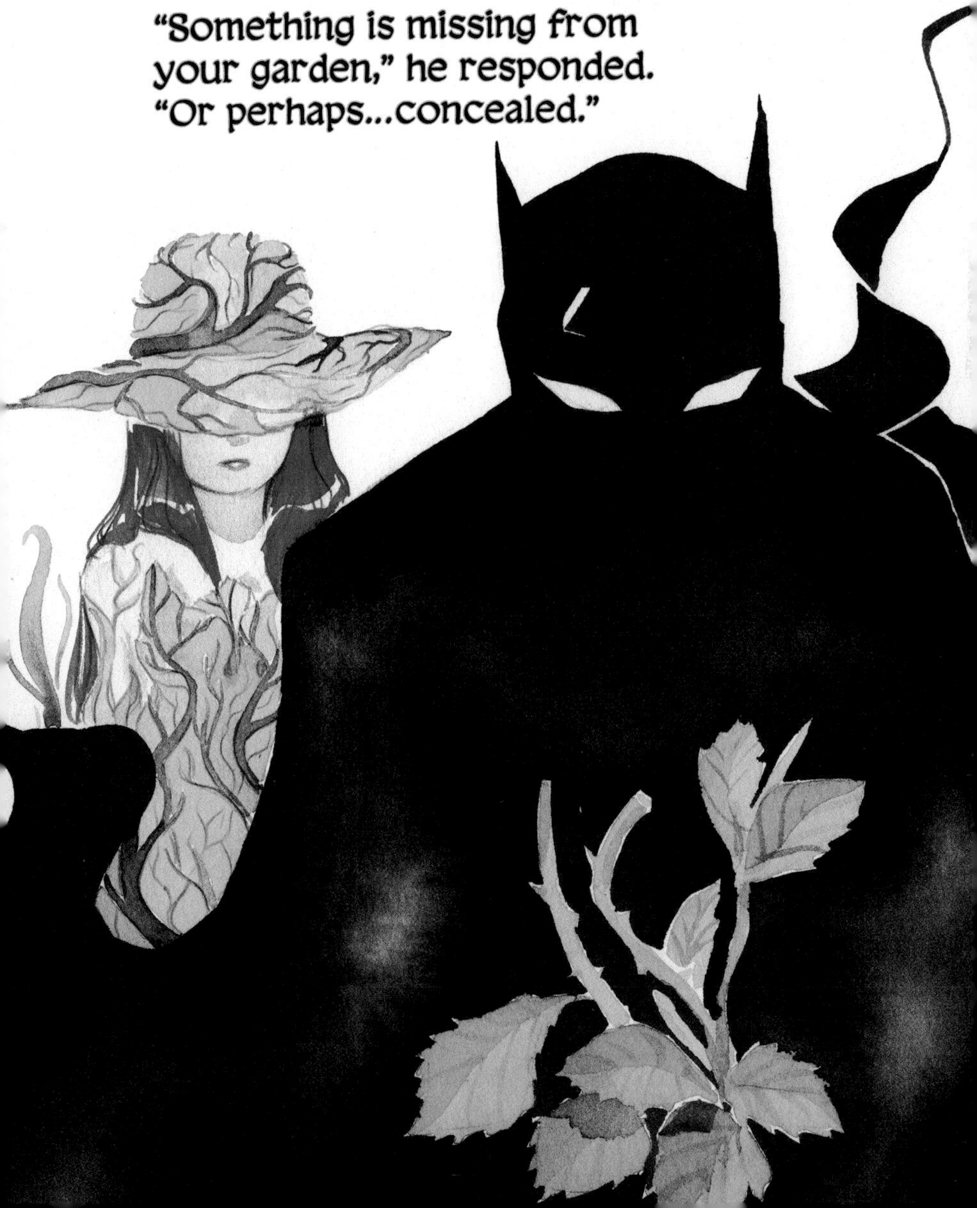

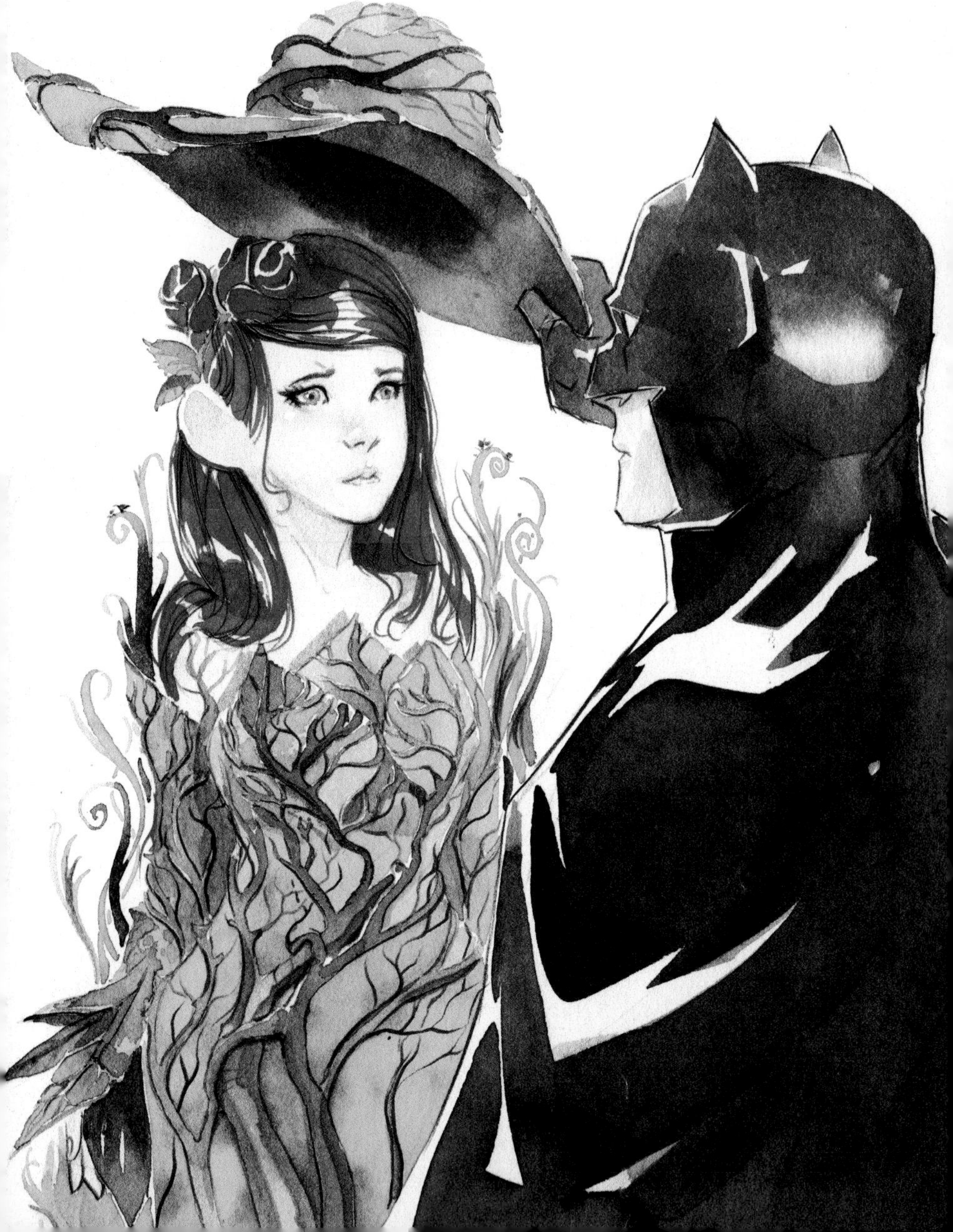

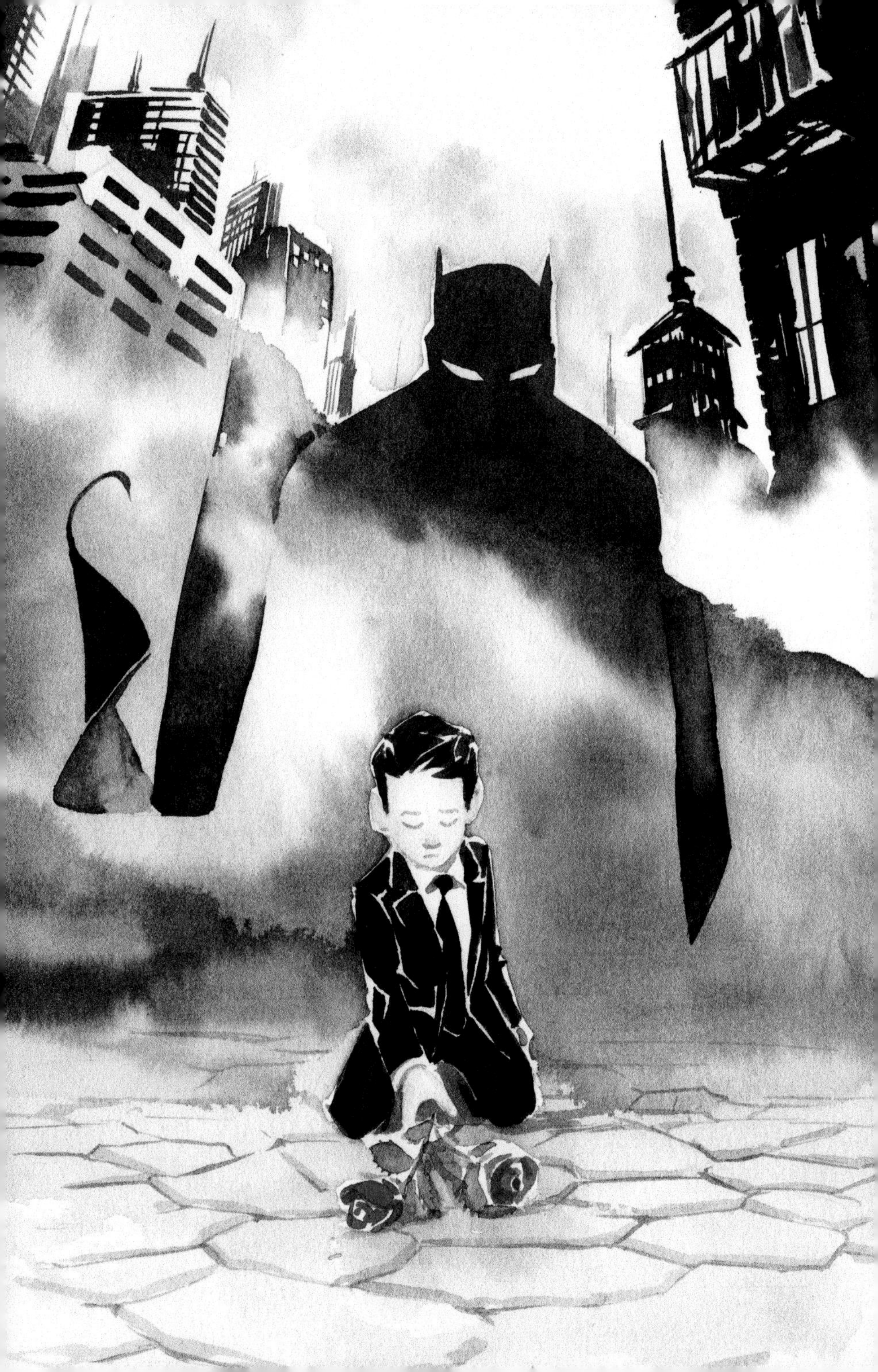

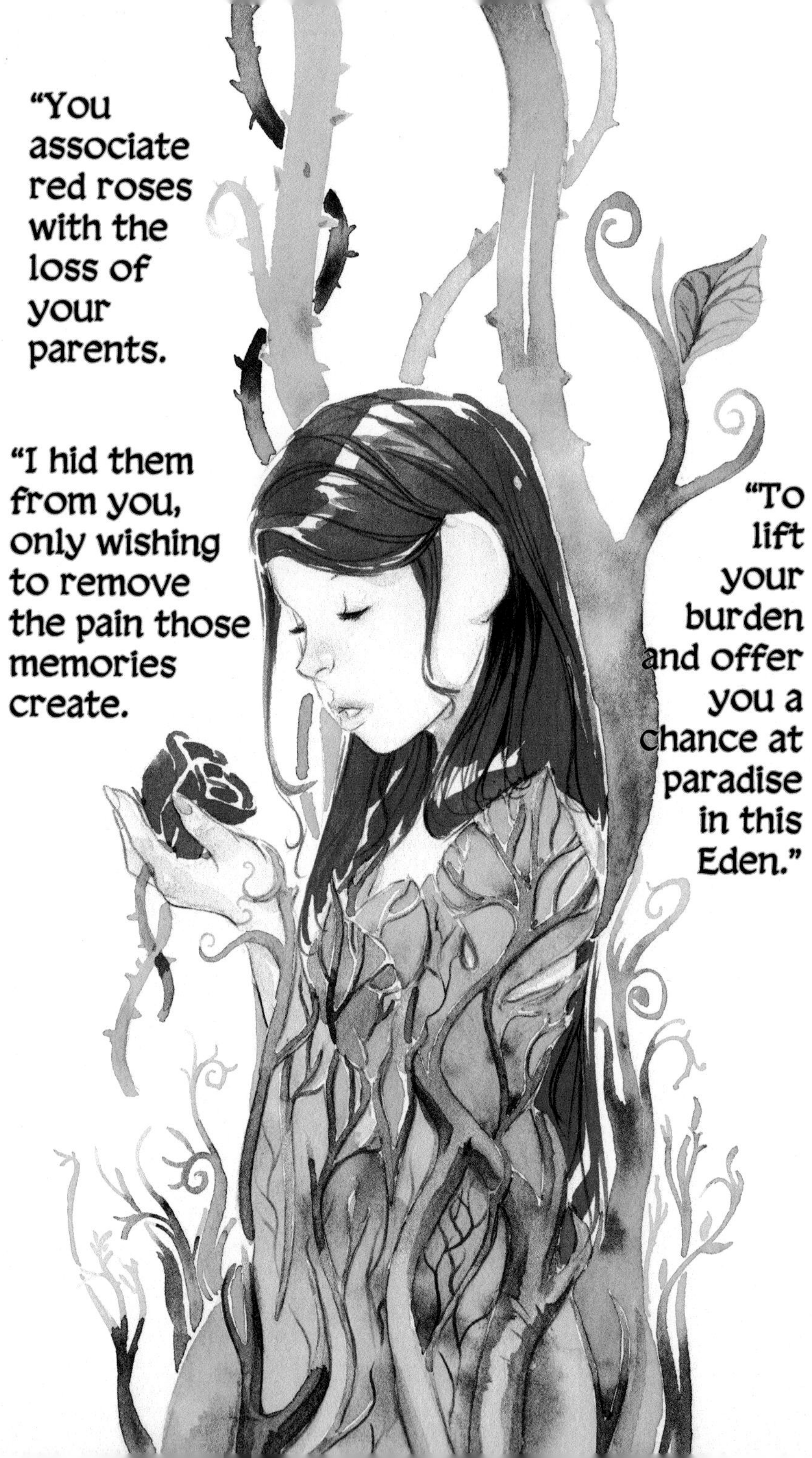
"You associate red roses with the loss of your parents.
"I hid them from you, only wishing to remove the pain those memories create.
"To lift your burden and offer you a chance at paradise in this Eden."

"I can't stay," he said with resolve. "Something remains unfinished. I'm still needed elsewhere."

"Then take these with you," spoke the green woman.

"And may you find what you are searching for."

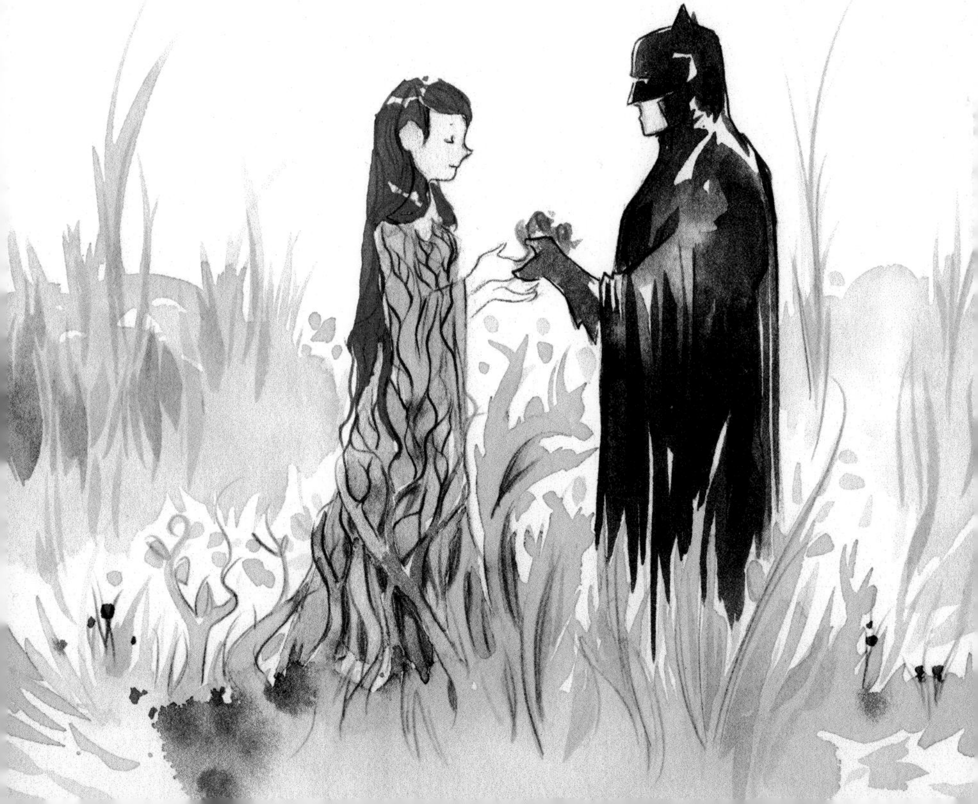

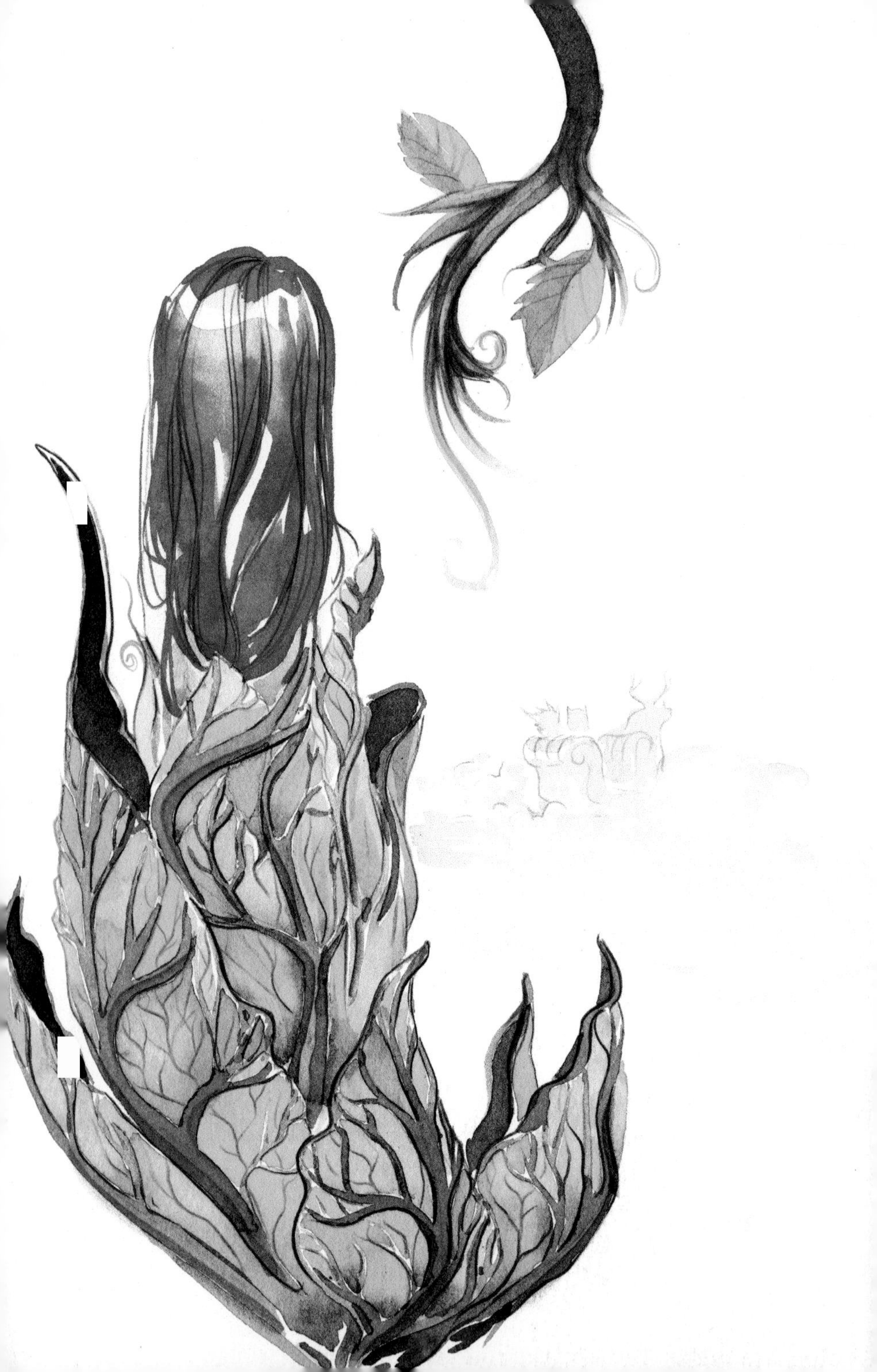

As they continued on their journey, they were visited from above.

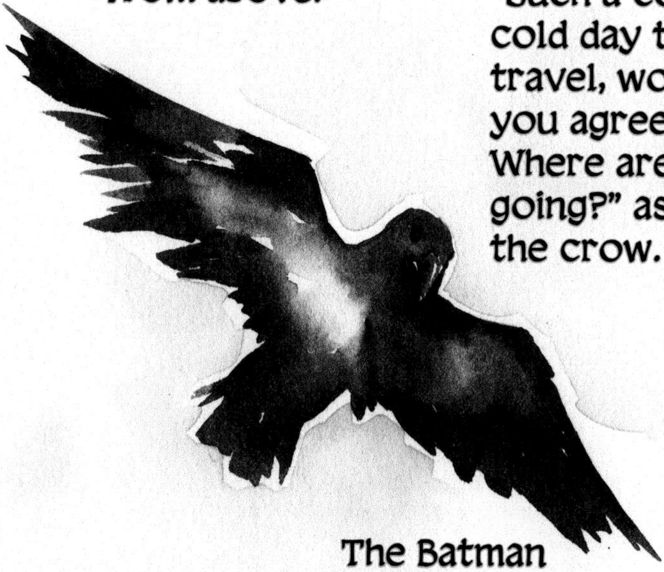

"Such a cold, cold day to travel, wouldn't you agree? Where are you going?" asked the crow.

The Batman looked at the Snow Queen before he answered, "I'm still not quite sure."

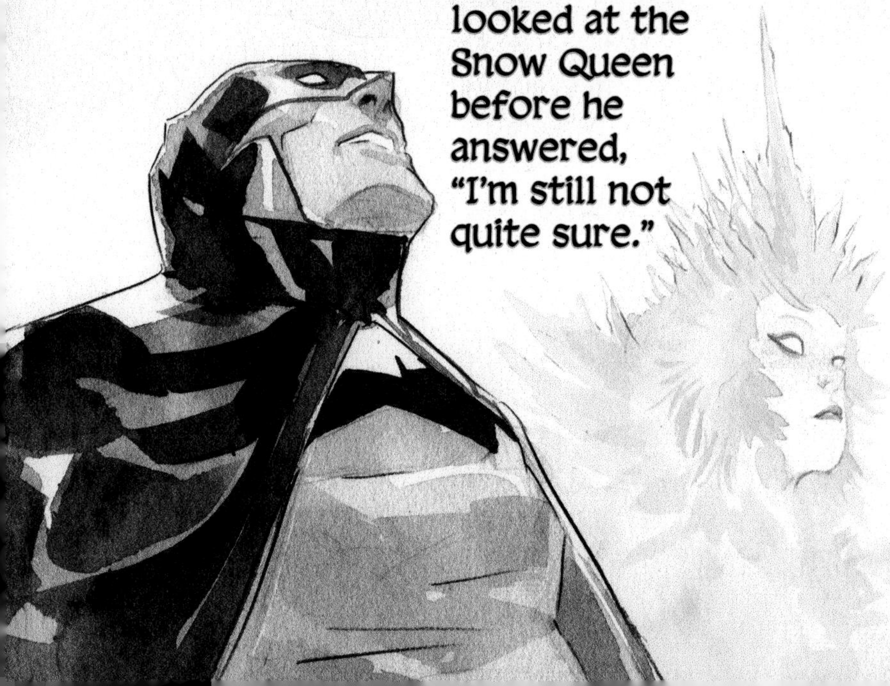

The crow hopped excitedly, unable to keep its secret.

"I know, I know!" exclaimed the crow. "What you're looking for is up ahead at the Ice Palace.

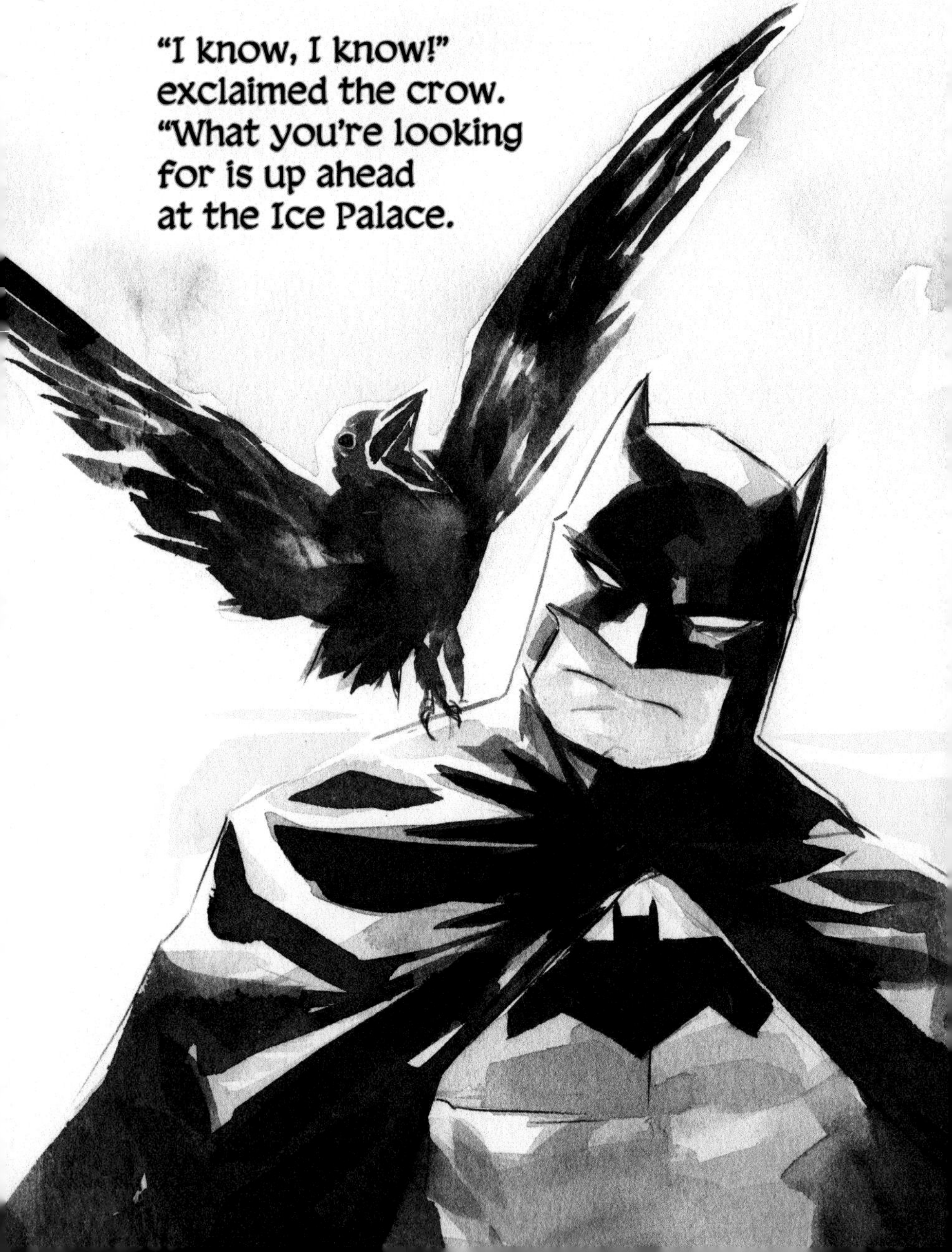

"Just wait, just wait," said the crow.
"First let me tell you a story.

"There's a man who would do anything to save the one he loved.

"But now ***he*** is the one who needs saving."

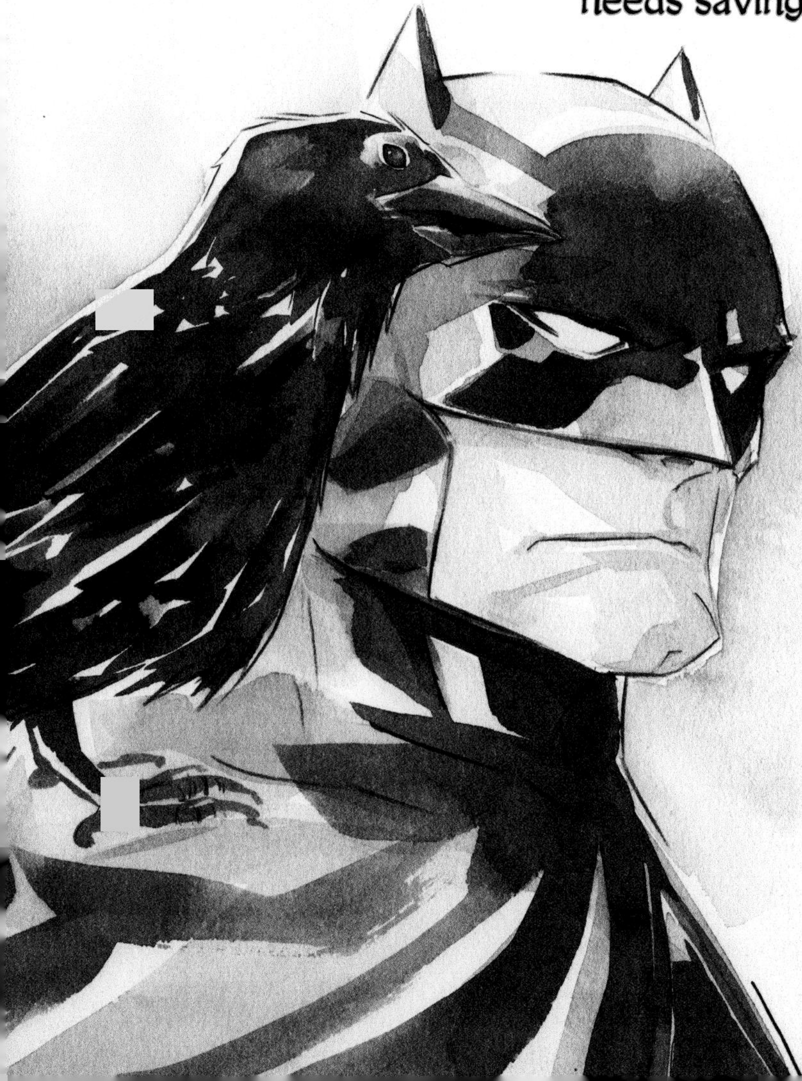

Growing impatient, the Batman asked, "Is this who we're looking for?"

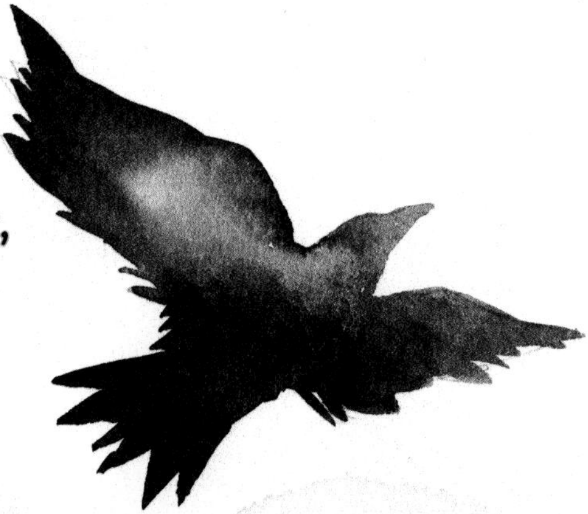

"Could be, could be. See for yourself," answered the crow. "But you'll never get inside."

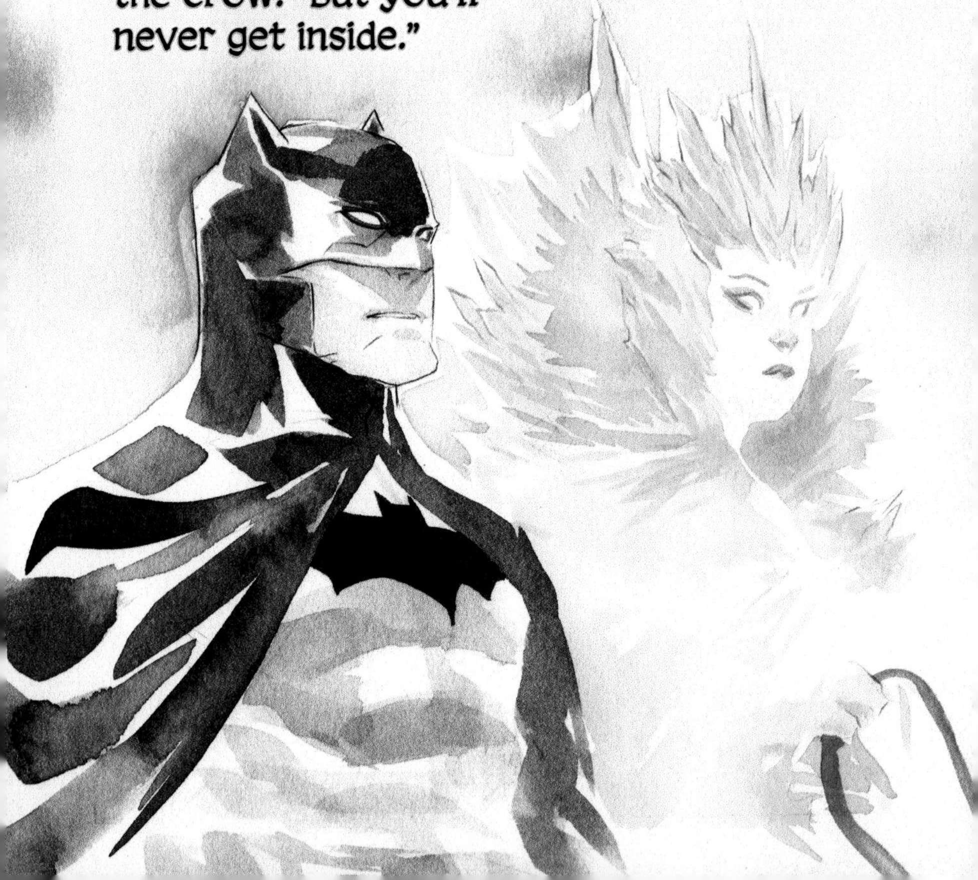

Before them towered the palace in all its icy splendor.

Giant stalagmite columns rising up to touch the sky.

Walls formed by drifted snow and window slats cut from the cold winds.

A fortress of impenetrable ice. Their final destination.

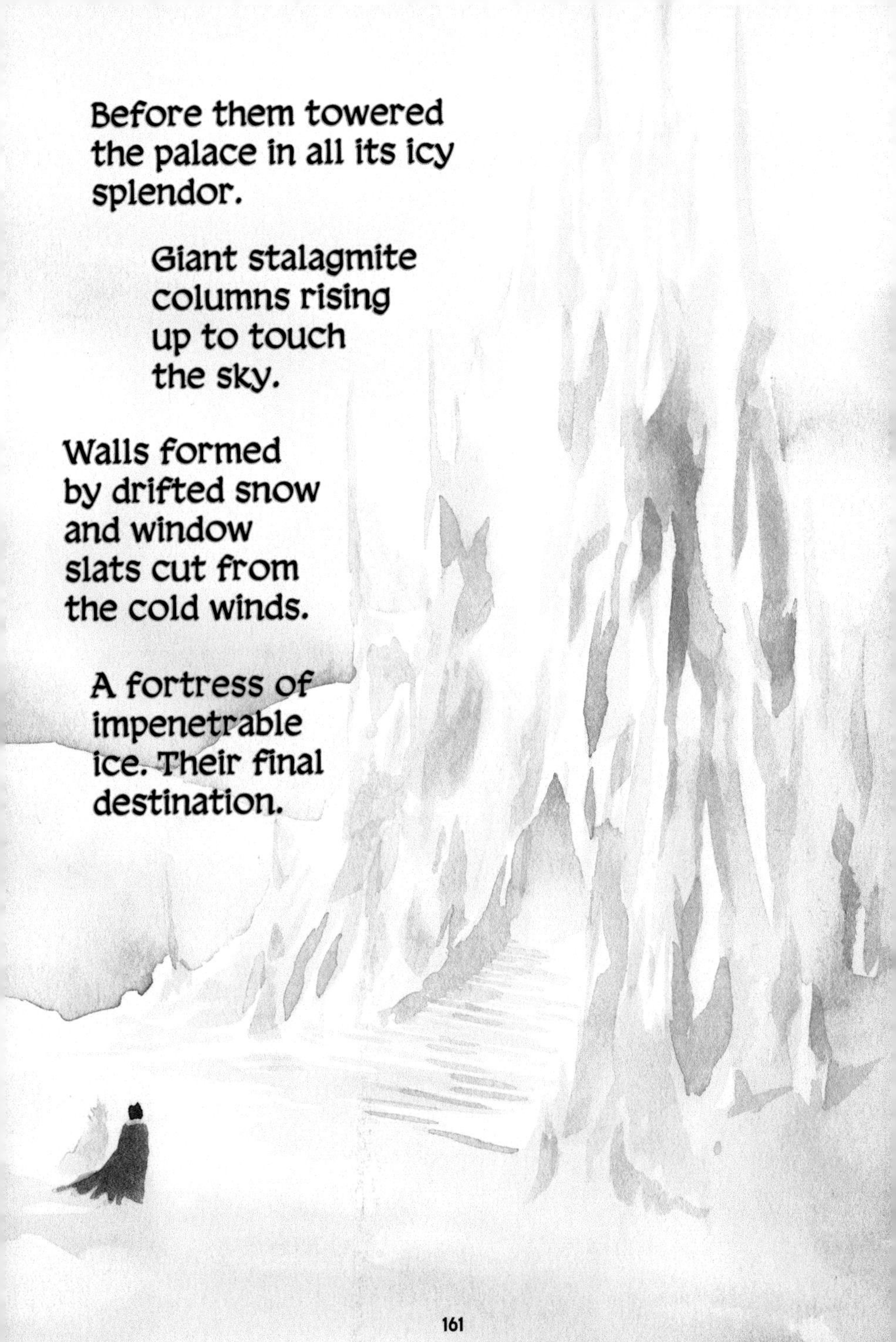

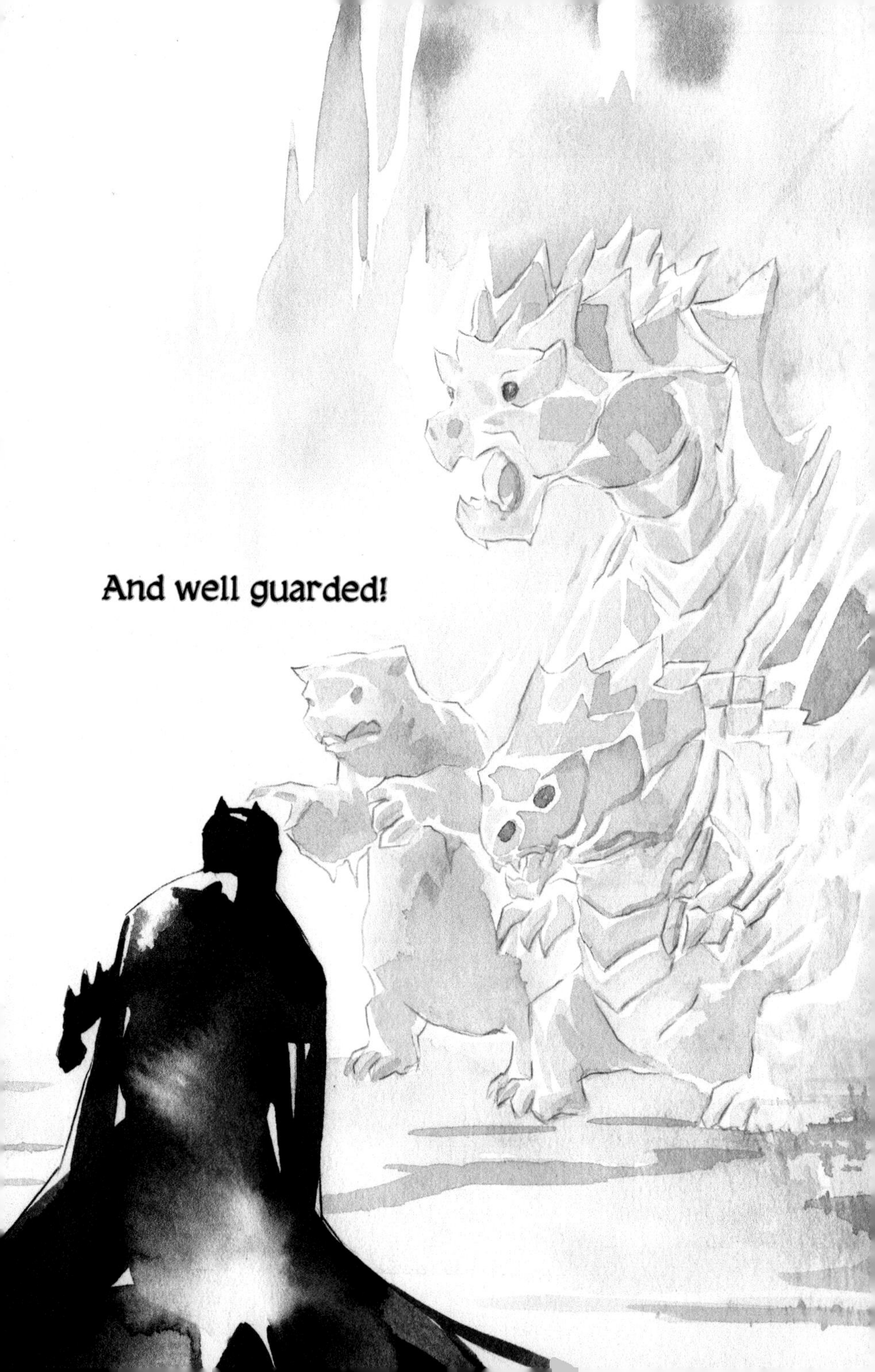
And well guarded!

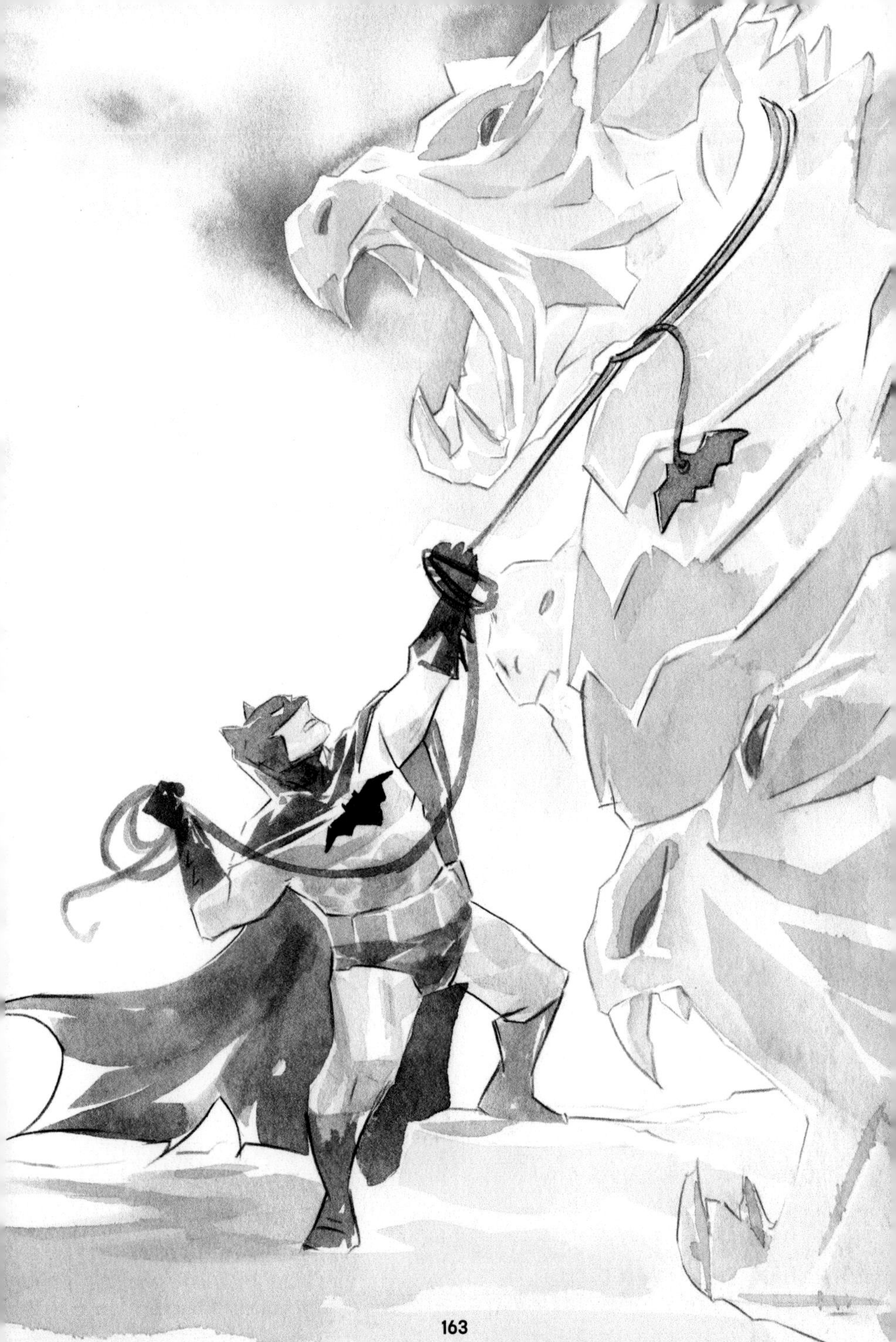

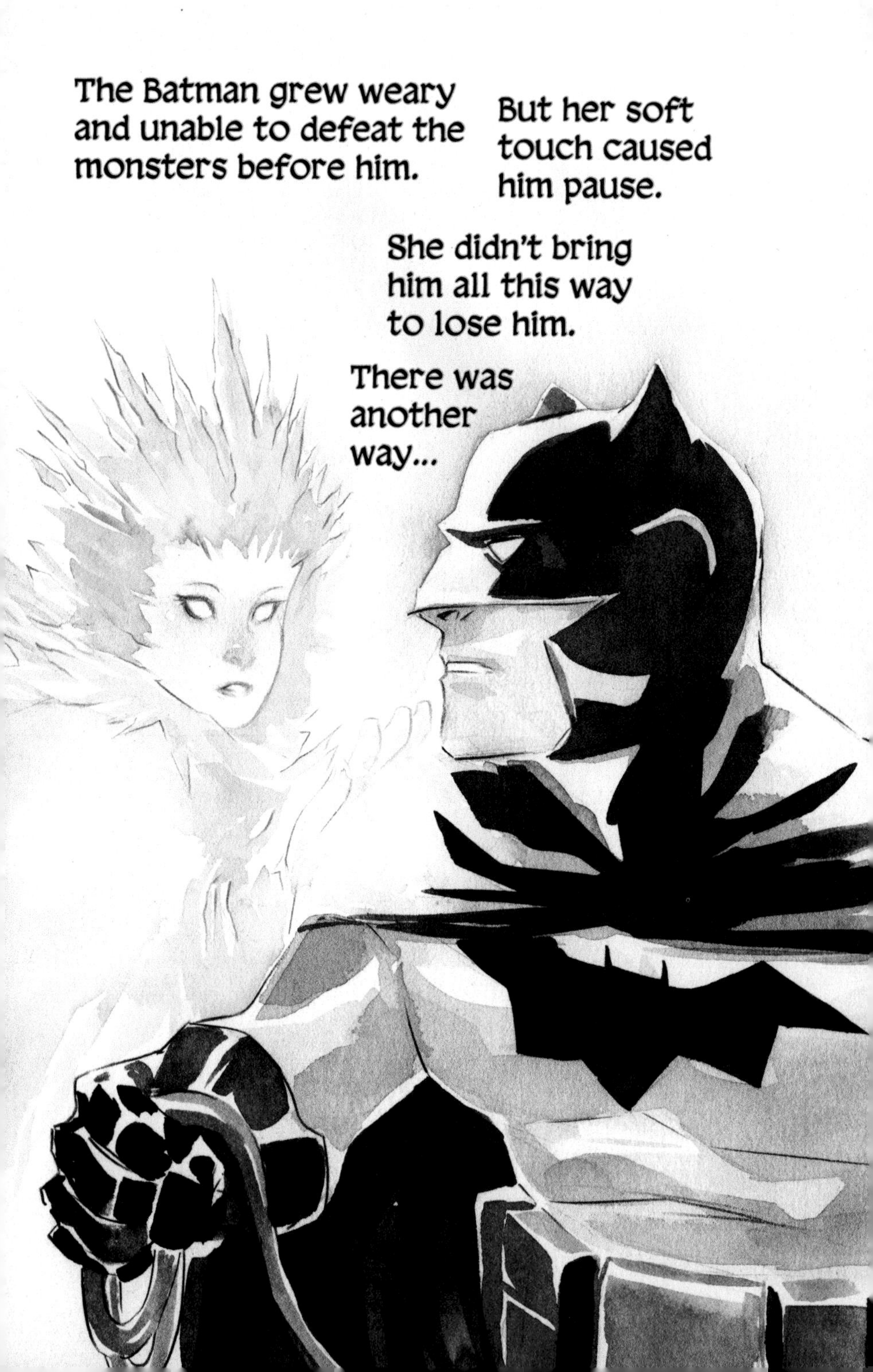
The Batman grew weary and unable to defeat the monsters before him.
But her soft touch caused him pause.
She didn't bring him all this way to lose him.
There was another way...

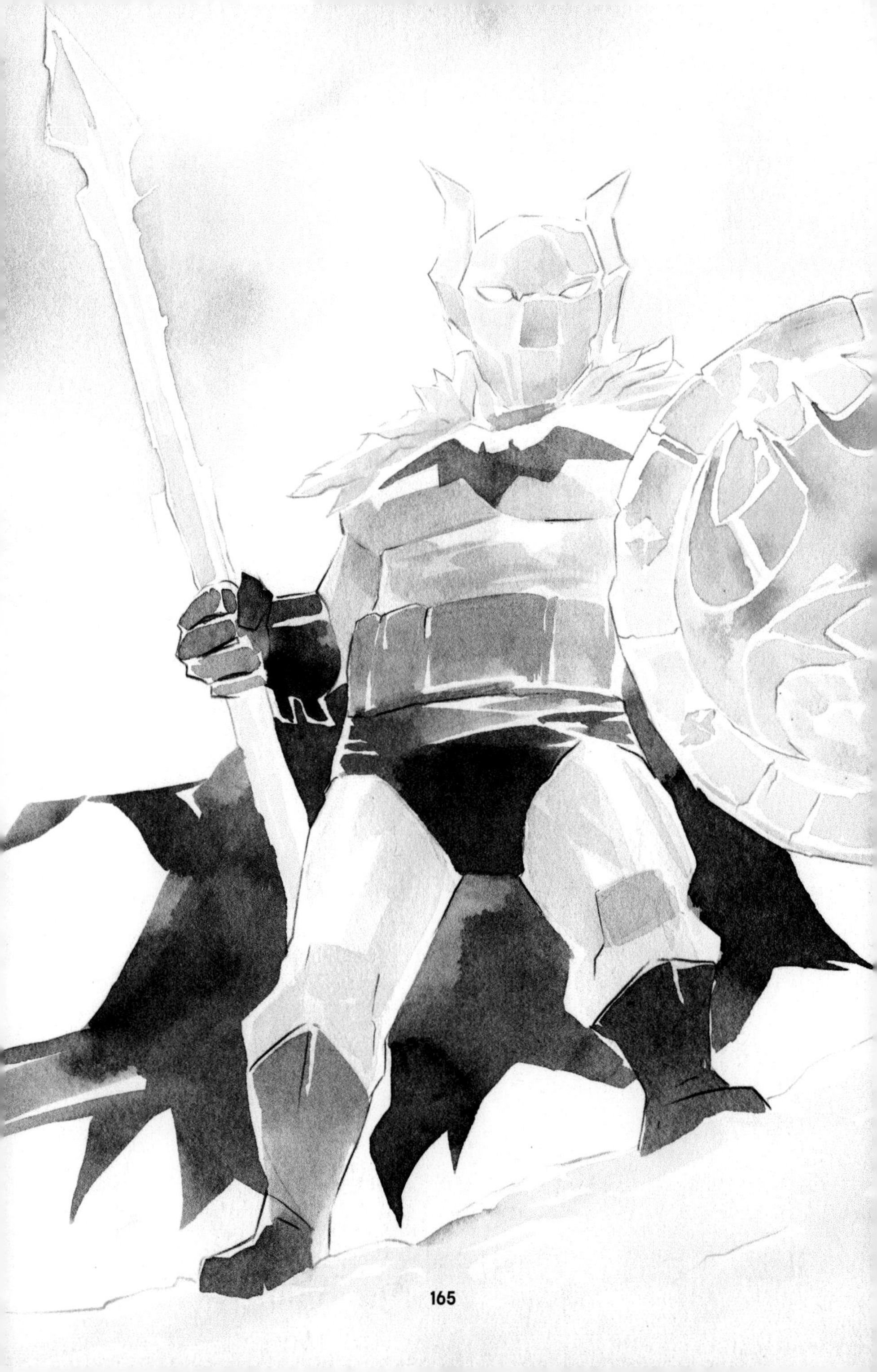

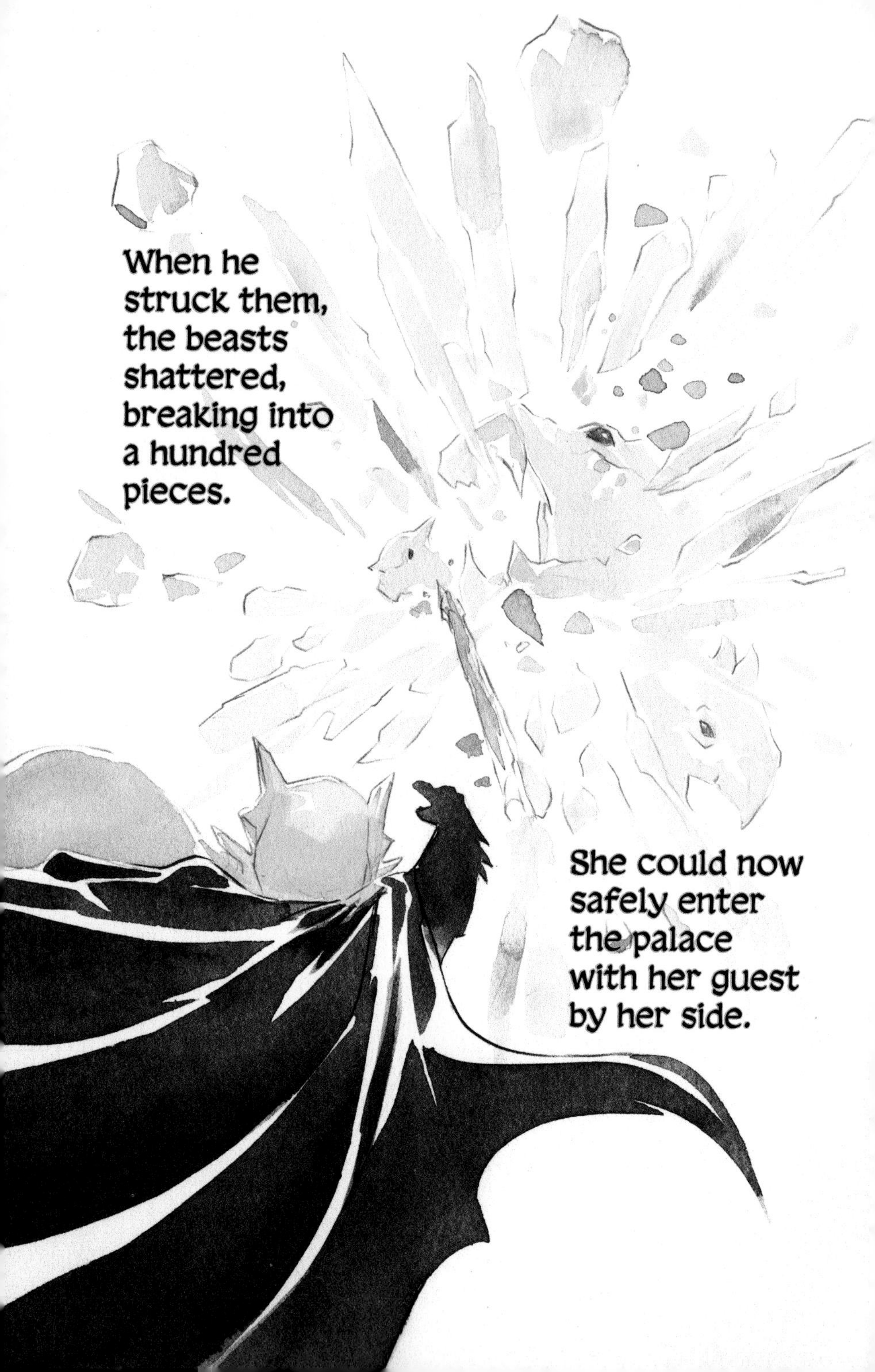
When he struck them, the beasts shattered, breaking into a hundred pieces.
She could now safely enter the palace with her guest by her side.

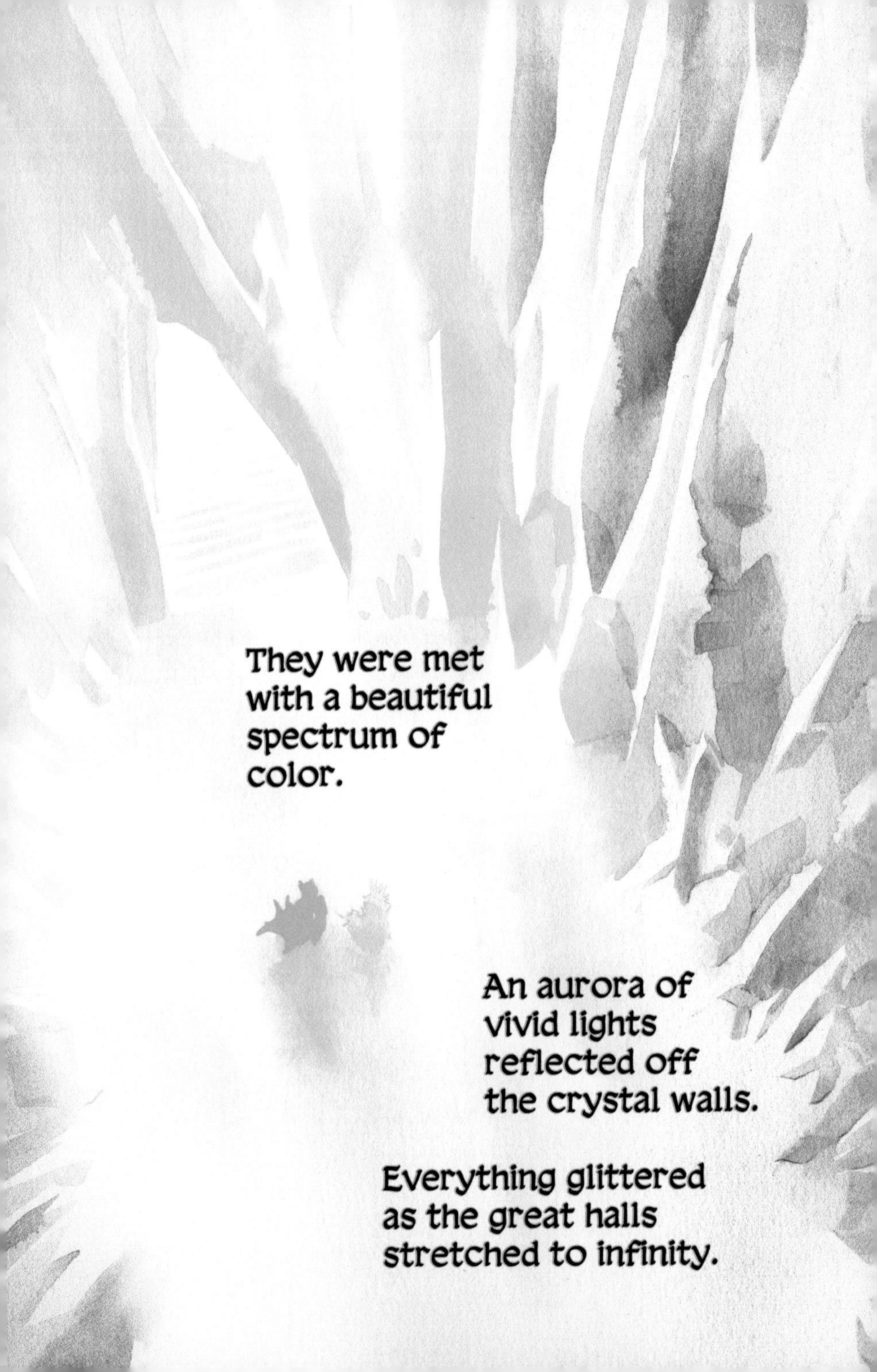
They were met with a beautiful spectrum of color.
An aurora of vivid lights reflected off the crystal walls.
Everything glittered as the great halls stretched to infinity.

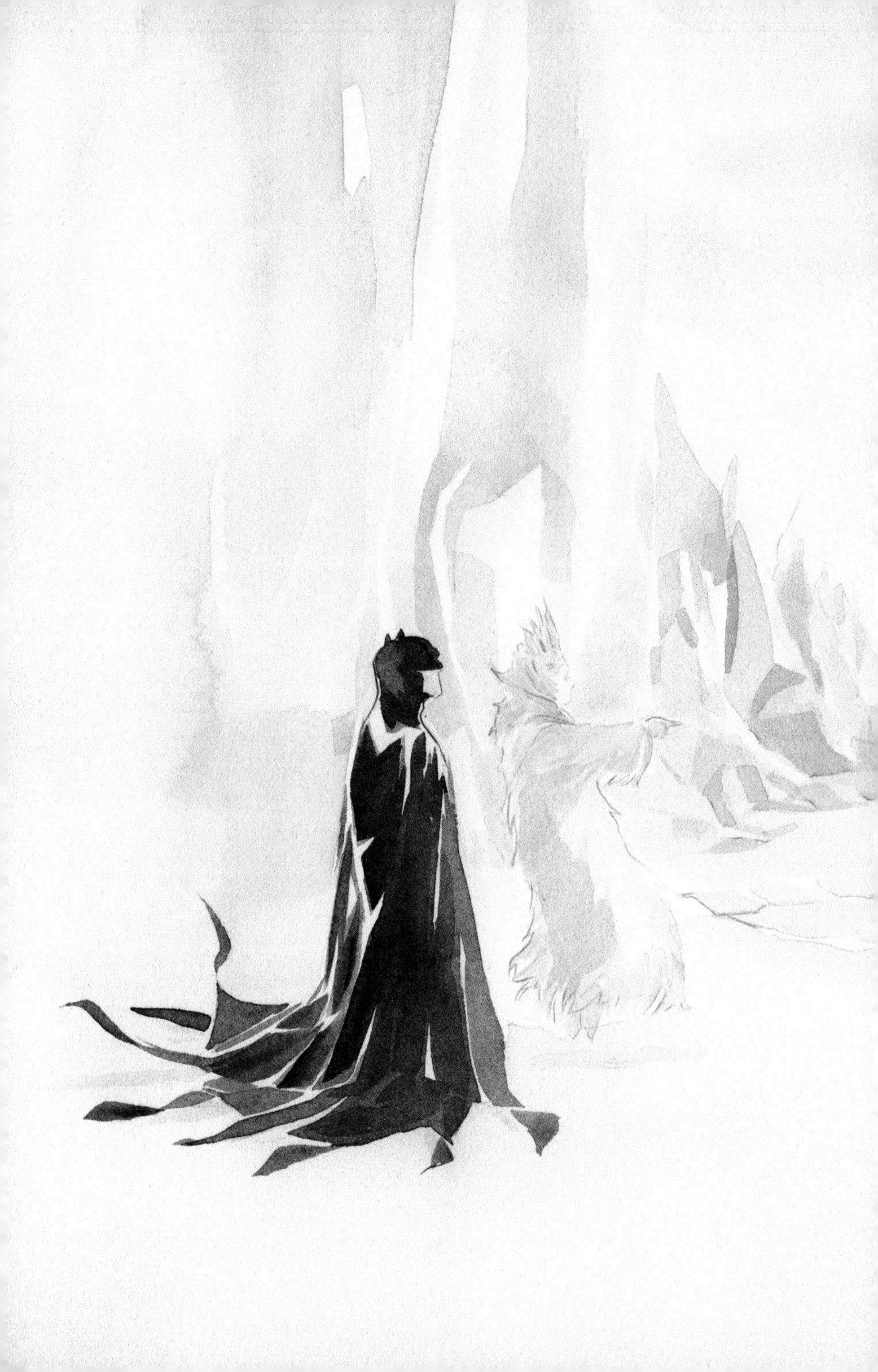

His exposed skin was cold to the touch.

His heart was silent.

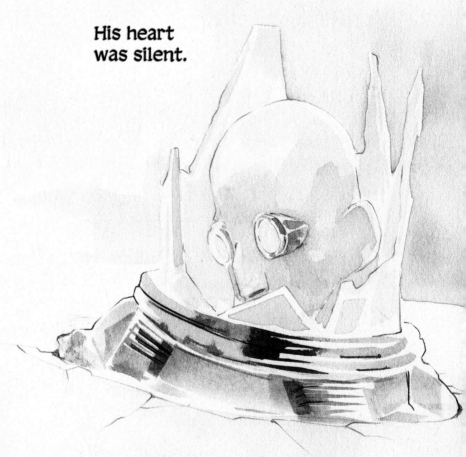

The missing man did not move.

But the other
man did.

And was joined
by majesty.

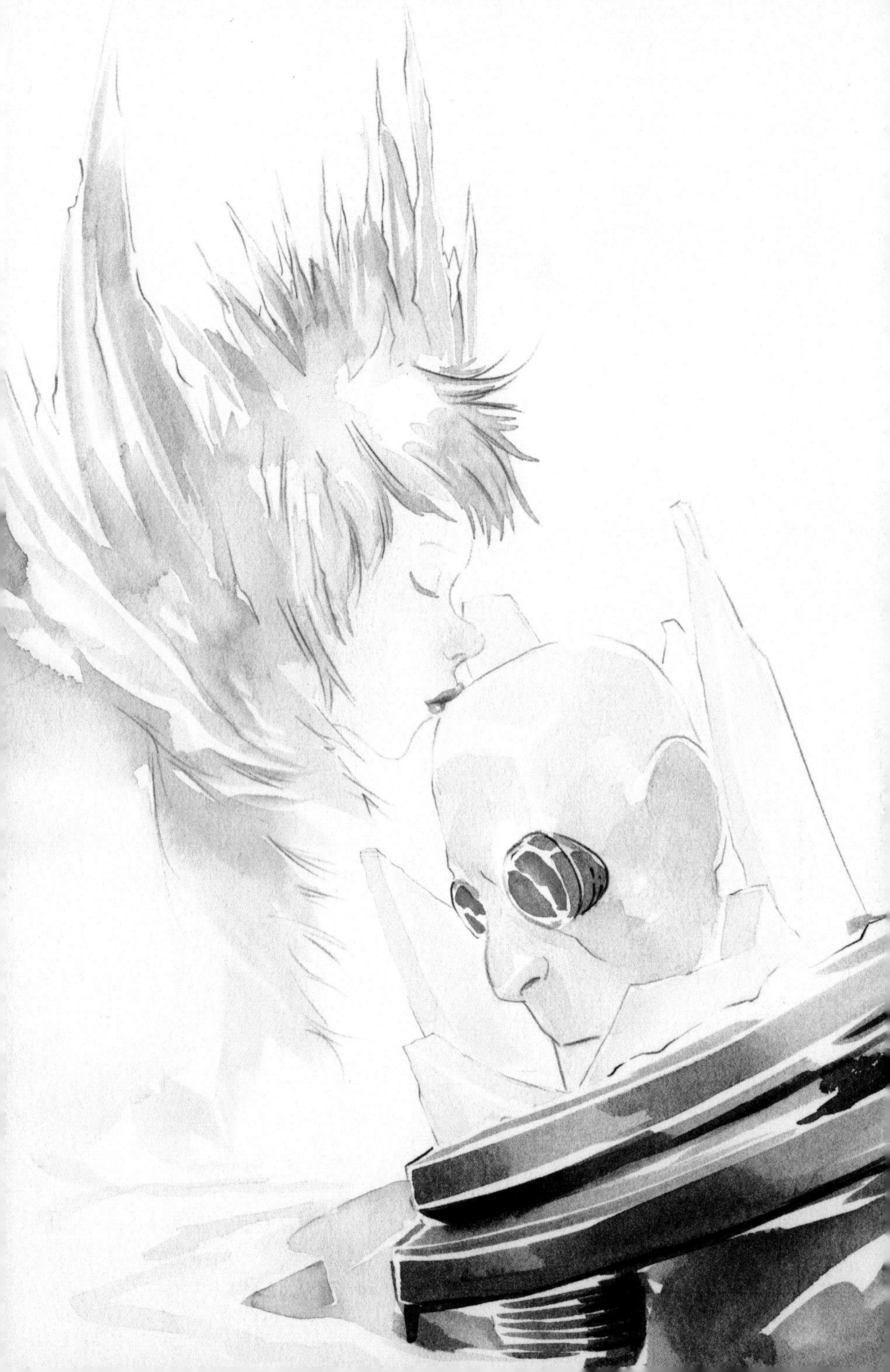

One prison opened.

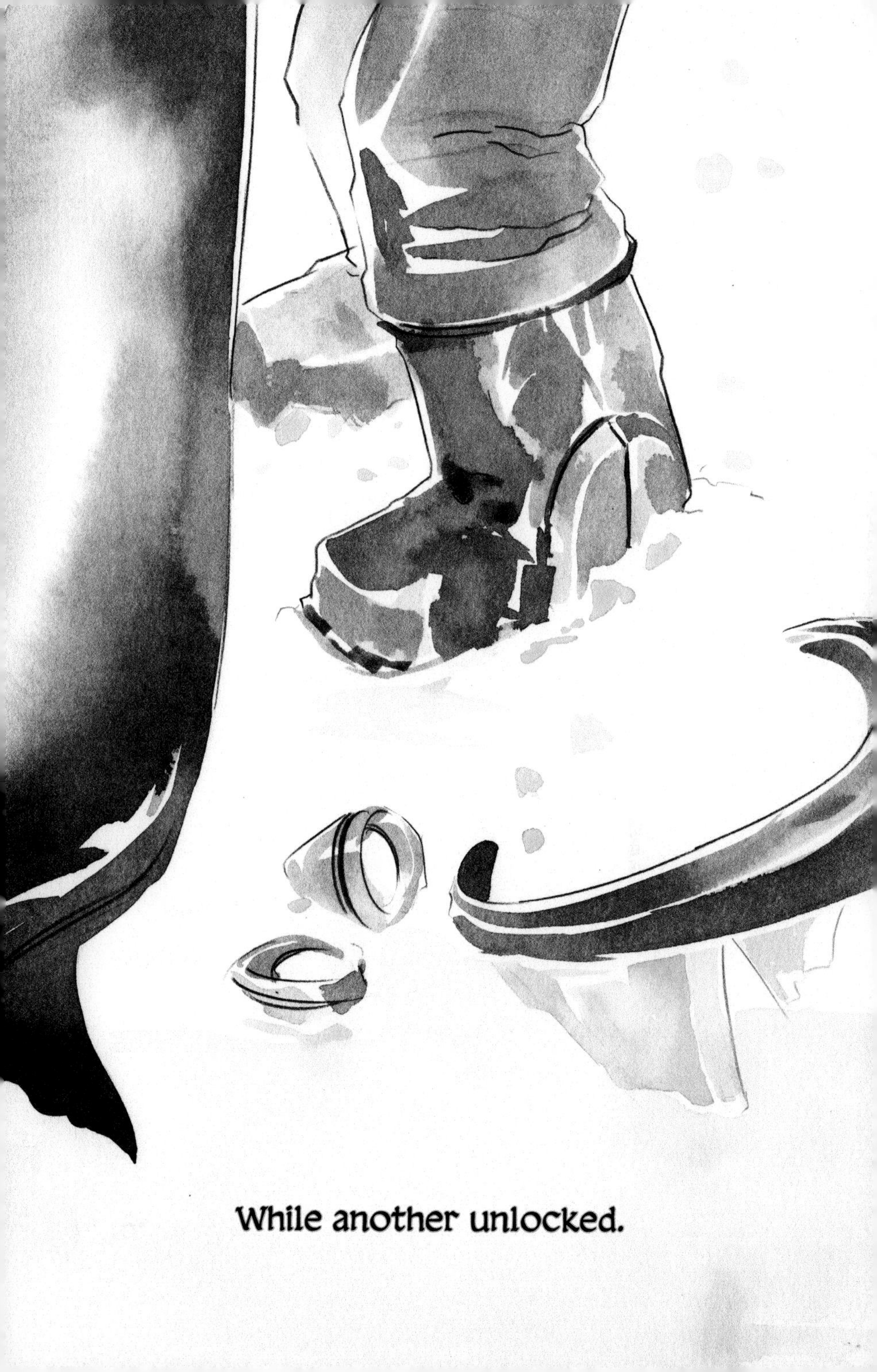
While another unlocked.

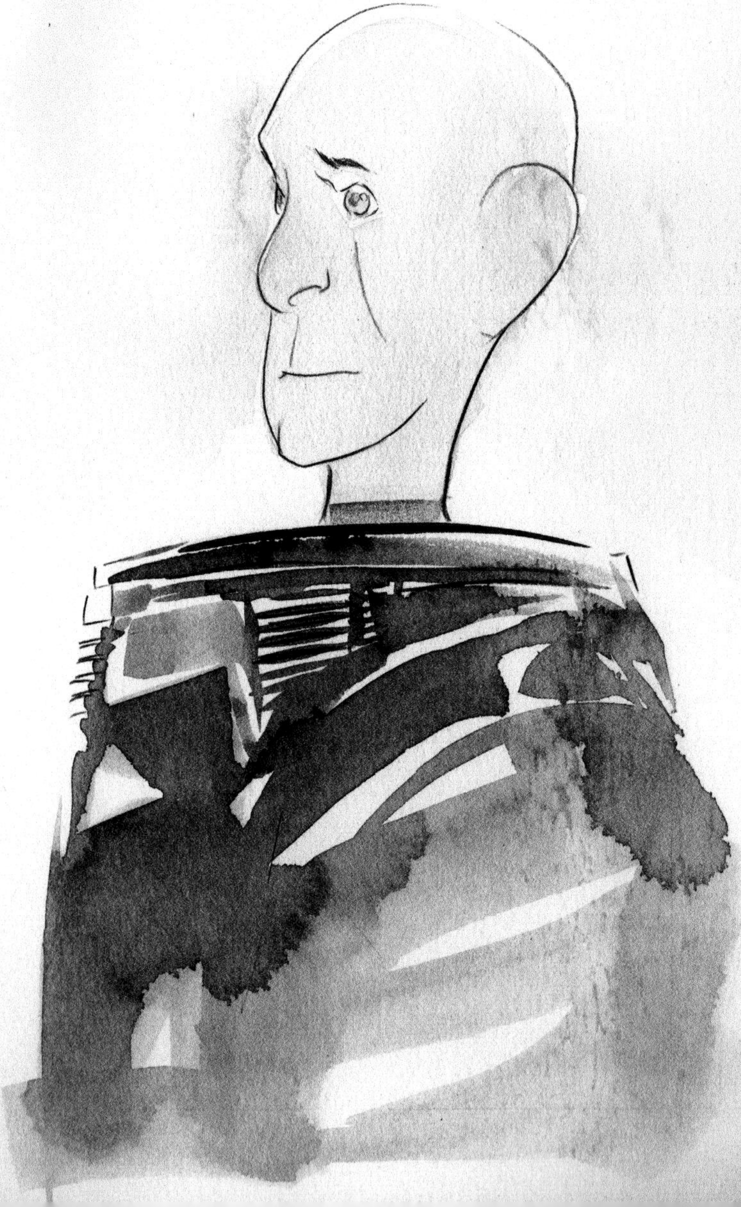

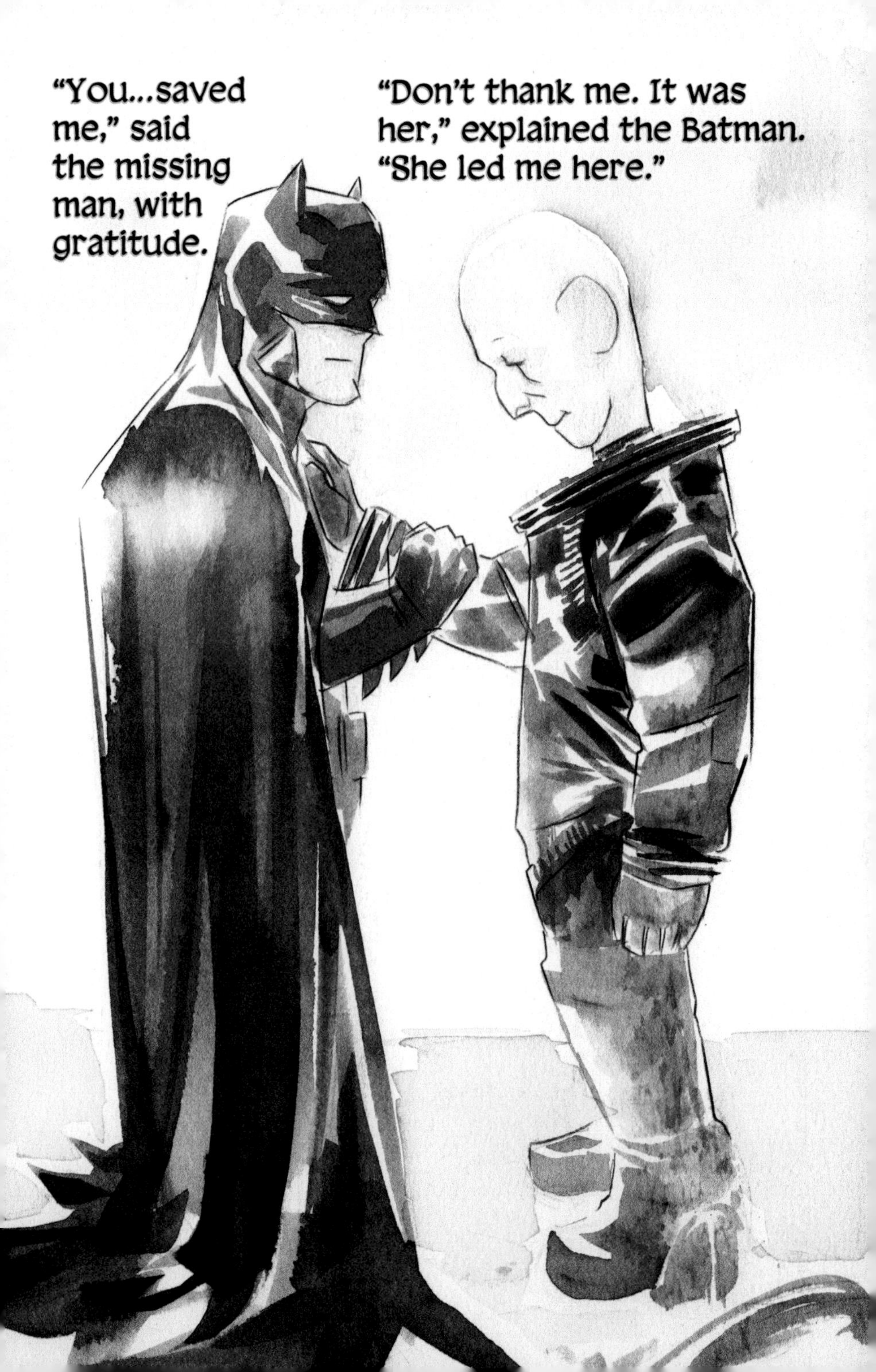
"You...saved me," said the missing man, with gratitude.
"Don't thank me. It was her," explained the Batman. "She led me here."

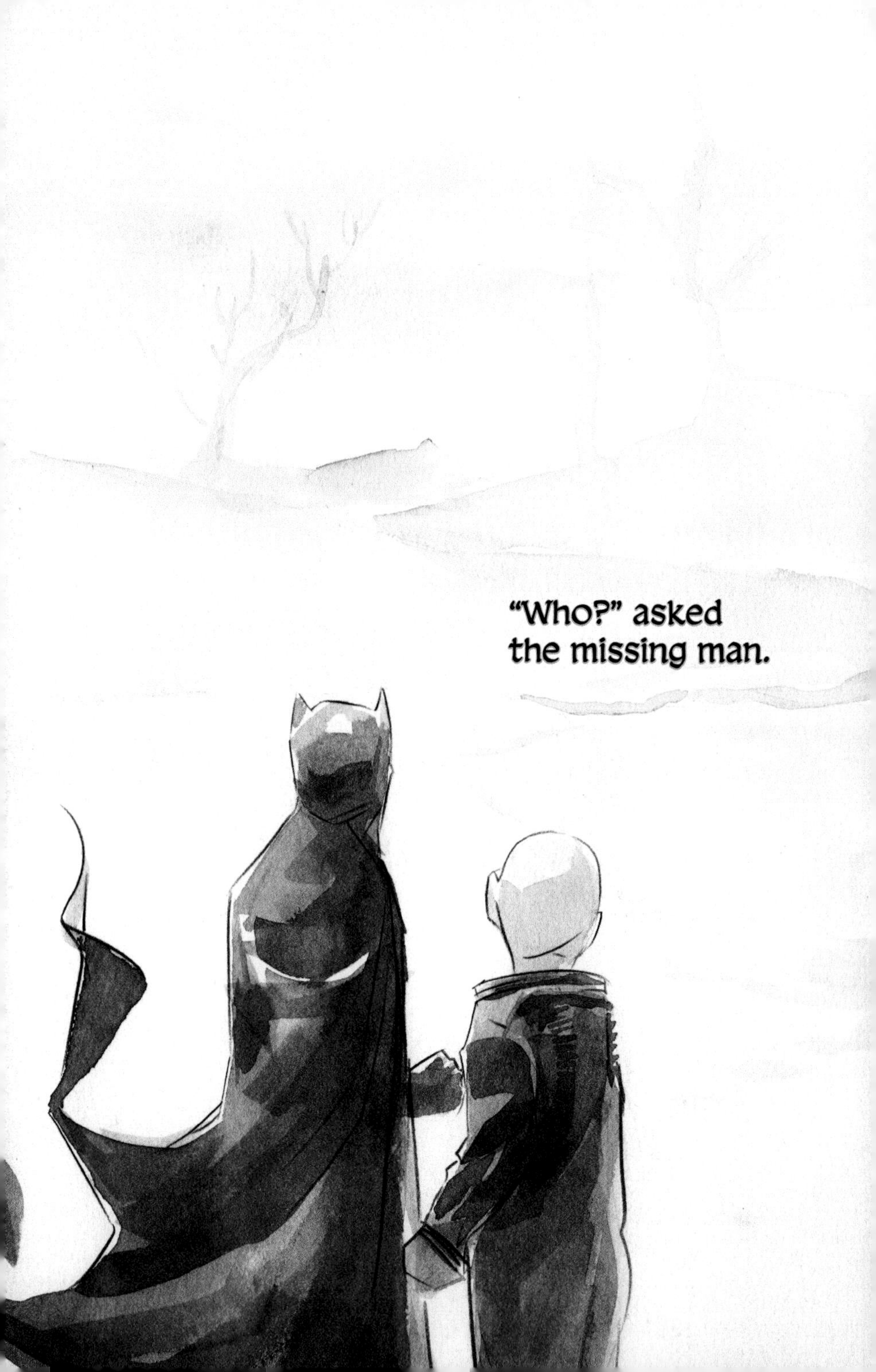
"Who?" asked
the missing man.

"Why were you here?" asked the Batman.

"This place holds special meaning," the missing man expressed. "It's where she first skated. It's where we first met.

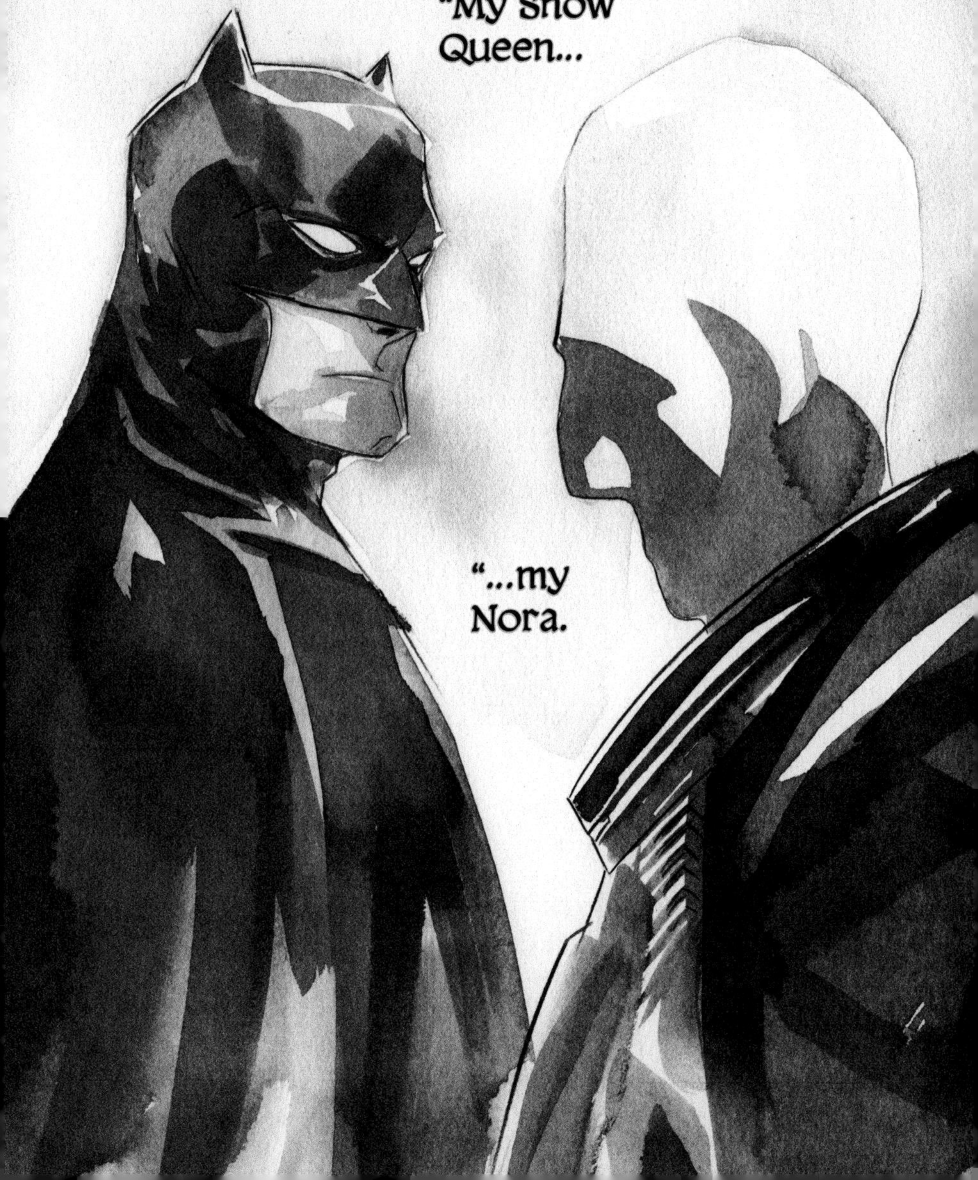
"My Snow Queen...
"...my Nora.

"I realize now, my memories of her have kept me frozen in time," said the missing man.

The Batman agreed. "Sometimes it's not just bad memories that stop us from living, but good ones, too."

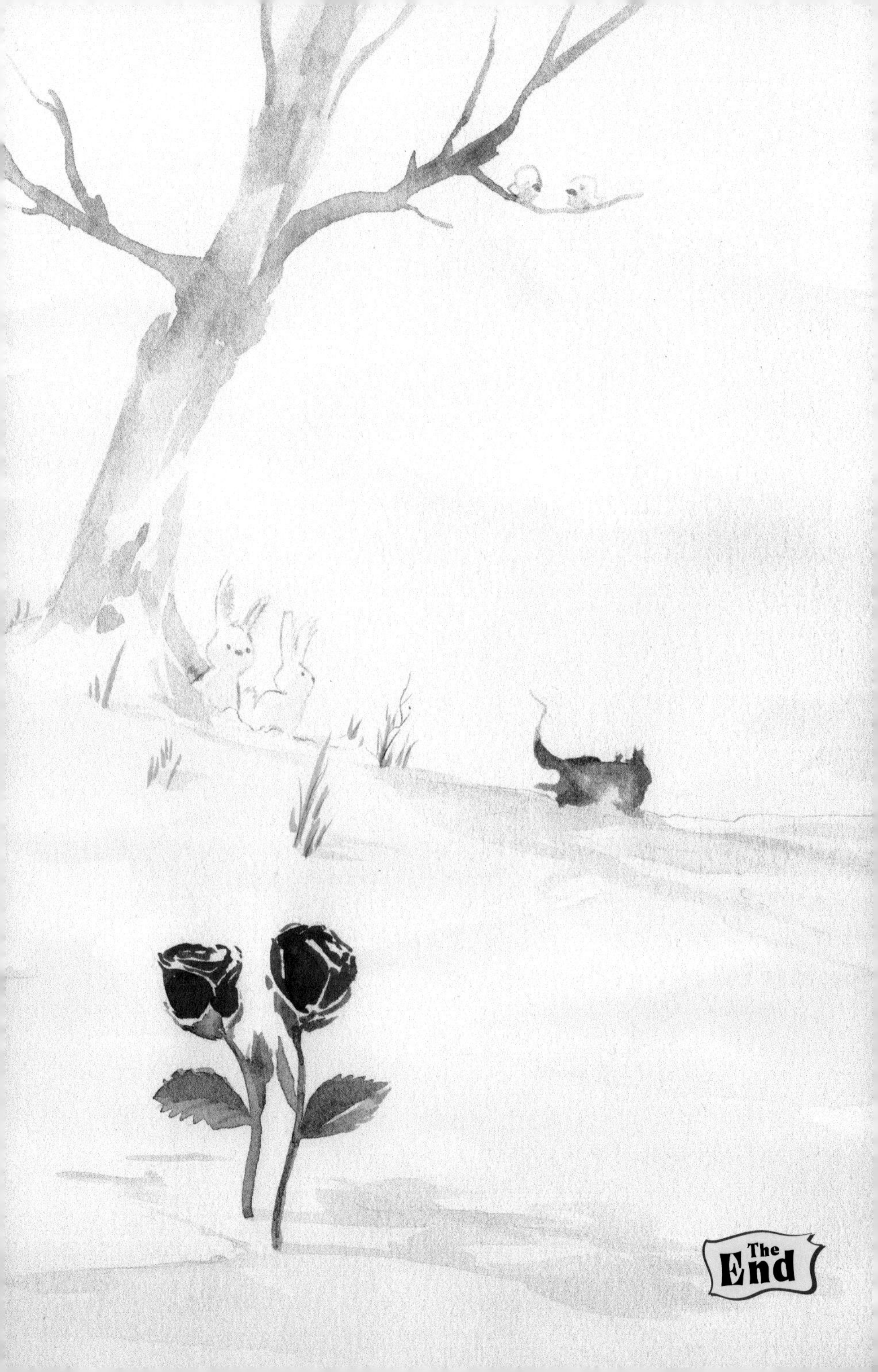
The End

Derek Fridolfs has been nominated for an Eisner Award
for co-writing *Batman: Li'l Gotham* and is the #1 *New York Times*
bestselling writer of the DC Comics: Secret Hero Society series.
In addition, he's written and provided art for titles including *Teen
Titans Go!*, *Scooby-Doo, Where Are You?*, *Looney Tunes*, *Adventure
Time*, *Regular Show*, and *Teenage Mutant Ninja Turtles*.

Dustin Nguyen is a *New York Times* bestselling and Eisner
Award-winning American comics creator best known for his work
on Image Comics' *Descender* and *Ascender*, DC Comics' *Batman:
Li'l Gotham*, Scholastic's DC Comics: Secret Hero Society series,
and many other things Gotham-related.

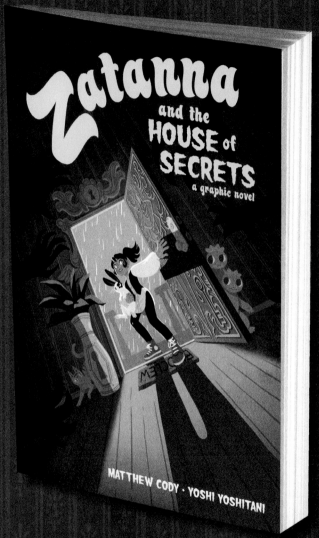

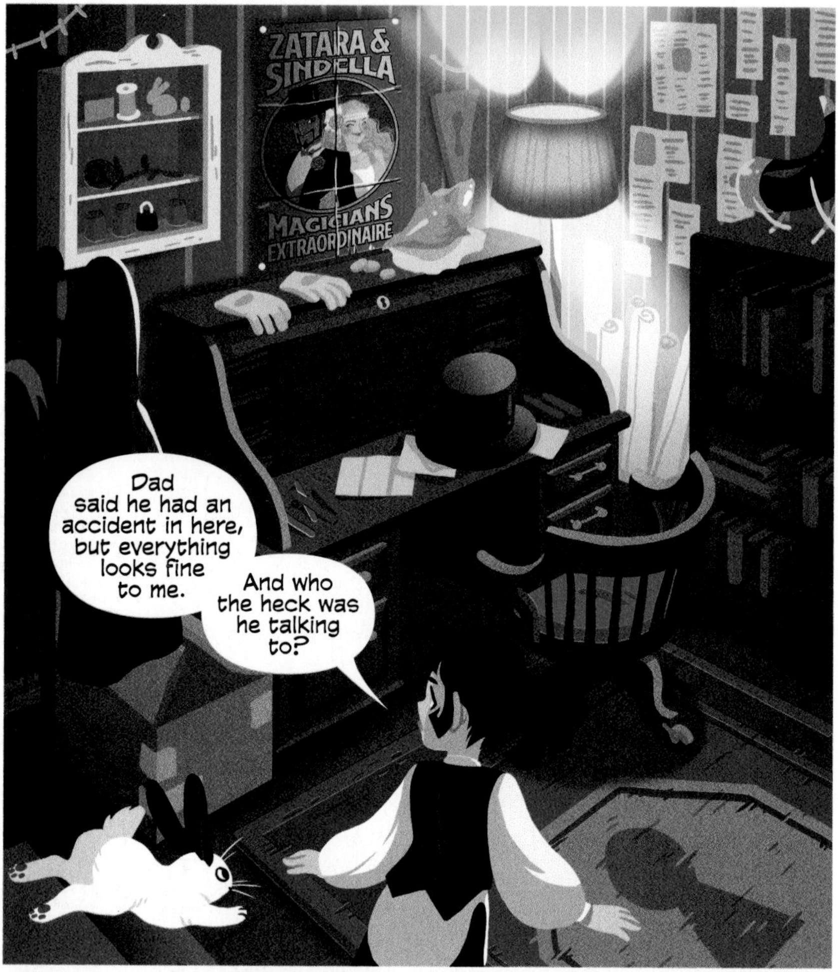
ZATARA & SINDELLA
MAGICIANS EXTRAORDINAIRE
Dad said he had an accident in here, but everything looks fine to me.
And who the heck was he talking to?

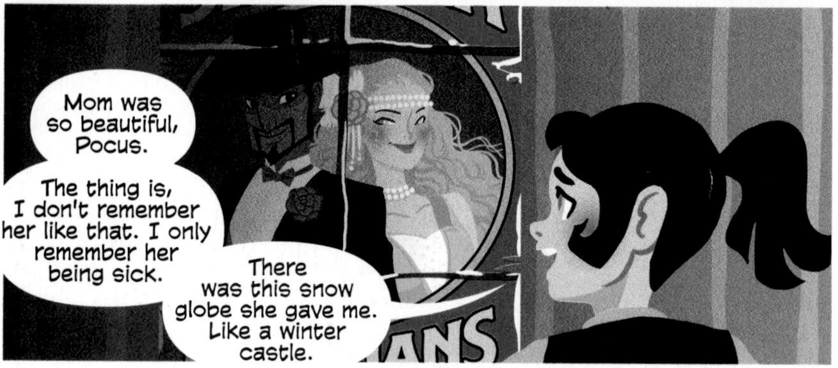
Mom was so beautiful, Pocus.
The thing is, I don't remember her like that. I only remember her being sick.
There was this snow globe she gave me. Like a winter castle.

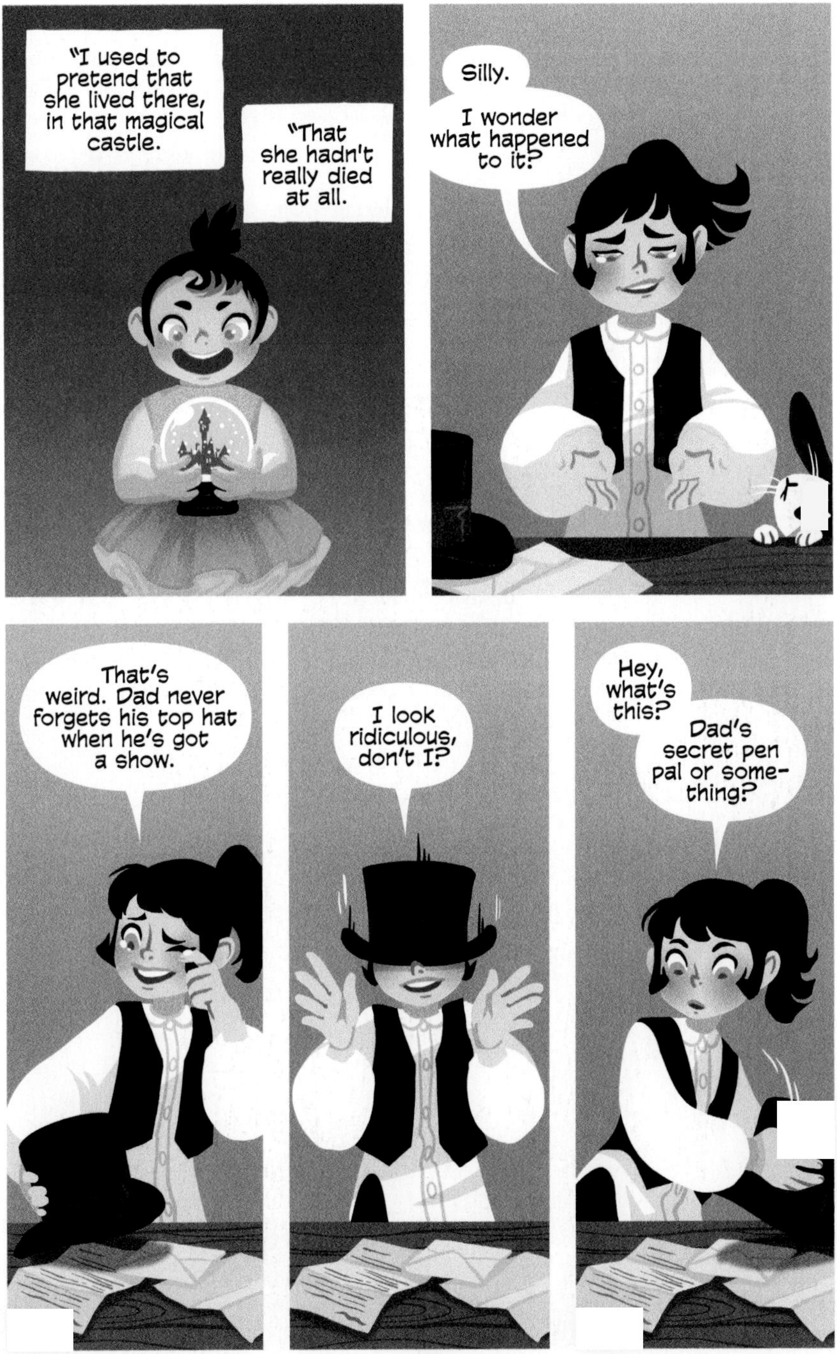
"I used to pretend that she lived there, in that magical castle.
"That she hadn't really died at all.
Silly.
I wonder what happened to it?
That's weird. Dad never forgets his top hat when he's got a show.
I look ridiculous, don't I?
Hey, what's this?
Dad's secret pen pal or some-thing?

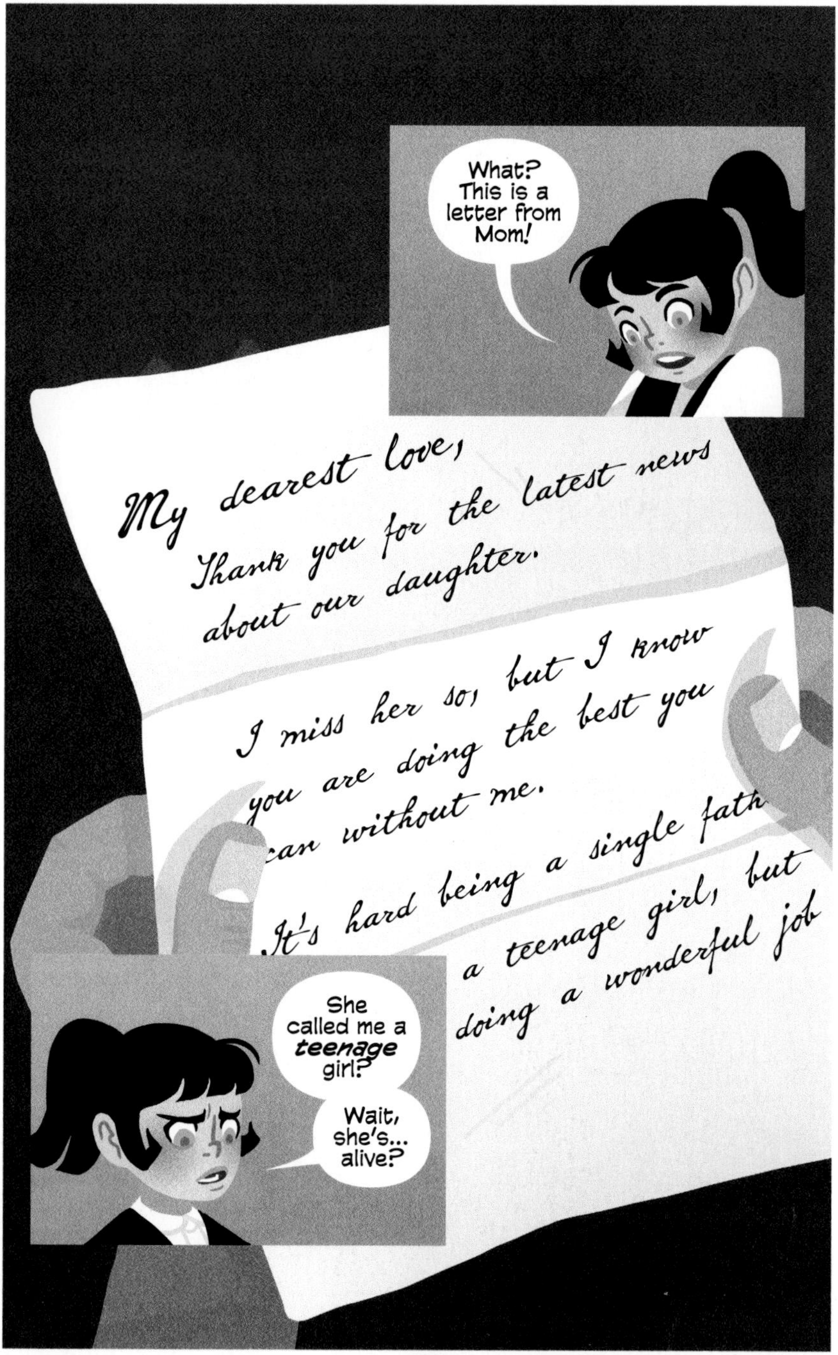

What? This is a letter from Mom!
My dearest love,
Thank you for the latest news about our daughter.
I miss her so, but I know you are doing the best you can without me.
It's hard being a single fath
a teenage girl, but
doing a wonderful job
She called me a *teenage* girl?
Wait, she's... alive?

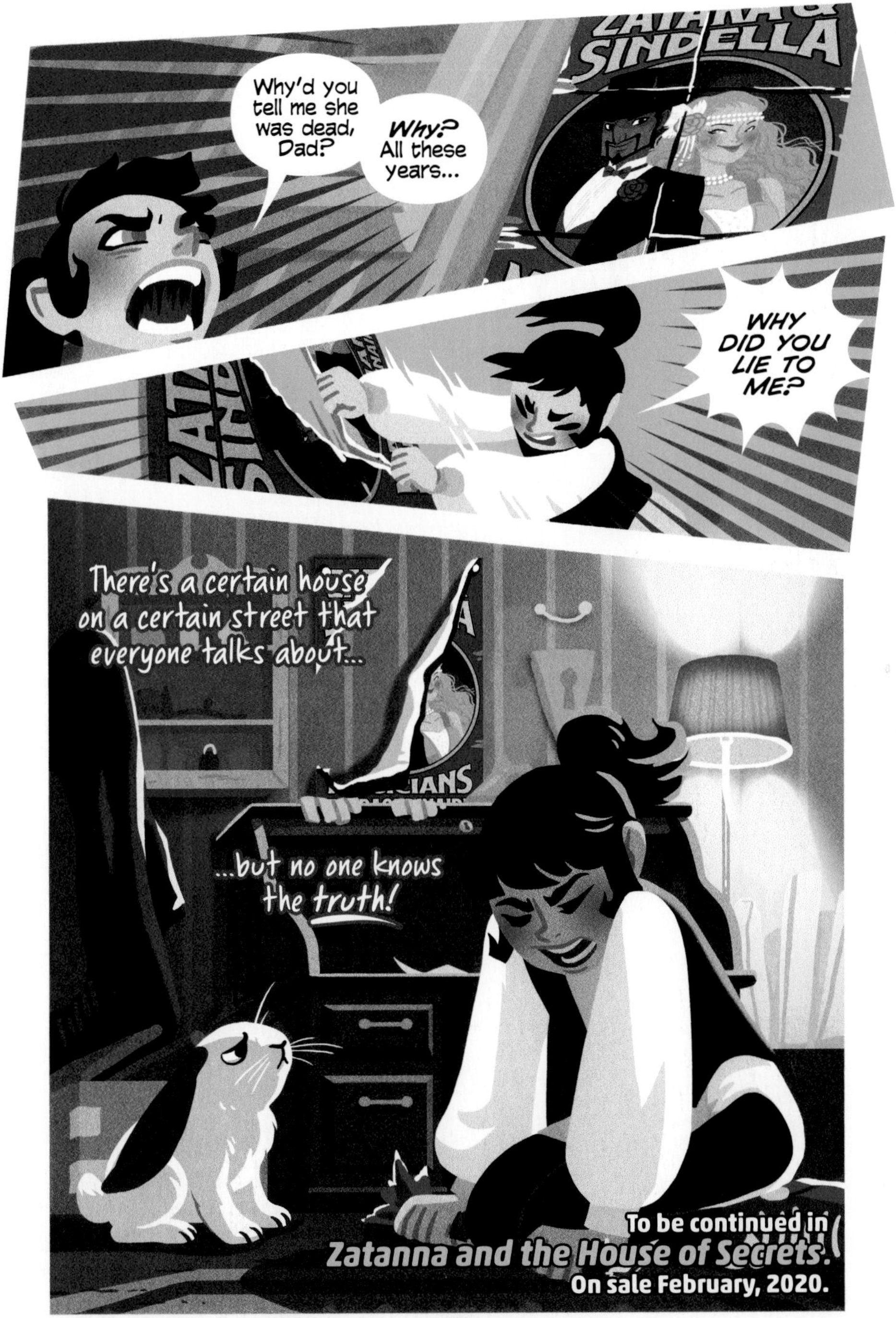
ZATANNA &
SINDELLA
Why'd you tell me she was dead, Dad?
Why? All these years...
WHY DID YOU LIE TO ME?
MAGICIANS
There's a certain house on a certain street that everyone talks about...
...but no one knows the *truth!*
To be continued in
Zatanna and the House of Secrets.
On sale February, 2020.

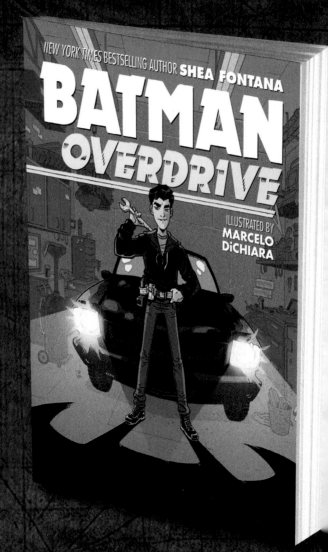

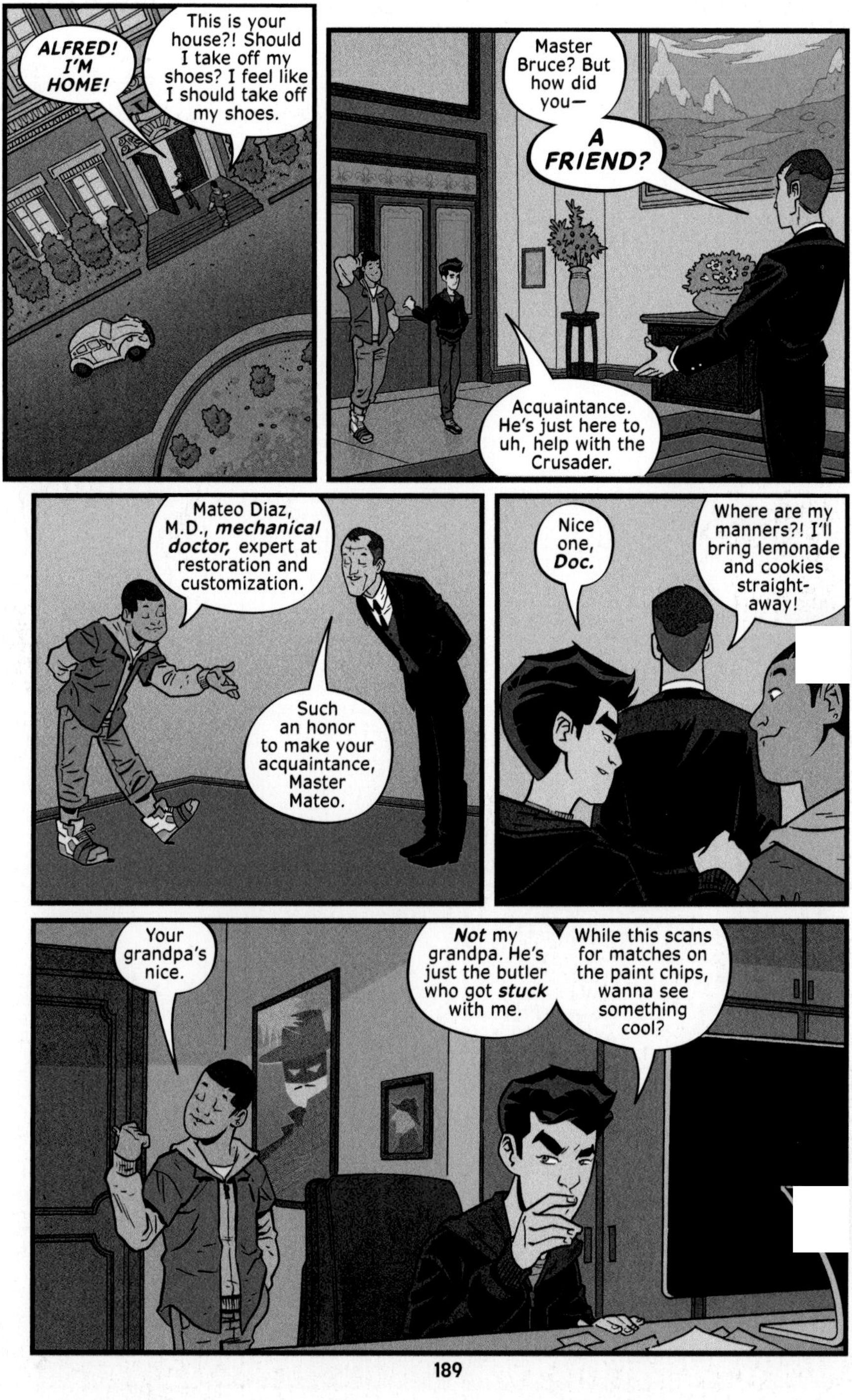
ALFRED! I'M HOME!
This is your house?! Should I take off my shoes? I feel like I should take off my shoes.
Master Bruce? But how did you—
A FRIEND?
Acquaintance. He's just here to, uh, help with the Crusader.
Mateo Diaz, M.D., mechanical doctor, expert at restoration and customization.
Such an honor to make your acquaintance, Master Mateo.
Nice one, Doc.
Where are my manners?! I'll bring lemonade and cookies straight-away!
Your grandpa's nice.
Not my grandpa. He's just the butler who got stuck with me.
While this scans for matches on the paint chips, wanna see something cool?

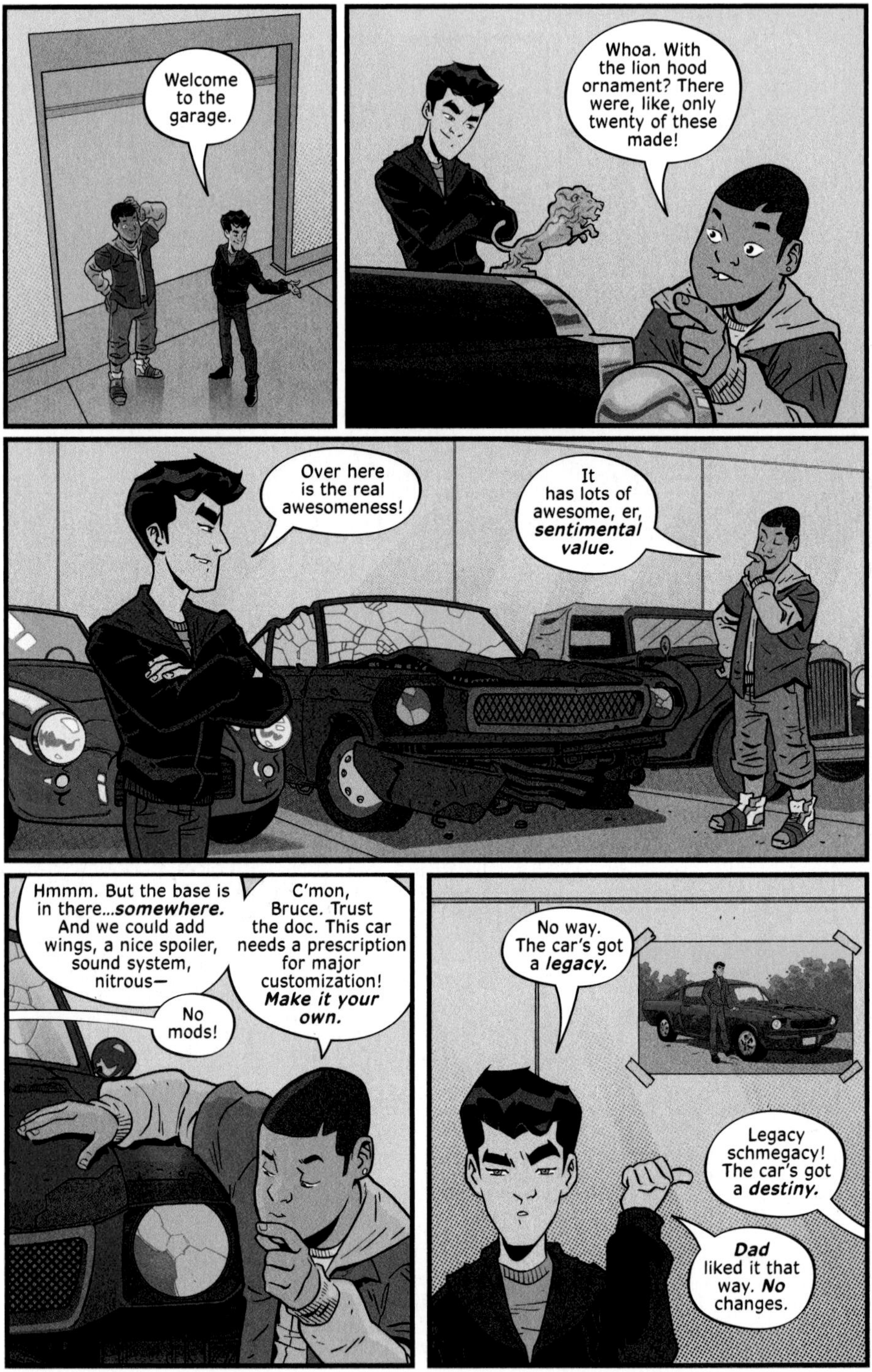
Welcome to the garage.
Whoa. With the lion hood ornament? There were, like, only twenty of these made!
Over here is the real awesomeness!
It has lots of awesome, er, ***sentimental value.***
Hmmm. But the base is in there...***somewhere.*** And we could add wings, a nice spoiler, sound system, nitrous—
No mods!
C'mon, Bruce. Trust the doc. This car needs a prescription for major customization! ***Make it your own.***
No way. The car's got a ***legacy.***
Legacy schmegacy! The car's got a ***destiny.***
Dad liked it that way. ***No*** changes.

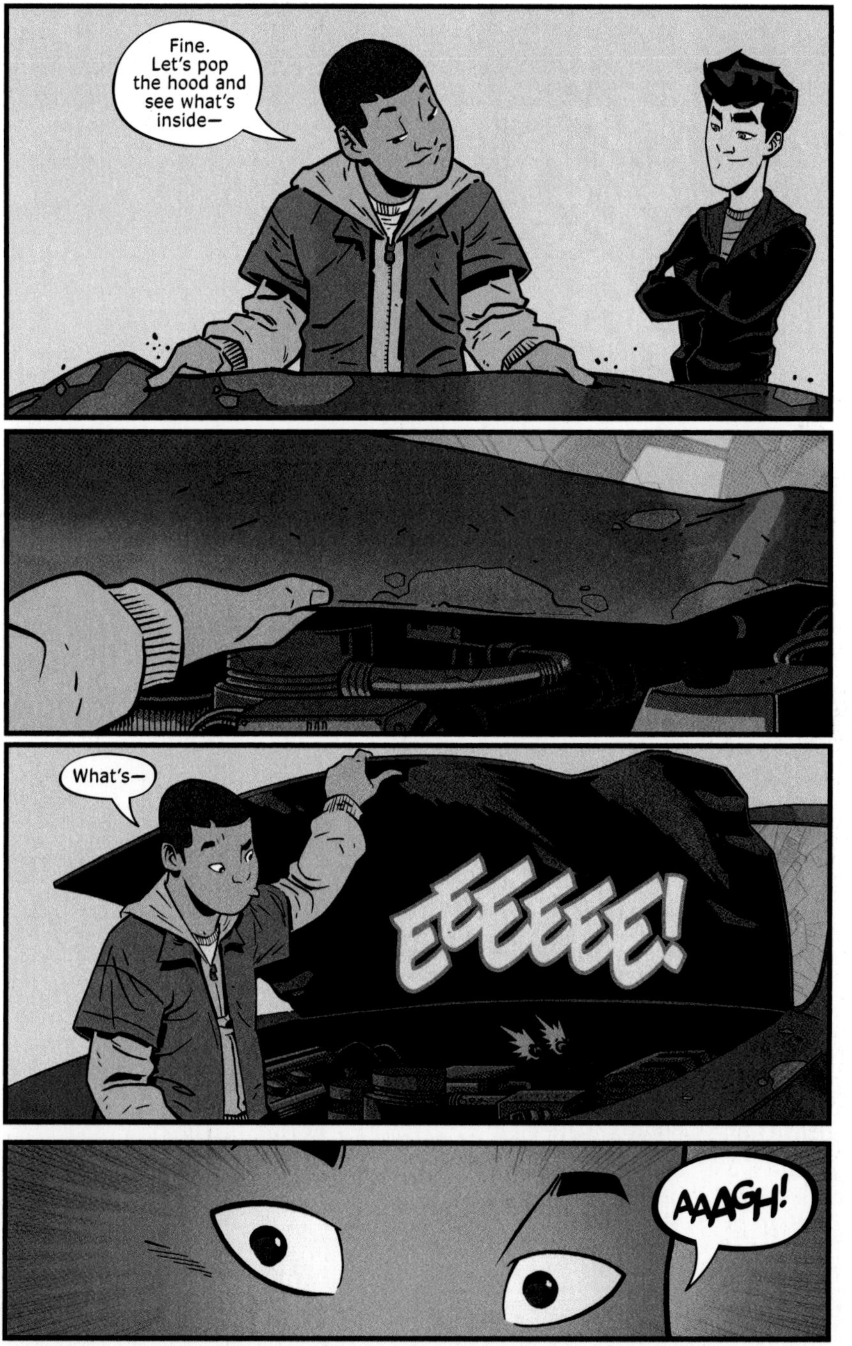
Fine. Let's pop the hood and see what's inside—
What's—
EEEEEE!
AAAGH!

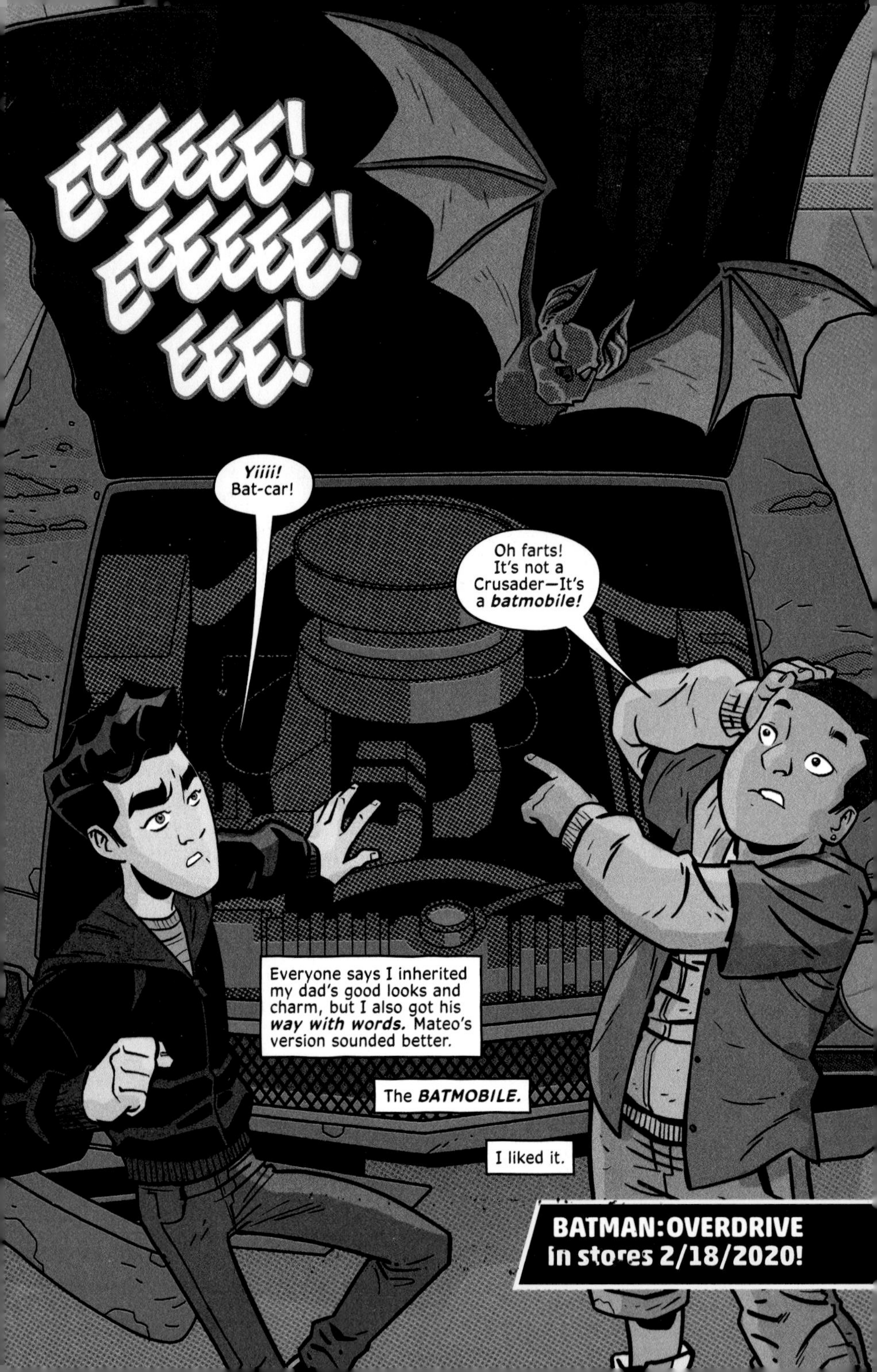
EEEEEE! EEEEEE! EEE!
Yiiii! Bat-car!
Oh farts! It's not a Crusader—It's a batmobile!
Everyone says I inherited my dad's good looks and charm, but I also got his way with words. Mateo's version sounded better.
The BATMOBILE.
I liked it.
BATMAN: OVERDRIVE in stores 2/18/2020!